# Also by Laura Thalassa

# BESPELLED

## LAURA THALASSA

Bloom books

Published by Bloom Books, an imprint of Sourcebooks
P.O. Box 4410, Naperville, Illinois 60567-4410
(630) 961-3900
sourcebooks.com

Cataloging-in-Publication data is on file with the Library of Congress.

Printed and bound in the United States of America.
KP 10 9 8 7 6 5 4 3 2 1

*To Ali,*
*Remember, remember…*

# Content Warning

Bespelled contains some themes and depictions that might be sensitive to certain readers. Please go to my website for a full list of content warnings.

# A BRIEF RECAP OF THINGS I MUST NOT FORGET (IN THE OFF CHANCE THAT ASSHOLE MEMNON SCREWS WITH MY MEMORY AGAIN)

*I am Selene Bowers. Age twenty. My parents are Olivia and Benjamin Bowers. My best friend is Sybil Andalucia. I attend Henbane Coven. (Finally!) Despite the coven's reluctance to admit me (they didn't like that my magic eats my memories), they did so after they learned I used my magic to land a plane in the middle of the Amazon rainforest. That's a long story. The only really important parts of it are that (1) while there, I found my familiar, Nero—he's the grumpy panther hanging around you like a shadow. Yes, that's his legitimate personality. Don't hold it against him. He's secretly a really good boy. And (2) I...woke a dude.*

*Okay, so he's not just any dude. He's a tit-sucking whoremonger. Memnon the Cursed is a two-thousand-year-old sorcerer who believes I'm some long-dead wife who shoved him into a musty tomb two millennia ago and forced him to sleep away the centuries. In the plot twist that no one* saw coming, I am his long-dead wife. (I'm sorry if you're relearning this now. You have my endless sympathies.)

Memnon and I are—brace yourself—soul mates, fated from birth to be together because fate was drunk the day it decided to make this decision. Before you even consider thinking this situation is romantic, please note that Memnon is terrible and ruthless, and he hates me. He literally burned my journals, the ones that hold my memories.

The sorcerer also framed me for a series of murders. The victims were witches—some of them coven sisters. One of them I knew, Charlotte Evensen. (Nero and I had the misfortune of discovering her body.) I am innocent, though the Politia, the supernatural police force, now believes I'm some rampaging serial killer. Despite all appearances, Memnon is not the killer either. The true murderer is still at large, and the bodies of their victims were mauled and coated in dark magic. Whoever or whatever is responsible is truly evil.

The Marin Pack shifters consider me a friend of the pack, and they are willing to help prove my innocence. ~~If~~ When my name is cleared, I'll need to meet with the pack to discuss another matter I have to deal with: a spell circle gone wrong.

Two weeks ago, on October 14, the night of the new moon, I participated in a spell circle in the persecution tunnels beneath the Ravenmeade residence hall (a.k.a. my house) because I was broke and needed some cash.

Yeah, terrible idea. The high priestess tried to force a bond on a shifter girl named Cara who was extremely intoxicated. I broke the circle before the spell could be completed, and I managed to get the girl out of there, but there was a violent magical fight, and now at least one

2

witch, Kasey, is missing. The other witches who participated in the spell circle all wore masks, so I don't know who they are, but it's entirely possible some of them live in my house. Which means I might be eating and sleeping alongside my enemies.

Memnon had been helping me sort out how to handle the fallout from the spell circle, and honestly for a few seconds there, I thought maybe I could get past his many, many issues. He does have a few things going for him:

(1) Bad boy attitude

(2) Muscles and tattoos

(3) Worships the ground I walk on when he's not vengeful

(4) Gorgeous

(5) Is giving when it comes to…never mind

Unfortunately, he nearly asphyxiated an entire room of supernaturals and forced me to remember my past when I explicitly told him I didn't want that. So he sucks.

Oh, and I'm now engaged to him. It's an unbreakable oath, so…sorry about that.

Good luck.
XO,
Selene

# CHAPTER 1

**Well, this night fucking blows.**

I sit on the concrete floor of one of the Politia's dimly lit cells, my arms slung over my knees, my dress from the Samhain Ball pooled out around me.

I stare at the ground absently, my palm still throbbing from where I cut it earlier this evening to lift my *curse*. It's not the only thing that hurts.

A migraine like no other is pounding beneath my skull, thanks to overusing my magic earlier tonight. But even that isn't the most painful part of my body at the moment.

I can barely breathe around the ache in my chest and the memories that now fill my head.

I woke up this morning as Selene Bowers, a twenty-year-old witch with magically-induced memory loss. I'm ending this evening as Selene Bowers, a twenty-year-old witch who has two complete sets of memories—one from this life and one from another.

A wave of nausea rolls through me, partially from the

migraine, partially from the sheer quantity of memories that have been shoved back in my brain. All of them demand my attention, but especially the strange, alien, *old* memories.

I now focus on that other life, Roxilana's life.

*My* life, I correct myself. My first one.

It unspools behind my eyes like some awful movie. The battles, the death, the sheer desperation to survive.

The sweetest, most beautiful part of that life was Memnon, that insufferable bastard. I hate that tonight, on the heels of one of the worst evenings of my life, when I should revile the sorcerer more than ever, my head is filled with memories of his touches, his whispered pledges of undying love, and his sheer *magnetism*. It drew me to him over and over again when I was Roxilana, and damn it, it draws me to him even now.

Back in that ancient life, he fought for me and fiercely loved me. He crossed Europe to find me then made me his queen. And he became one of the most powerful, monstrous men in the ancient world so that I could have my heart's desire. We had the sort of love that's so sharply wonderful it borders on pain.

Until, of course, the moment it all fell apart.

And it fell apart just as spectacularly as it began.

In the distance, a metal door hisses open, the sound scattering my thoughts.

I lift my head, wondering if I'm about to be questioned. My exhaustion surges at the thought. I don't think I have the energy to effectively plead my innocence, even though I now have the memories to prove it.

I hear the low tones of an officer speaking to the man on duty down here. Then two sets of footfalls head toward my cell. One of them I'd recognize from anywhere, the

5

sure, heavy sound of that stride drawing out goose bumps. A moment later, a ribbon of twisting, indigo magic moves toward the bars of my cell.

Memnon.

The ache in me deepens. Yet after all he did tonight, I have anger to match my hurt. It's buried under the pain of my migraine, but how it burns.

Memnon's magic reaches between the iron bars of my cell, but instead of passing through, his power sizzles against some ward, the wispy blue smoke recoiling from the contact.

"These are neutralizing cells," a masculine voice explains. "No magic gets in or out. They're spelled to keep inmates from using their power."

Inmates like me, he means.

"You've subjected my *fiancée* to this?" Memnon says, menace dripping from his voice. My stomach bottoms out at that word. *Fiancée*. I think I might've liked *inmate* better.

"I assure you, there was a warrant for her arrest—"

"She was arrested and detained under false allegations," Memnon cuts in, his tone sharp as a blade. "I expect your department to make amends for this."

The fucking *audacity* of this man to demand anything from the Politia when he was the one who truly placed me here.

His heavy, ominous footfalls come to a stop right in front of my cell. Even with the jail cell suppressing my magic, I can sense the throb of the sorcerer's presence, his power spilling out of him.

It's that staggering power that got me into this mess in the first place. A sorcerer's magic eats away at their conscience, so the more powerful they grow, the more heartless they become. And my soul mate is both very, very powerful and very, very heartless.

"*Est amage.*"

I don't react. I'm too exhausted *to* react.

The officer unlocks the cell, the door clanging as he opens it.

"Miss Bowers, it seems the department made a mistake with your arrest," he says dispassionately. "Please accept our apologies. You are now free to go." He steps aside to make room for me.

I draw in a long and defeated breath. I don't like sitting in this cold, dank cell, where my power is muted, but I'm even less eager to run into the arms of my vengeful soul mate.

"Pouting is so very unlike you, fiancée."

That damn word. It makes my temples pound harder.

I lift my head to stare at the cinder-block wall ahead of me. "I don't want to leave with him," I say to the officer.

I sense the man looking between me and Memnon. "Miss," he finally says, "you don't—" His words cut off suddenly.

"Hey!" another officer on duty shouts. "What do you think—?" His voice, too, abruptly cuts off, and a moment later, I hear the dull thud of his body hitting the ground somewhere in the distance.

Finally, I glance over, only to see my soul mate gripping the first officer by the back of his neck. The man's eyelids flutter, and I know with stomach-curdling clarity that Memnon is altering yet another mind tonight. He already did this to a room full of my peers shortly after he nearly killed them all.

Once Memnon finally releases the officer, the man

calmly walks back the way he came, not bothering to look at either of us. Nor does he stop to check on the other officer on duty down here.

And now I'm alone with the sorcerer.

I still don't meet his eyes. "I'm not going with you," I say.

"I'm not giving you a choice," he says.

He takes an ominous step forward into the cell, then another and another. Before I can think better of it, I scramble to my feet. The action wakes up all my aches and pains, and I nearly collapse under the onslaught of them all.

Cursing, Memnon closes the distance between us and catches my swaying form.

And now, cradled in his arms, I do finally look at my soul mate.

I drink in his bronze skin, his black, wavy hair, and those mesmerizing eyes which are dark brown at their edges and light like bourbon near the pupil. It's only been hours since I saw him last, but my gaze roves over his subtly hooked nose and full, curving lips, his high cheekbones and knife-sharp jawline. Finally, they snag on the scar that runs up from that jawline to his left ear then cuts across to the corner of his left eye.

It's like seeing a specter, and for a moment, old memories eclipse the new ones. I reach out, my fingers grazing his cheek.

Memnon's expression softens at the touch, and that's all that's needed for the rest of our past to overtake my addled mind.

"*Est xsaya. Est Memnon,*" I whisper. "*Vak watam singasavak.*"

*My king. My Memnon. You survived.*

Some terrifying emotion wells up in me. It feels like a

8

serrated knife, carving me up from the inside out. I can't place what it is I feel or why I feel it, but I do know that if Memnon wasn't already holding me, my legs would buckle.

This close to me, I see his pupils dilate, and he goes still. "You remember," Memnon says almost desperately.

"Of course I remember. You forced me to."

And now all that anger swells back up in me. I pinch my eyes shut and weakly try to push away from him, even as my skull throbs and my stomach churns.

"Oh no, little witch," he says softly, *fondly*. "I'm not letting you go now." He hoists me more fully into his arms and strides out of the room.

The moment we cross that magical threshold that separates the neutralizing cells from the hallway, my power floods my body, the sensation so sudden and sharp that I gag.

In an instant, Memnon's own magic swarms me, slipping into my mouth and down my throat, settling my nausea.

I release a shaky breath and lean tiredly against the sorcerer's chest. I note absently that he's changed out of his tuxedo, exchanging it for a black fitted thermal, black jeans, and boots.

"Does anything else hurt?" he asks, his tone gentle—far too gentle.

*Everything* else hurts—my head, my joints, my very skin. But most of all, my heart.

"Isn't this your moment to gloat?" I say instead as I'm carried down the empty cellblock. "You've defeated me in all ways."

Memnon's magic stretches out and opens the heavy metal door ahead of us. "I will gloat when my future wife feels better."

*Future wife.*

I make a face at that, then wince when my head throbs harder. Fucking *hate* unbreakable oaths and this farce of an engagement.

Next to the door out, the officer on duty lies sprawled on the ground, his eyes closed and his chest steadily rising and falling. Memnon pauses a moment to crouch next to him and, balancing me in one of his arms, he uses his other to touch the man's forehead.

*"You drank too much tonight and fell asleep while on duty,"* he murmurs. *"You're embarrassed and will tell no one of this."*

Memnon rises, cradling me in his arms once more. If I felt better, I would've had some acidic commentary about what he just did. But honestly I'm too tired and in pain to care.

"Where do you hurt most?" Memnon asks as we exit the cellblock, as though he read my thoughts.

"My head." What point is there in lying? It feels like someone is trying to jackhammer their way out of my skull.

No sooner have I spoken than Memnon readjusts the arm wrapped around my back so that his hand cups my forehead.

*"Ease the pain,"* he murmurs in Sarmatian.

His magic sifts out of him, some of it slipping up through my nostrils and some of it sinking directly into my skin.

Immediately, the migraine fades, each pulse of pain less intense than the last, until it's gone completely.

I sigh, settling deeper into Memnon's arms for a momen—

Wait. No, he's still the enemy. I'm not going to enjoy being carried when he just ruined my life.

"I can walk," I insist as Memnon carries me down the Politia's lonely hallway.

Not actually sure about this one, but fuck if I'm going to let Memnon continue to haul me around like I'm helpless.

"All right then, little witch," he says, almost indulgently, like I'm being cute and ridiculous.

Goddess, but I'd love nothing more than to stab this man with a spork.

He bends, letting my feet touch the linoleum floor and holding me stable as I stand. I'm still wearing the heels I borrowed from Sybil earlier this evening for the Samhain Ball, and as soon as Memnon lets me go, my legs wobble like I'm a newborn fawn. For a second, I'm positive I'm going to face plant, but then I find my balance.

Memnon moves around to my front and kneels at my feet.

My brows pull together. "What are you—?"

He reaches for one of my legs and lifts it, setting my foot on his thigh. I hop around for a moment before resting my arms on his shoulders and leaning my weight against him.

I consider kicking the man in the teeth when he pulls Sybil's stiletto from my foot.

I frown down at him. "What are you doing?" I demand.

"Removing these ridiculous shoes so you can walk," he says, massaging the pad of my foot.

My frown deepens.

The sorcerer presses a kiss to my ankle, then sets my foot down.

My heart flutters, and oh no, I do not like this.

Right now, I have Memnon slotted into a tidy category I like to call *Evil-Ass Monsters*. It's a good category, an *accurate* category.

If he starts being nice, my bond and my past life memories

11

might team up to recatalog him into some other category much less suited to him.

Memnon removes my other shoe, then collects both heels. He rises, forcing my hands to slide off his shoulders. Suddenly, all six something feet of him looms over me.

"Better?" he asks.

"I didn't need your help taking my own shoes off." I glare at him to drive the point home.

The man smirks a little, his eyes twinkling. He's not put off by my anger in the least.

Should've kicked him when I had the chance.

"Come, little witch," he says, placing a proprietary hand on my back. "Let's finish getting you discharged and leave this place."

# CHAPTER 2

*I step out into the chilly night air, the door to the Politia* station hissing shut behind me. My hair feels limp, my skin is sticky with sweat and blood, and my black gown is torn in a couple of places.

I am the picture of defeat.

Memnon steps up next to me, his hand moving to the small of my back. If I am defeat, then he is pure, unadulterated victory.

"So what are your plans for me now?" I ask.

There are undoubtedly plans. This is, after all, his night. I'm just along for the ride.

A wisp of blue smoke curls around my midsection like a phantom embrace, and I hear his voice inside me, cruelly intimate.

*You and I are going home.*

I would wager all the money I have to my name that he doesn't mean *my* home. Which means...I get to see his place.

A shiver courses through me. I don't want to go there, but I'm also perversely curious to see where he's been living.

"As long as there's a bed"—I gesture in front of me—"lead the way."

I'll rally some sort of revenge plot tomorrow. Right now, however, this is a full-fledged surrender.

Gritty asphalt digs into the pads of my feet as Memnon guides me across the parking lot toward a sports car.

"*That's* your car?" Disbelief coats my voice. I knew the man had acquired some money, but not this much. "Just how many heads have you rifled through?" He must be extorting money from people like it's no one's business.

His fingers press into my back. "Feisty mate, always believing the worst of me."

"You're less disappointing that way." Well, almost. The bar is *constantly* lowering itself.

I expect to sense the heat of Memnon's anger through our bond. Instead, he lets out a loud, amused laugh.

"*Est amage*, the world can turn and the times can change, but thank the gods, some things remain the same."

I scowl at him. Not going to address that.

I eye the car. "Do you even know *how* to drive?"

There's a conspiratorial gleam in his eyes. "I speak your language and wear your modern clothing. I own a car and a home, and I have a bank account full of money. What do you think, Empress?"

"I think you stole this car along with a memory or two on how to drive it."

"Those who hold the power make the rules," he reminds me, ever the ruthless warlord.

This is what made Memnon move through the ancient world with such ease. Not only was he smart, strong, and unscrupulous, his ability to glean knowledge from others allowed him to assimilate fast.

I just never appreciated how fast until now.

He opens the car door for me. Inside the vehicle, a shadow moves, its amber–green eyes glinting in the darkness.

"*Nero.*" I all but fling myself onto my familiar, my body draped over the leather bucket seat so I can reach the panther better. We've only been apart for a few hours, but I'd been anxious about my furry dude.

He must've been anxious about me too because he nuzzles against me awfully intensely for a panther who prides himself on being aloof.

While I'm snuggling my familiar, Memnon neatly tucks my legs into the car and closes my door.

When the sorcerer opens his own door, he inhales sharply.

"*Nero,*" he growls.

I pull away from my panther, and only now do I notice what my soul mate already has.

Nero has torn apart the inside of this car. The rear seats are in shreds, the foam interior littering what's left of them. He's clawed up the back side of the front seats, the leather hanging in ribbons. Even the center console I'm leaning on has been gouged at.

I don't know how much my panther understands about the situation between me and Memnon, but this feels like a feline *fuck you*, and I am here for it.

"You are such a good familiar," I say softly, stroking Nero down his flank while he rubs his head against me. "I'm sorry for leaving you like I did," I whisper, referring both to this evening and to another, fateful evening long ago, when my familiar and I were forced to part ways.

Nero continues to rub against me, the big cat in an unusually forgiving mood.

I hear Memnon sigh as his magic floods the interior of the car, thickening in the air until I can't see much beyond Nero's fur. When it clears, the car's interior is unblemished once more.

The sorcerer gets in then, folding his massive body into the driver's seat. Suddenly the space feels very, very small.

I release Nero, letting him resettle into the back seat while I buckle myself in. The engine roars to life, and Memnon smoothly maneuvers his fancy car out of the lot and onto the street.

I guess the sorcerer really can drive.

Leaning my head against the window, I stare tiredly out at the dark night, watching streetlights and shadowy foliage blur by.

"When are you going to marry me?" I ask softly.

I can't *not* ask it. Right before I was arrested, Memnon said we were to wed immediately. It's been hours since we made that unbreakable oath, and I feel like a fish caught on a hook, waiting to be reeled in to my death.

Memnon reaches over and takes my injured hand in his, turning it so my sliced palm is facing up.

"Not tonight, *est amage*, when you still bear the marks of our battle."

I release a shuddering breath.

*Not tonight.*

That's a relief.

I glance down at the wound from earlier, when I cut my palm with his blade and said my oaths and lifted the curse. The wound has begun to scab, though the flesh around it is red and angry.

"When then?" I press.

Memnon's fingers graze the cut, his touch whisper soft. A wisp of his magic curls out, brushing against it. Almost instantly, the flesh pulls together and seals itself up until even the seam of the wound fades away.

"Look at me, Selene." It's a command, yet all I hear is a plea. Memnon wants connection, reassurance. This was his grand plan after all. He couldn't resurrect the past, but he could at least draw forth my memories of it. I suppose, at the heart of all the sorcerer's vengeance, he simply wanted to feel less lonely.

My gaze reluctantly moves to his. He's torn his own attention briefly from the road ahead of us.

"It doesn't matter when we marry, little witch." He squeezes my freshly healed hand. "Neither magic nor time can keep us apart." His eyes are luminous. "We are like the stars. Eternal."

———————

I mean to stay awake. I have every intention of noting the streets that lead to Memnon's place and then every detail of the house itself. But the winding roads that cut through the mountains north of San Francisco rock me gently, the clock says it's after three in the morning, and my fatigue is overwhelming me. It might even be that despite my hate for Memnon, something deep in me is supremely comforted at being in the car with him and my familiar.

Whatever the case, I make it maybe three miles before my eyelids start drifting shut and another mile before I close them for good.

I stir twice more—once to the feel of my body being

gathered into strong, warm arms and again when I'm placed on a soft mattress and tucked in.

Memnon's voice echoes inside me as I slip off to sleep.

*Be at ease, fierce queen. You don't have to fight any longer. You are safe with me.*

# CHAPTER 3

*I blink groggily and stretch, basking in the feel of dappled* sunlight on my skin and the masculine smell clinging to my sheets.

I reach for the owner of that smell, but my hand lands on nothing but blankets.

My brow creases, and I sit up, stifling a yawn I have a destabilizing moment where I'm confused, because I've never laid eyes on the massive, glass-encased room I'm now in, and I can't remember how I got here. I remember last night all too well, no thanks to the sorcerer, but my memory does a nosedive after I got in the car with him.

Memnon must've carried me in and placed me in this bed. *His* bed. That makes my spine straighten and my eyes sharpen. I must be in his house, though the man himself is nowhere to be seen.

My gaze greedily takes in the room. The first thing I notice is the space. You have to be a rich bitch to afford something bigger than a tin can here in Northern California.

Memnon is definitely a rich bitch.

The room is massive, and it's made all the more cavernous by the lack of furniture. There's this bed, a bookcase on the wall to the left, and a side chair next to it. Beyond that, there's nothing, save for the panoramic windows that take up most of three of the room's walls. Out the windows directly across from the bed, I can see the rolling coastal hills, and out the ones to my right, I see several evergreen trees that flank the house. Past them, the forest looms dark and lonely. I don't know how far we are from Henbane Coven, but these woods look similar.

Also along the right wall is a massive en suite bathroom, and to my left is the doorway out.

"Memnon?" I call out.

The building remains silent. A minute later, however, Nero pads into the room, his coat looking particularly sleek as he moves in the soft light. He walks right up to the bed, then hops on.

I reach out and pet him. "Have I told you that you're the best familiar in the whole wide world?"

He gives me an uncomfortable look, his ears twitching a little. I imagine this is the expression teenagers give their parents. I guess he used up all his sentimentality last night during our reunion.

I run my hand down his neck. "Memnon?" I call out again.

Where in the seven hells is the sorcerer? He finally has me in his bed where he's been apparently angling to get me this whole time, yet now he's the one missing.

I throw the sheets off, biting back an oath once I realize that I'm in an oversize shirt—*his* shirt—and my panties from earlier.

He undressed me. Of course he did.

Bastard.

A small, reasonable part of me is willing to throw the guy a bone—he probably just wanted me to sleep comfortably. But fuck him and the fact that he saw my tits while I'm still angry with him. I seethe at the thought.

*Memnon,* I all but growl down our bond.

The first thing I sense is his smile.

*You're awake, fiancée. Did you sleep well?*

I grimace at that word. Fiancée. I swear he keeps using it just to rile me.

*You better have closed your eyes when you undressed me,* I say.

All I feel is that persistent grin from his side of the bond, damn him.

*And where are you?* I demand.

*Is someone upset that I wasn't in bed with them when they woke?*

I grind my teeth. He's so cavalier and *playful* at the moment.

*When are you coming back?* I ask.

I feel glee from him. *Miss me already?*

*If that keeps your fragile ego from shattering, then sure. I miss you so desperately I might die if I don't see you again.*

On the other side of our connection, things go quiet, still.

Finally, Memnon says, *Speak to me like that again, and I will give you your heart's greatest desires.*

*My heart desires to be rid of you. If you can give me that, sure, I will whisper some empty platitudes in your ear.*

On the other end of the bond, Memnon is no longer jovial. If anything, I swear I sense a flicker of woundedness. I nearly cackle at the thought. I might not be defeated yet.

*I will be home soon,* he says instead.

Soon? Soon? The fuck does that mean? Fifteen minutes? Two hours? I need to know how much time I have.

But to him, I merely say, *Oh good, then I'll get the knives out and sharpened for your return.*

His amusement returns. *Empress, you're speaking my love language.* With that final, disturbing thought, he pulls away from the connection.

How does he even know about the concept of love languages? Never mind. It doesn't matter. I need to get out of here.

I glance at the oversize black shirt I wear.

Well, first change, then escape.

I head for the walk-in closet next to the bathroom. Halfway there, a scrap of lace hanging inside it catches my eye.

My stomach bottoms out as, for an instant, I'm filled with dread that some other woman has been here with Memnon.

No, that can't be right. Can it?

I hate that I care. He and his poor life choices can rot.

Still, my pulse pounds between my ears as I hustle toward the closet, drawn by a horrified fascination at what I might find inside.

Women's clothing? Weapons? Bodies? Who the fuck knows.

The walk-in closet is about as big as my entire room at the coven. *He's such a rich bitch.* Despite the space, there's not much inside as far as Memnon's clothes go. I see a handful of suits hanging up as well as some folded shirts and pants on the shelves.

Not that I'm paying much attention to those.

My eyes are pinned to that single scrap of lace, which now that I'm closer looks like a slip dress. I reach for it, my stomach plummeting at the thought of someone else wearing this around Memnon until I notice it has a tag still attached.

I exhale, my breath shaky. Okay, so it's not some mystery woman's. What a relief. For her, of course. Best not to get within striking distance of this dude.

Letting it go, I tug out another dress. This too has a tag still attached.

All the women's clothes seem to have tags.

They're also all roughly my size.

*These are meant for me,* I realize.

That really shouldn't stun me—Memnon intends to marry me, after all. Still, this is…a lot.

An old feeling, one that belongs to Roxilana, rises.

This would've won her over. Easily.

Before Memnon took her away and married her, she had little to her name. Even for me, independent though I am, being doted on is alluring.

*This is blood money, Selene. And the price is letting the asshole get his way.*

Dicks will sprout wings before that happens.

I stare at the clothes a moment longer. I do have to get dressed, I concede. I rifle through the women's clothing until I find a pair of jeans and a simple white shirt.

*Goddess, forgive me for taking from the devil.*

On a shoe rack below, there are three different pairs of shoes in my size, one of which happens to be a set of Doc Martens.

I grab the combat boots.

*Forgive me, Goddess, for taking these too. And for keeping them.*

I mean, it's not every day one gets new Doc Martens.

Grabbing the items, I head into the bathroom and quickly pull on the clothes, my agitation growing. I don't know where Memnon is, but the time I have before he returns is limited.

When I straighten, I notice that tucked into the bathroom mirror is a photo. *Of me.*

In it, I'm clinking a champagne flute with a few people who are off camera. I know from memory that it was taken this last New Year's Eve, when Sybil and I and a few of her coven sisters were all at an apartment party. It's an action shot of me, one where I'm genuinely smiling and my eye just happened to catch the camera.

My heart does a funny thing, finding this picture in Memnon's otherwise bare bathroom, knowing he must've taken it from one of my photo albums and placed it here where he'll see it every day, alongside his own face.

I stride out of the bathroom and snatch up my phone, which rests on one of the bedside tables. It clings to a mere five percent of battery life.

I slip it into my back pocket and survey my surroundings once more.

There's not much to see in this room, nor was there much to the bathroom and closet. For some reason, I assumed there would be. Memnon is good at playing the game of rulers, and in the modern world, so much of that is owning lots of expensive things. But so far, there's really not that much that screams self-involved.

I guess my warlord ex is a little too rugged to bother

with more creature comforts. That, or he's still amassing his wealth, one victim at a time.

I need to go, now.

Yet my attention moves to the one place where Memnon has accumulated items: his bookshelf. Without intending to, my feet lead me over to it.

There are books from Pliny the Elder written in their original Latin, alongside the Greek versions of *The Iliad*, *The Odyssey*, and Herodotus's writings, and some ancient poetry. There's a biography of Nero, as well as some histories of Europe, Asia, Africa, and the Americas that span the time frame when Memnon and Roxilana lived.

My eyes move to the lower shelves, where they snag on the familiar spines of my notebooks.

I don't breathe.

*It's not possible.* Memnon burned them. I *watched* him burn them.

I drop to my knees, disbelief and hope—painful, awful hope—riding me, and I pull one notebook out. This one is covered in gold foil constellations. I open it up, and a little sound slips past my lips when I see my name and the date range in my handwriting. On the next page is a set of notes about how to get to the restaurant where I was working at the time. Alongside it is a spell I scribbled in for removing wrinkles from clothes.

I flip through several more pages, which are full of Polaroids, sticky notes, to-do lists, directions, spells I thought were worth remembering, and hasty sketches.

My thumb runs over one such sketch, this one of a Sarmatian griffin. I swallow down the strange rush of emotions it brings forth before moving through the rest of the notebook.

It is, without a doubt, mine. Somehow, it's whole once more.

This is a trick. It must be. I saw these notebooks burn, and I touched their charred remains. I remember the acrid, smoky smell that clung to the room once they were nothing more than cinders.

I grab another journal and flip through it. Then another.

I pinch my eyes shut, my throat tight with emotion. Despite my efforts, a rebellious tear slips out.

I don't know how Memnon managed to weasel these out of my room or fake their fiery demise, but *they still exist*. He saved them.

For one-point-five seconds, I feel a rush of tenderness toward the sorcerer. Then I remember that he still manipulated and coerced me. He still framed me for murder and forced me to lift that curse against my will.

So screw him and his small kindnesses.

Moving back over to the closet, I look for anything that might be able to hold my notebooks. Tucked away in a far corner, I find a black duffel bag that has a knife, rope, and some zip ties.

Not fucking suspicious or anything.

Emptying the bag, I haul it over to the bookcase and dump all my books into it. There are so many of them that I can't zip the bag up. Instead, I heft the thing onto my shoulder, smiling a little at the weight of them. I suddenly feel more like myself, having them close.

I pull out my phone and, ignoring the slew of messages and notifications, order a car for Nero and me.

"Nero," I call out to the panther, who's still sprawled out on our enemy's bed. "It's time to go."

I don't wait for him to follow. My body is jittery with

nerves and resolve. I've got my notebooks. Now I need to get back to the coven and ward the shit out of my room so that pushy sorcerers can't approach me.

I leave the bedroom, Nero at my heels. The two of us pass by several rooms that branch off the house's hallway as well as a sprawling living room. I lament the fact that I have to get out of here. I really am curious about the rest of Memnon's home.

The front door is a bronze monstrosity. I reach for the handle, only when I go to open it, it doesn't budge. It's then that I notice the ward shimmering on both the lock and the door handle's surface.

I glance down at Nero, who's come to a stop at my side. "Memnon has a bad habit of locking us in places while I'm unconscious."

The big cat blinks up at me, clearly bored.

I lay my palm on the door and simply wait. After a few seconds, deep blue tendrils of the ward leave the door to crawl up my fingers. Like last time I did this, Memnon's magic can't seem to help but draw near. They wrap around my wrist like they're desperate to hold on to me, and as they do so, the spell's structure warps and melts until the whole thing slides off the door and up my forearm.

It lingers there on my skin for several seconds, then dissipates.

When I try the handle again, it gives, sunlight slicing through the opening. Success!

In my pocket, my phone vibrates, and I know without looking that my car is approaching. The timing couldn't have been more perfect.

My gaze drops to Nero, and I run my teeth along my lower lip. He's going to be a problem for whoever picks us up.

Lightly, I place a hand on the big cat's head, causing his ears to twitch. "*Do ulibad povekomsa pesagus diveksu kuppu mi'kanutgusa buvekatasava.*"

*Hide this great cat from all eyes but mine.*

My power, which is still recovering from last night, sluggishly sifts out of me and pours down Nero's body. The spell is not accompanied by the usual prickling or throbbing in my head I've come to expect, the one that took memories from me.

My memory loss really is no more.

At the reminder, I feel the burn of betrayal all over again.

Yesterday might've been Memnon's day, but today fucking isn't.

I glance back at the foyer and living room. It really is a lovely house. Shame.

Closing my eyes, I focus on what little magic remains. It's not much, yet I only need a spark.

Memnon made a mistake, leaving me and my wrath here in his inner sanctum.

I extend my arm palm up, and my eyes snap open. "*Elements of old, feel my ire. Light this fucking house on fire.*"

Down my arm, my magic trickles and gathers until a wisp of pale orange smoke rises from my extended hand, curling and transforming into flame.

I toss the ball of flame into the living room, where it lands on a fringed rug. In a matter of seconds, the fire smolders, then grows, consuming what it can of the rug and anything else nearby.

"C'mon, Nero," I say. "Let's get the hell out of here."

# CHAPTER 4

*By the time Nero and I return to the coven, the sun has disap-*peared behind a thick layer of clouds, and I feel like I've been hit by a cauldron.

Memnon's pain-numbing spells must've worn off, and my body is feeling all the aches of last night, as well as the deeper exhaustion that comes from overusing my magic.

Once I enter my house, I head toward the dining hall, lured in by the smell of soup and fresh bread. Halfway there, I feel a prickle at the back of my neck. I glance around and notice a couple of witches staring. And when I enter the dining room, a witch who had been playing a fiddle now stops, and the chatter in the room quiets as my coven sisters glance my way.

I've been distracted by my wicked fiancé, but for these women, my arrest must've been the drama of the night—especially since Memnon spelled them to forget their own brushes with death.

Ignoring the looks, I grab a bowl painted with vines

from the stack at the buffet line and fill it with steaming soup. Snagging a bread roll from a nearby basket, I beat a hasty retreat from the room, Nero at my side.

All I really want to do is snuggle into my bed and binge-watch something on my laptop, but I haven't spoken with my best friend Sybil since last night, and so much has happened since we parted that it feels wrong to hole up without at least stopping by her room first.

I don't bother knocking when I get there, I just step inside, Nero trailing after me, and set my bread and soup down on her desk.

Sybil's back is to me while she tends to her wall of plants, her lilac magic threading through the room. She's lost in her own world, humming something under her breath that the leaves are swaying to. Merlin, her barn owl familiar, rests on a perch over her bed, his eyes hyper focused on Nero.

"Sybil," I call out.

My friend startles, nearly dropping her watering pail.

"Goddess's wrath," she curses, turning. As soon as she sees me, she gasps. "Selene!" Now she chucks the pail aside, causing Merlin to flap his wings as water sprays him and his perch. She crosses her room and throws herself at me. "I've been *so* worried," she says, holding me tightly. "I heard you were arrested, but when I called the station, they told me you'd already been released. But then you weren't answering your calls, and you never showed up here." She pauses to inhale a breath. "Where have you been?"

"I've been with Memnon," I say tiredly. I shrug off the duffel bag I've been carrying, nearly clobbering Nero.

My familiar gives me what can only be described as a dirty look.

"Sorry, bud," I say to him.

His ears flick at the term. You just cannot please everyone.

"*Memnon*?" Sybil says, making a face. "Last I checked, we hated his guts."

"We *still* hate his guts," I confirm.

"Oh good. I mean bad." Her brow furrows. "But last night when he was carrying you out of the dance, you guys seemed like you'd ironed things out. What happened?"

I let out a jaded laugh that ends as a sob.

Hell's spells, where to begin?

I sit down heavily on the edge of her bed, Nero curling up at my feet. "If you have an hour, I'll tell you everything."

She nods, pulling her computer chair over to sit. "I'm listening."

So I tell her the whole, sordid truth, from Memnon asphyxiating a room full of supernaturals and altering their minds, to framing me for the murders to forcing me to agree to his shitty demands.

Sybil keeps saying "What the fuck?" over and over again, her eyes glued to me.

Once I finish, she lets out a hysterical little laugh. "So let me get this straight: You're no longer a suspect"—I nod—"but you're engaged to a psycho"—another nod—"and you can now remember your past?"

I give her a sad smile. "Yeah, that's about where the situation is."

"I don't believe it," she says, staring at me intently.

I probably wouldn't either, if roles were reversed.

"Ask me about a memory, one you know I've forgotten."

Sybil sits back in her seat. "Um…okay." She drums her fingers on the armrest. "What did we do on the night of our high school graduation?"

Easy. "We got drunk off cheap booze and skinny-dipped in the Irish Sea. It was tit-chappingly cold too."

Sybil's mouth parts with her surprise. "Holy midnight," she says softly. "You remember." The lights in her room flicker, punctuating the statement. "And your magic won't take any more memories the next time you cast a spell?"

I shake my head. "No."

Sybil's eyes well as they move over my features. "How do *you* feel about that?"

I sigh and get up, grabbing my bread roll before returning to her bed. Bread will help, right?

"Awful. Angry. A little hopeful and then guilty that I feel hope." I rip the roll in half, then take a bite of it. "I don't know. I'm so conflicted."

Sybil moves next to me on the bed and rubs my back. "I'm sorry," she says softly. "Now is probably not a good time to tell you what's been happening here."

I glance over at her, my brow creasing. "What are you talking about?"

"Another witch was murdered."

It's my turn to stare at her in disbelief.

"What? *When?*"

"I think someone discovered the body sometime in the middle of the night out in the Everwoods."

A shudder runs through me when I realize this must've been Memnon's doing. He'd moved the previous bodies into the Everwoods when he was framing me for murder. He must've spent the hours I was incarcerated unframing me for murder. After all, he didn't scheme to marry me just to leave me behind bars. Not when he's busy stocking up his closet with clothes for me.

All at once, fear floods my chest, making it hard to

breath. I place a hand over my heart, choking a little on the sensation. I can't understand my own extreme reaction—

*SELENE!* Memnon bellows down our bond.

Speak of the fucking devil.

Panic continues to grip me, and I realize it's *his* emotions I'm feeling, not my own.

*Answer me if you can!* His tone is frantic. *Tell me you're okay.*

"Are you okay?" Sybil says, parroting the sorcerer's words. Her brow crinkles as she eyes me.

I nod. *I'm fine*, I push down our bond, just to beat back this terror pouring from Memnon. It clicks then. *You found the fire.*

I sense the instant realization strikes him.

*You set this?*

I feel relief spreading down our bond, and it's like a balm to his previous fear.

He begins to laugh. The hairs along my arms rise at the sound.

*Clever, vicious woman. I should know by now that you would have vengeance to match my own.*

Only he would find arson funny.

"Selene?" Sybil snaps her fingers in front of my face. "What is going on? You're zoning out."

"Memnon's found the fire," I say distractedly.

"What fire?"

"The one I started in his house."

"You started a fire?" she squawks.

I nod.

*Where are you now?* Memnon asks.

*Home.*

*I don't see you,* he says.

33

My *home*, I clarify.

"You're not serious, are you?" Sybil says. "You can't just light people's houses on fire."

"You can if they suck."

"Selene." Sybil gives me a patronizing look.

*Give me one good reason why I shouldn't come over right now and haul you back here,* Memnon says.

*I will light your house on fire again,* I say, doubling down on my actions. *Assuming any of it still stands.*

When will this man learn not to fuck with witches?

*How are you doing?* Memnon says, pivoting the conversation. *Getting uncomfortable yet since we made that oath?*

*Why would I be uncomfortable?*

There's a spark of amusement. *You'll find out soon enough. Once ignoring it becomes intolerable, soul mate, you can come find me.*

*Tits will talk before that happens,* I say. *In the meantime, have fun figuring out where you'll sleep tonight.*

I withdraw from the connection then and glance at Sybil. "I should get back to my room." I have the rest of my dinner to eat and notebooks to put away.

"Whoa, whoa, whoa, you can't just leave after you casually mention that *you lit some dude's place on fire.*"

"Not 'some dude,'" I say, grabbing my soup. It's long since gone cold. "My evil soul mate. And I'll tell you more about it later."

I lift the unzipped duffel bag of notebooks onto my shoulder, and Nero is getting up.

"I'm holding you to that," she says after me as I leave her room.

Nero and I make it up to the third floor and past a random bat flying down the hallway.

The door to my room hangs slightly ajar—no one bothered to fully close it last night after I was taken away. My heart twists at that.

I push it open and step inside. The space is still covered with sticky notes, and my newest journal sits wide open on my desk. It's a time capsule of my life before my memory was restored. This version of me—the one who meticulously crafted her life to work with her memory loss—I feel like I lost her when I gained these memories.

And even though there's a lightness to me where the curse once bore down, I feel a bit like a ship without an rudder, forced to drift aimlessly.

Nero prowls over to my bed, then hops on it, completely uncaring that I'm having a moment.

He stretches out his forelegs, then sprawls out on his side, closing his eyes.

"Clearly, you're super torn up about last night," I mutter, dropping the duffel bag with my notebooks. A few of the books spill out.

I move to my desk, looking over the open page of my newest journal. I run my fingers over one of the last notes I left myself:

**Do not trust Memnon the Cursed.**

I can still remember the anger and the panic I felt in the moment. Strange to be on this side of it. My eyes slip away from the warning to the sticky note placed in the center of the page. I smooth a hand over it before I realize the penmanship isn't my own.

Narrowing my gaze, I pull the sticky note off the paper.

*You might've forgotten what happened at the spell circle, but we have not.*

I drop the note on my keyboard, staring at it before looking first to my window, then to my previously open door. The wards I made are still in place, the spidery threads of them still softly glinting in the air.

I exhale. Whoever wrote this got past those wards. A chill runs down my spine. How? Someone who meant me ill shouldn't have been able to, not without ripping the spells down.

I glance back at the note. They're aware of my memory loss but not that the magic causing it was lifted.

*And they won't learn of this*, I decide.

Something ancient and buried stirs within me. Enemies ended me once, long ago. I didn't endure that to be played once more.

I pull out my chair and sit down, opening my notebook to a fresh page. I might not need this journal to remember my tasks, but there are other things it can be useful for.

Grabbing a pen, I jot down the disturbing events that have happened on campus since the school year began:

*Murdered witches*
*Monthly spell circle with illegal binding spells*

I've been connected to both of these events. Until now, I was too busy trying to stay one step ahead of the shitstorm to actually address either of them. But now I can. I glance at the sticky note again.

I *must*.

Returning my attention to the notebook, I tap my pen

against the paper. Many of the murdered witches attended Henbane Coven.

There are so many questions I have about these murders, starting with Memnon's involvement, but before I can get too distracted by that, I force myself to look at the other incident listed. The spell circle happens every new moon, and if my experience was typical, then they all center around forcibly binding  an unwilling supernatural—in my case, it was a shifter—to the high priestess running the circle.

According to the sticky note, she and the other witches haven't forgotten that I fucked their spell to shit, and unfortunately for me, I don't know who those witches are. They'd all worn masks. But I do know they can get past my wards and into my room.

A bit of that old, iron-fisted spirit of mine rises in me again.

If I want to live in peace, I'm going to have to deal with these enemy witches before they deal with me. Removing whatever threat they pose to me is more important than even my studies.

My pen moves to write the information down, and only halfway through scribbling my plans out do I realize it's unneeded. I won't forget.

I will, however, need help.

I tap the top of my pen against the paper.

In the past, Memnon was just as keen to discover these witches as I was. I don't think his interest had anything to do with revenge. Even then in the depths of his anger, I believe he still sought to protect me. I'm nearly positive he would be willing to get his hands dirty on my behalf once more.

But he might simply use this request as leverage to get something else out of me. The thought leaves me cold.

No, that will not happen. I won't let it.

My mind strays back to the last of my ancient memories, the truly painful ones,and I press my lips together. I have leverage of my own.

*Memnon,* I reach out down our bond.

I feel warmth from his end of the magical cord. I'm sure he thinks this is me caving to his wishes.

Before he has a chance to speak, I say, *Meet me in the Slain Maiden's Meadow in an hour. I...* I close my eyes, forcing the next part out. *I need your help.*

# CHAPTER 5

*The ache in my bones is getting worse.*

Earlier, I assumed it was exhaustion and the aftereffects of overdrawing my power. I assumed the spells Memnon cast to remove my pain wore off. I assumed, I assumed, I assumed.

But I was wrong.

This is what Memnon had been hinting at when he wanted me to come to him.

I'm starting to feel the effects of the unbreakable oath.

I blow out a breath as I weave my way between the massive evergreen trees, dread gathering in my stomach. I knew there were consequences to not upholding a magical oath. I didn't realize they made you feel like shit.

I don't know how much longer I will be able to ignore the vow before I end up begging the sorcerer to marry me, just to ease the pain.

Between the boughs of the trees ahead of me, I catch sight of Slain Maiden's Meadow. The last time I came here,

I wasn't yet a student. The field looks lovelier now, in the dying light, the sunset painting the dead grass golden.

And there, in the middle of the field, my soul mate waits, his back to me.

Memnon is the sound of straining leather. He's the smell of horse-sweat, grass, and man. He's sun-warmed skin and wind-tousled hair. He's a part of me just as much as Roxilana is, and no amount of magic or anger can change that.

As though sensing my gaze on him, he turns, his eyes lighting when they meet mine.

*Memnon kisses me fiercely as he sinks into me. There's only me, him, the endless grasslands around us, and the heavens above us.*

*"I am yours forever," he breathes against my lips. He pulls away to search my gaze, his features bathed in the soft orange glow from my magic. "Forever."*

Can he feel it? The past pressing on us like it has a presence of its own? Does it close up his throat like it does mine? Or am I the only one drowning in these memories?

"Little witch," he says, watching me as I cross the last of the distance between us. "You beckoned."

A shiver courses down my back at the low, honeyed sound of his voice.

"We need to talk," I say, switching to Sarmatian. Out here in these woods, we have more seclusion than my residence hall, but anyone could be listening.

I let my magic pour out of me. The pale orange glow wraps around us like a blanket, forming a magical barrier to block out sound. I don't incant the spell, but it's there nonetheless, woven into my magic through my intent alone.

Memnon reaches out, stroking my power like it's a cat.

40

"I'm listening," he says, his eyes flicking from my magic to me.

"When the curse was lifted, did you see into my past?" I ask.

The sorcerer's brow furrows. Whatever he thought I was going to say, this isn't it.

"I saw your recovered memories from this life," he responds slowly. "But once the curse moved to your first life and you started to weep, I lost the connection."

He'd been wiping away my tears and reassuring me I was okay. I'd almost forgotten those details.

"So you didn't see how that life ended," I say, just to be sure.

His gaze moves between my eyes and my mouth. "No, I didn't."

"What do you think happened?" I ask.

Memnon's expression grows grim. "I haven't the faintest clue. That is what I still wish to know. Why you cursed me to endless sleep and what you did after I was gone."

I can hear other, more personal questions that he won't voice but still echo down our bond.

*Did you regret burying me alive? Did you betray me for another? Did you fall in love with someone else? Were you happy?*

"How did I betray you?" I prod him. "Tell me exactly the steps you believe I took to entomb you."

Memnon's eyes narrow as he looks at me, a muscle in his cheek jumping. "Selene, if this is some sort of trick—"

"Oh, there's a trick involved, but it wasn't made by *my* hand."

His brows rise, caught off guard by my response.

"Tell me," I insist. "How did I fuck you over? I want to

41

know every detail you believe I carried out to place you in that sarcophagus."

The sorcerer's jaw tightens with indignation. "This is my life you ruined—"

"No," I say viciously. "It is *my* life that *you* ruined. Two thousand years ago along the banks of the Amazon River, I *died* to keep you safe from a horrible fate! There was no grand plan. There was no *life after you.* I protected you, and what did you do when you woke? You blamed me. You attacked me. *You* betrayed *me* and everything we once were with your vengeance."

Memnon looks as though I've struck him.

Goddess, but my bones ache, and I'm breathing heavily. All around us, my magic twists and writhes with my churning emotions.

"What?" Memnon finally says, his voice hushed.

"You wish to understand the past and my motives better?" I grab his hands and place them on either side of my head. "See them for yourself."

Memnon's hands flex against my skin, wisps of his magic curling out from beneath his palms as though he can't quite contain his emotions. Down our bond, I feel the first tendrils of his rising horror.

I don't think he wants to believe me, nor do I think he wants to read my mind. Not now that he knows he might not like what he finds.

"*Do it,*" I insist, shaking his hands a little from where I still grip them. My eyes are pricking, and I didn't mean to get worked up over this. I just wanted his help, but this is how I get it without owing him anything. This is how the sorcerer understands that he owes me. The truth of our past—and our first demise—makes everything he's done to me so much worse.

Memnon works his jaw, his scar tugging a little at the action. His smoky amber eyes hold my gaze for several seconds.

Finally, he bows his head, then nods, his fingers flexing against me again. "All right, Empress. As you wish." He adjusts his hold. "Repeat after me," he says. "*Pes datapzaka kubiwapsasava vi'savva ziwatunutasa vak mi'tavekasavak ozakos detgap.*"

*I bare the last memories of my first life for you to see.*

I recite the incantation, gripping his hands tightly, my heart beating fast as I prepare to relive this particular memory.

Memnon's magic rushes from his hands, the blue tendrils of it slipping into my mouth and up my nostrils. I arch my back as it moves to my head, my hands tightening against his.

And then that final, fateful day of my last life unfolds right before my eyes.

# CHAPTER 6
# Roxilana

*59 AD, Bosporus, Crimea*

**Roxi...**

My eyes snap open, and I stare at the dark ceiling of the palace bedroom, Memnon's voice ringing in my ears. A deep, inexplicable sense of dread has lodged itself in my marrow. Was it a bad dream that I dragged with me from sleep? Something else?

I take several shallow breaths, trying to get my bearings, then I reach for Memnon. The other side of the bed, where my soul mate should be, is empty.

*Memnon?* I call down our bond.

All that comes back to me is silence.

He had woken me, I'm sure of it, so where is he?

"Memnon?" I call out softly, thinking maybe he's somewhere in this dark room. But the space feels empty, and no one answers me back.

Did he stay up late to strategize future battles with his

blood brothers and other high ranking officials? It wouldn't be the first time.

But if he *were* awake, he would answer me. He doesn't.

I try again.

*Memnon?*

No response.

My heart begins to gallop, and the unsettled feeling I woke with amplifies.

Perhaps my husband fell asleep somewhere else. He doesn't usually do that, but it's entirely plausible. He's been overworking and undersleeping, his mind consumed with war.

At the foot of the bed, Ferox, my familiar, lifts his dark head, his form merely a deeper shadow among the rest. My anxiety must be loud if it's roused him from sleep. I want to tell my panther to be at ease, but I cannot—not when I'm still trying to figure out what has set me on edge.

Out the palace window, I listen to the call of a starling as I steady my breath. Even the birdcall pricks at my skin. Damn this relentless unease.

Throwing my sheet off, I move to the window and rest my hands on the stone sill, drawing in a deep breath of the briny air. I gaze down at the royal harbor and the moonlit shores of the Black Sea.

Another starling call joins the first. If I had woken up less agitated or had I not woken up at all, I would've easily missed it.

*Starlings come in the winter, not the apex of summer, and they come in swarms of millions, not in lonely pairs.*

The groan and creak of wood has me glancing down at what I can see of the vessels moored at our docks.

I frown as my unease ratchets up.

Were those ships there earlier today? It's too dark to be sure.

I strain my eyes in the darkness, making out a few figures on those docks. The longer I stare, the more figures amass, all of them silent as the grave.

*Something's wrong.*

Deeply, deeply wrong.

*Memnon? Why won't you answer?* I plead, more to myself than to him.

Does he know something is afoot? Could something have happened to him?

No. I refuse to believe that. I sense him on the other side of my bond, even if his end of it is subdued. He lives still.

Moving away from the window, I pad to the chest at the foot of my bed. I open it, and by feel alone, I grab a shirt and breeches. I don't dare illuminate the room as I dress in case my worst fears have come to pass.

We have enemies. We have always had enemies. Never more so than now. Memnon has always made sure to be one step ahead of them, but I don't believe he anticipated this.

As I finish pulling on my boots, there's a soft rapping near the portiere, the curtained doorway to my room.

"Roxilana!" a masculine voice whispers urgently. It takes me a moment to recognize that it belongs to Zosines, Memnon's closest and fiercest blood brother. Another insistent rap. "Roxilana! Wake up!"

I'm crossing the room to draw back the curtains when Ferox growls softly. I go still.

Very slowly, I glance at my panther, feeling that disquiet in my stomach. I can see little beyond my familiar's general form, but as I stare at him, I can just make out that Ferox's eyes are fixed on the portiere.

I follow his gaze. The wards that cling to the curtained doorway like cobwebs now shine faintly in the darkness, as though they've been activated. Zosines must be trying to get in—and he cannot. That threshold is warded against malevolent intent.

Chills skitter down my spine.

I glance back down at Ferox, my body still steeped in unease.

"Roxilana!" Zosines calls out again. His voice is louder, more panicked and insistent.

My familiar lets out another low growl, then drops soundlessly to the floor, prowling forward like he's homing in on a kill, his belly low to the ground. I slip down our bond and into Ferox's head, curious about what is alarming him.

I'm not even fully seated in his mind when I first scent blood. So much blood. The acrid tang of it is ripe enough to taste.

"Roxilana!" Zosines pleads. "We're about to be under attack! We need to get you out now!"

I touch the closed curtains between us lightly, imagining the tall warrior in my mind's eye. Zosines and Memnon have been fierce friends since they were children; the two are bound by a blood oath and many, many battles. My mate trusts him with his life.

But intuition and observation are telling me something else altogether.

"*Asphyxiate*," I whisper.

I don't see my magic wind around Zosines's throat, but I hear his surprised chokes and then the clatter of something heavy, followed by the thump of his body hitting the floor.

Only then, once he's sufficiently distracted, do I dare push aside the curtained partition.

On the other side of it, Zosines claws at his throat, trying uselessly to pry away my power. Those who don't wield magic cannot stop it. Next to him lies a wicked-looking dagger, one he must've been holding when he called for me.

Wordlessly, I command my magic to draw the blade to me. The weapon rattles against the ground for a moment before it streaks across the space and into my hand.

Stepping up to Zosines, I kneel next to him and indolently press the blade to his throat.

His dark eyes glare up at me.

"What are you doing?" he rasps.

I honestly don't have the faintest clue, but panic still laces my blood, and my intuition has never steered me wrong.

I command more of my power to wrap around him, tethering him in place. The last thing I want is for Zosines to get away now that I have him in a vulnerable position.

"Where is my husband?" I demand as Ferox comes to my side, his gaze unerringly trained on the warrior.

"Can't breathe." Zosines's eyes are starting to bulge.

I ease up on the spell. "Where?" I press.

Zosines gasps in a few lungfuls of air. "*Safe*," he hisses out. "But you are not. The palace is about to be breached, my queen. There is not much time. We need to go."

Distress is contagious, and I want to agree, I do.

The faint scent of blood catches in my nostrils, and I remember all over again how even sequestered in our room, Ferox could smell the iron tang of it. Zosines said the palace was about to be breached, but violence has already happened here.

My gaze roves over him, and I notice then the fresh

speckles of blood on his clothes. Violence he must've partaken in.

I lift my eyes. The rest of the hallway is eerily silent, save for the soft hiss of torches in their sconces. In the distance, I can hear something else. Voices?

Refocusing on Zosines, I gather my magic and force it down his throat. "*Only the truth shall cross your lips,*" I incant.

Zosines jerks and fidgets against the magic holding him in place. He's seen enough of my power to fear it.

"What is happening?" I demand. As I ask it, I retract my magic completely from his throat.

He presses his lips together.

"Speak." My magic bears down on him. "*Now.*"

"A coup, you cunt," he bites out.

My blood runs cold. A *coup.*

"Where is Memnon?" The question is more pressing than ever, now that I know there's a price on his head.

Zosines laughs. "Wherever the fuck that crazy bitch Eislyn took him."

Eislyn…took him? During a coup? To hide him? He wouldn't have allowed that. Not when his closest family and friends are here in the palace under attack. But then again, I haven't heard from him since I woke.

"Is he alive?" I ask.

Zosines snickers, and I focus on that callous reaction. "I doubt for long."

I can't breathe. Not when I'm drowning in panic.

Later. I can be sad later. He's apparently alive for now. With Eislyn. Probably in that land beyond the land.

My fingers twitch a little as I fight the urge to hunt my soul mate down.

"Why is this happening?" I demand.

"The Romans held this territory for a century before Memnon took it. They want it back."

There are enough clues sprinkled about. "Who made a deal with them?"

Zosines's throat works as he fights against the words. He pulls futilely against the magic binding him in place.

"Memnon's plans would have killed us all. I wanted what was best for our people."

"Who did the Romans make an offer to?" I press. Someone was promised something.

"*Me.*" The word rips from his throat. "They came to *me*. Eislyn brokered the deal."

I didn't think it was possible to feel worse about the situation, but I do. Eislyn turned on Memnon as well. Unbelievable. I always assumed it was me she'd fuck over.

In the background, I can hear more voices. They sound louder, bolder. Whatever precious time I have, it's slipping through my fingers.

"Tell me the rest of the plot."

Zosines laughs weakly. "You cannot hope to outmaneuver it."

I pull the warrior's dagger away from his throat. There's a flicker of curiosity in his eyes, maybe a little victory, as though the futility of my situation is finally sinking in.

I study him, meeting those dark, devious eyes. Now I'm not mistaken—triumph does flicker in them. Unfortunately for him, he cannot see the thick plumes of my magic wrapping around us.

Adjusting my grip on his dagger, I shove the blade into his side.

He begins to scream, but it does him little good. My power swallows up the sound.

"Stop fucking with me, and tell me the full plot," I command, "and maybe I'll heal this wound."

He gasps, but an unholy excitement dances in his eyes. "You'll pay for that later, my queen," he vows, spitting out my title like it's an oath.

I twist the knife, and Zosines screams between clenched teeth.

"*Answer me.*"

"Half of Memnon's top warriors were in on it. Itaxes, Rakas, Tasios, Palakos, Thiabo, Dzoure—and more," he gasps out. "You were both to be drugged at dinner. Once you were sedated, the plan was for Eislyn to take Memnon away—she had very specific plans for him—and you were to come with me. But you left dinner early, so here we are. There are five hundred Roman soldiers and mercenaries ready to descend on the palace—if they haven't already. Another thousand mercenaries, mainly Cimmerians, are at the ready, should anything not go smoothly."

I try not to feel as hopeless as Zosines is making the situation sound. Memnon has single-handedly defeated worse odds. It's not over yet.

"What else?" I ask.

Sweat has begun to bead on his forehead, and his breathing is coming in short, shallow pants. "The royal family and any loyalists were to be killed. We can't have anyone avenging the fallen king and causing unrest."

Terror rolls through me then. Tamara and Katiari, Memnon's mother and sister, are certainly at the top of the list.

"What do you get out of it?" I ask.

The corners of Zosines's mouth twitch and spasm as

though he's trying to hold a gloating smile back. "I would be king."

Ah, there it is. He sold his dearest friend out for power.

His mouth continues to twitch.

"Anything else?" I prod.

Finally, he adds, "You. I would get you as a war prize."

My eyebrows lift. Me? It's such a preposterous thought.

"Why?" I finally ask.

The look in his eyes shifts, turning...covetous is the best word for it. I've seen that look from him before. I just never paid it much attention. The man has six wives—already more women than he must know what to do with. *If he had it his way, I would be the seventh.*

Revulsion moves through me. He clearly never thought this through. I'd curse him to death sooner than he could lay a finger on me.

The distant sounds of commotion grow louder. I think...I think I hear the massive palace doors groaning open. Shit.

"Besides you," I say, "is anyone else coming for me?"

Zosines laughs. "*Everyone* is coming for you. Memnon and your allies are dead. Those who would follow you have perished. Some still sit in that dining hall, their corpses rotting away in their chairs. Their bodies will remain unburied, their flesh left out to rot. But if you come with me, I can save you. I can make you queen once more."

Queen? That's what he intends? If it weren't for the truth spell, I would doubt his words, especially now that I have buried a dagger in his side.

He must want me for my power. He must think that his benevolence sparing me from certain death tonight will make me feel indebted to him. Such are the ways of Sarmatian warriors. That's just not *my* way.

"This is your only chance to live," Zosines adds.

His words are punctuated by distant battle cries. The soldiers are inside.

I search his eyes. "You think I am scared of the Romans? Of death? Or that I would cling to my throne if Memnon didn't sit beside me?" I shake my head. "I would follow him to the ends of the earth. I would follow him even into death. But I think you shall go there first."

With a flick of my wrist, the power that encircled us now rushes for his head.

*Snap.*

His neck breaks, and my magic releases him, his body going limp on the ground.

I glance up when I hear the sounds of furniture crashing and wood splintering. The soldiers must be raiding the bottom floor of the castle. The cries of the encroaching legion are getting louder.

I straighten. I need to get going if I wish to stop Eislyn before it's too late, but first...

I look down the hall to where Tamara and Katiari's room is. The curtains of the portiere are partially ripped away. My heart beats faster and faster. There's no time left, but I need to be sure.

Ferox steps in close, his head nudging my hand so that my palm rests on it.

*I'm here with you*, the gesture seems to say. I draw in a deep breath then head toward their room. Halfway there, I can hear the slow drip of something.

I'm not even to the doorway when I see Tamara's body in the shadows of her room, her torso slumped against the wall, a bloody, gaping wound in the center of her chest where someone ran her through with a sword.

My knees nearly give out, and I have to stumble the rest of the way to Tamara to stop myself from falling. I pass through the still-intact wards shielding the room and fall to her side, cradling her cold body in mine. Her head slumps listlessly against me, and though the shouts and screams are closing in, for a moment, I cannot bother with them.

This is a Sarmatian *queen*, a woman who led armies into battle and made life-and-death decisions on behalf of her nomadic peoples for years before Memnon took over. She deserved more than a traitor's blade through her chest.

I continue to hold her body against mine, even as I hear boots on the stone stairs. My eyes scan the room, looking for Katiari, Memnon's younger sister, dread coiled in my belly. I have to cast an illumination spell to see the rest of the room.

Beneath the soft orange glow of it, I see the slumped body of Katiari. She lies on her back, four arrows jutting from her chest, a pool of blood beneath her.

Carefully, I release Tamara and move to my sister-in-law's side, touching her skin lightly. It has the same deathly chill clinging to it as Tamara's does. The Sarmatian princess is gone as well.

A disbelieving breath shudders out of me. She was not just a sister by marriage but by love and choice as well.

I am a child again. Soldiers have invaded my home, killed my family. My sobs turn into an anguished cry.

Roman sympathizers did this. Rome once again *took* from me.

I can hear them at the end of the hallway, knocking over braziers and ripping at the hanging tapestries.

Poisonous rage builds in my veins, devouring my grief and turning it into something darker, deadlier.

I am reliving old pain, but I am no longer a child, and these men shall suffer.

Another cry rips from my throat, but this one sounds feral, *wrathful*.

I rise, Ferox near my side. I place a hand on his head.

I whisper a spell aimed at my familiar. "*Impenetrable armor for your body,*" I incant.

My magic billows over the great cat, coating him in a protective ward. Heedless of the few seconds I have left, I turn the same spell on myself, my power moving down my form and readying me for battle. It won't hold forever, these spells never do, but it will protect us for now at least.

There are a dozen or more sets of feet rushing toward the end of the hall where we are, likely drawn in by my scream.

Quickly, I place a curse on my mother-in-law and sister-in-law's bodies. "*Skin like death, liquefy the innards of any who dare touch these corpses.*" My voice breaks on that final word. My mind knows these women are gone; my heart cannot fathom it.

I cast the bodies one last grim look. The soldiers will try to desecrate their remains. I smile malevolently at the thought of the pained death that awaits such fools.

My power gathers beneath my skin, my muscles and joints throbbing from it. Rage makes even that pain feel good.

I glance at my familiar. "Ready yourself, Ferox. Everyone beyond this room is an enemy. Kill whatever you can."

I step out of the room as the first of the Roman soldiers closes in on me. This soldier is a youthful man with rich, golden skin and thin, lithe legs.

His eyes widen a bit when he sees me, and he slows just

a little. Behind him are more than a dozen others. I raise a hand, my magic gathering.

"*Annihilate.*"

*BOOM!* The entire castle trembles as power explodes out of me, blowing the soldiers in front of me apart. Bloody limbs fly, smacking into other soldiers farther back, knocking them down.

All that's left of that golden-skinned man is a bloody splatter mark on the ground.

I stride forward as more soldiers pour into the hallway off the stairs.

I waited too long to leave this place, but I no longer care. My rage burns in me, scalding my magic.

I storm down the hallway while Ferox rips out the throat of a soldier struggling to push off the mutilated torso of a fallen comrade.

More magic gathers. "*Annihilate!*"

Another explosion. More scattered bodies. Those pretty Roman helmets are blown from the heads of their soldiers, or else they're blown away *with* the severed heads of their owners still inside them.

The sight of the scattered remains of soldiers soothes something primal in me. I never thought of myself as particularly malicious, but apparently, for my soul mate and my family, I am. Ruthlessly so.

So focused on the carnage am I that I don't notice the first arrow that strikes me. It hits me in the right shoulder, and though it doesn't so much as tear the fabric of my warded tunic, the force of it still nearly knocks me off my feet.

Archers. There are archers inside the palace despite the close proximity of this space. The thought has me casting out another annihilation spell. Bodies burst apart, and dust falls from the ceilings and the walls shake. I don't care if this whole, massive place falls on our heads so long as it takes these men out with it.

I try not to think about the grief and sorrow that claw up my throat at what I've lost this evening and what I might still lose.

*Need to get to Memnon. Gods, I need to get to him.* I still haven't heard from him, and I sense little down our bond.

There are many places Eislyn could've taken Memnon, most of them entirely inaccessible. But if she and my mate are still here in this realm, then there is one place above all others where she would take him.

When I get to the stairs, I blow apart another cluster of soldiers, the spell taking out a large section of the stone steps with it.

I descend down what remains, recasting the ward I placed on Ferox, who clings close to my side.

The palace temple, then. That's where I must go.

Down on the first floor, the sounds of battle cries and anguished screams are louder. And when I catch sight of the melee, it takes my breath away. A few loyal Sarmatians fight back against the soldiers, but they're *vastly* outnumbered. The Romans are also cutting down innocent palace servants, who have no battle training, and smashing or carrying out royal items, most of them relics of the rulers who lived here before us.

As soon as I'm noticed, the atmosphere in the main area of the palace shifts entirely.

"The queen!" someone shouts.

I can't place the voice, and I have no clue whether it's from friend or foe. But then I catch sight of Rakas, one of

Memnon's named betrayers. He's pointing his sword at me and shouting orders.

All my rage is directed into an unnamed curse, one I aim for that traitorous Sarmatian man. The pale orange magic that barrels toward him is threaded through with oily black stains. When it hits Rakas, it lifts him into the air, great plumes of orange smoke upwelling beneath him. Never have I made such a spell or committed such a feat as lifting a person into the air. This is fueled by rage and pain and my power's own sentience.

The fighting slows, and people stop to stare as Rakas writhes above them, slashing his sword at thin air to try to break himself free.

The magic still swarms around him, hugging close to his skin, and it's only once it's sunk into him that I clearly see his flesh begin to boil and bubble, until all at once his body explodes, bits of cursed flesh raining down on the room. People begin to shriek as the curse lands on them and burns their own flesh.

The Roman soldiers are screaming, horrified. They signed up for war, not witchcraft. Some run, but most cast new, deadlier gazes on me. That's when the fighting begins in earnest.

I blow those nearest me back, then cast two more annihilation spells. Many, many bodies go flying.

Beneath my impassioned feelings, I begin to feel the drain of my magic. It's running out; it *will* run out. Rather soon if I keep attacking as I am. It's hard to care. Not when my cheeks are wet and a soul-deep ache has taken root inside me.

The moment the room recovers from their panic, a dozen arrows rain on me and Ferox. My familiar yelps when one of them hits his flank, and I lash out, my magic slicing a whole row of soldiers nearest me.

*The temple*, I remind myself. I need to get there if I have any hope of reaching Memnon.

I raise my arms to the room. "*Incinerate.*"

Fire billows from my palms, blowing out at those nearest me. Soldiers catch fire, and smoke and the acrid smell of burning flesh fill the room.

I cannot think about those I'm leaving behind. It's a bloodbath in the palace, and Memnon's forces have either been slaughtered or co-opted by the enemy. Any hope of us winning this fight will come only once I have my husband at my side.

My arms shake as I carve a bloody path for myself and Ferox. My panther lunges at anyone who comes too close, ripping out throats and slashing legs. I'm feeling the first true strain of my power. Sweat drips from my brow, and—

I choke as an arrow lodges in my back, throwing me forward. Another hits me near the armpit.

The protective ward I cast must've disintegrated.

A soldier rushes at me, sword swinging. I jump out of his way, but his blade slashes me across the abdomen.

I gasp, then rasp out, "*Impenetrable armor for my body.*" The ward returns once more.

It's too late though. Blood is seeping between my fingers and dripping down my back, and there are dozens of soldiers closing in on me.

*The temple*, I remind myself. Just need to get to the temple.

Closing my eyes, I draw on my pain and my blood and then the blood of anyone nearby. My power reaches out, drawing on the suffering and building in my veins. Dazedly, I release it, only half noticing the people it rips apart.

*The temple. The temple.* It's become a chant.

Ferox sticks close, and I can feel his inquisitive, worried gaze on me as I manage to pass through the double doors and leave the palace, my power blowing the enemy back many arm spans.

Several more arrows hit my body, though they bounce off my skin and clothes and clatter uselessly to the ground, leaving nothing behind except for ugly welts. Unlike the two others I carry. They protrude out of me almost comically.

Outside the palace the world is unnervingly silent, save for a few skirmishes and a couple of soldiers hauling away a chest of something or other. But the teeming scores of soldiers are following me out. It's all I can do to cast my magic behind me, pushing them and their weapons back, back, back, even as the wordless spell drains my quickly depleting reserves of power.

Off to my left, I can see the shadowy silhouette of the abandoned temple. The priests maintaining it left once we moved in, and no one else besides the odd palace servant has used it since. Sarmatian gods don't dwell in temples, and I have no use for Roman ones.

I stagger to it, moving as fast as I dare and leaving a trail of blood in my wake. I need to heal my wounds, particularly my abdominal injury, but I cannot focus on more than keeping my magic up at my back, where it protects me and Ferox. Even now, I sense the soldiers battering against it, their shouts and footfalls far too close.

It feels like an agonizing eternity before I reach the temple steps. As soon as I'm inside, I hastily ward the threshold against intruders, the magical strings of my casting somewhat sloppy. My hand shakes, and my pain is distracting me. I add another layer to the ward, this one to block weapons from entering the space—it was a ward we forgot to place on the room of Tamara and Katiari, and Zosines and the other traitors found a way around it.

I spell it just in time too. The first of the soldiers slams into the ward not a moment later. I jerk back at the sound, and my body sways a little. Ferox presses against my side, clearly trying to help me stabilize my balance.

"Thank you," I say softly, delving my fingers into his fur. One of my hands is still clutching my midsection. "*Mend the wound, heal the flesh*," I whisper.

Thick, syrupy magic spreads out beneath my palm, sinking into my skin. I hiss as it tugs on my injury, but already the pain is lessening as the wound repairs itself. I still have two arrows protruding from my torso, but for now, I let them be.

"*Illuminate*." The light I cast is faded, watery. My magic is faltering.

I half stride, half stumble toward the back of the temple, where the innermost sanctum is. Where the entrance to the ley line will be.

When I see it, my relief makes my knees weak. It's barely visible under the light of my magic, but I can just make out the strange distortion in the air where the ley line entrance bends the light.

Far on the other side of the temple, I hear the bangs of weapons and fists against my ward, then the haunting sound of it shattering.

I place my hand on Ferox. "We'll step onto the ley line at the same time. Ready?"

The panther dips his head, which is the closest thing I'm

going to get as assent. Behind us, soldiers clamor toward us. Seconds. We have seconds.

Taking a fortifying breath, Ferox and I cross onto the ley line.

Immediately, the noise quiets, and our surroundings—what little I can make of them in the darkness—smear. Nonmagical humans cannot traverse these roads, at least not without aid. Which means that for now, Ferox and I are safe.

I cannot, however, say that about anyone else who remained devoted to Memnon. To me. They are still locked in battle, getting butchered by an enemy they didn't see coming.

I need to get to Memnon. Need to save him from whatever fate Eislyn has devised. Need to avenge our people.

My gaze flicks to the walls of the ley line. It's shaped much like a tunnel, though you wouldn't know it at the moment. The darkness hides everything except for the faint smudges of starlight far beyond.

With my free hand, I reach around and pull out the arrow from my back, grinding my teeth together and swallowing a scream as I pry the head of it from my flesh, its edges ripping through more muscle. I toss the bloody projectile to the rippling tunnel walls.

"I offer you my blood, violently spilled by an enemy," I gasp out as the open wound at my back begins to bleed in earnest, "in exchange for the safe passage of me and my familiar to the Khuno River palace."

What little I can see of the walls ripples, then smooths.

Fuck. It didn't work.

Without the help of the ley line itself, I won't be able to find my way to this destination. Instead, Ferox and I will wander along it, hopelessly lost until I either find a way out, or we perish.

Adjusting my hold on Ferox, I reach for the other arrow and dig my fingers into the skin around it. A scream rips from my throat as I pull the second arrowhead out and throw it at the wall. "I offer you my blood, violently spilled by an enemy," I repeat, "in exchange for the safe passage of me and my familiar to the Khuno River palace."

This time, the walls hardly even ripple.

"I offer you a memory," I say to the fae magic, my desperation growing. "In exchange for the safe passage of me and my familiar to the Khuno River palace."

The walls of the ley line ripple around me, further obscuring the scenery outside.

I take a few steps forward, bringing Ferox with me, but then the walls around me smooth, denying me passage once more.

I cry out, "For gods' sakes, what do you want? Tears?" With my free hand, I gesture to my cheeks. "You can have them."

The ley line's strange, foreign magic brushes against my face, taking the offered tears.

Still, the wall doesn't open. I want to scream.

"You already have my blood and my tears. What more do you want?" I ask the darkness. My magic is failing, my blood is streaming down my back, and my body is faint with exhaustion. There's not much left of me to give.

Why had I not learned to navigate these magical roads without selling little pieces of myself? My ignorance is costing me.

A thought comes to me, one that has me pressing a

quivering hand to my stomach. I swallow. There is one more thing—

"Fine, I'll tell you a secret: I think I might be pregnant."

# CHAPTER 7
# Roxilana

*59 AD, somewhere in the northwestern Amazon Basin*

***We're spit out onto wet soil, mud oozing beneath my boots.***
It worked. My body sags with relief. It worked.

I stand, glancing at my surroundings. The sun is setting here, and though the jungle around me makes many sounds, there's a peaceful, quiet element to this place that's jarring compared to the shrieking violence of Bosporus.

Ferox's growl is all the warning I get.

I'm about to turn when a blade is shoved clean through my back. It happens so fast I don't have time to do more than choke on my own surprise as I glance down at my abdomen, where the bloody tip of a sword juts out.

Roughly, it's withdrawn, and with its exit I collapse to my knees, a cascade of blood pouring from the wound. It's—it's right where—

"You cannot know how long I've wished to do that." Eislyn's beautiful, lilting voice is laced with malice.

With a snarl, Ferox lunges for the fairy. But before he can make it anywhere near her neck, Eislyn brings the hilt of her weapon down on his head. There's a sickening crunch, and I choke out a scream as my familiar collapses in a heap at my side. The ward that had protected him only minutes ago must've disintegrated.

The fae woman walks around to my front, tapping the bloody sword against her thigh as she appraises me. "I had hoped you'd survive the attack long enough to come here."

She tilts her head, appraising me. I imagine she's debating whether to stab me again, though I'm too distracted to notice. My mate is missing, my familiar is unconscious, and blood is pouring out of my abdomen at an alarming rate.

I can barely think over the pain in my gut, yet I have rage to spare. My body is shaking with it. I gather my magic, preparing to strike.

"Ah, ah," Eislyn chides, using the bloody sword tip to tilt my chin up. "Think about harming me, and I'll drive this sword through your throat, then that of your familiar, and you will die never knowing what became of Memnon."

I go still, terror replacing anger. "Where is he?"

Her eyes flick to the palace to my right for the merest of instants before she casually says, "I thought you were his soul mate. That you could find him through your bond alone." She tilts her head again. "Apparently not."

As she speaks, I focus my magic on my gut wound. It's a mortal wound, but only if it cannot be repaired. I *can* repair it. I'm already clutching it, and now I slowly trickle my power into it. All I have to do is live, then I can save both Memnon and Ferox.

"What did you do to my mate?" I ask.

She stares down at me stoically. "He will sleep for a

hundred years, until all he knows and loves has passed on. When he wakes, all that will be left is me."

My brows come together, even as I feel the nauseating tug of internal injuries sealing themselves up.

She continues. "I already warned Memnon several times that you would prove treacherous. I told him that a civilized Roman girl like you would never fully accept the warring ways of Sarmatians. That his bloodthirstiness would eventually drive you to do something desperate to stop him from all the killing and conquering. He didn't believe me then, but I'm sure when he wakes and finds you long gone, he will remember my warnings."

Eislyn's warnings would hold weight with Memnon. She'd been an advisor to Memnon's father as well as several kings who came before him.

"And," she continues, "I will make sure to tell him how you, his dear mate, made a deal with the Romans for peace and how you couldn't bear to kill him so you left him to sleep. I'll make sure he knows that you lived a long life— that you remarried, had children, and you didn't once try to wake him."

I can barely breathe over my disbelief. Who *is* this woman?

"He'll be heartbroken," she continues, "but in time, he will recover."

I search her features. "Why are you doing this?"

Her eyes glitter, and the corners of her mouth curve into a sly smile. "That's a secret you'll have to die without knowing."

Instinct rather than eyesight has me noticing the infinitesimal shift of Eislyn's weight and the adjustment of her grip on the sword.

I call on my anger and my power. "*Annihilate*," I breathe.

The spell blasts out of me, the power blowing off her sword arm. She screams, reaching for the gaping wound at her shoulder. Her wings unfurl, thinner than linen and far more delicate. She uses them to rush herself to the ley line portal.

I'm already gathering the scraps of my magic, readying them in my hand.

"*Annihilate.*"

Her form disappears a moment before my spell does, though the ley line absorbs it as well.

My breathing is ragged.

Eislyn is gone. For now.

I stare down at the ruin of my abdomen, and I bite back a sob. If there was a baby, the odds of it surviving such a wound…

I have to dig my teeth into my lower lip to keep from screaming. Tears slip down my cheeks. Don't think about that. Then there's Ferox…

I reach out a hand and pet my panther. Beneath my touch, my familiar stirs, then turns his head to weakly lick my hand. I strain for enough magic to heal him. It leaves my palm sluggishly, but I sense the spell take root, and it slowly mends my familiar's injuries. Once I'm sure he'll be okay, I let my hand slide from him.

*Memnon. Need Memnon.*

I force myself to stand, and the world goes dark for a moment. Blood loss, this must be blood loss. It physically hurts to draw out more power and funnel it toward the last of my wounds, and my magic is tired, reluctant.

*I'm dying.*

It comes to me with detached clarity. I'm dying faster

than my magic can heal. And Memnon is cursed to sleep for a hundred years, and once he wakes, he will be Eislyn's pawn for whatever bigger scheme she's concocting. Perhaps it's love she wants from him. Perhaps it's power. Whatever it is, she was willing to have his family murdered and entice his friends to betray him. She was willing to twist my motives and my love for him, all so she could see her awful plan through.

I cannot leave him to whatever fate she intends.

I stagger forward, toward the palace, leaving Ferox where he is so he can sleep off his injury. Ahead of me, the river palace gleams among the trees; it's so unnaturally beautiful it sets my teeth on edge. It always has.

I pass the marble pillars fashioned like trees and the golden vines with their sharp-edged glass flowers that decorate the walls, leaving a trail of blood in my wake.

Eislyn had looked to this place when she spoke of Memnon, and warded as the palace is, it is the perfect place to hide someone undisturbed for a hundred years.

But where?

I close my eyes and focus on my connection to Memnon. She had mocked our ability to find each other through it, but it *was* how he first found me in Rome. I can find him through it too. I just need to focus.

Closing my eyes, I breathe in deeply, trying to ignore the screaming pains of my body and the cold chill that has set in my bones. I let my mind take a back seat to my magic, and then I begin to walk.

I'm so dazed, I nearly fall into the hole in the ground. I stagger back and draw in a startled breath at the sight of the square opening in the ground. Next to it is a massive stone slab that's been cast aside.

I eye the torchlit walls descending from the opening. Memnon's down there. I can feel it like the beating of my own heart, and if I focus again on our shared bond, I can feel it tugging me closer, closer...

Eislyn had rigorously planned this entire situation, but she'd been careful not to tell me where Memnon was. I don't think she was finished.

The thought gives me a whisper of hope. That's all I need. Just a whisper.

Carefully, I descend the stairs, bracing myself against the wall to keep my fatigued body steady.

At first, the decorated walls around me barely register, but then my fingers cannot help but notice the divots where words have been carved. I stare at the writing.

*...containing the might of the gods within him, Memnon the Indomitable drove the Dacians from their lands...*
*...charged into impenetrable Rome with nothing more than his blood riders and captured his queen...*

The writing doesn't sound like me, but I'm one of the few who not only know these events but also how to read and write Sarmatian with the Latin lexicon. It would be easy to assume I helped secretly commission a vault like this and oversaw its creation.

A shiver racks my body that has less to do with blood loss and more to do with the disturbing lengths Eislyn went to to carry out her plot.

*What does she want with my husband?*

The question will plague me.

All thoughts of her motives vanish the moment I step into the burial chamber. And there's no mistaking that's what this is. In the center of the torchlit space lies a white marble sarcophagus, the lid of it removed. From here, I can only make out a glimpse of scale armor, but I know—it's Memnon. Even if the bond wasn't indicating it, the slope of that chest and the sheen of that bronze armor would.

A ragged sob rips from my throat. I hadn't believed he was asleep, not truly, not until now.

I drag myself to the stone coffin, the blistering pain of my wounds dulled by the deeper ache in my heart. My gaze barely touches on his arresting, sleep-softened features before my legs give out. I'm awash in pain—pain so dark and bleak I don't know how I'll surface from it.

*He's already out of my reach.* Enchanted to a hundred years of sleep. If it were mortal magic, maybe I could break the spell, but Eislyn is a fairy, and their magic is different, *incompatible.*

Even if the spell could be broken, I'm dying. Beyond that, Memnon's empire is now overrun by battle-ready Romans, his traitorous warriors, and a scheming fairy.

We have too many enemies and not enough time. A tear slips out.

I place a hand lightly on the ruined flesh of my abdomen. I want retribution, but more than anything, I want peace. For me, for my soul mate. A single lifetime where we can love each other without the fear of our enemies killing us.

I struggle to pull myself up, gnashing my teeth together against the pain. There's darkness pulling at my vision, and at this point, my magic is likely the only thing left keeping it at bay, but I do manage to get my legs locked under me. I've got life left in me yet.

I glance into the coffin, where Memnon rests, still as death. Not even his chest moves with his breathing. I can tell through our bond that he still clings to life, but he gives few signs of it.

I stroke his hair back, drops of my blood and tears hitting his armor.

"This is not how we end," I whisper. "We are eternal."

Something dark and resolute moves through me.

*We are eternal.*

If we cannot have this life, then we shall have another.

Eislyn isn't the only one capable of using extraordinary measures.

I am as well.

And whatever spell she's placed on Memnon, I can make one stronger. It might not break the enchantment he's under, but it can usurp it.

Some final fire stirs in me, rousing me.

I can do this, for him, for us.

I *must.*

I just need a little help.

My grip on the sarcophagus tightens as I draw my magic together. There's precious little power left in me and nothing my body wants to give up. But there are other sources of magic—in the air and, more notably, in the ground. The earth is already feasting on the trail of blood I've left. I can sense the magic beneath me clamoring for it. *Hungry.*

There are things that rule that magic, things that have whispered to me every so often. They might be willing to help me cast a spell of the magnitude I need...but they always exact a price.

I bow my head over the sarcophagus and draw the words out. "I call on any god who will answer: Memnon the Indomitable shall sleep the sleep of immortals. And he shall awake *only* by my hand. I bind my soul to this vow. Even in

72

death, I shall be beholden to it. Take what you must to make it so."

For several moments, all I hear is the soft, reverent hiss of the torches. Just when I'm nearly sure it didn't work, a low moan starts up in the distance, rattling the torches in their sconces. It builds into a howling wind that tears through the room, blowing my hair back. As it moves through me, I feel it pull away bits of my essence. The blood on my skin vanishes, as do the tears on my cheeks. Something dark and hungry slips inside me through my wounds, and I gasp at the insidious intrusion.

Once this essence is in me, it begins to spread. I choke on my own breath, my hand going to my abdomen. Whatever god answered my plea, it's named its price. I can feel it feasting on what's left of my life.

The unearthly wind circles the room several times, then sweeps out, gone just as quickly as it came. The pain, however, eating me from the inside out, is still there.

I stagger, struggling to catch my breath. I lean against the sarcophagus, my eyes drawn back to Memnon.

Always Memnon.

Beautiful, monstrous Memnon.

I touch his cheek, my fingers slipping a little. "We will get another life. A better one," I promise.

I lean into the sarcophagus, ignoring the way my body screams in protest, and press a kiss to his lips. They're still warm.

I pull away, my mouth lingering right above his. "I will find you again, my king. I am eternally yours."

I can feel hot tears slipping from my eyes as I straighten. All I want is to crawl inside that coffin and spend my last few moments with him. It would be a good place to die.

Unfortunately, if I mean to see this through, I can't do that.

I lift a trembling hand, my breath ragged as I force my reluctant magic to lift the coffin lid into the air. I shift it over the sarcophagus and gently lay it down.

Another tear drips, and I can feel my lower lip quivering with sadness and exhaustion. My tired eyes rest on the inscription carved into the top.

*For the love of your gods, beware of me.*
MEMNON THE CURSED

It's a terrible epitaph to leave him with—not that it's inaccurate—but it will scare off almost anyone who can read it. But in case it won't, I will need to ward it.

Just the thought of doing so has become heavy. I splay my hand over the lid, preparing to wrangle more magic. Yet when I call it forth, my power surges forward, stronger than ever.

A gift from the unnamed god.

I bite my lip to keep from crying out my relief. Though my mind is addled with pain and encroaching death, the ward I cast is strong; the many threads of it have a smooth sheen. As soon as I finish it, another forms and another, until my focus becomes the room at large. This too requires a ward.

I move around the coffin, though my legs don't feel as though they'll keep me upright. That noxious presence is spreading, withering me away from the inside out.

Something presses against my legs, and when I glance down, I realize it's Ferox. At some point, my familiar dragged himself off the ground and ventured into this cursed tomb to find me. He leans against me now, his eyes large, concerned.

I place a hand on his head. "I'm so sorry," I whisper brokenly. "I didn't mean for any of this to happen."

He pushes his nose into my palm, nudging it, as though demanding reassurance. I run a hand down his black fur.

"I release you, Ferox," I tell him. "You shall not be bound by my curse," I say, invoking my magic and weaving it into my words. "With my death, our bond shall sever, and you shall be free."

He hisses at me then, as though I have committed some great and terrible act.

"I'm sorry," I whisper again, my throat tightening. "You were always too good for me."

He growls, like even my apology displeases him.

I stagger over to a wall and lean heavily against it.

More spells seep from my palms, coating the room in pale looping threads like some shoddily woven garment.

I heave from the effort, my bones aching, brittle. So tired.

Cannot give up now. Not when the biggest spell is yet to come. It's a race against this thing inside me. Gods may occasionally be benevolent, but they are almost never merciful. Particularly not the bloodthirsty ones. I doubt this god will extend my life longer than they see fit.

I struggle up the stairs, and though Ferox is obviously still mad at me, he presses his body against mine to prevent me from falling.

"Thank you," I say, my voice weakening.

The two of us make our way out, the overcast sky so much brighter than the dim room we were in. Once I'm out, I turn around and lift my arm, my tears coming faster.

Leaving him in there feels like a betrayal all its own, like another knife sunk into my flesh.

I straighten my spine, drawing on my will.

"*Seal the opening.*" The stone covering slides over the... *tomb's* entrance, then with a thud sinks into place.

Ferox makes a low, baleful noise, scratching at the stone like he can unearth it. I have to stifle another sob, drowning in sorrow.

My heart seems to skip a beat, then stall. After a terrifying few moments, it begins to thump again.

I have precious little time to commit one final spell. A curse that will eclipse Eislyn's magic with my own.

If my desperate plan is to truly work, it is not enough for Memnon to outlive the enchantment. Eislyn must forget her fevered fixation so she might never come back for him. And those who could remind the fairy of Memnon's existence, their memories too must be expunged.

I think of the soldiers pouring into the palace and the many cities Memnon has violently conquered. There are thousands who would want to kill my slumbering husband if they ever learned the truth. One whispered word into the wrong ear—it wouldn't even have to be Eislyn. Other supernaturals could access the ley lines and end the king while he lies vulnerable.

*Everyone* must forget my sorcerer, so that none may come searching.

Only I shall have that power.

That insidious dark force closes in on the last of me, and my heart seizes again.

*One...two...three...*

Sluggishly, it resumes beating.

I take a shuddering breath and gather together all that I can of the power at my disposal.

"*With all that is left in me, I demand this world and everyone in it forget Uvagukis Memnon. Every last person who carries a memory of him shall lose them, beginning with Eislyn.*"

I give the last of myself up to the curse.

Pure, raw power bursts from me, sweeping out across the jungle until I can no longer see it. I sense when the first mind has been struck. It must be Eislyn's. I take a perverse amount of pleasure knowing I'm peeling away her memories.

She's the first, but it's the beginning of the curse.

Across the world, a thousand upon a thousand people carried some memory or awareness of Memnon. One by one, my magic devours every last memory of him. Memnon the Indomitable simply becomes some vague, cruel commander of legions who came and went.

In my mind's eye, I can see the petroglyphs bearing his name chip away until the recordings vanish. The ink on papyri rearranges itself to remove Memnon; where his presence is too frequent, the papyri simply burn up.

Across every land he conquered, his name disappears, cast from the record.

I take the memory of Memnon from everything and everyone.

I scream as my magic and that foreign essence consume me. The years of my life fall away like a fever dream as the magic leaving me thins out to just a wisp.

My heart stutters as that last thread of magic darkens, then doubles back on itself, moving back toward me.

Must hold on until the curse is finished. For this to work, no one can remember him.

No one...

*Not even me.*

My magic strikes then, sinking into my flesh and closing in on my memories. With a final, choked cry, my heart stops, and the last mind is wiped.

# CHAPTER 8
# Selene

*Present day, somewhere north of San Francisco*

**The last memory of my previous life fades away. I blink several** times as Memnon comes back into view. His cheeks are soaked as though he's been crying while reliving most of the past, and his hands tremble against my cheek.

"*No.*" The ragged word tears from his throat. His eyes search mine, his expression desolate. "*No,*" he says again, this time more broken.

Memnon's knees give out, and his hands drop from my face as he falls to the ground.

For several long seconds, all I hear is the sound of his heavy breathing as he bows his head, his hand pressed to his heart. I can feel the sharp blade of his grief through our bond, and I catch a few of his fragmented thoughts.

*…watched her die…alone…protecting me…powerless… What have I done?*

Finally, I hear a sound that is somewhere between a sob and a moan.

"*Roxi*," he says quietly, his voice thick with anguish. He looks at me then, horror written all over his face. "What have I done?" he says, echoing his earlier thoughts.

I stare down at him dispassionately. "A lot, Memnon. You've done a lot."

He draws in a shuddering breath. "You *died*."

"I did."

"You were alone in the palace when they came—" His voice breaks off, and he rubs his eyes. "My mother, my sister—" He presses his lips together, and his expression nearly crumbles again. "You had to fight your way out alone."

Memnon bows his head again and covers his eyes with his hand, and the man who has done so much and felt so little now weeps, overcome with emotion.

"Eislyn...you had warned me about her. I didn't listen. She almost...she destroyed everything. If you hadn't..." He draws in a shuddering breath. "If you hadn't placed the curse—if you hadn't given your *life*..." His voice breaks on that word. "I would've surely been damned to some awful fate. Instead, you did something miraculous. You bought us another life together."

I gaze down at him as the shadows around Slain Maiden's Meadow grow longer and darker.

"I see everything now," he says. "I *understand* I punished the one person who tried to save my wretched life. My best friend and soul mate, the love of my life. I have treated you like an enemy and made you hate me, and I relished it all in the name of vengeance. But this whole time you were

80

my savior." He turns his face up, his glittering eyes rising to mine. "I'm sorry, *est amage*. It is not enough, but I am sorry."

I study him for several moments, and then I do something I didn't think I was capable of doing, given all that Memnon has so recently done to me: I reach out and wipe away his tears. The action makes him close his eyes tightly, and a few more unbidden tears slip out.

I've only seen this man cry a precious few times, and the sight of him broken and vulnerable twists my gut.

Memnon catches one of my hands and cups it between his. "I have committed too many evils against you to repair with a few simple words or actions. They will never be enough to repay the debt I owe you. There is only one thing I can offer you."

Still kneeling, Memnon unsheathes his gold-hilted dagger from his side. I tense at the sight of it, my palm still stinging from the memory of that blade cutting through my flesh last night when I made my unbreakable oath.

Memnon offers up his own healed palm, and faster than I can follow, he slices it open once more.

"What are you doing?" I ask, alarmed.

His smoky eyes are steady on me as he says, "*With blood I bind, with bone I break. Only in death shall I at last forsake.*"

My lips part with surprise.

Birds take flight from the trees around us as he finishes, "*Your bidding be done, under moon and sun. My will is yours until your heart is won.*"

# CHAPTER 9

***I stare in horror at the proffered hand.***

He's giving me far more than a simple apology. This is a bond he's offering up.

I don't know much about bonds besides the fact that some are fated and some are chosen, and Memnon and I share the former connection.

But if I heard him correctly, he's offering me another one, only the terms of this one grant me control over his... free will.

My heart beats fast. I was hoping for his help, but this is so much more than that. If the sorcerer were bound to me, he would very literally have to follow my orders.

Memnon stares at me with those steady, calculating eyes, waiting on me as his blood drips to the grass. I know he knows all this. The powerful, vengeful Memnon, who's wiped out entire armies with his magic, is handing all that control over to me.

*He wants to tie you as close to him as possible.* This is just one more way. Even defeat he uses to his advantage. And then there's the terms of the bond.

*My will is yours, until your heart is won.*

The bond would break if I ever fell in love with him.

I gaze at his hand a little longer, debating, debating…

It's a mistake to think Memnon's a tamable thing, but I'm discovering that I'm not what I appear to be either.

I need help, and I need power. Memnon has both.

Resolve straightens my back. Kneeling in front of him, I take his blade from his other hand. My own magic is already unspooling out of me, the smoky tendrils of it straining for Memnon's dripping blood.

I take a deep breath, then before I can reconsider my actions, I draw the dagger down my palm, grimacing as I cut my palm for the second time in two days.

I reach for Memnon's hand, pausing just short of it. My gaze flicks to the sorcerer.

"This doesn't mean I forgive you," I warn him.

"I'm repaying a debt. No forgiveness is needed."

Scowling, I finally clasp his hand in mine.

The moment our blood touches, our powers hiss to life, streaming out from between our clasped hands and swirling together around us.

In the trees around us, birds take flight, their forms dark silhouettes against the deepening sky.

I drop Memnon's blade as his magic enters me through my wound and makes its way up my arm. It reaches my chest, and I suck in a breath as his power takes root beneath my ribs.

As soon as the magic settles, Memnon releases another wave of power, and I feel the cut on my palm seal itself up.

I release his hand, running my fingers over my newly repaired skin, smearing a little of the residual blood.

Memnon sits back on his haunches, resting his forearms on his knees. He watches me quietly for several seconds. I can't look at him. I now control a man—my own soul mate. Shame blooms in me. I shouldn't have agreed to this.

"Test it out, Empress," he says softly. "Compel me to do your bidding."

I stare at him, my dread rising. This sort of bond is what I fought against only two weeks ago. It was the fate I saved the shifter girl from.

Yet this is also what Memnon freely offered. And it is what I wanted.

Finally, I look at Memnon, ignoring the sad, wondrous way he appraises me.

"Stab me." I say the words softly, casually. No magic accompanies them, and a part of me is sure the command won't work.

Memnon blanches. "*Selene,*" he protests. But already his hand reaches for his discarded dagger.

Dimly, I'm aware of my magic forcing him through the movements, but I cannot see the plumes of it at work. It's all happening within him.

I lift my chin. "Right through the heart."

"No." But even as he speaks, his hand curls around the hilt of the blade, and his body is angling toward me. Panic clouds his eyes, and I can feel an echo of it through our connection.

One of his hands braces me by the back of the neck while his other arm draws back.

For an instant, that arm trembles. "*Please,*" he begs.

Then he lunges at me, his arm driving forward, the dagger aimed right for my heart.

"*Stop.*"

Memnon's blade freezes inches from my chest. He's breathing hard, and his arms are trembling.

I don't realize until then that I'm shaking as well. I don't think I fully believed that the binding spell worked until that moment.

"Put the blade away," I say softly. "You won't be stabbing me tonight—or any other night."

Oh Goddess, I've traded my memory loss for a new complication: needing to be precise with my words.

Memnon banishes the blood from his blade, then sheathes it, his breath still a little ragged.

"I don't want to marry you," I say. My whole body still aches from the unfulfilled oath.

The sorcerer hesitates. When he finally looks up, his eyes are conflicted. "It's an unbreakable oath, *est amage.*"

"You don't need to keep calling me that."

His jaw clenches. "Then command me to stop."

The two of us stare each other down.

I blow out a breath. "Fine, if I cannot undo the oath, then we're going to work with that other part of the vow."

How had we worded it?

*As soon as circumstances allow,* Memnon says to me through our bond.

I give him a look. "I want the 'circumstances' in question to be that we have to fall in love." I can live with that.

His eyes flash. This is what Memnon thought he had in the bag yesterday.

"Or," I add, "if you'd prefer, we could simply get

married—" I feel an instant spark of hope from the sorcerer. "Then immediately have it annulled."

Spark gone.

I smile. Oh, I think I could easily relish this.

Reluctantly, he nods. "We might have to make another vow for it to work, but let me see if the magic will simply adjust to the new meaning behind that clause."

He closes his eyes, focusing on the vow, and after a moment, I shut my eyes and do the same.

*The circumstances needed for us to get married are that we must first fall in love.* I repeat it over and over until I believe it. That malaise that has clung to me all day gradually lifts.

When I open my eyes, Memnon is studying me curiously, his head tilted, a small smile of his own curving up one side of his mouth.

"Do you feel better?" he asks.

I nod, sitting back on my haunches in the tall grass. "I think it worked. Did the vow…affect you too?"

Memnon gives a sharp nod. "I was under its compulsion as much as you were. I don't feel its effects any longer, but if they come back, we will need to make another vow."

Or marry. But he's smart enough not to propose that.

He's still studying me with that peculiar look on his face that's part amusement, part curiosity. It's tempered by the somber air he has about him, but it's making me oddly self-conscious.

I tuck a lock of hair behind my ear. "What are you thinking about?" I ask.

Memnon's gaze is steady. "That I should've given you control long ago." He stops speaking, and I think that's it. However, after a protracted moment, he frowns as more words are pried from his lips. "I'm also replaying your last day as Roxilana over and over again in the back of my mind," he adds unwillingly, "but I'm trying not to let you see how I'm slowly suffocating on my own pain." After he finishes speaking, he grimaces. For all that we are connected, Memnon still has his secrets.

Or he did until now.

I didn't really want to hear that either, if I'm being honest. Memnon is more palatable when he's heartless and cruelly devious. Now that we have this arrangement, that's where I want to keep him.

"I'm fine," I say, trying to brush over the events. "I'm alive." But Memnon also violently lost his mother and sister, and unlike me, they're not coming back. He has to come to terms with that as well.

I clear my throat, eager to turn the conversation away from the past.

"I don't want you to hurt my friends ever again," I say.

Memnon's eyes sharpen. "You're going to need to nuance that command."

My knee-jerk reaction is to argue with him, but I can begrudgingly admit he has a point. I literally just showed him a memory of two supposed friends betraying him. I fought them both, and if I hadn't been able to hurt them, I would be long dead.

"You are not to hurt my friends unless there's a reasonable cause for it," I amend.

Shit, there's definitely room for Memnon to abuse that rule. Whatever. I can fine-tune the command later.

I draw in a breath. "Now that you know what happened between us long ago, I want to talk about the other reason I called you here." The real reason.

He waits, arms casually slung over his knees, watching me again with that look in his eye as dusk bleeds into darkness.

"You told me not so long ago that I have enemies."

Memnon watches me carefully. "I did."

I think back to the threatening note left in my notebook. "Those witches, the ones who were after me the night I saved the shifter girl—when you lent me your power—they are still out there."

His expression darkens. "Not all of them."

Right. Because between me, Nero, and Memnon, a few of them definitely kicked the bucket that night.

Okay, so at least he knows what I'm referring to.

"There's also the murdered witches," I say. "The ones whose deaths you framed me for." I don't mean for the bitterness to enter my voice, but there it is. And it's going to be there for a long time, regardless of Memnon's efforts to repay his debt.

"I'm linked to these two separate issues. And I know you know more about the murders than I do."

He's gone quiet, but his eyes are cutting like daggers.

"I want you to help me learn everything I can about both the murders and those spell circles, and I want *you* to help me stop them both."

There's a certain poetic justice to the idea of Memnon, who drove me into all this misfortune, now helping me resolve it.

Once I've said my piece, I tense. If Memnon were anyone else, I know they'd scoff at me. I'm no detective, and even if I were, these are no ordinary mysteries.

To Memnon, however, I'm more than just Selene, Henbane student with prior memory issues. I'm also

Roxilana, queen of a nation of warriors, coruler of an empire. Inserting myself into deadly business comes naturally to me. Almost as naturally as it does to Memnon.

A bloodthirsty, pleased look spreads across his face. "I can do that, my queen."

# CHAPTER 10

*He's going to help me. I don't have to marry him, and he's* now going to help me.

I exhale a long, relieved breath.

I can tell he badly wants to touch me, hold me. There's a hollowness in his eyes, and regret is starting to creep into the rest of his features.

Finally, I think he gets it.

He fucked up.

He really, really fucked up.

Memnon rises, then reaches out a hand for me. "I have a lot to tell you, and I think you'd find your room a more comfortable place to hear it all."

I take his hand and let him help me up, noting that he holds my hand for a second longer than necessary once I'm on my feet.

"Is it safe to talk about this stuff there?" I've been played too many times in the last few weeks not to be paranoid.

"No," Memnon says. *But fortunately for us,* he continues down our bond, *we can speak of it like this.*

Fair point.

I stare at him a little longer, then reluctantly begin walking back toward my residence hall. Memnon sidles up next to me as we hit the tree line.

"I just want you to know that I actually want nothing to do with you ever again, and I'm only doing this now—"

"Because you want my help," he finishes.

"Because I know you won't leave me alone," I correct, "and putting you to work seems better than letting you run wild." It's not entirely a lie.

Memnon stays quiet.

"You have nothing to say to that?" I ask as we weave between trees, our shoes crunching over pine needles.

"Oh, I have plenty," he says.

"Then say it."

The sorcerer shakes his head, but my words carry their own compulsion. Memnon forces out the admission. "I *loathe* hearing you say you want nothing to do with me, but after being in your head, I understand it all entirely, so I must eat my feelings on this. But yes, I have no interest in letting you go. None at all. So I will help you with these mysteries, though the extra scrutiny may very well place you in more danger, and that means I will likely have to kill more people, and I don't want to admit that to you because I have a reputation to redeem. And I need to redeem it because I want you to crave me the way I crave you. You are the air in my lungs and the blood in my veins, and all the power and glory in the world are useless without you—" His voice breaks off.

Great Goddess's tits, that's…a lot to take in.

After a moment, he mutters, "*Fuck*."

I think the situation is sinking in for him as well.

"No, no, keep going and tell me how you really feel," I say sarcastically, though my words ring a little hollow.

Memnon makes a pained noise. "I hurt for all that I lost and how I lost it, and I'm despairing that I will ever get it again. I'm drowning in self-loathing at the moment."

I glance over at Memnon, my eyes wide, before I realize that though I made a joke, he was forced to take the command literally.

After a moment, the sorcerer groans. "Gods, what have I done?"

Despite the heavy admissions, I smile, just a little. I might actually like Memnon this way. He's disarming, which is a step up from hateful.

*You're not supposed to like him.*

"You *are* supposed to like me," Memnon says. "That is the entire point of being soul mates."

"Get out of my mind."

"*Est amage*, it is *you* who are in *my* mind," he says.

I glance down at my boots. "You were right last night," I admit softly. "There is so much about you I don't know."

It's silent for several seconds. Then—"Please don't make me give another confession. I can hardly stand the thoughts when I say them out loud."

I swallow a laugh.

"How did you come to live in that house?" I ask.

"It's a rental," Memnon replies.

"How did you get the money to pay for it?" I ask.

"I know you remember my power," he says. "With a touch and my will, I can get into anyone's head. I can learn their secrets, such as account numbers and routing numbers. And I can use them to my benefit."

So he's been stealing money. It's not the worst crime he's committed, so I guess I should curb my horror.

"And how did you learn about bank accounts, routing numbers, passwords—"

"—and mortgages and the stock market?" Memnon finishes. "I am still figuring out most of these, but once you touch enough minds, the information fills itself out. Assuming, of course, that the minds correctly understand the concepts. I'm pretty sure most people have no idea how the stock market actually works—myself included."

Ahead of us, the trees thin out, and I can just make out the conservatory and, farther on, my residence hall.

"So you've been using your powers to take what you need?" That explains how he learned English so fast.

"I can hear your disapproval, Empress."

"I don't actually," I say, surprising even myself. But it's the truth. "You woke two millennia later than when you went to sleep. I'm glad you took care of yourself."

In the darkness of the woods, I sense Memnon's eyes on me. He doesn't say anything, but down our bond, there's this honeyed softness coming from him. It makes me think of all the parts of us that I really don't want to focus on.

I press my lips together and say nothing else for the rest of the walk back.

As soon as Memnon and I enter the residence hall, the air in the house shifts.

But as we pass my house's library to our right, a few witches gaze curiously at the sorcerer. He gets more looks from the witches heading to the dining hall and a couple more from coven sisters coming down the staircase.

I glance over at Memnon, struck all over again by his appearance. His bronze skin, his black hair, and that beautiful, unforgiving face are arresting to look at, and that's saying nothing about his massive stature. He's built like the warrior he once was, and it shows.

He quirks an eyebrow at me, the corner of his mouth curving up. His lips part, and he sucks in a breath to speak.

"Whatever you're about to say, don't."

The sorcerer closes his mouth, bound by my order. That doesn't stop him from continuing to appear highly amused.

When we get to my room, Memnon's assessing gaze sweeps over the place.

"Where is Nero?" he asks when he sees the empty cat bed.

"Out hunting." I close the door behind me. "I didn't name Nero after the emperor," I confess. It was one of the things Memnon and I argued about weeks ago. "I named him after the era I first found him." Romans included the reigning emperor's name in their dates. I lived and died during Nero's reign, and though I hadn't consciously realized that when I gave my familiar his name, I was still unknowingly paying tribute to it.

"I...see." I sense the frayed edges of Memnon's guilt all over again. That's his only tell.

The sorcerer moves to my computer chair and sits down, his legs splaying out. His eyes still look a little haunted, and he's definitely acting more reserved than usual, but there's this menacing energy about Memnon that he can never fully shake. I feel as though I caught myself a monster. One who looks at home in this cramped room.

He swivels a little in the seat, peering over the knick-knacks on my desk. The action makes me twitchy, and

I have to remind myself that I can actually control the man now.

His eyes snag on my keyboard. Abruptly, he stops moving.

"*Who wrote this?*" His voice is entirely different, low with rage. He picks up the sticky note with the threatening message, strands of his power snapping and coiling out of him like lunging serpents. When his eyes meet mine, he looks ready to murder somebody. He probably *is* ready to murder somebody.

"The people who survived the spell circle—I think."

His eyes begin to glow, just a little. He slides the note into his pocket.

"What are you doing?" I say, sitting down on the edge of my bed.

"Saving this note so that I can nail it to their body when I find them."

Hell's bells. Involving Memnon is already turning out to be a bad idea. I'm trying to tame a creature far more intense than even my panther.

My soul mate leans forward, the tense set of his features making his scar appear extra visible. "I will tell you everything I know about the murders and the spell circle, but, *est amage*, the knowledge comes at a cost. If I involve you, we run the risk of our enemies discovering our connection—not just that we're soul mates but also that you now control me. That is…dangerous knowledge to have. It can be used against us. Do you still want my help?"

"I'm already involved. I want to know."

Memnon bows his head and nods. *Which should we focus on first?* he says, speaking directly down our connection.

95

Right. This discussion is a bit too sensitive to be voicing out loud.

I jut my chin toward his pocket, where the threatening note rests. *The witches involved in the spell circle.* They are the more immediate threat.

Memnon's eyes glow again. Those glowing eyes, along with rustling hair, are signs a sorcerer is giving in to their power. When that happens, they run the risk of losing hold of their humanity and their control over the power they wield. This is when a sorcerer's magic truly eats at their conscience.

But just as quickly as my mate's eyes illuminate, they return to their normal hue.

*They entered your room, even with the wards?* Memnon asks. His gaze moves to my door.

I nod.

More of Memnon's magic slithers out of him with my admission. It moves across the room and scours the door, and I'm sure that the sorcerer is setting yet another ward.

*About the spell circle,* I say down our bond, my gaze wandering to the panther tattoo that's peeking out from his neck. *This is what I know: The circles happen every new moon beneath this house—or at least they used to.* I don't know if they will move them after the shit show that happened last time. *The only woman I know by name who was involved in it was Kasey. She was the witch who recruited me to attend the spell circle. Now she's missing.*

Memnon rubs his lower lip, watching me. *The night they chased you through the woods, how many were injured?*

I shake my head. *I don't know—at least a dozen.*

*Did anyone die?*

I hesitate. *At least one.* Nero...Nero ripped out one

woman's throat. *There might've been others as well. I wasn't paying attention.*

Memnon nods. *When I went back to exact revenge, all the women—both alive and dead—were gone. Whoever got the dead and injured out of those woods made sure to scrub the area of their blood and any other evidence I might use to hunt them down. They were ready for a counterattack. Whatever is going on, this isn't just some monthly gathering. They are organized, they have resources, and they know how to make bodies and evidence disappear—and they have access to the persecution tunnels beneath the house.*

The thought is nauseating, now that I know these people have gotten through my wards and into my room. The persecution tunnel that leads out from beneath this building connects to a vast network of subterranean tunnels. No one in this house is entirely safe if these tunnels are being exploited for nefarious purposes.

Memnon threads his fingers loosely together, his forearms resting on his thighs. *Why would a well-organized group of supernaturals do their business in the tunnels beneath your coven?* he asks down our bond.

I sense he knows the answer to this. I turn inward, thinking about it. The only thing that comes to mind is the most obvious answer, the one I already know.

*Most of the members must live here.*

Memnon nods. *Or they're trying to recruit witches from your house.*

That is what happened to me. I just didn't go along with it.

Memnon's eyes flick over me, and though the conversation is a bit dark, a small smile curves his lips.

*What?* I say through our connection, trying not to notice the lock of hair that's fallen in front of one of his eyes. I have to physically restrain myself from reaching out and tucking it behind his ear.

*I like this,* he admits.

*You like what?*

*Us, studying our enemies, plotting out our next moves.*

I frown, even though my heart speeds up, just a little.

The sorcerer stands, rescuing me from the moment. He moves to my door and angles his head, studying the protective spells.

*They shouldn't have been able to get in here with all these wards in place.* Memnon turns back to me. *If I told you it wasn't safe to stay here—*

*There is no way I am staying with you in that burnt husk of a house,* I say.

*If it weren't burnt?*

*That would also be a* no.

The sorcerer stares at me, eyes narrowed, for a long beat. Then he smiles, like he relishes my anger. Turning back to the door, he murmurs in Sarmatian, "*Guard this door against all those who wish Selene harm.*"

His indigo power flows out of him, spreading out over the door as he adds yet another ward to the growing knot of them. The plumes of his magic condense into lines of what looks like writing. The markings glow as they sink into the frame of the door, then dim until all that remains is the barely perceptible sheen of the spell.

*If you want to find out more about the people behind that note, then there's one place we should definitely explore,* Memnon says down our bond. *The persecution tunnels.*

# CHAPTER 11

***"This is not how I planned to spend my evening,"* I say as the** two of us enter the Ritual Room.

The windowless room, with its walls and ceiling painted black, was where coven sisters gathered for certain ceremonies. Currently, a circle of partially burned white candles sits at the center of the room, the box they came in pushed off to the side.

"Yes, well, mine didn't quite look like this either."

"How *did* your plans look?" I ask him curiously.

"I expected to be enjoying the fruits of my vengeance. Namely, I thought I'd be married to you and well on my way to eating your pussy out."

I make a face as I step up to the spelled wall, shivering a little at the thought. I'd like to say that the shiver comes from a deep-rooted fear, but that's not true. Mostly, I'm remembering what being married to him was like, which was lots of love and good sex.

"I see you're still deluded."

"Am I, now?" he says behind me, and the mocking tone of his voice sets my teeth on edge. He and I both know I have a weakness for his mouth when it's on certain unmentionable parts of me.

"I still cannot believe you proposed to me by threatening the lives of my friends. Talk about the least romantic proclamation of love."

Memnon comes around to my front. "Yesterday, I sought revenge," he says slowly, walking backward toward the far wall. "Today and for the rest of my life, I will seek to make you happy. If it's romance you want from me," he says, his eyes too bright, "then that's what I will give you."

I scowl. "That's not what I meant."

"Isn't it?" he says. "You want a soul mate who can love you as you mean to be loved."

I raise my eyebrows, trying to ignore the tug of those words. "This might come as a huge shock to you," I say, "but I am actually fine not being in a relationship with anyone. Especially you."

"Mmm," he says noncommittally.

I can tell he's disregarded my words as soon as he hears them.

Memnon turns to the wall and places a hand against it. "*Ifakavek.*"

*Reveal.*

The doorway fades away, exposing a hidden room and a spiral staircase that descends from it. The two of us set that spell what feels like lifetimes ago. Good to know it still works.

The sorcerer steps through, then glances back at me. "Coming, Empress?"

I cross the room and step into the small antechamber where the spiral staircase waits.

I turn to face the exposed wall.

"*Buvekatapis*," I murmur.

*Conceal.*

And I seal us inside.

---

Unlike the last time I visited the persecution tunnels, I'm no longer afraid of what's down here. Perhaps it's because then, I was interested in running from those who had hurt me. Now I'm interested in finding them.

My gaze sweeps over the subterranean room where the spell circle was held only two weeks ago. It appears just as it had the last time we visited.

"What are we looking for down here?" I ask.

"Anything at all. We can start with figuring out where the witches entered from," Memnon says. "The night of that circle, did you notice anyone in your house going to that room above us?"

"The Ritual Room?" I think back to the night in question. I'd waited in the library for Kasey. The rest of the house, however, had been quiet. I shake my head. "I don't think so... Wait," I say as something comes to me. "Some of the tunnels were lit."

As opposed to right now, when the torches sitting in the sconces are dark.

"Then it's possible they were meeting somewhere else and then entering these tunnels from that point."

The trouble is there are so many branches of tunnels moving in all directions.

"Which way should we go?"

"I don't think it matters, little witch."

I can't quite suppress the pleasant shiver that endearment evokes.

I decide to head down the same one I took when I last fled this room. We haven't gone a hundred feet when the tunnel splits apart.

Did I go left or right last time? I'd been so hyped up on adrenaline, I don't remember.

On a whim, I go right, Memnon close behind me. Then I make a left. Then a right, the torches flickering to life as we go. Eventually, we hit a staircase that lets out into the Everwoods. We backtrack, then begin again. Ten minutes later, we hit another exit, this one leading into a crypt that smells like mold and old bones.

"Hey look," I say, nodding to the stone coffin as I drag away a thick web. "It's my second lover"—I squint at the name—"Ephigenia. I'll wake her in another year when I get tired of you. I do so like burying my lovers."

When I turn to look at Memnon, his face is displeased.

Too soon for jokes apparently.

We retrace our steps and try again, the torchlight making our shadows dance. The futility of what we're doing is starting to set in. I don't even know what we're looking—

*Thump.*

The sound echoes off the walls from somewhere far ahead of us.

Memnon and I look at each other, then we both quicken our pace.

*This is probably a bad idea,* I say silently.

*Don't tell me you've lost all your courage now.*

In the distance, the tunnel dimly glows, the light growing

brighter the closer we get. Either we are recrossing our old tracks, or another person is down here.

*If someone else is down here, we shouldn't assume the worst of them,* I say. *It could be literally anyone. Maybe Henbane's staff uses these passageways.*

*For what?* Memnon challenges me. *Casual get-togethers? These tunnels were created for illicit purposes.*

*They weren't,* I argue. *They were created to avoid capture.*

*Yes,* Memnon agrees. *That would be considered illicit behavior.*

Fuck, I guess it would.

The two of us finally get to the previously lit hallway. A little farther down it opens up into another subterranean room similar in size and structure to the one beneath the residency hall. But where the latter room was empty, this one is full.

I pause as I take it all in. It looks almost like a witchy clubhouse. There's a lit candelabra hanging from the ceiling. Along the right wall is a series of inset cabinets and shelves. On several of them rest moth-eaten grimoires, their clashing magic pooling in the air above us. On another shelf is a crystal ball and a scrying bowl and a bust of a woman with a very large nose and a determined air about her. Across the room is a massive tapestry depicting an enchanted forest. Beneath it are several chests and an armoire painted with flowers and serpents. A few broomsticks lean together in the corner.

There's a worn green velvet couch, a plum-colored wingback chair, and a table between them stacked with books. I drift over to the stack and rifle through them, reading their titles as Memnon continues past me, cutting through the room toward another chamber that houses a spiral staircase.

*I'll be back in a minute,* he says as he heads up the staircase, clearly determined to find whoever was down here.

"Mmm..." I say noncommittally as I look at the book titles. *The Sisterhood: The Dynamics and Culture of Witches*; *Ancient Symbols and Their Meanings*; *Into the Dark: An Exploration of Forbidden Magic.*

The book titles are somewhat interesting but not revealing in the least. Abandoning them, I wander around the rest of the room, peering at the items. The grimoires on the shelves are old, and their magic has a musty, rotting smell to it as though it's unmaking itself. I pause when my eyes land on one of the grimoires. It's a small, thin tome, its spine mostly gone. Threads of dark magic waft off it.

Before I can think better of it, I pull the book off the shelf. I flip through the spellbook, but there are no bookmarked pages or obvious spells of interest. Only disturbing drawings of dismembered fingers and eyes. Real cozy reading.

I put the book back, wiping my hands on my jeans to get the oily feel of the magic off me. Turning my attention to the cabinets that run along the lower part of the wall, I crouch down and open them one by one.

Inside all of them are baskets filled with bars and snack packs of chips and trail mix and mini bottled water.

This is definitely a clubhouse of some sort. And while it's unusual, I've seen nothing here that's overtly nefarious— dark grimoire aside.

Closing the cabinets, I move to the other side of the room, drawn to the armoire simply because the painted serpent and flowers on the front of it are so beautiful. I run my hand over the image of the snake, noting how the phases of the moon have been detailed on its body. Beneath my touch, it seems to come alive for a moment, the delicately painted scales rippling as it slithers a little. I hear a click, and then one of the armoire's doors swings open slightly.

I did not even realize it would do that.

I nudge the door open even wider.

My eyebrows rise.

Dozens of black robes hang inside. Reaching for one, I rub the fabric between my fingers and breathe the material in. It smells faintly of that cloying draught I was given at the spell circle. More incriminating still, there are a few nearly transparent white shifts hanging inside as well. Cara the shifter had worn something similar when she'd been brought to the circle…

I back away from the closet, my pulse pounding loudly in my ears. I mean, it *could* be a coincidence. There are probably similar robes and shifts stored somewhere in the residence hall as well. These are pretty basic ceremonial regalia.

I turn and take in the room again, my gaze sweeping over the space before settling on the chests.

I move over to one and attempt to open it. The lid doesn't budge.

I wonder if stroking this one would work?

I try doing just that. When the lid still doesn't budge and I feel faintly like I committed some sort of sex act against the chest. I focus my attention on the iron latch at its center. There's a keyhole beneath it, one my iron room key would probably fit—though I left it back in my room.

"*Open,*" I command in Sarmatian.

My magic unfurls, a thin line of it flowing into the keyhole. I hear a latch tumble, and then my power is pushing the lid up against the wall.

What is the point of a lock if a spell can…

Hell's spells.

Stacked inside the chest are many, many masks identical to those worn at the spell circle. On top of them all is the high priestess mask.

Well, this is no longer a coincidence. Whoever's been involved in the spell circle is storing the items for it here.

# CHAPTER 12

*I reach inside the chest and lift the high priestess mask out.*

"Memnon!" I call.

When I don't hear him, I lower the mask and glance down the chamber he exited through.

He's been awfully quiet down our bond since he disappearedup the staircase.

*Memnon?* I reach for him through our connection.

*I'll be there soon, Empress. I'm almost finished.*

*Finished?* I say, alarm bells going off in my head. *With what?*

*The interrogation.*

Oh, fuck.

Dropping the mask, I dash toward the wrought iron spiral staircase. I glance up it, hearing the low notes of Memnon's voice from somewhere up above.

Bloody boils. I take the stairs two at a time, the structure shivering as I pound my way up it in my haste to get to Memnon.

The stairs lead to a narrow antechamber with an open archway out. On the other side of it, I can see what looks like some sort of teacher's lounge, and on the far side of it, I see Memnon holding a woman by the throat, her feet flailing as she tries to rip away at the sorcerer's hand. Her pale green magic snaps at Memnon, but whatever spells she's casting, they're not deterring my mate in the slightest.

"Memnon!" I cannot leave this man alone for five fucking seconds. "*Put the woman down*," I say in Sarmatian.

Memnon glances over his shoulder at me while he lowers the woman back to the ground.

"Hello, my queen," he says smoothly, like he wasn't just choking a witch. A witch he *still* holds by the throat.

I stride forward. "You cannot accost people and treat them like threats," I say.

I don't mean for that to be a direct order, but in response to it, Memnon's hand opens, and he releases the woman, who then tries to bolt. Memnon blocks her escape with his body.

"You may want to qualify that command," he says, sending his magic to the door the witch is rushing toward. When she gets to it, the handle won't turn. Her own magic flares out to combat Memnon's spell. "We might be stumbling on a lot of bad people."

*She knows things*, est amage.

Aw man. I can feel a stress headache already brewing.

*Fine, disregard my last command. Just be gentle with her.*

As soon as I give the silent order, Memnon's magic wraps around the witch's midsection and gently drags her to a nearby couch.

"*Stay*," he orders. His magic flows out of him at the command and he restrains her against the seat.

Goddess, but I *hate* that spell of his. I'm also trying not to hyperventilate at the fact that I'm now allowing Memnon to manhandle people on my behalf. Considering we're somewhere inside the Henbane Coven's main buildings, this witch is likely an instructor.

My misgivings overwhelm me. I'm about to call the sorcerer off when he speaks again.

"I think you'll be very interested to hear what Lauren here has to say."

The woman, who looks to be in her midthirties, glances between each of us, her light brown hair disheveled and her eyes frightened. More of her magic sifts out of her as she fights Memnon's hold. It's an exercise in futility.

"Let me go," she demands.

Memnon folds his arms and tilts his head. "Tell her"— he nods to me—"what you told me, then maybe I will."

This is so wrong. This isn't what I meant at all when I asked for Memnon's help.

*Is it not?* he responds. *I think you needed an excuse to be unleashed, and I'm it.*

The witch in front of us interrupts our silent conversation. "I—I was just down in the tunnels restocking it with supplies."

My brow furrows. "Why does that room need to be stocked with food?"

The witch, Lauren, shifts her attention to me, and there is a flicker of recognition. Unfortunately, even with my memories back, I don't recognize her.

"We always keep the tunnels stocked with f-food. In c-case of emergencies."

Memnon laughs low. "That's not the reason you gave when I peered into your mind."

She opens her mouth, but when she tries to speak, nothing comes out. Her shoulders curl inward a little. "I can't talk about it."

I frown. That doesn't exactly scream innocent to me.

"Please," she says to me, her eyes beseeching, "let me go. You know this is wrong."

*Yeah, this is definitely wrong,* I say down my bond.

"Tell her why you cannot talk about it," Memnon says.

"I c-cannot talk about that either."

Memnon looks over at me.

*Is that supposed to mean something?*

*Doesn't that sound like a magical compulsion? Because it is.*

My eyebrows rise as Memnon says to Lauren, "Where's your phone?"

The witch's eyes dart briefly to a purse sitting nearby. Memnon walks over to it as the witch fights her restraints.

He withdraws her phone and holds it up to her. "Unlock the device."

Before she can resist, her phone recognizes her face and unlocks on its own. The sorcerer glances down at it, then taps on a few buttons. He takes a picture of something, taps on a few more buttons, andthen I hear the phone in his pocket buzz.

Tears begin to slip down the woman's cheeks as Memnon returns her phone to her purse. She looks first to my mate, then to me. "You don't understand," she says softly. "Thank the Goddess you don't."

"But I do understand," he says dangerously, moving back over to her. "You were there that night Selene was attacked, weren't you? You helped attack her."

She shakes her head. "I had no choice."

The sorcerer looks pityingly at her. "I doubt you did. And you leave me with no choice now either."

Memnon steps into Lauren's space and grasps the sides of her head. The woman begins struggling anew.

"Memnon," I say, a note of alarm in my voice, "you will not hurt her."

He inclines his head toward me, but that's the only sign he gives that he's heard my command.

To Lauren, he says, "You never saw us, and we are not here now. You are going to grab your things and go home."

He releases the witch and backs up.

Lauren stands, looking somewhat baffled to find herself here. Her eyes sweep across the room, passing over me and Memnon without really seeing us. Her gaze catches on the still-exposed doorway to the persecution tunnels, but only for a moment. She turns, grabs her purse, and heads out the door she tried to escape through minutes ago.

I wait until the sound of her footsteps fades completely.

There's a bitter taste at the back of my throat. Something about this is off—more off than having my mate pry secrets out of witches.

"I have bad news for you, *est amage*," Memnon says, still staring at the door.

I glance his way. "What is it?"

"That woman?" He jerks his head in the direction Lauren departed. "She's bonded."

# CHAPTER 13

*My head snaps to him so quickly. "What?" I must've* misheard him. The possibility that merely hours after Memnon and I formed a bond, we run into a witch with a bond of her own...

"She answers to a woman who goes by the name of Lia. She has a weekly call with this Lia where she's forced to divulge information about various witches." Memnon's eyes grow cold. "Lauren is a recruiter."

My breath catches in my throat. "What do you mean by that?"

"She uses her position as an instructor here to scout for witches this Lia might like." After a moment, he adds, "She was there that same night you were. I *watched*"—his voice breaks off as he spits the word out like a curse—"her chase you in her memories. She tried to kill you several times."

I can't breathe. I must've misheard him. "She's—she's an instructor," I try to argue. I don't want to believe that the instructors here could be in on this.

Memnon continues. "When Lauren finds witches who are promising, she passes along their information to Lia, and in some cases, she arranges for them to either participate in a spell circle or be subjected to it."

I stare at Memnon's mouth. "What does that mean?"

"It means," he says softly, "those women get bonded."

I press my lips together.

"There's another spell circle already planned for the upcoming new moon," he says. "It didn't look like they'd decided on a location, but they still mean to hold one."

Suddenly, Memnon's aggressive tactics don't seem so overblown. Not in light of what he discovered.

"Selene," he says, searching my face, "that's not the worst part."

There's more?

His gaze is steady on mine. "This Lia woman is looking for you."

---

The two of us step out of the teacher's lounge and into the corridors of Cauldron Hall. Dazedly, I note the doors of various classrooms and faculty offices on either side of us, but my mind is lingering on what we just learned.

It's a systemic thing, these bindings. I figured as much, but to hear it confirmed, to hear that an instructor here at Henbane Coven is involved in it? Suddenly, all the witches here feel marked. Me, Sybil, the witch speaking with her cardinal familiar down the hall, the group of women lurking in front of the massive bubbling cauldron that dominates the main entryway.

Memnon pulls out his phone and dials someone. He places the phone to his ear, but I can feel his eyes on me as we make our way out of the building. I can hear an automated voice placidly ask Memnon to leave a message.

The sorcerer curses and hangs up. "No one answered Lia's number," he says, tucking his phone in his pocket. "I'll try to call it again later."

But why bother? It's likely no one will answer. Or maybe someone will. Then what? We threaten them over the phone? Tell them what they're doing is bad and wrong? Continue to call them until they block us? It's likely a burner phone or a temporary number or…or …

I am halfway down the marble steps outside Cauldron Hall when I decide to sit down there and then.

Memnon pauses ahead of me, then glances back.

"Selene?" he asks, concerned.

I shake my head, trying to catch my breath, though I haven't been running. I don't know why I'm so *winded*.

I hear his heavy, deliberate footfalls back up the steps. When he gets to my side, he pauses. Then he proceeds to step up next to me and sit down heavily. His leg bumps against mine.

"Please don't."

*Don't what?* he asks down our bond.

*Don't act concerned.* I press my palms to my eyes.

Despite the command, Memnon places a hand on my back. When I don't immediately knock it off, he pulls me into his side.

I guess his concern is genuine. The realization sours my stomach, even as I lean against him, taking shameful comfort in the warm, solid feel of him.

*Because of you, I have to clean up this mess.* It's such a blatant lie; Memnon might've taken part in moving the bodies of murdered witches, but he had nothing to do with this.

*We're going to clean it up. Together,* he says, not bothering to call me out on the lie.

My annoyance spikes…along with a traitorous warmth that loosens the tightness in my chest.

Memnon glances out across the lawn and toward the coven's main entrance and the thick forest beyond.

*You told me not to hurt Lauren,* he says. *If you lift the order, I can—*

*If I lift the order,* I finish for him, *you'll kill her.*

He's quiet. He knows as much.

After a moment, he adds, *If I don't stop her, more witches will get bonded against their will.*

I pinch my eyes shut. *I know.*

Killing her would be convenient, but I can't just order her death. That takes a sort of coldness that I don't have.

I shake my head. *We need to find this Lia and stop her.*

She's the puppet master pulling the strings here. It doesn't help that she's apparently taken a keen interest in me.

*We'll find her. I was able to get her number off Lauren's phone. I'll see what I can do with it.* Memnon's gaze flicks down to me. *But be warned, whoever Lia is, if she is truly forcing bonds on these witches and making them recruit more victims, she is likely highly evil and very dangerous.*

What he means is that eventually, he will likely have to kill her. I'm glad he doesn't voice it, because I don't think I would stop him, and I'm not ready to deal with *that* awful truth on top of everything else.

Instead, I say, *There's no one worse than you.*

His eyes twinkle menacingly.

*Est amage, I'm counting on that.*

Eventually, we make it back to my room.

Nero has also returned and has ditched his cat bed to instead sleep sprawled on my bed, letting out adorable little huffs that I think are cat snores.

At least one of us is at peace. I'm still turning over the fact that an instructor at Henbane is luring witches to the same spell circles I was lured to. That this instructor fought me as I tried to escape with Cara, the shifter girl.

I feel the sorcerer's eyes on me, and I turn to look back at him. He lingers in the doorway, a lock of his black hair hanging over one eye. Gone is the aggressive, angry man I've gotten so used to over the last several weeks. I can still sense his violence—that's as much a part of him as anything else—but it's tucked away at the moment.

Instead, I can feel the sharp ache of his love through our bond. Somewhere during our evening, his eyes lost their haunted look. But now the hollowness is back.

There is a huge part of me that wants to reach out and touch him just to remove that expression from his face.

*Do you want to discuss the murders now?* my mate asks.

I'm tired to my bones. And hungry.

"Another night." I want to pick Memnon's brain on this when I'm sharp enough to ask the right questions.

Memnon's expression has shifted a little. Now he's looking at me like he's caught sight of salvation. Tentatively, he reaches out, his knuckles a hairsbreadth from my cheek.

"Don't," I say.

He swallows, his hand still extended. "I'm sorry," he says, his voice rough.

I want to tell him that his help changes nothing. That being bound to me changes nothing. That his remorse and even his friendliness and every other disarming part of him changes *nothing*.

Even if it does.

Instead, I step back from him. "I'm not going home with you."

I know staying with him would be the safer option, but Memnon is still the man who nearly killed a room full of my friends to force me to marry him, and he's still the man who made me release my memories against my will, and I'm still rabidly angry at him. I'd sooner stay with a pack of hungry wolves than with him.

Memnon nods pensively, not bothering to fight me on this. Gone is the victorious man from the night before.

His eyes drop to my stomach, and they linger there for several long seconds. The room is so quiet that I catch a single whispered word.

*Child.*

I place a hand on my lower abdomen, swallowing. I don't know what to say about that. It's one more tragedy between us.

"I cannot believe a child—our child— existed at all," he says softly, "and that I must simultaneously celebrate and mourn their life."

I draw in a shuddering breath. This feels so unresolved, and a deep, ancient part of me wants to close the distance between us and grieve this loss together. But while I might've lived and died as Roxilana, that's not who I am anymore, and Memnon is no longer my husband. So I wait for the moment to pass and for the sorcerer to tuck away the pain in his eyes.

Eventually the moment does pass and Memnon turns to leave. He pauses when his eyes catch on something.

I follow his gaze to the unzipped duffel bag I took from his house. My notebooks are spilling out from it.

"You didn't truly burn them," I say. I can't decide if that's an accusation or a question.

His look softens as it returns to me. "I know I can be heartless, but even when I thought the worst of you, I never sought to destroy all that you are just to get what I want."

The silence in the room is so, so loud.

"You could've fooled me," I eventually say.

"I did fool you," he agrees. "You believed them gone."

"That doesn't make you any less cruel." He still got what he wanted.

Now Memnon does reach out and touch me. He cups my jaw, tilting my head up to his. "What if I told you that I feared one of your enemies would come in here—just as they have—and look through those journals? What if I told you I worried they might find some piece of information they could use against you?"

I give my head a shake. "You did it to prevent the Politia from reading them and finding something that might elimi- nate me as a suspect," I argue.

"I did," he agrees. He searches my eyes, almost willing me to understand. "I *also* didn't want them to read your journals."

"Because it would prove my innocence."

"Because the corruption in your city runs deep."

I study him for a long moment. "You think the Politia is in on this?"

He releases my jaw. "Information can be bought from anyone, Selene. Even the authorities."

I…I think I believe him.

"If that's true, why didn't you just tell me?" I could've easily hidden my notebooks.

"Because I also wanted vengeance on you," Memnon says. "Gods forbid my vengeance look like protection."

I frown, searching his face.

I hate that what he's saying makes sense.

"Answer me truthfully," I command him. "Was any of what you said a lie?"

He holds my gaze. "*No.*" Before I have a chance to respond to that, Memnon's gaze returns to my stack of notebooks. "Burn those or ward them, but don't leave any of them exposed here for others to pick through. Because I can assure you, if given the opportunity, *they will.*"

I walk over to the duffel bag. I don't really know what I'm thinking when I shove the books back in, pick up the bag, and carry it to Memnon. He's about as trustworthy as a hobgoblin—no offense to hobgoblins—but...I don't know. Maybe the evening is getting to me, or maybe it's feeling overly confident about this new bond of ours. Or maybe it's simply the fact that even when he was seeking retribution against me, he was still trying to protect me and the things most sacred to me. Whatever the reason, I decide to trust my gut over all the bad blood between us.

"You want to earn back my forgiveness?" I ask. "Then you can start by taking these with you and protecting them like you intended to." I hand the notebooks over.

Memnon watches me carefully with those smoky, calculating eyes as he takes the bag of journals from me, and I try not to think about what his own sleeping arrangements are. The last glimpse I had of his house was of it on fire. I press my lips together to avoid asking about the state of it or whether he'll be okay. The sorcerer is nothing if not ruthlessly effective. If the house isn't okay, he'll simply find another. It's everyone else around him who needs to be worried.

He gives my lips a lingering look before backing up toward the door. "Stay safe, *est amage*. You are powerful and capable, but even that can be bested by treachery."

I know both of us are thinking about Eislyn and Zosines.

I nod. "I'll be careful."

"Reach out to me when you want to discuss the murders—or if you need anything at all," he says, his eyes lingering on mine. "I am yours to command."

I frown, not liking how serious everything suddenly is or how my heart feels uncomfortably bereft now that he's leaving. Ridiculous, foolish heart.

He waits for a moment for me to say something—anything—but I'm ensnared in my own mixed feelings.

"Um, okay...see you later then." Not sure I could've made that any more awkward, but all right.

Memnon gives me one last penetrating look, and it feels like a promise. He raps his knuckles on my doorway. "Later, little witch." He dips his head and leaves, a little of his indigo magic lingering in the air after him before it dissipates away.

# CHAPTER 14

*Memnon's wards seem to do the trick. No one but me enters* or exits my room, and two days later, as I sit in my Intro to Magic class, I'm beginning to think that maybe I'm safe for the time being.

I tap my pen against my notebook as I wait for Professor Huang to enter. I haven't reached out to Memnon since he left my room. I still intend to discuss the murders and follow up on the weird clubhouse shit we stumbled on...but I chickened out yesterday, and today...well—

I glance down at the skeleton catsuit I'm wearing. I've kept this costume around for years for this very day.

All Hallows' Eve. Samhain. Halloween, for the uninitiated.

The night when the barriers between worlds are their thinnest. The Samhain Ball three days ago was in honor of the holiday, but tonight, the true celebration takes place.

Outside the lecture hall, witches in costumes are moving pumpkins and unlit lanterns across the back lawn and into the Everwoods. If they're at all afraid of going into that shadowy forest, they don't show it. But they must feel this oppressive tension that hangs over the coven.

Everyone is feeling the weight of the killings. From the rumors I've overheard in the last two days, Henbane's administration is considering placing a campus-wide curfew. And if things get worse…there's the possibility that Henbane will shut down, either temporarily or for good. Already there's talk that the school is going to get sued by several of the victims' families. This moment is precarious.

A few darting looks from some of my classmates drag me from my thoughts. I shift uncomfortably in my seat as I remember all over again that only three days ago, I was a wanted suspect for murder.

*I still hate you,* I say to Memnon. It's a super shitty way to reach out to someone you haven't spoken with in days, but I think Memnon's earned this sort of greeting.

Down our bond, I feel a flush of amusement.

*Are you just randomly musing on this, or—*

*Everyone around me still thinks I'm guilty,* I say.

That's not technically true. They might be aware that my name's been cleared, and they're simply curious. Either way, it sucks.

*Want me to come over there and wipe everyone's memory of those events?*

It would be a hilarious offer if I didn't know he was serious.

*Goddess, Memnon. Can you not go feral for five minutes?*

I feel his grin through our bond, the sensation of it warming me from the inside out.

*Stop smiling. It's annoying.*

Memnon does stop smiling, and I somehow hate that

even more. I'm about to withdraw the command, feeling like a big meanie, when Memnon says, *Let those witches fear you. They should. You are powerful and terrifying, and you have made yourself a formidable opponent. Maybe then people will think twice before they fuck with you—just as I have.*

Before I can respond to that—what do I even say to that?—Professor Huang walks in, their long black hair flowing like a curtain behind them.

My professor lays their notes out on the podium, looking a little askance before they face the class. "Happy Samhain to you all."

A few people cheer in response.

They nod to a few witches seated in various rows. "I see many of you are already wearing your costumes. I'm glad to see you all in the celebratory mood. This night is your birthright to claim, but I want to take this time to caution all of you to be safe during this evening's festivities. A campus-wide six p.m. curfew will go into effect starting tomorrow, November first. Witches will be expected to be inside by sundown and to remain indoors until sunup. Any assignments requiring nighttime spellcasting will be altered to respect this curfew."

The room is lethally silent, but that tension has ratcheted up.

"Your safety is of the highest priority to all of us instructors here at Henbane."

I think of Lauren and how she chased me through the woods two weeks ago and how she's scouting students for binding ceremonies. My stomach gives a sick twist. Not all instructors here are looking out for our safety.

Professor Huang glances down at their notes and clears their throat. "I would like today to be just another lecture," they say, "but in light of the recent deaths, I don't feel as though I can stick to the scheduled discussion. So instead, I want to use today's lesson to focus on dark magic—what it is, how it is used, and why it is considered forbidden."

The room goes uncomfortably silent. This is the part of witchcraft we don't speak of, the part that we're supposed to pretend doesn't exist at all, even though it's always been there, lurking on the periphery of our world. It's the aspect of our power that has gotten witches into trouble through the ages.

"With that," the professor continues, "I'd like to ask you all: What is the first lesson all witches must learn?"

"*Primum non nocere*," I call out.

*First, do no harm.*

The Hippocratic oath. Physicians aren't the only ones who follow it; witches do as well.

Professor Huang steeples their fingers in front of where their arms rest on the podium, and they nod their head. "Do no harm," they repeat, enunciating each word.

I mean, it's a good idea for witches—in theory. In practice, what does that really mean? If someone makes a tincture for success, maybe it helps them, but in the process, it fucks over a colleague? Or someone brews a love potion, and it works—does that rob their significant other of an experience they should've had with another? Is it fair to meddle? Where do you draw *that* line?

"One of the better known dark magic users was Elizabeth Bathory, who wove spells from the blood of hundreds of people whom she tortured and killed to maintain her youth and beauty. Less well known is Gretta Gimbley, who extended her own life by cannibalizing the spelled flesh of her victims.

What she didn't consume, she used to prepare deeply cursed potions, which she then sold as medicinal tonics."

She obviously sounds like a super fun human being.

I go to jot the information down, but...I don't feel that same pressing need. Now that my memories have returned, my notetaking doesn't have to be quite so diligent. After a moment's hesitation, I write it all down anyway. There's something unbearably comforting about falling back on these old habits. I'm not ready yet to make new ones.

Professor Huang continues. "We sense intuitively what dark magic is—we hear these stories, and we know these witches were utilizing it—but what actually *is* dark magic? What is blood magic? How do curses and hexes tie into this?"

Everyone is quiet, tense.

"To answer the first question, dark magic is any power that deliberately draws on or causes the pain and suffering of another. This can be a spell whose outcome is for another to feel pain and misfortune—such as a curse or a hex, the latter of which is more of a minor misfortune. Then there's *where* the power is drawn from. If it is drawn from an unwilling source or taken using unnecessary cruelty and force, then that will draw out dark magic."

My pulse spikes when I remember that some of my fights over the last two weeks drew on or caused pain. I sink a little lower in my seat.

The professor continues. "Dark magic is a perversion of the natural flow of the universe, and in order to correct for it, magic exacts a price from whoever wields it. This is why the Law of Three exists. Good begets good, and bad begets bad. So I gave you all some clear, basic examples of dark magic, but there are other, more murky aspects of it as well. Collecting power from already dead and decaying things might also draw out dark magic, even if you didn't kill that thing." Professor Huang's eyes sweep over the room as they speak. "All this is further complicated by the fact that sometimes you might have to cause pain to stop a greater suffering—like incapacitating someone who is hurting another. Would that be considered dark magic?"

No one answers, but we're all waiting with bated breath to hear what Professor Huang has to say.

They give the room a rueful smile. "This is where the headache-inducing nuances of magic lie. The unhelpful answer to this is that it might be considered dark magic and it might not. Ultimately, however, the biggest factor that determines whether your magic is dark or not is your own intentions. So much of this has to do with intent."

One of my classmates raises her hand. "Why would anyone prefer dark magic to light?"

Our instructor's gaze is steady on my classmate, their expression grim. "Power, my dear. Dark magic may be dangerous, but with it comes lots and lots of power."

---

Once class lets out, I slide my notebook into my bag and make my way to the podium, where a few other witches are currently speaking with Professor Huang.

Once the students ahead of me are finished, I step up to my instructor, fidgeting with the strap of my bag.

Professor Huang raises their eyes. "Yes?"

"I have a question regarding...bonds."

If my instructor is surprised by the topic, they don't let on.

"I'm confused about the different types," I clarify. "I know there's fated bonds…"

My professor jumps in. "So," they say, "there's a lot of nuance to this subject because fated bonds—think soul mates and familiars—do not require binding *spells*. Fated bonds are intrinsic, magical connections. They get lumped together in name, but truly, in most regards, they are their own thing. As for binding *spells*, these occur all the time among witches and mages. They're so normal that they get overlooked. Unbreakable oaths, for instance, are a type of binding spell. There are also other, more unnatural things that can be bound together. Take love spells, for instance. The target of a love spell may have no initial interest in the person who pines for them. A love spell binds the two—for a time. Just long enough to create an opportunity for some real chemistry."

Okay, this is way more information than I needed, and it hasn't really answered the heart of my question.

"What about bonds people form between one another?" I ask.

My professor hesitates, then sighs. "You want to know about forged bonds and forced bonds."

I nod, chewing the inside of my cheek.

"Supernaturals can form magical bonds with one another outside those that are fated from birth. The two types are called forged bonds and forced bonds. They sound similar but they are fairly different. Forged bonds are the lesser of two evils. With these types of bonds, all the parties involved give their explicit consent to the bond formed. Not that this makes the terms of forged bonds necessarily *equal*. Selling your soul for some heart's desire is technically a forged bond, though it's commonly understood that this is no equal exchange. For this reason, forged bonds are heavily discouraged, even between family members or romantic partners."

Professor Huang gives me a meaningful look, like they can see right through me.

I shift my weight. "Why?" I ask, my anxiety spiking.

*Should've considered this before I took Memnon up on his own binding spell.*

"People change. Hearts change. Involving immutable oaths with mutable things can make for hard, unhappy lives."

"And the other type of bond," I say hoarsely, unwilling to peer too deeply into that sobering warning. "Can you tell me about that?"

My professor grimaces. "We don't speak much about forced bonds because of their evil nature. Forced bonds are, as their name implies, *forced*. They only require the consent of one of the individuals involved, and they can be placed on any other supernatural. There is nothing redeeming about these bonds. They are made to subject their victims to another's control entirely. Fortunately, they require more power to complete, so the only time these can really happen is with a spell circle."

I think this is supposed to be reassuring, but it leaves me cold. There are spell circles already in place, and these forced bonds are routinely occurring.

"Needless to say," Professor Huang adds, "they are the highest class of criminal offense, right up there with murder."

Unfortunately, that doesn't reassure me either. "What happens if a forced bond is placed on you?" I ask. "How do you undo it?"

"It depends on the terms. But there's a reason forced bonds are dangerous, forbidden spells. Because if such a spell is placed on you unto death, then only death shall break the bond."

―――――――――

I cut across Henbane's main lawn, passing by a coven sister feeding a murder of crows. Several other witches head across the grass with massive, spelled pumpkins bobbing in the air above them like witchy balloons; they make dull thunking noises as they bump into one another.

It's a cute display, but my mind is still in my classroom, lingering on what Professor Huang said. Did Cara, the shifter girl I rushed away from the spell circle, really come that close to being forever under the control of the woman leading it? Is Lauren, that instructor Memnon interrogated, currently under such a bond? Is Lia solely behind all of it? Was she the high priestess? The questions are going to pick at me.

My eyes still linger absently on those bobbing pumpkins when I feel an unnerving tingling at my back, like a finger stroking down my spine.

Immediately, I look toward the Everwoods, scanning the tree line for the source of the sensation. Amid all the costumed witches, I catch sight of a shadowed individual on the edge of campus. I swear I see a swath of pale gray skin, but no sooner have I blinked than the person is gone.

I hurry the rest of the way to the residence hall, trying to convince myself that I'm not being watched.

My mind drags back to Cara and to the werewolf pack she belongs to. It's been several days since I last spoke to Kane. I meant to call him before now, but he's still abiding by the rules of the Sacred Seven, the week surrounding the full moon. That's when a werewolf's powers are most potent—and most unpredictable. The pack seques-ter themselves during this week for their safety and that of everyone else.

As I cross the foyer and head up the stairs to my room, I grab my phone and scroll to Kane's number anyway.

It's time we talked.

# CHAPTER 15

*"Selene?"*

"Kane, hey," I say as I close the door to my room, caught off guard by his low, gravelly voice. A large part of me wasn't expecting him to answer the phone.

"How are you doing?" he asks. "I meant to reach out. I heard about...the arrest the other night." The one he warned me about. "I'm sorry."

I shake my head, even though he can't see it. "It's fine. They released me and cleared my name."

"Yeah, I heard about that too."

Goddess, but there's nothing like casually talking about being a murder suspect with your former—current?—crush to really make things awkward.

I clear my throat. "Anyway," I say, "that night, you mentioned that your pack wanted to speak with me about the night I found Cara."

"Yeah, we did want to talk to you about that. Tonight is the last night of the Sacred Seven. I'd need to check with my pack's alpha, but I could probably call a meeting tomorrow if that works for you? I know there's sometimes festivities following Samhain, so we can always push it—"

"Tomorrow works," I say. I can prioritize celebrations another year, when supernaturals aren't getting bonded and murdered around me.

"Great," he says, his voice growing a little less gravelly. "Then assuming the pack approves the meeting, I'll wait for you at the boundary line between our properties at five p.m. tomorrow."

"All right. I'll see you then."

Kane hesitates, then admits, "And in case you forgot some of our call that night, I would still like to see you again."

My breath catches. I *had* forgotten, but not in the way he assumes. The memory got buried under everything else I had to deal with in the last three days.

"I still think about that night I came over to your place," Kane continues. His voice deepens with the admission.

He can't possibly be referencing the night Memnon tossed him out my bedroom window.

"I'm still so sorry about that—"

"I shouldn't have left you after the officers came," the shifter interrupts me. "I should've stayed."

My heart thunders at the thought, but I shake my head. "I wouldn't have let you." Memnon was all too willing to hurt Kane.

He's probably *still* all too willing.

"That asshole doesn't scare me."

I think of the legions of soldiers who lay slaughtered on long-ago fields of wheat, all of them killed by Memnon's power. I think of the way my former husband took a

132

palace—and the kingdom that came with it—on whim alone. And how dizzyingly easy it was for him to force me to capitulate to his demands. He was raised to be a warrior, and his magic has only made him more lethal.

"He *should* scare you, Kane. He really should."

---

I spend the afternoon in the Everwoods with Sybil and my other coven sisters, setting up the decorations for the festivities tonight. We all either grow or move hundreds of pumpkins along the edges of a makeshift pathway. Though it's not obvious to the naked eye, a ley line runs along this path. Fairies and spirits often travel these magical roads, and tonight, we're inviting them onto coven land as honored guests.

Once we're finished with the pumpkins, we spell lanterns to float in the air above the path, the candles inside each one still unlit.

After the last of the items has been positioned, I dust off my hands and back up.

Sybil skips over to me, her butterfly wings fluttering behind her.

"So remind me again what's going to happen later?" I say as she links her arm through mine.

She shakes her head. "No way am I going to ruin the surprise. You're just going to have to see it firsthand." Sybil glances at the growing shadows. "C'mon," she says, tugging my arm in the direction of our house. "We should hurry up and eat and get you changed."

"Get *me* changed?" I say uncertainly.

"Babe," she says, pulling on my skeleton suit, "you're not going to want to wear this."

"What's wrong with my costume?" I say, somewhat defensively.

"There's nothing *wrong* with it, but it's going to be constricting as fuck when you start drinking witch's brew later. I would know. Last year, I literally ripped mine apart to get out of it."

I look at her askance. "What's in the witch's brew?" I cannot imagine anything would cause me to rip my clothes apart.

She flashes me a secretive smile. "I can't tell you, but you just have to trust me that it's all a part of the celebration."

Cutting loose does sound fun…

I run a hand over my spandex catsuit. "This is the only costume I have," I say.

She gives my arm a squeeze. "Luckily, you have me for a best friend."

# CHAPTER 16

*"What am I supposed to be?" I ask, staring at my reflection.*
I look exactly the same, except for some shimmery makeup and a white satin slip dress that leaves me feeling more exposed than covered.

"You're a sexy ghost—or a dead bride. Whichever you prefer."

I want to laugh a little. The whole point of dressing up on Samhain is to mask your true identity so that malicious spirits won't recognize you. But in this outfit, I look like me, only in white.

"Wow, you truly do work wonders," I say mockingly.

The joke goes entirely over her head; Sybil looks thrilled.

My eyes linger on my chest.

"You can see my nipples," I state.

"Babe, we're going to be seeing *everyone's* nipples by the end of the night. But if it's a big deal to you, I have pasties. We can also use *magic*." She wiggles her fingers dramatically to emphasize her point.

I tilt my head back and forth, trying to decide if I want to just wear a white dress—for the ease of stripping later, apparently—or put back on my skeleton costume and get an earful from Sybil.

"Do you think ghosts get offended when we dress like them?" I ask. "Seeing as how it's the day the spirits cross over?"

"You were going to dress as a skeleton," she says.

Yeah, but my point still stands.

Sybil lifts a shoulder. "I don't think the spirits care, but if you want to play it safe, you could always be a living bride."

At her suggestion, my mind moves to Memnon and his plans to marry me.

I look in the mirror again, my heart beating fast at the thought.

"I could be a bride." That seems like a more respectful option.

Sybil squeals and claps her hands. "Yay! Then let's find you a veil!"

---

We do end up finding an old, moth-eaten veil in some forgotten chest downstairs, though the long train of it that trails on the ground was clearly beautiful back when it was new. I *very* reluctantly put it on after dousing it in a few sanitizing spells.

Just before sunset, I leave Nero in my room with instructions to stay inside tonight since the woods will be crawling with drunk witches in a few hours.

Sybil and I head downstairs, where the rest of our housemates have gathered. Dozens of my coven sisters are taking off their socks and shoes and making their way to the front door in all manner of costume. Goblins, leopards, fairies, mummies, vampires—the already magical company looks even more unearthly in costume.

"Shoes off!" one of my sisters calls out to the room. "We'll need to ground ourselves during the spell circle."

"Spell circle?" I glance at Sybil as unease blooms in me.

She smiles secretively. "Don't look so nervous, Bowers. This is the fun part."

It probably is. I've just been burned by the last spell circle, so I now assume the worst.

Begrudgingly, I remove my shoes and tuck them into a corner, the floor feeling chilly against my bare feet.

One of the witches throws open the door, and another cries out, "Let's party, bitches!"

Then there's clapping and laughter, and all of us begin to funnel out of the residence hall. In the process, several witches step on my veil, making my head jerk back and nearly ripping it. Eventually, I have to murmur a spell to make the thing float like fog behind me.

We make our way across the grass behind our house before plunging into the Everwoods.

Here, under the thick shadows of trees, it feels as though night has already fallen. There's an electric heaviness to the air like a storm cloud about to break.

We make our way to the pumpkin-lined path while above us, the unlit lanterns bob in the evening breeze. An owl hoots in the distance, but besides that, a solemn sort of silence has descended over the forest and our group along with it.

Ahead of us, the pathway opens up onto Slain Maiden's Meadow. Only days ago, Memnon pledged himself to me here. Now, the field is filled with countless costumed witches. In the center of the clearing, there's a massive pile of wood and kindling.

The moment the sun dips beneath the horizon, a strong wind cuts through the clearing, stirring our hair and costumes.

"In a circle!" an older voice calls out. "Witches, grasp one another's hands, and take position. It is time!"

Time for what is still unclear, but I follow orders anyway, grasping the hands of a witch with long, wavy black braids and another with cropped blond hair.

Once we've arranged ourselves, that grave silence takes over again. I can hear the soft snap of our outfits blowing in the wind, but everyone is so quiet and so still. Even our magic seems subdued, the air almost entirely clear of it.

"Welcome, honored sisters, to our one hundred and eighty-seventh annual Samhain ceremony!" an older feminine voice shouts. I can't tell who the voice belongs to, only that magic has been used to amplify it. "Samhain is the holy night when the veil between worlds thins. Tonight, we have gathered to welcome guests from these other lands who wish to visit earth for an evening. We will invite them through the doorway here, but in order to do so, we must call on our communal power to help open it for the evening."

So there it is, the reason for the spell circle. We're to pool our magic to help widen the rift between worlds. Sounds totally safe.

"Then," the witch continues, "we will make our way down the path to Last Rites Cemetery, where a feast awaits both us and our honored guests. Beware," she warns. "Not all spirits are benevolent, and not all guests are dead—"

What in the seven hells does all *that* mean?

"—so use caution even while enjoying the revelry

tonight. Other than that, dance, drink, sing, and mingle with our honored guests, and allow yourself to give in to your own innate wildness."

In the distance, wolves begin to howl, as though acknowledging our wildness with their own.

Another witch now speaks. "Let's commence the celebrations by calling forth our guests. *Air above and earth beneath, here at last our worlds meet,*" she incants. "*Goodfellows and the dearly deceased, come and join our hallowed feast.*"

Down the line of our hands, I feel the current of her power run up my right arm and down my left, and I remember absently that magic moves in a clockwise direction for creation and counterclockwise for destruction.

She begins the incantation again, only this time, the rest of us join in. "*Air above and earth beneath, here at last our worlds meet. Goodfellows and the dearly deceased, come and join our hallowed feast.*"

I jolt as what began as a small current now amplifies. The magic that would normally waft off us funnels itself down the line of witches, the throb of it startling and decadent as it passes through me.

Again we repeat the phrase. And again and again, until the air is electric and my body is a live wire.

Est amage, *what is happening?* Memnon says, cutting through the magic-induced haze of my mind.

*Witch stuff, Memnon.*

I don't know if he says anything after that. Magic is filling the space where my mind is. There's only this moment and the touch of my sisters' hands, and the world is magic, all magic, I think as my limbs tremble from the power and heat engulfs me. *We are magic.*

"...come and join our hallowed feast—"

All at once, the nearly unbearable power flowing through me is sucked toward the center of the circle.

With a crack like thunder, the air rips apart. From it pours forth a wave of some translucent substance. It takes a moment for my eyes to realize it's not a substance but spirits. Dozens of them. They cut across our circle, heading for the lantern-lit pathway.

"*Welcome!*" one of the witches shouts, her greeting trailing off into a cackle as more and more specters cross over, their ephemeral forms streaking across the clearing. More laughter rises around me, and I feel it bubbling up in my throat too. The aftereffects of the communal magic have left me lightheaded and euphoric.

The unlit bonfire at the center of the clearing now lights, the wood snapping and smoking as it goes up in flame.

None of us witches have released our hands, and now we begin to sway and dance as one, moving in a circle. I don't know who decides this. Maybe it was me? I can't tell if my thoughts are my own or *ours*, the collective whole of our coven.

Someone begins to hum, and the melody catches, until we're all humming the same wordless tune.

The song grows louder, and the dancing becomes erratic until some—or maybe all of us—decide to release hands. The magical current cuts off abruptly, and what's left in my body leaves me tingling and high off power.

"To the feast! To the feast!" a witch shouts, and though the group's magic is no longer linking us together, I still feel that shared unity, and carelessly, I laugh.

At the sound of it, a nearby witch dressed like a wraith comes in close and gives me a hug, pressing a kiss to my cheek. "Merry Samhain," she whispers before dashing off.

More laughter fills the space as sisters dance and embrace, their eyes and hair a little wild. I'm sure I look the same.

I was wrong to worry about this spell circle. *This* is how they are meant to be. A moment of unification between witches and a reminder that we are all one.

Sybil appears out of the crowd. "C'mon, my nubile bride!" she shouts, grabbing my hand. The bonfire's flames dance in her eyes, giving them a moonstruck look. As soon as my fingers entwine with hers, she cackles. The sound is contagious, and I begin laughing with her, feeling lighter than air. And then we're running, racing alongside dozens of other wild-eyed witches and eager spirits, all of us following the magical road.

As we careen down the path, a deathly chill moves through me. A spirit emerges through my abdomen, and I let out a startled scream at the sight of its transparent form.

The spirit, a young man in a three-piece suit with slicked-back hair, lets out an echoing laugh and streaks ahead of us.

Sybil laughs and laughs at my reaction, her spelled butterfly wings beating behind her, until a spirit passes through her body. Then her laughter turns into a choked cry as a hag on a spectral broom flies out from her body before careening through the group of witches ahead of us. Now I'm cackling and Sybil's reluctantly giggling, and our feet are stepping on sticks and rocks, and I know I'm getting nicked but the wind is smoothing my satin slip over my body like a lover's touch and raking its fingers through my hair and the veil floating behind me, and I'm caught up in the magic of the moment.

That all ends when hoofbeats—then screams—erupt behind us. Sybil glances over her shoulder, her eyes going wide.

"Seven hells!" She veers off the path, dragging me with her. She's not fast enough.

I hear the pound of hoofbeats a moment before someone snags my veil from behind me, lurching me backward. I stumble, about to turn around, when a hand catches me around my waist, lifting me off the ground and onto a steed.

I cry out as my ass lands on an oiled leather saddle. I glance up at a man with sharp, dark eyes and inky hair that seems to be decorated with raven's feathers. My gaze lands on his pointed ears.

A fae.

Did he come from the portal we opened?

"There's been a mistake," I say, pushing against the man's chest, my dress riding up my legs.

His arms tighten on me. "I don't think so. You're dressed like a bride."

My eyes widen. "A b-bride?" I echo. What had Sybil said long ago? Something about stories of fae snatching witches from these woods to be their brides? "No, no. This is not an *actual* wedding dress, and I'm definitely not looking for a groom. I already have one of those in fact. This is a costume." I squirm some more in his arms as his horse cuts down the path, nearly trampling dozens of other witches. "Seriously, let me go."

"*No.*"

My gaze snaps to his. The fae lifts his chin, as though he doesn't think a witch like me will do anything.

Maybe it's the side effects from all that communal magic. Maybe it's just that I'm tired of bossy men. Maybe it's that the last fairy I crossed paths with tried to kill me. Or maybe it's the fact that this pretty asshole is openly trying to abduct me.

I rear back a little, then punch the fucker in the face.

The fairy's head snap back, and his whole body recoils, falling away from me. I must've added a little power to the hit. Whoops. I shake out my throbbing hand as the fairy slides off his horse, hitting the ground with a dull thump.

Witches jump out of the way, a few of them letting out startled screams.

*What is going on,* est amage?

*Why do you only ever talk to me when there's a problem?*

*I'm trying to give you space. Now, what's wrong?*

While the fairy regains his bearings, I hop off his horse and sprint for the cemetery, my terror eclipsing any pride I feel at that punch.

*I threw a man off his own horse.*

*That's my queen,* Memnon says, immensely pleased and not at all bothered by the fact that I assaulted someone.

As I run, I rip off my veil and toss it aside so that no one else can assume I'm actually on the market. *Fuck.* I'm trying to drop the engagement I already have. I do not need a second one forced on me.

"Selene!" Sybil shouts from far behind me. "Selene!"

Everything in me is demanding that I continue to flee—

*Flee?* Memnon's voice is no longer playful. *Who are you fleeing from?*

*I'm fine, Memnon,* I insist, even as I glance past my friend, toward that black-haired fae rider far behind me. He's remounting his horse and scanning the crowd of witches.

I dart behind a tree. Goddess, but if he tries to grab me again...

*Who tried to grab you?* Memnon demands.

*Stop eavesdropping on my thoughts,* I respond, my breath coming in quick pants.

"Selene!" Sybil is still shouting.

"Over here!" I call out.

*I will gut your enemies from navel to throat.*

*You won't,* I correct him, *because like I said—*

I pause to peer around the trunk of the tree. When I catch Sybil's eye, I wave her over.

*—I am fine.*

Memnon doesn't respond to my words, but I sense his skepticism.

Sybil jogs over just as I hear the fairy's horse snort.

"Why didn't you warn me about that?" I whisper. Around us, other witches are still heading toward the cemetery, many of them glancing back at the rider.

"Because that didn't happen last year!" she says, her eyes wide. "Goddess," she says, grabbing my aching hand, and I have to smother a wince. "Are you all right?"

I sense Memnon still eavesdropping.

"I'm *fine,*" I say, more to him than to her.

She searches my features, then glances back at the fairy. "Fuck!" she curses as the hoofbeats start up again. "Duck!"

I don't know what good ducking will do, but I drop to the ground anyway.

The fae rider and his steed pound past us, my floating veil clutched in his grip. He doesn't notice me at all as he veers off into the woods.

I'm breathing heavily. "Who thought letting him in was a good idea?"

"He'll leave by dawn," says an older witch passing by. "The bride he takes will have agreed to go."

Oh really now? Because he didn't seem super into consent when I was in his clutches.

"Those are the rules for hunting on coven property," the elderly witch finishes as she moves away from us.

"*Hunting?*" I echo, horrified as Sybil and I begin walking again. I keep scanning the woods where I last saw him. "We're not deer to be caught."

The older witch gives her head a shake. "To some of them, you are."

Maiden, Mother, and Crone.

"What will happen to the witch who goes with him?" I ask.

"The same thing that happens to all brides the fae steal away," the witch says. "They are taken back to the Otherworld, and the union is made official."

*Sex* is what she means. Sex followed by…whatever fae do with mortals.

"Sounds hot," Sybil says.

I give her a traitorous look.

"*In theory*," she adds, smoothing out her costume. "Anyway, you should've seen that fae's face when his ass hit the ground. Pure disbelief and outrage. You knocked *years* off his life. Where did you learn to hit like that?"

*Memnon.*

It felt like muscle memory—being on the horse, throwing the hit. It didn't seem to matter that millennia separated those memories from this evening.

"It's just one of those things that came back with my memories," I say evasively.

I give the dark woods one last glance before turning my attention ahead of us. I can make out the end of the pathway and the gravestones and crypts beyond it, the stone markers lit up by yet more lanterns.

Once we enter the cemetery proper, it's clear this is

where the party is at. There are more pumpkins stacked around gravestones, along with marigold flowers. A fiddler on the far side of the cemetery has struck up a tune, and large tables rest between grave markers, all of them set with candelabras and laden with food spelled to be accessible to both spirits and mortals. On one side of the cemetery, a large cauldron bubbles away. I veer right for it, dragging Sybil along after me.

"Someone is super eager," she mutters.

"You would be too if you just barely escaped getting kidnapped seconds ago." We weave our way through the graveyard, passing headstones covered in moss.

"Yes, it sounds so awful to be chosen as an immortal's bride. Real tough life you have there."

I stop at the cauldron, knocking some of the marigold flowers at its base askew as I turn to gape at her. "He picked me because I wore white and was easy to grab! That's all! That's, like, the most unromantic way to get a girl."

Sybil looks unconvinced as I grab a glass and reach for the cauldron's ladle, pressing my lips together at the steady throb still coming from my hand.

"If the dude is so in need of a female companion that he has to travel to a whole different realm to snatch one away without even getting to know her," I say, filling up the glass and handing it to my friend, "he probably sucks."

Sybil tilts her head as she takes the glass from me. "You *may* have a point."

"Thank you," I say, feeling vindicated. I fill myself up a glass of witch's brew, down the cup in a few long gulps, then refill it once more.

I hear the baying cries of wolves in the distance.

Sybil looks positively thrilled. "Looks like your kidnapper might've made it to shifter territory."

That thought pleases me for two-point-five seconds before I remember that if the lycanthropes manage to scare the fairy off, he'll just return.

I chug my second drink, only vaguely noting that this version of witch's brew tastes strongly of star anise and clove.

"You're going to want to chill on how fast you drink that," Sybil cautions as I refill my glass again.

"Or you can just make bad decisions with me," I say, looking pointedly at her glass.

She cackles, then knocks her own drink back.

"Fine," she says, handing over her cup. "I'll join the bad decision train with you, you freak. Now, refill our glasses, and let's grab some food!"

---

I understand Sybil's caution only once it's too late.

We end up drinking another glass of witch's brew and gorging ourselves on the foods set out for this outdoor banquet.

It's only once I'm sitting on a crypt alongside Sybil and several other housemates of ours, nursing my fourth glass of brew, that I feel the first stirrings of desire.

I shift a little to ease the sensation, only now remembering that *espiritus*, the active ingredient in witch's brew, makes witches extra lusty. It's just an inconvenience, nothing too distracting.

Around us, ghosts and other witches sit on crypts and tombstones, enjoying one another's company. Many have also taken to dancing around tombstones.

"You guys thinking about going to the bonfire?" asks

Yasmin, a petite witch with brown skin and curly hair cropped in a bob. She daintily eats a caramel-dipped apple in one hand and sips brew from the other, completely unaware that one of her tits has slipped out from between the linen bandage mummy dress she wears.

Next to her, Olga stands in a Victorian dress, her once-coiffed hair now tugged mostly loose and the high-necked collar of her dress gaping open, a few buttons missing. That's not the only thing missing. Her Ledger of Last Words, a book dedicated to collecting the final words of the dying, is also absent tonight. Olga's eyes are a little glazed from the witch's brew, and she's tugging absently on the back of her corset as though she might be able to loosen the lacing.

Another wave of desire slams into me, this one much more insistent, and I white-knuckle my glass, nearly moaning at the throbbing sensation between my legs.

Mai, a witch with pale skin and wide, high cheekbones, eyes Olga. "You ladies can do whatever you like," she says, "but I'm going hunting for wolves. I want to get eaten like I'm Little Red fucking Riding Hood."

"Oh, count me in," Sybil says from where she sits next to me on the crypt.

"Count you in for what?" I say dazedly, only half following the conversation.

I tug at the low neckline of the satin slip. Two hours ago, this felt like a wisp of an outfit, but now my skin is hot and overly sensitive, and the dress chafes in a way I cannot stand.

Around us, other witches have begun to strip, the outer layers of their costumes haphazardly tossed over the gravestones.

Sybil rubs her neck absently, her wings fluttering behind her. "Getting fucked by a lycan."

My body viscerally tightens at that word. *Fucked.* Goddess, how much *espiritus* did they put in the brew this time? This is like a lust potion gone wrong.

I swim through the haze of my thoughts, finally refocusing on the conversation.

"Wait, *what*?" That's her plan? "But the shifters...they're still in seclusion."

Sybil holds her thumb and forefinger close together. "They're just a teeny tiny bit feral. That's all. It's not like it's the full moon." Her words slur together a little.

My skin is hot, so hot, and not even the chill in the wind can cool it.

"When I said I wanted to make bad decisions, I didn't mean *that!*" I say, shifting again. Damn this throbbing. I want to sob at the coiling sensation growing in me that demands all sorts of friction.

Sybil looks me up and down, her own cheeks flushed. "I think you need to go wolf hunting too, Selene. Or find yourself a pretty witch. You drank a lot of brew."

I swallow and shake my head, hopping down from the crypt. Only as soon as I'm on my feet, the brew hits me all at once. I sway a little.

"Sacred Seven," I say, my voice coming out breathier than usual. "The lycans are still observing it. And then there's that—that *fae*." Unless the shifters chased him off, he's likely still prowling the Everwoods.

"Oh!" Yasmin squeals. "You think he's close by? I want to see him. Fairies are so pretty."

"Only look for him if you want to marry him and have lots and lots of kinky fae sex," Sybil says, smiling salaciously. "Apparently he likes girls wearing white, so your mummy costume will probably do the trick," she says, tucking Yasmin's boob back into her mummy wrappings.

As Sybil and Yasmin discuss the nuances of becoming a kidnapped bride, I press my legs together, my need rising. Goddess, but I've drank way too much. What was I thinking? The lust is no longer manageable. Nowhere near it. I was a fool to think otherwise. My desire has ratcheted up to a painful need.

*Est amage, I feel how you ache…*

*Memnon,* I nearly gasp down our bond. I should be irritated by his voice. Instead, my lust seems to find its target.

My king. My soul mate.

I don't want to throw myself to the wolves or to the fae. I want *him.*

*I was wrong earlier,* I say down our bond. Even my internal voice sounds breathy, wanton. At least I'm thinking a little more clearly. *I'm not fine. I need… I want…*

Fuck, I'm having trouble saying it. I want him, but I don't want to beg. Not when he's finally the penitent one.

*Are you all right?*

*No,* I nearly moan as a wave of desire rolls through me.

The other end of our connection is disturbingly quiet. Then—

*Gods, little witch. What was that?* His tone is all wrong. Deeper and—and surprised.

Another wave crashes into me, and I press my thighs together, but that movement is too much. My pussy seems to have a pulse point of its own, and I can feel it with each beat of my heart.

Around me, the group of witches is splintering apart. Sybil's hand clasps mine, and she tugs me along with her as I drown in my own lust. As soon as I begin to walk, I let out a soft gasp. Even that small movement is heightening the throb at the juncture of my thighs.

I nearly weep. Going to hex whoever made the brew tonight for being so cruel. I wanted to get smashed, not to smash someone.

*Memnon!* I call out again. Where did he go?

*I'm here,* est amage, he reassures me.

Thank the Goddess.

*What do you need?* he asks.

Can he not tell?

*You.* I nearly weep the word out. Cursed brew.

He's quiet for several agonizing seconds.

*If you need me, little witch,* he finally says, *then command it of me.*

Command it of him? What in the actual fuck?

The growing ache in my core overwhelms the last of my sense and my pride. Shoving away my embarrassment, I straighten my back and steel my resolve.

*Come to me, Memnon.* I sound less like Selene and more like fierce, strong-willed Roxilana.

I feel the sorcerer's mood shift, warmth spreading out from his end of the bond. *As you will it, Empress. For you, I will always come.*

I pinch my eyes shut. Fuck, he's being noble—about a booty call no less. I start to laugh but end up moaning.

"Babe, you going to make it?"

I glance over at Sybil, who is pulling me along. Next to her are Mai and Olga. My gaze moves to the trees and the dark forest. I'd been so singularly focused on speaking with Memnon that I tuned out what was happening with my friends.

"Where are we going?" I ask. I can't tell exactly where

we are in the Everwoods, only that a fae rider might be somewhere out here, and at this point, I'm likelier to climb him like a tree than I am to fight him off.

"To get laid!" Mai says, lifting her glass of witch's brew into the air like she's making a toast.

Absently, I glance at my own hand, noticing that I too am still carrying my booze. As is Sybil. And Olga, who has now lost her dress and is clad in only a corset and a sheer skirt. Her hair hangs mostly unbound.

"Whoo!" Sybil cheers, raising her glass.

Olga joins in, and all right, guess we are toasting. I lift my own cup and clink it with the others, our brew sloshing about. I hesitate only a moment before I take another drink of it.

Is this irresponsible? Yes.

Is Samhain a celebration that revels in witchy debauchery? Also yes.

Apparently it's also a low-key orgy-fest, judging by some of the witches we're passing. The forest is alive with the sounds of moans and pleasured cries. Each one of them seems to reach inside me and twist me up tighter and tighter.

I have a two-thousand-year-old soul mate who is coming to take care of my needs, I remind myself when I feel like I'm going to burst from the ache of it all. I can probably command him to do kinky shit. Bet he'd be down.

"Bottom's up, girlies!" Mai shouts.

Another pang of lust hits me, and I covertly pour my drink out. I'm all for being irresponsible, but I have zero desire to black out. That story ends with me waking up in the bed of some douchey fae lord who now thinks I'm his wife because he's decent at kidnapping drunk girls.

Thank you, no.

"We can leave our glasses here," Mai says, taking our cups from us and placing them at the base of a nearby fir tree. "They're spelled to eventually return to the cemetery."

We leave them behind and resume our drunken march forward. I glance at the rest of the group—Sybil with her flushed cheeks and her spelled wings fluttering madly, as though they're trying to get away, and Mai, who was dressed as a knight but is now dressed as a topless knight, and Olga, who is skipping along and singing some creepy song about corpses.

Oof, we are a ragtag bunch.

"So where are we going again?" I ask Sybil.

"Hmm?" she says, swaying a little.

"Where are we—"

Deeper in the woods, an ominous howl goes up, followed by another and another, the sound raising the hair along my forearms.

Olga decides now is a fantastic time to stop singing creepy songs and howl back like a demented wolf.

"Did you forget already?" Mai says, noticing my shocked expression. "We're hunting for wolves."

I release my friend's hand, even as my skin still throbs. Fuck, *all* of me throbs. I'm a mass of overstimulated nerve endings. "We cannot be on lycanthrope territory during the Sacred Seven," I say adamantly. Doing so is essentially consenting to being bitten and turned. Which can happen, especially during the Sacred Seven when a shifter's animal instincts often overwhelm their human motives.

I back up from the group. "If any of us get bitten—"

Another howl interrupts me, this one much, *much* closer.

"No one's turning into a wolf," Sybil says.

I rotate in a circle, uselessly searching for the faint,

luminous blue line that marks the boundary between Henbane Coven and the Marin Pack. Did we pass it already? I place a hand on my head, distressed.

Sybil comes over to me, and she doesn't look worried. Why isn't she worried?

My friend lays her hands on my shoulders. "It's the seventh night of the Sacred Seven. This last evening of seclusion is basically a formality for lycans."

I shake my head. I heard Kane's rough voice only hours ago; he'd sounded like he was only partially holding on to his humanity. "This isn't a formality," I insist. "They need this night too."

Another bolt of desire courses through me. My panties are drenched, and this was an uncomfortable enough situation when I was lusty around a bunch of ghosts and coven sisters. But we must smell like sex and magic, and any shifter out tonight *will* notice. We're lingering out here like bait.

The lycans have extended me protection, but there is no protection against getting bitten on their land.

Fuck, fuck, fuck. "I don't want to be here."

I glance around again. Which way is home?

I can't tell.

Ahead of the group, a twig snaps, and my eyes flick to the sound. There in the darkness, I catch sight of three pairs of luminous eyes.

I freeze.

It's enough to temporarily cut through the haze of my lust.

Sybil follows my gaze, her hands falling from my shoulders as several shadowy forms prowl forward. Olga sends up an orb of light, and under the reddish hue of it, I can see—*fuck*—five wolves.

"Sawyer?" Sybil says.

One of the wolves flicks his ears. He stalks forward, past Olga and Mai, who look a little less eager to play with shifters now that their massive animal forms are this close.

Drunk Sybil, however, shows no such reservation. She rushes forward, causing some of the other wolves to growl. Heedless of the danger, she throws her arms around the wolf she thinks is Sawyer.

I go stone-cold sober for an instant as visions of my best friend getting mauled fill my mind. But shockingly, the wolf begins to lick what it can of Sybil's arm. It bows its head, nudging her with its snout, and its form shifts before our eyes. Hair recedes into skin, claws become nails, paws lengthen into hands and feet. The wolf's back broadens and its face rounds.

When it's over, a naked man kneels in Sybil's arms, his skin coated in sweat, his breathing labored.

He glances up, and yeah, it *is* Sawyer. Sybil squeals and hugs him tighter, gyrating against him while he breathes in her scent.

I nearly forgot about Sawyer—Sybil hasn't talked much about the shifter since they got together a couple of weeks ago, but it's obvious now that she has a thing for him…and that he has a thing for her. He nips lightly at her throat, and I tense, my magic beginning to pour out of me.

Infatuated or not, I will rip him off her if he dares—

A growl cuts through my thoughts, dragging my attention away.

The largest wolf of the pack slinks forward, its gaze fixed on me as it takes slow, tentative steps. I can feel power in its gaze—it makes me want to kneel, to bare my neck, to *submit*. The shifter is making it abundantly clear that I'm not to fuck with its pack mate.

I fight the compulsion—the last thing I want is to make myself even more vulnerable before a pack of wolves—but I do drag my magic back into me. Once I do, the growling dies down.

The shifter, however, continues to slink forward, and without meaning to, I tense all over again.

"Don't run," Sawyer says softly from where he holds Sybil. "If you need to back up, do it slowly."

I draw in a shuddering breath and nod. My skin is tingling in a decidedly unwanted way now that I've gained the attention of a fucking wolf.

*Not just any wolf*, I realize as I study its eyes. I remember looking at those lupine eyes only a couple of weeks ago.

"*Kane*," I whisper.

At the sound of his name, he goes very, very still. A low sound comes from his throat. It's close to a whine.

Shit, it *is* him.

Sawyer turns to Sybil and brushes aside one of her dark, silky locks. "I can't believe you came," he says quietly, though we can all hear him. "None of you are supposed to be here." He doesn't sound mad about that.

"My friends were interested in…getting to know your friends tonight," Sybil says.

In response to her words, Kane's ears flick.

He makes another whine that sounds almost…happy? His tail wags once, and I wonder if I'm supposed to feel reassured by this?

Out of the corner of my eye, I notice the other wolves approaching Mai, with her breasts bare, and Olga, whose corset is now loosened and partially sliding off her. They should be retreating—we all should be retreating—but instead Mai is beginning to stroke the valley between her breasts, and Olga is slipping her arms out of what's left of her outfit.

I can practically smell the sex in the air.

This is such a terrible idea. I'm drunk and my pussy is pounding with need, but even I can see that.

Unfortunately, no one else seems to think so. Sawyer has lifted Sybil into his arms, the two making out as he wraps her legs around his waist while those damn wings of hers flutter away. No sooner has he gotten her into his arms than he lopes away into the darkness. One of the other wolves is shifting, and a now topless Olga is petting one of the lycans who's remained in animal form.

I glance back at Kane, who has moved closer, his eyes fixed on me and his snout lifted as he scents the air.

I swallow, sure that he's smelling me. My scent and the wetness that's soaked my panties.

"Kane." I lick my dry lips. "I'm not…"

At the worst possible moment, another surge of desire floods my body, and I gasp, locking my knees to keep myself upright.

Kane's lupine form stills as though he's aware of exactly what's going on with me. Abruptly, he swings around to the rest of the group and growls menacingly at them, his hackles rising.

My heart ratchets up at the sound, and I begin backing up. Maybe while he's busy being weirdly territorial, I can just…disappear.

At the sound of Kane's growl, a freshly shifted lycan steps in front of Olga, guarding her with his body and slowly backing the both of them up.

"Relax, Halloway, we're leaving."

Leaving?

"Wait! No one needs to go!" But even as I speak, my coven sisters and the shifters who've caught their eyes slip away into the darkness. I hear a couple of breathy laughs, a handful of whispered words, a moan, then—nothing.

Un-fucking-believable.

I turn my attention back to Kane, who's studying me with those glinting blue eyes of his. My breath picks up, this time for entirely nonsexual reasons. It was distressing enough to face down my crush's wolf when he was injured, but now, when the two of us are alone in the woods and Kane's under the sway of the moon and his beast's instincts, it's somehow worse.

It doesn't help that I'm very drunk and even more aroused.

Kane approaches me, his eyes tracking my every move. The witch's brew is still hitting my system, and I can feel heat and need and magic moving through my blood. It's overwhelming my misgivings.

I put my hands out in a placating gesture. "I don't know how much you can understand, Kane, but we're friends, and I know I smell...weird." Read: like a horny badger. "I honestly just want to get back to my coven's festivities," I say slowly, fighting the urge to back up. "If you let me, I'll leave—"

At that, Kane gives a low growl.

"Or I could stay," I add.

His growl dies down.

I guess he wants company.

I try again, breathing through the throb of my desire.

"Kane, I know we didn't get our moment," I say, now edging back a little.

He prowls forward, aware of the distance I'm trying to create. He's having none of it.

"And," I continue, "I like you—a lot—but…" My words lapse into a moan as my arousal spikes once more. My breasts feel so heavy, and my core keeps clenching around nothing. "But it's still the Sacred Seven, and I'm waiting for someone else—"

At the mention of someone else, Kane begins to growl again.

If I weren't so drunk on witch's brew, and if Kane weren't an actual wolf at the moment, I'd know what to do. Instead, I edge back a little more, my heart thundering. I cringe when I feel my pussy pounding in time to it.

The lycan moves forward again, eating up the distance between us and then some. He's so close—close enough to touch. Close enough to get bitten. The thought has me backing up faster.

A low, warning sound rumbles in the shifter's throat as he heads after me once more.

"Kane, I know I'm on your territory, but you're making me nervous. Can you—"

I yelp when the back of my foot catches on a tree root, and I tumble to the ground. My hip hits the earth hard, and I hiss in a breath.

One moment, I'm laid out on the ground, and in the next, a massive wolf looms over me.

Maiden, Mother, and Crone.

I go absolutely still as Kane sniffs me curiously. His snout moves to my neck, and I feel his teeth graze my skin. I go very, very still.

"Please don't bite me," I whisper.

Sybil might've been blasé about it, but I don't have any interest in being a werewolf.

Kane pauses, then breathes my scent in once more, his tongue licking the flesh before his teeth graze it again, this time more deliberately, like he's considering the notion.

I lift my hand, readying a spell to push him away, when I see his pelt ripple. In the next instant, his form shifts, his fur receding into his skin as his torso broadens. His translucent magic hovers around him as he transforms.

In less than a minute, the shift is complete, and the wolf is gone. In its place is a very sweaty, very naked man, his heavily muscled body pressed to mine, his face buried against my neck.

He takes deep, heaving breaths as he recovers from the shift.

Unfortunately, all I notice is how fucking good he feels against me. Too good. I reach for him, needing more contact. My prior worries are distant things. Inconsequential, really. This is Kane. I like Kane. I wouldn't mind kissing Kane.

I drag him onto me, and he doesn't fight it. He shifts himself so his hips are settled between mine, pinning me in place, and his hand begins to languidly glide up and down the side of my torso, catching on my satin dress.

The lycan draws in a deep breath, then groans, leaning his forehead against my neck. "Fuck. You've had witch's brew, haven't you?" Kane's voice is deeper than usual, as though his wolf is barely banked.

"Mmm." I writhe a little against Kane. His body feels different than what I expected—his hair less coarse, his sweat-slicked skin less scarred. It throws me for a moment.

"You shouldn't be on lycanthrope territory," he says.

"I tried to leave. You wouldn't let me."

He huffs out a strained laugh. "Yeah, well, my wolf likes you, and he has fewer reservations about making that clear." He laughs again, then touches the side of my face. "I've been worried about you. You okay?"

I nod, then shake my head. "I don't want to talk about that." I can barely *think* over this driving need.

I feel Kane's cock trapped between us, and though he's acting gentle and concerned, his body is taut with arousal. I grind against him, causing the shifter to groan.

"Fuck, Selene," he hisses out, jerking his hips out of reach. "Please tell me you wanted to find me."

"No," I say, kissing the underside of his jaw and continuing to rub myself against him. "I had plans."

He growls at that, and the wolf is wholly in his voice when he says, "Seems to me like you're making yourself new ones."

With that, he finds my lips and kisses me.

Just like the last time I kissed Kane, it feels wrong. All wrong. Because I called out to another man, because I stumbled unwillingly into this situation, because it's the Sacred Seven and Kane's not in full control of his magic, and I don't want to get bitten. But most of all because *Kane isn't Memnon*.

I groan at the realization.

"I smell your need," Kane breathes against my lips, mistaking the sound for something more carnal. His mouth returns to mine, and he deepens the kiss, grinding himself against me, his hard cock rubbing against me through the thin fabric of my dress. I gasp into his mouth as sensation floods me, my hands moving to grip his hips. And yet—

Wrong, wrong, wrong.

The wrongness is screaming at me and cutting through my arousal.

"Wait," I say, breaking off the kiss, a note of panic entering my voice. My body is weeping at me for stopping, and I have to fight the urge to give in again. I place a hand against Kane's chest. "Stop." I force the word out, even as my traitorous hips grind against his.

Another growl rumbles low in Kane's throat, his instincts clearly not liking my words. "Stop?" he says. He dips his nose to my neck and breathes in. "Your body, your very scent itself is telling me to fuck you. You're dripping in arousal."

I pinch my eyes shut. "I know, but…" I draw in a deep breath and force my limbs to untangle themselves from his. "I can't do this."

I can't. The longer I lie here, the more obvious that becomes.

Kane rears back a little, but he doesn't get off me. Instead, he searches my features. "You can't, or you don't want to?"

I open my mouth—

"It doesn't matter what my mate meant," a deep voice answers. "She said *no*. Now get the fuck off my fiancée."

# CHAPTER 17

**Memnon looms like a god behind me, his magic pressing at** my back like a storm cloud as he glares down at the shifter.

"Fiancée?" Kane echoes, gazing down at me. I can't see his features well, but from what I can make out, he looks both confused and heartbroken. "*Mate?*"

I swallow, glancing away.

I didn't tell him everything about the night I was arrested, nor have I mentioned that Memnon and I are soul mates.

Memnon's magic wraps around the shifter's body and rips him off me, throwing him against a nearby tree. Kane hits it with a grunt. Before he can move away from the tree trunk, the sorcerer's power pins him to it.

Memnon strides forward, murder in his eyes. He looks like he's going to rip the shifter's spine out through his chest. "If it's not the lycanthrope who thought to touch what's mine."

*Memnon, I am not a piece of meat to fight over.*

*Of course you're not,* he says smoothly down our bond. *You are the reason for my existence. But I will fight over you.*

"Do you remember what I told you when I saw you last?" Memnon says, stepping in close to the bound lycanthrope.

While he speaks, Memnon's power brushes against me, wrapping around my midsection and slipping beneath my back. I think it's supposed to be a reassuring caress, but the sensation of his magic against my overstimulated skin has me gasping.

Whoever made that brew should be arrested. This amount of arousal feels criminal.

Memnon continues, "I said that if you ever touched Selene again, I would cut off your dick and feed it to you. And what have I found here? You touching my *unwilling* fiancée."

A low growl starts up in the shifter's throat. "Unwilling? *You* want to talk about unwilling? You stalked her and broke into her room. You threatened to hurt me to get her to do your will. And now you'd have me believe she's *engaged* to you?" He laughs in Memnon's face. Kane's eyes move to mine. "Tell me you willingly agreed to *that.*"

I don't know how Kane so easily sees through this engagement of ours.

The sorcerer's magic is gathering; I can see the agitated ends of it lashing around him like whips, and I know he's about to do something awful.

"Memnon, don't hurt him," I gasp out.

My mate doesn't so much as flinch at the order, but his magic rapidly descends back into his body until the night air is entirely clear of it. Knowing all that violent magic is now bottled up inside the sorcerer unnerves the shit out of me.

When Memnon glances over his shoulder at me, the

corner of his mouth curving up, I can tell my order doesn't matter. He has something else up his sleeve.

"I'm guessing Selene hasn't told you about our past?" The sorcerer faces Kane again. "Our love stretches back two thousand years. You wish to compete with that, wolf? My soul mate and I have endured horrors you cannot imagine to get to this moment."

"I think I have a helluva lot more chance than a tool like you," Kane says.

Memnon steps in close, his form towering over the shifter's. "Is that right? Because I thought I heard her say *fuck no* to your offer, but maybe my ears are just ba—"

Kane's fist swings out, hitting Memnon square in the cheek, and the sorcerer's head snaps to the side.

Aw fuck.

Memnon stays in that position for an extra moment. When he straightens, a little line of blood drips down from the corner of his mouth. The sorcerer smiles, the expression tugging on his scar and making him look malevolent.

"Foolish little pup. Thinking of stealing people's mates."

Kane hits him again.

Memnon groans, stumbling back. The shifter lunges for him, taking the sorcerer to the ground. Kane's fist slams into the sorcerer's face again and again. He just takes it, not even bothering to protect himself from the hits.

"Kane, stop!"

Kane lifts his head and growls in response, the alpha in him chafing against my order. He does, however, lower his fist, his chest rising and falling with his exertion.

Beneath him, Memnon's face is a bloody mess. The sight of it causes a bolt of sheer terror to course through me.

*I'm all right, little witch,* he says. *Healing it already.*

"Why isn't he fighting back?" Kane says, his eyes still focused on Memnon. "I know this motherfucker loves to."

*I really do,* Memnon says down our bond. My soul mate sounds more than a little self-satisfied, despite the fact that he just had the crap beaten out of him.

Tentatively, I move toward the two. Arousal is still soaking my panties, and honestly, the fighting did nothing but deepen the ache.

"Because I told him not to," I say to the shifter. Of its own accord, my magic slips ahead and presses itself against Memnon's wounds. It ignores Kane's bloody knuckles entirely. "But if you keep hitting him, I'll let him have at you, and, Kane," I say softly, "you don't want that."

The lycan looks between us. "So he listens to you now?" he asks me, getting off Memnon.

The sorcerer sits up and wipes away what blood my magic hasn't already cleaned from his face, then rests his arm on a bended knee.

Memnon leans back a little, a mischievous twinkle in his eye. "Are you going to tell him or should I?" he asks me, oddly gleeful for a man who just took several hits to his face.

"*Memnon,*" I caution. Why must this entire conversation happen while I am blazingly drunk and in *desperate* need of an orgasm?

"What is he talking about, Selene?" Kane asks. I can see his wolf staring at me from the backs of his eyes.

Hell's spells.

My stomach churns as I admit, "Memnon is bound to me."

Uncertainty flickers in his eyes. "You mean through your...bond?"

"The soul mate bond doesn't compel me to do

anything," Memnon says. "The one we made a few nights ago, however…"

It finally registers. "You *bound* him?" Kane says, horrified.

My stomach twists. I became a friend of the pack in the first place *because* I stopped a binding spell from happening. To suddenly now have one myself doesn't look good.

Kane stares at me like he's never seen me before. Like maybe I am the bad guy.

Memnon stands up, stepping in front of me. "Don't look at her like that," he says, menace back in his voice.

"Why would you do such a thing?" Kane says, ignoring Memnon entirely.

Memnon answers anyway. "I asked it of her. I am earning back the trust I broke."

Kane looks from Memnon to me, aghast. I cannot tell what is running through the lycan's mind, but Goddess, I am too drunk to adequately address it anyway.

Another wave of desire washes though me, and a soft moan slips out.

Ugh. And horny. Crone's cane, but I'm far, far too horny to be having this conversation.

Kane's nostrils flare, and his eyes fully shift, and Memnon glances back at me with an arched eyebrow, and fuck, everybody is very aware that I'm one throbbing erogenous zone.

"Well," I say, inclining my head a little. "It has been lovely, Kane. We will chat again soon. Memnon and I are leaving right now," I say, directing this last bit to the sorcerer.

Memnon immediately moves toward me with a possessive glint in his eye.

Kane's gaze searches mine. "Selene…"

I hear the hurt in his voice, and it guts me.

I didn't intend for any of this. Not the confrontation,

not the meeting with Kane, not even the arousal. It's still my fault, but I hadn't wanted it all to play out so messily.

The shifter's attention moves to my soul mate, and his pain transforms into anger. "How does it feel to be forced to do another's bidding?" Kane calls out.

Memnon gets to my side and turns around to face the lycanthrope. Though the shifter is deliberately baiting him, there's no longer any rage in Memnon's eyes. Instead, he flashes the shifter an amused look.

"Like foreplay, pup."

# CHAPTER 18

*We walk for several minutes in silence, the only noises the* crunch of our feet over leaves and the harsh sound of my breath.

Behind us, a howl goes up, the sound mournful. I rub my eyes, a sob stuck in my throat.

Never meant to hurt him. Love sucks. Witch's brew sucks. This situation sucks.

I'm still drunk and so, so aroused, and it makes everything that much worse.

"How much of that did you see?" I say.

I feel Memnon glance over at me, his bourbon eyes flicking to my mouth. "Enough."

I run my hand over my face. Goddess, but this evening has gone tits up.

"I don't know how to do this," Memnon admits.

"Do what?" I say, my fingers finding their way to the low neckline of my dress. I'm absently starting to tug on it.

"Fight for the right to be yours."

I glance over at him just as he looks up toward the shrouded sky, my eyes tracing the line of his jaw.

"Before, when you were Roxi, you were mine and mine alone. I never needed to prove my worth to you." He stops and faces me. "And now that I must, I feel my own inadequacies rising to the surface. I can fight and kill for you, but I cannot be whatever that man is."

Even in the darkness, I can see there's still a bit of swelling in his face. Neither of our powers fully healed him.

I step up to him and place a hand against his cheek, letting my magic sink into his skin. I don't utter a spell, but my power understands my intention, and it goes about healing his remaining wounds.

"I'm still so angry at you," I admit. "So angry it's hard to breathe through it." If I had spoken these words days ago, they would've rung true. Right now, however, the heat of my hate has banked. "But tonight, I called out for you. *I wanted you.*"

*I still want you.*

Another wave of desire punctuates my confession, and under the force of it, I close the last of the space between us. For once this evening, my desire doesn't feel like the enemy, like something working against me. It feels…if not natural then at least magical. Wondrous. Something to be celebrated.

My hand slips from Memnon's cheek and moves to his chest, my fingers digging in at the solid feel of him beneath my palm. I want more. Need more.

"I am yours to command, my queen," he says in Sarmatian. "So if you want me to please you like I was made to, *command it.*"

The two of us stare at each other, the moment taut with tension.

I drop my gaze to his chest and deliberately place both my hands on his pecs. My pulse is pounding between my ears, my blood is roaring in my veins, and an evening's worth of want is gathered up in me.

I push him gently. Memnon is as immovable as a mountain, but he lets me force him back, back, back until he bumps against a tree trunk.

My eyes rise to his neck, where I can just make out the panther tattoo that peeks out from above the collar of his shirt.

Rising onto tiptoes, I wrap a hand around his neck and pull him to me. Gently, I graze my lips over the inked animal. Long ago, he got the tattoo in honor of Ferox, my familiar. My heart squeezes at the memory.

Memnon's hand comes up, holding my face to his neck, like he wants to keep me there forever.

"*Est amage,*" he says softly, reverently, his free hand lightly stroking up and down my bare arm.

"I don't want to command you," I whisper into his ear. That's what *he* wants. I want him to be at my mercy in an entirely different way.

So when I pull away, my hands slip to his pants, and I undo the button at the top.

"*Selene,*" he says, his voice roughened with surprise. He captures my wrists, trying to stop me. He can have my wrists. I don't need them for what I'm about to do.

My magic rolls out of me, unzipping his pants and tugging them and what he wears beneath down his legs.

"When was the last time someone bowed to you, *est xsaya?*" *My king.*

Memnon goes preternaturally still, and when I meet his eyes, his expression is feral.

"*Selene*," he says again, and his voice holds a dangerous edge.

He wants control? He wants strategy? He won't get *any* of it right now.

I drop to my knees, my wrists still caught in his grip. The throb in my core has reached a fever pitch. I don't know if it's possible to come from arousal alone, but apparently I want to find out.

The sorcerer's erection juts out proudly, a bead of precum glistening in the darkness. I have countless memories of taking him in my mouth, yet I've technically never experienced it in this life. That strange contrast only sharpens my desire.

I lean forward, wrapping my lips around the head of his cock. Memnon hisses in a breath. I draw my tongue up his slit, the taste of him nearly sending me. Shit, I might actually come this way.

"*Selene*," he groans, his hips jerking forward of their own accord.

I take him deeper into my mouth.

Better than memory. So much better.

He still holds my arms captive, and honestly, it's doing nothing but heightening my own arousal.

I pull away from his cock long enough to say, "If you don't want this, release me."

I stare up at him, waiting. His hands flex on my wrists but don't let go. "Selene, you are the one who needs—"

"I need *this*," I interrupt. "I need you."

With that, I lean in, taking Memnon's cock as deep in my mouth as I can.

"*Gods*, Empress," he curses as his hips begin to move in tandem with my mouth, "Feels like heaven. I'd almost forgotten."

I smile around him, pleased by his reaction—pleased by him.

Slowly, I retreat from his cock until only the head of him remains in my mouth. Then I move back up his shaft, enjoying the feel of him against my tongue. I fall into a rhythm, one that has my own core throbbing harder and harder. The longer I work him, the more my jaw burns with the effort. Even that ache is familiar. And somehow, the memory of it is breaking my heart and filling it up all at once.

Through our bond, I sense his knees growing weak. My desire roars in my veins, but through our connection, I also catch wisps of the pleasure I'm giving him. My breasts feel too heavy, and the ache between my thighs pounds harder than ever.

Memnon finally releases my wrists so he can dig his fingers into my hair. "My queen, my mate, this is rapture... cannot last much longer."

I can sense it too. Goddess, I can. It's stoking the heat inside me, ratcheting it up and up.

*I should leave you unfinished like this,* I tell him, running my hands up his thick thighs. Feels so damn good. *Just as you left me so many nights.*

He'd sent me so many sex dreams, edging me without release night after night.

*You'd be justified doing so.* Memnon groans, thrusting a bit deeper into my mouth. *I enjoyed cruelly teasing you.*

*I'm tempted,* I say, my own core still throbbing as I release him from my mouth. *But what I really want,* est xsaya, *is to see you lose control inside me.*

Memnon is breathing heavily, staring down at me from where he leans. In the moonlight, his eyes glint like coins, his scar a darker shadow than the rest. He looks as though he were born from the darkness, the angles of his features sharp and wicked.

"I wanted to wait until you didn't hate me so much," he says softly.

Is that why he's always stopped short of sex with me? If so, that's…annoyingly noble.

I shake my head. "I called you here tonight for some quick, meaningless sex," I say. "If you're not up for that, you can leave." It hurts to say this last part, but my arousal will pass. I'm not going to use our bond to force him to stay if he doesn't want to.

Memnon crouches in front of me, not bothering to pull up his pants and tuck himself away.

"*Est amage*, you and I both know I don't do fast fucks, and I definitely don't do meaningless ones." He regards me for a long moment. "I can eat you out until sunrise and beyond, but if you want me inside you, those are my terms."

I narrow my gaze at him, my breath ragged. "You do know I can command you." I think he's forgotten who has the upper hand here.

He tilts my chin. "Then command me," he challenges. "I willingly gave you that power over me." Memnon stares at me a little longer. "Otherwise, *those are my terms.*" When I don't say anything, he leans in. "I think, even caught up in whatever potion you've taken, you *do* still want deep connection, and you want to feel safe when everything else is out of control." He pauses for a moment. "That's all I ask for, Empress."

There is a lot of nuance to his demands; it would probably

be simpler if I sent Memnon away or stuck to oral. I don't want that.

My eyes drop to his lips. "Kiss me," I breathe.

In an instant, his mouth is on mine. His lips are a memory, and with every stroke of them, I awaken. I'm Roxilana, and I am Selene.

"Do you still want me?" he whispers against my lips.

I nod against him, wrapping my arms around his neck.

He grins against me, pleased, so pleased. Like he's gotten everything he wants. His hands hook beneath my arms, and he lifts me up, twisting us so that it's my back that hits the tree. The sorcerer lifts me high, high up over him, his magic twisting around my waist and beneath my thighs to keep me pinned there. I stare down at his face, confused at why I'm so much higher than even he is.

Until, of course, I realize my pussy is eye level for him.

"Nice panties," he says a moment before he snaps them off. "Now, legs over my shoulders," he commands.

"Wait, what?" I say dazedly. "I want you to fuck me."

He leans forward and nips my dress and what he can of my pussy, and I yelp, bucking against him.

"We'll get to that eventually." He gives my ass a squeeze. "Over my shoulders, feisty witch," he says again.

I do as he says before I can think better of it, only slightly miffed that he's the one bossing me around.

He steps in close, forcing my legs farther apart. While his magic holds me in place, his hands caress the outsides of my thighs, pushing my dress up to my waist.

Cold air hits my pussy.

"*Memnon*," I gasp, staring down at him.

"Hold on to my hair, *est amage*. I want to feel your pussy grinding against my face."

Goddess, but he's such a dirty talker. My chest is heaving faster and faster with my arousal. The anticipation has taken me right to the edge. He could barely touch me, and it would set me off.

My hands thread through his hair. Flashing me a hungry look, he leans forward.

Mere inches from my core, I tug on that hair, pulling him away.

"Mercy, little witch, do you want to feel good or not?"

I glance down at the sorcerer and take in his ferocious, violent beauty, and my heart is beating fast, so fast, and I feel vulnerable.

"This is just for tonight," I say, watching him carefully. "It won't be a regular thing."

"Of course," Memnon says smoothly, his gaze unfaltering. I should be skeptical of his easy agreement after all his earlier demands, but honestly, I want this too bad to peer closely at his reasons.

*Just for tonight,* I repeat to myself silently. *Just because of the brew.*

"Now," Memnon says, running a hand up and down my outer thigh, "will you let me taste you?"

"Yes."

I've barely gotten the word out when Memnon's mouth is on me.

I gasp as his lips move against me, my hold tightening on him, and I'm rising, rising, rising—

"*Memnon!*" I cry out as I come.

He continues eating me out as I come, and holy fucking Goddess, it's too much. I make tormented, helpless noises.

"If you think I'm stopping just because you came quick, here's your notice—*I'm not.*"

I don't know whether to curse him or thank him, because no sooner has my orgasm begun to ebb than my arousal comes roaring back.

He teases all my sensitive spots before slipping a tongue in me. I moan, pressing my core closer to his mouth. My world has come down to the point of contact where Memnon's mouth meets my pussy.

"Tastes like fucking ambrosia, mate," he says as he works me with his mouth. The man eats me out with a hunger reserved for starving men, his hands kneading my thighs.

His mouth moves to my clit, and he is *merciless*. I move against his face, grinding against him like he wanted me to, my body desperate for more of him. I pinch my eyes shut, leaning my head back against the rough tree bark, writhing against him as sensation rapidly builds in me all over again.

Before it can pitch me over the edge, Memnon moves away from my pussy, lowering me.

I cry out at the loss of his touch, my eyes opening.

The sorcerer's own eyes are taking in every inch of my face like he's committing it to memory. "Do you still want me, *est amage*?" he asks when we're at eye level.

I nod, my core feeling painfully empty.

"Then command me," he says.

"I want you inside me."

He gives his head a shake. "Command me."

I hesitate, searching his gaze. I don't want to take the sorcerer's agency from him, and my orders do just that. Yet he *wants* my commands pressed onto him, I think. I think his demand for them *is* his consent.

My hand drifts to his neck, where my snarling familiar is inked on his skin. I trace the lines of it. "If you don't like anything I order you to do, say 'Ferox,'" I whisper.

Cannot believe we're about to have the sort of sex that requires safe words.

Memnon's eyes shine. "All right, Empress, I can do that. Now, *command* me."

I wet my lips, then lift my chin. "Fuck me, Memnon."

"That's my queen."

He spreads my thighs, lining us up. I can feel his heavy, throbbing cock at my entrance.

Memnon pauses. "This changes things."

I open my mouth to argue, because it doesn't change anything—it's just sex, a simple physical act. But before I get a word out, Memnon drives into me.

I gasp, my grip tightening on my soul mate's neck as his massive cock fully seats itself inside me. I'm speared on the thing, and despite my dripping pussy and all the foreplay, I am stretched nearly beyond my limits.

Memnon exhales sharply, a shiver running through him.

"Are you good?" he asks softly, sensing my tension.

I nod, swallowing a little. "Just give me a moment." I had forgotten how big he was.

For several seconds, all I can hear are our ragged breaths and the distant pleasured cries of other witches. The sorcerer leans forward, pressing a kiss to the underside of my jaw, then my cheeks, then my nose, then my eyelids. With each gentle brush of his lips, my body relaxes, and my core stretches, accommodating him.

"Gods," he murmurs in Sarmatian. "Two thousand years and I'm finally home."

I don't want to admit it, but I feel it too. Those gentle, reverent kisses, the fullness in my core—this feels right, so right.

This is more intimate than I'd planned, but a deviant part of me enjoys this.

"Don't move," I whisper. "Not yet."

His lips brush against my mouth. "I'm not going anywhere," he murmurs.

My body has already stretched for him, but I stay there a few extra moments, just to relish it a little longer. Eventually, my arousal takes over, and I shift against him, now needing the friction of his thrusts. Only...they don't come.

Memnon presses his forehead to mine, letting out a husky laugh. "Amazing as this feels, *est amage*, you're going to have to release me from your last command if you want me to continue."

Oh, right.

"You can move," I whisper, too overcome by the feel of him to be embarrassed.

He pulls away to kiss me under my jaw. Memnon drags his cock almost all the way out of me before thrusting back in.

I gasp.

"You feel so godsdamned good," he murmurs, grabbing my hands from behind his neck and threading his fingers between mine as his hips continue to rock against me. "My fierce little *fiancée*."

The reminder drags away some of the lust-driven haze that I'm under.

"This means nothing," I insist.

"This means *everything*," Memnon says, squeezing my hands. His next thrust is punishingly deep, and I moan as it hits every nerve ending inside me.

The sorcerer still wants something soft here; he's tried to angle this to his advantage.

But he isn't the one in control.

I meet his eyes. "Harder," I demand, lifting my chin. I don't want to be reminded that we were married once or that we might be again someday. Terms be damned, right now, all I want from him is sensation alone. "Fuck me like you're determined to get me to come as fast as possible."

Memnon groans as his own pace picks up. He bites his bottom lip as he looks at me. I don't think he's aware of the action, but it has me mesmerized. I moan at the sensation, tilting my head back as I begin to climb once more.

The sorcerer leans in. "Just so we're clear, Selene, I want to give you soul-devouring sex," he says as he slams into me, his hips pumping faster and faster. He fucks me like it's the one thing he's been made for. "Not this hasty shit." Each punishing stroke of his cock sends me closer and closer to the edge. "I want you to see the life we once shared—the one I still want to give you," he says, squeezing my hands.

"You'll give me what I ask for," I tell him. "Isn't that what you want from your queen?"

Memnon holds my gaze, his thrusts relentless. "I live to serve you, Empress."

I can't read his expression, not in the darkness here, but there's no trace of mockery or disappointment in his voice. I think he's being wholly sincere. But it is a reminder: I will only get my way like this so long as the bond remains and I don't fall in love with him.

The sorcerer pulls down one of the straps of my dress, exposing the breast beneath. Bending down, he sucks on my nipple and teases it between his teeth.

That's all it takes.

I cry out as my climax explodes through me, clouding my vision. I squeeze his hands as wave after wave of it crests.

180

Memnon groans against my skin. "Missed the feel of you coming around me." He hisses in a breath. "Squeezing my cock too good," he says as he continues to mercilessly drive into me.

Memnon has barely uttered the words when I feel him thicken. I cry out again as the extra pressure extends my climax.

"*Gods, Selene.*" He pistons hard into me, abandoning my breast in favor of my lips.

And then he's coming.

He kisses me through wave after wave of his own orgasm. I can feel an echo of it through our bond, amplifying the receding edge of my own. He's in my mouth, in my pussy, and wrapped around me, pressed against me as closely as he can get. I sense if he could, he would simply melt into me.

I like the thought. Right now, with the brew still burning like fire in my veins, I wouldn't mind Memnon sinking into me and never leaving.

Eventually, his thrusts gentle, and he gives my mouth one last kiss as he pulls out of me. He clutches my body to his as he lowers me to the ground.

"Can you stand?" he asks as he sets me on my feet.

My unsteady legs immediately fold.

He catches me. "All right, that's a *no*," he says, lifting me back into his arms.

"I'm fine," I insist, but Memnon is already wrapping my legs around his waist and holding me so that we're chest to chest.

The two of us gaze at each other. I lock my ankles together and twine my arms around his neck.

"This is nice too," I admit.

Memnon's eyes twinkle. "Good, *est amage*, because I have no intention of putting you back down."

I hear the rustle of his jeans and the sound of his zipper being done up as his magic redresses him. And then he begins to walk.

"Where are you taking me?" I ask.

"Back to your room. Unless you'd rather stay out here?"

I can't tell if he's teasing me or if it's a legitimate question, but I shake my head. "My place is good."

His gaze drops to my lips, and he nods. "Good."

Memnon hasn't taken twenty steps when he makes a tortured noise and glances down between us.

Heat rises to my cheeks when I realize what he's noticing. Memnon's come is leaking out of me and getting all over his shirt.

"I'm going to make a mess of your clothes," I say softly.

"If you think I'm *anything* but pleased," he says, "you're mistaken."

My cheeks burn hotter, even as I tighten my grip. Given this position, the two of us are painfully close. As close as we used to be when we'd ride together—closer, technically, since then I always faced away from him.

On a whim, I press my face into his neck and breathe in. The action causes his hold on me to tighten.

"You don't smell like grass or horse anymore," I say, surprised and maybe a little dismayed. He doesn't even smell like sweat. He used to. I close my eyes, and I can remember with striking clarity that other version of him. His low-slung pants and kurta, which he'd peel off the moment his torso got too sweaty from training. The bow and gorytos he wore in addition to his blades. The warm, sunbaked feel of his skin after a long day out on the steppe.

"That must be a welcome relief." Memnon's voice has that husky, intimate quality to it.

I shake my head against him, playing with a few locks of his hair at the nape of his neck. "No, it's not." I frown to myself, then breathe him in again.

Memnon does still smell like himself in the most innate way. And it's that smell that makes me lean my head against him.

My old friend. My fiercest enemy. My newest lover.

After a moment, he says, "I'm unused to hearing you speak of our past as…ours." He pulls me away from his neck to gaze at me. "It fills me with no small amount of joy."

I stare back at him uncertainly, my emotions tangled up, when that goddess-damned witch's brew stirs in my veins, and my core begins to ache all over again.

No, no, no. Please, not again.

I press my lips together to stifle a moan, but I don't manage to stop my hips from grinding against him.

"Again?" Memnon says, surprised.

I duck my head, a little embarrassed. Instead of responding, I lean in and press a kiss to his neck, then another and another. Memnon draws in a sharp breath, his hands gripping me tighter.

Despite my own misgivings about my soul mate, I'm absurdly relieved that it's him who's with me tonight. The sorcerer is as natural and familiar to me as my own skin. Perhaps it is like this with all soul mates, but I suspect so much of it has to do with the life we lived together long ago. That one was built first out of friendship.

He makes a low sound deep in his chest. "What did you take?"

"What do you mean?" I ask him, even as I continue to trail kisses along his skin.

"You have a healthy appetite for sex, little witch, but this is something else," he says as I continue to rub myself against him. "I can feel your need clawing at me through our bond."

"Witch's brew," I say. There was no such equivalent in the ancient world. "It draws out our magic, but it has some side effects." Though they're not usually this potent.

We break through the tree line, the moaning noises growing more numerous.

"This sounds like our camp after a celebration," he says, harkening back to his people.

The sounds intensify the closer we get to my residence hall. By the time we step up to the door of my house, it sounds like there's an orgy happening on the other side of it.

Once we enter, it's clear that there *is* an orgy happening in the library—RIP to any nearby books. Several other couples are scattered in the house's den. I can hear more in the spell kitchen and the dining room.

Somehow, even with my panty-less attire and my pussy juices all over Memnon, we're still looking like the most modest couple here.

The sounds follow us up the stairs and down the hall.

It's only once we enter my room and Memnon kicks the door shut that the sounds grow muffled. Sort of. I can still hear rhythmic thumping from a nearby room.

Memnon's magic pours out of him and covers the walls, muffling the sound until it's just us. Well, us and Nero.

The big cat is curled up in his bed, looking miserable at all the commotion. He gives me a betrayed look as Memnon finally sets me down.

"I'm sorry," I say defensively. "I didn't know it was going to be like this."

His tail twitches with annoyance.

Apology apparently not accepted.

"The woods are full of more of the same stuff. You can go out there, but you're still going to be annoyed."

That's all the permission he needs. My familiar gets up from his bed and lithely leaps onto the windowsill.

"Just be careful. There are ghosts and werewolves and at least one douchey fairy out there. If anyone tries to get close, protect yourself."

Nero glances back and blinks his amber-green eyes at me. It's the only indication that he heard my words at all. Then, with a final flick of his tail, he leaps onto the oak tree outside, and then he's gone.

I turn my attention back to Memnon, who's already gazing at me with naked longing in his eyes. My skin is becoming uncomfortably hot again. I don't know when the brew will eventually let up. And now trapped in this room with Memnon, our past is reaching for me from the grave.

"Stay with me tonight," I repeat. "That…is an order."

The command feels wrong, yet Memnon looks at me like a man who's been given a second chance at life.

"Don't read into this too deeply," I caution. "Tonight— this is all just empty sex," I insist, driving home my earlier point.

Memnon gives me a husky laugh as he closes the space between us. I tilt my head back to look at him, reminded all over again about just how huge he is.

He leans in and presses a kiss to the point where my jaw meets my ear. "A lie you'd like to be true," he breathes against my skin. His magic tugs at our clothes, pulling my dress up and over my head. He moves away from me while it comes off, his indigo magic removing his own attire.

There's a fire beneath my skin, one the witch's brew ignited and Memnon has only stoked, and at the sight of him adorned in only his tattoos, my desire spikes so sharply it's almost painful.

I only have a moment to admire him in all his glorious nudity before he wraps a hand around my waist and drags the two of us onto my bed.

We've barely hit the mattress when Memnon pulls away and flips me so that my ass is in the air.

"On your hands and knees," he commands.

*I hate bossy men—hate them,* I think as I do as he says.

*You're lying again,* Memnon says, clearly overhearing thoughts that were not meant for him.

His hands go to my hips, gripping me fast. With a brutal thrust, he's inside me once more.

I cry out, nearly coming from that contact alone.

He must sense how close I am because he leans in and says, "Not yet, little witch. We have barely started having fun yet."

He then proceeds to fuck me slowly, only giving me these shallow, teasing thrusts until my orgasm moves out of reach.

"You bastard," I murmur.

The devil laughs at my back. "You have no idea."

Once he's sure I won't immediately climax, he drapes his chest over my back and wraps a hand around my neck, his pace picking up just a little. "I'm going to take care of you, *est amage,*" he vows, "until every last need of yours is met. But in return, you're going to listen to me. If you're a good little witch, I'll reward you for it."

I feel the heavy brush of his magic against my clit, dragging me rapidly toward an orgasm. But just as quickly as it comes, it's gone.

"And if you're a bad little witch, I'll give this pretty neck of yours a squeeze."

Lightly, he constricts my breathing, and for reasons I don't fully understand, that too brings me closer to orgasm.

"*Memnon*," I moan.

He squeezes my neck again. "Naughty witch. You're going to call me *husband* or *soul mate*. Anything else gets punished."

I'm the one with the power over him. I can stop this at any moment, yet I don't stop it. I don't even give it more than a passing thought.

The sorcerer's hold loosens on my neck, but his thrusts slow again. Why is he slowing?

"Harder," I insist.

He begins to pick up speed. "If you want more, then address me properly."

I whimper, my pussy throbbing.

"Don't be cruel—" Don't say it, Selene. Don't say it. Don't—"*Husband*."

There's a rush of magic against my clit, and I nearly collapse against the sensation. Only Memnon's bracing hand on my neck keeps me in place.

"Do you like that?" he says. "Tell me that your husband understands your needs like no other, and I will give this to you until you come."

"That's so fucking manipulative," I say, even as he hammers into me.

He squeezes my neck, presumably for disagreeing with him. Maybe for cursing.

I gasp reflexively, my pussy tightening around him.

"If you don't like it, you can always come the good old-fashioned way," he says.

I bow my head, wanting to sob because I'm so fucking turned on, and he's so goddess-damned evil.

"You understand my needs like no other." I gasp out the sentiment. It doesn't sound like a lie because Memnon does, indeed, seem to know every trick of my body.

He leans in near my ear. "*Who* understands your needs?" he presses softly.

This monster.

I turn my head to meet his gaze, our faces inches apart.

"You, *my husband*," I spit out.

He holds my gaze for a second longer before he remembers himself.

"Good woman," he praises me, his lips curving into a smile. And then his magic is scouring my clit and sliding up my stomach and over my breasts, teasing my nipples as well.

My arms buckle, and Memnon releases my throat so that my upper body can collapse onto the mattress.

The sorcerer brushes my hair off the nape of my neck and presses a kiss there. Between that and the relentless rub of his magic, I shatter, arching back against him as I come and come and come.

His hips slam into me, pumping harder and faster, trying to give me everything I crave all at once.

"*Fuck*," I hear him curse under his own breath, even as I feel his cock throb inside me. Then, with a roar, he comes, his own climax lengthening my own.

I press my ass against Memnon even as I place my forehead on my hands. My orgasm hasn't even ended, but the pulsing ache from the cursed witch's brew is back again.

I make a frustrated sound, wanting to weep. My body is tired, but it doesn't seem to matter; it's demanding release again.

"Memnon, I think…" *I think I need more.*

The sorcerer smooths a hand down my sweaty spine. "I know, *est amage*. I can feel it through our bond. As long as you need me, I will take care of you."

And he does. Many, many times over.

# CHAPTER 19

*I know I've done a bad thing before I even open my eyes.*

A very, very bad thing named Memnon.

The room smells like sex, and my body is sore everywhere. My wicked soul mate lies asleep in my bed, holding me like I'm his own personal teddy bear. His leg is draped over mine, and his arm is wrapped around my chest, as if in sleep he fears I might escape him.

If I could scream at drunk Selene, I would. My pussy feels swollen and bruised, and my body feels sticky with sweat and come. I pinch my eyes shut, willing it all away. Especially the pretty things he said between bouts of sex. Those linger with me even now.

The man deserves my ire, *not* my interest.

I turn over in his arms so I can look at him. He makes a noise low in his chest and pulls me tighter against him.

"Again?" he murmurs, his eyes still closed and his voice thick with sleep.

I want the earth to swallow me up. "No," I say hoarsely, a blush creeping up my neck.

"Thank the gods." He sounds legitimately relieved, which only makes me flush deeper. "Much as I want to fuck that pretty little pussy of yours, I think you broke my dick last ni—"

I cover his mouth before he can finish the sentence. Memnon's eyes blink sleepily open, and I can feel his lazy, languid grin beneath my hand.

He reaches out and strokes my cheek. *Aww, is my mate embarrassed?*

"Last night never happened," I say. Just sex. It was just some casual, highly erotic sex. That's all.

*Oh, it* definitely *happened. That memory is up there with finding you and marrying you the first time around.*

I close my eyes and inwardly wince. I see he's taking last night in the complete other direction.

He runs his knuckles over my bare flesh. "Are you sore?" he asks, his brow furrowing.

I open my eyes and shake my head, even as I feel the throb from between my thighs. "I'm fine."

Memnon frowns, studying my features. "Fine," he echoes, testing the word out. I think the sorcerer is coming face-to-face with this expression for the first time. "I don't believe you. We fucked a lot—I wasn't gentle."

I remember. I asked him not to be.

I groan and bury my face against his chest. The things I said, the things we did...

Definitely hexing whoever made that batch of witch's brew.

Memnon laughs softly, rubbing my back and pressing me

in close against him. It's strange that these types of touches are new yet also old and familiar.

"My little witch *is* embarrassed," Memnon says, sounding both surprised and delighted by it. He kisses the top of my head, the action oddly endearing. "I also don't believe you're *fine*."

As he speaks, I feel warmth spread out beneath his palm and along my skin. It soaks into my flesh, and my various aches and pains vanish.

I lift my head and give him a grateful look. Now is when I push him away. Only...I don't want to. And I know this is how all bad ideas begin when it comes to Memnon—giving the guy a chance—but right now, as I stare at the sorcerer's scarred, inked torso, the past feels like it's rising up from the depths.

On a whim, I run my hand over his skin, tracing his various tattoos. I had asked him not so long ago to tell me what they all meant.

Now I don't need to.

"Your first hunt," I say softly, tracing a ram with a twisted torso on his arm. "And your first animal kill," I say, moving my fingers over a fallen deer. My hand moves to a horse whose body is decorated with swirls and stripes. "Your first battle," I say. My fingers move to another fallen ram with designs on its body. Looming over it is a fanged predator. "Your first human kill," I say. "*And* your first brush with death." My touch moves up to his neck. "Here's my familiar, and—" My fingers glide to his other shoulder. "These are the various tribes you unified, and here are more whom you defeated." My hand drifts to the skin above his heart. "Here's your family crest," I say, tracing the dragon, "and..." He was planning to add the tree of life around the dragon as a representation of me and the bond that ties us together, but he was cursed before he got the chance.

Memnon watches me like he's hanging on to my every word. I realize how truly lonely it must be for him, living in this modern world where no one understands who he is or where he came from or what his life was like. His people are hardly more than a shadowy smudge in history books.

"It's still surreal that we had an entire life together," I murmur.

Memnon's eyes turn sorrowful, and his hand slips down my torso, his index finger tracing a design over my abdomen, right where, long ago, I carried his child, and right where, long ago, Eislyn shoved a knife through me and ended that possibility.

"But we *didn't* have an entire life together, little witch," he says softly. "Look at me. I may have been in my prime by ancient standards, but by yours, I am young. *We* were young when things ended. You and I were robbed of our life before we could fully live it."

I have to breathe through my nose, just to alleviate a sudden tightness in my chest. Once the feeling abates, I exhale. That was then. This is now. He and I may have once shared something real and amazing, but things are different. *I* am different. And Memnon has been unforgivably cruel to me.

I pull away a little, gathering my blankets against my chest like a shield. I clear my throat. "We should talk about the witches who have been murdered," I say, trying to get the focus off our relationship and on to something else.

Memnon raises an eyebrow. "Now? You'd like to discuss this now? When the taste of your pussy still coats my tongue and your thighs are still slick with my—"

I cover his mouth again before he can finish the sentence, my cheeks heating. His eyes go right to my blush, and I feel him laugh beneath my hand.

"You will tell me about the murders," I command him, removing my shaking hand. I don't know what I'm thinking, insisting on this. I'm in no state to solve anything—not when I'm in my problem-making era, the man in my bed case in point. But last night keeps playing on loop in my mind, and if we don't focus on the most sobering topic I can think of, I might just fixate on how good it felt to be fucked again and again by this man.

I need a distraction.

Memnon must feel the grip of my magic, because I see his throat work almost immediately.

*All right,* est amage. *All right.*

He pushes himself up in my bed, leaning against the headboard. *I have been trying to establish myself in this city since I arrived.*

With that admission comes something else down own bond, something that feels like maybe desire, only this isn't a lust for flesh *but for power.* It unnerves me, especially because I've felt this sensation from him before, when I was Roxilana.

*There are other supernaturals here—sorcerers like me,* he says.

*Okay,* I respond, not sure where this is going.

*A family of them—the Fortunas—hold most of the power in this area. On paper, their business, Ensanguine Enterprises, is an investment firm, but in reality, it's...a shell company?* Memnon sounds confused about this, like he's still figuring out these concepts and terms. *It's a criminal organization masked as a corporate entity. Shortly after I arrived in the Bay Area,* he continues, *I began working for Ensanguine Enterprises. I don't know if this is how they approach everyone looking for a job, but I was taken to a mage named Patrick, who works directly with the Fortunas. He tried to bind me.*

My heart begins beating fast. *He tried to* bind *you?* What is with everyone trying to bind others?

*He believes he* did *bind me,* Memnon says, rubbing his lower lip, his eyes distant. *As do the other supernaturals who were in the room. I touched their minds, altered a few memories, and now when Patrick gives a command, I do it.*

Inwardly, I cringe. It was bad enough when I was the only person who was ordering Memnon around. To know someone else is demanding things from my mate... An angry, sick feeling stirs up in me.

*Can't this Patrick tell there's no bond?* If I focus hard enough, I can feel the forged bond I made with Memnon.

*He hasn't questioned it yet.*

Lingering in the air between us is the possibility that one day he might. And despite all the resentment I still hold toward Memnon, a spark of fear blooms in my chest.

*Just...be careful.*

Memnon's eyes twinkle. *My queen, are you concerned for my well-being?*

*Yes.* I frown, disturbed by my own concern. *Finish the rest of your story,* I command.

*Patrick is the head of security for the Fortuna family,* Memnon says. *The Fortuna empire is run by the patriarch of the family, Luca, and he's who Patrick takes direct orders from. But the security staff covers Luca Fortuna as well as his wife, Annalee, a few mistresses, and his three children—Leonard, Juliana, and Sophia. There are also a few distant relations, though it seems Luca's siblings and their children are either dead or on the other side of the world.*

I barely notice Memnon's magic unfurl around him. Its presence is so common in my memories—memories of talking in bed just as we're doing now—that I barely bat an eye at the tendrils as they brush against my skin and weave through my hair.

*Because Patrick believes he exerts total control over me through the bond,* Memnon continues, *he's had me stand guard outside buildings and suites where Luca Fortuna and his son, Leonard, have illicit dealings. These aren't normal meetings. People come out of them bloody—if they come out at all.*

I feel myself pale. *Is that where you found the murdered witches?* I ask.

Memnon gives his head a shake. *Those bodies come out of the Equinox Building in San Francisco. It's one of Ensanguine Enterprises' properties, and the Fortunas tightly control who goes in and who comes out. Patrick's called in to dispose of those bodies, which he then has me and a few other men deal with. That's how I've gained access to the murdered witches.*

What were those witches doing there in the first place? *So you haven't seen who murdered the witches or how it's done?* I ask.

Memnon shakes his head again. *The bodies are usually waiting for us in a car in the parking garage.*

I try to hide my disappointment. I was hoping for more. I'd figured all-powerful Memnon would know more.

At least I now know the bodies are linked to that family. That's not nothing—especially since I *have* heard of the Fortunas. They're an old San Francisco supernatural family, and they raise a lot of money for charities and civic causes.

*Is there anything else you know about the murders?* I ask.

*Only that ultimately, the Fortuna family is behind them.*

Somehow, in the course of our conversation, either Memnon has scooted toward me, or I have moved closer to him.

But now as Memnon speaks, his hand strokes up and down my spine, and I feel myself arching into that touch just a little, and my nipples have pebbled, and I'm fantasizing about what it would be like to just give in to the monster, once and for all. And this is all so supremely fucked up because we are discussing *murders*.

*There's something big going on in the Equinox Building,* Memnon continues, *but I've been unable to figure out what it is. Patrick doesn't know, nor do the other members of his team. And I haven't been able to get close enough to the Fortunas themselves. Luca doesn't let anyone get near him, not even his own security team.*

His hand is still moving up and down my back. A residual flare of lust bubbles up at the touch. Those hands were all over me last night, drawing out my pleasure like it was magic.

I clear my throat. "Will you tell me if anything else comes up?"

With his free hand, Memnon reaches out and lightly rubs my lower lip. "Command it of me and I will."

"And if I don't?" I ask, trying my damnedest to ignore his hand.

He drops his hand. "You'll be forced to trust me then. Are you ready for that?"

The two of us stare at each other, and my pulse begins to race.

"I don't know," I admit.

The fact that he gets anything but a flat-out *no* is gracious of me.

Memnon is quiet, and I realize our little murder chat is over.

Now that there's no longer the somber topic to distract

either of us, I'm painfully aware once again of the fact that we're naked in a tiny bed, the smell of sex thick around us, and Memnon's hands are stroking me like I'm a cat.

I stiffen, not sure what to do or how to handle this.

I should get away from him. Put some distance between us. I can barely even think when he's this close.

Memnon leans forward and presses a kiss to my ear. Before I can bolt like a skittish deer, he wraps his arms around me and drags me down to the bed, rolling us a little so that I'm caged in his arms.

"I can hear some of your very loud thoughts, little witch," he murmurs against my ear. "Let's not make this awkward. If you want to keep me here, imprisoned in this room, so I can suck on your tits and play with your very abused pussy some more, I will *gladly* do so. We can even pretend you're still under the thrall of that potion you drank."

He nips my ear, and I make an outraged noise, both by his words and his bite.

"Or you're going to send me away so you can get on with your day. But we're not going to make this weird, okay?" he says, catching my eyes. "We did not fuck like animals last night to act like strangers today."

I close my eyes. "*Memnon*," I say, embarrassed all over again.

"And the gods know we didn't survive the ages to be uncomfortable in each other's presence."

"Your point has been made," I say, opening my eyes.

"Good." He gives the tip of my nose a quick kiss, then releases me.

I sit up, eyeing him like he's some great predator. "I want you to leave," I admit.

If he stays, I will probably cash in on those tit kisses, or worse, keep him in my bed and have my way with him until he's fucked the forgiveness out of me.

Memnon rises out of my bed, gloriously naked. The dappled morning light lovingly showcases his powerful physique.

*He's mine.* For the first time, that thought takes my breath away.

His hair is tousled from sleep and sex, which gives him an unguarded look. My fingers itch to thread themselves back in his hair so I might tug his head to me and kiss his neck.

No, no, no, Selene. Lock those thoughts up. Last night was a one-time thing. That's all.

I get out of bed and drag on a pair of stretchy shorts and a T-shirt. Across from me, Memnon pulls on his own shirt, and I wince a little when I see the massive stain at the bottom of it.

*A one-time thing*, I repeat like a mantra. Maybe if I say it enough, all the erotic highs and embarrassing lows that came with it will smooth away and I really will feel indifferent about the whole thing.

Once Memnon finishes dressing, he steps up to me and tilts my chin up. All thoughts of indifference vanish at that touch and the look in his eyes.

It's impossible to be indifferent about Memnon.

"One last thing, Empress."

"What?" I say, my gaze drifting down to his lips before I jerk my attention back to his eyes.

"Don't share what we've been talking about with anyone else," he says solemnly.

I think he's not just referring to the murders but the spell circles too.

I stiffen. "I'm going to have to. I'm meeting with the lycanthropes tonight to discuss what I know."

His eyebrows rise, the action tugging at his scar. "You have a meeting with them?"

*The local pack offered me their friendship and protection after you framed me for murder.*

*Ah.* Memnon has the grace to look a little uncomfortable.

*Just be careful,* he cautions, his eyes hard. *The Fortunas have eyes in a lot of places. If any of them discover that you are trying to pry their secrets free, I will have to butcher a lot more people to keep them from coming after you. I trust you don't want all those... needless deaths.*

I barely breathe. The sorcerer would do it too—he's already killed entire armies. A few spies and criminals would be nothing to him, though they'd mean something to me. Those deaths would be on my head.

*I could order you to not kill anyone,* I say.

Memnon's eyes begin to glow, a sure sign that I've touched a nerve. *Do that and you'll make me desperate to keep you safe. And,* est amage, *you don't want me desperate,* he warns.

I suppress a shiver. Beneath the surface of my soul mate lives a monster, one who loves me and little else. If Memnon believes he can't kill those who are a threat to me, he might simply torture them endlessly or break their minds or bodies so completely death won't matter. Or he might pick another tactic, one that forces my hand in some way.

*I won't leave you vulnerable,* Memnon says, only driving his point home further. *I cannot bear another Bosporus.*

That final battle, he means. The one that began with a betrayal by his oldest friend and his closest aide.

He leans in, then hesitates, waiting for me to command

him to stop. When I don't, I see a shadow of a smile a split second before his lips brush mine.

*Last night will happen again,* he vows. The words are spoken in Sarmatian, and I don't think they were meant for me. They sound far too distant and quiet to be deliberate. *Only next time, you'll be mine in earnest.*

His kiss deepens then, the action echoing his silent sentiment.

When Memnon pulls away, his eyes search my face. "Call to me whenever you need me next, Empress," he says. "I'll be around."

He presses a final, chaste kiss to my lips, then leaves the room.

I sit down hard on my bed, just as the tree outside rustles. The next moment, Nero hops through the window, looking thoroughly disgruntled.

"Hey, have you been out there this whole time?" Shoot, now I feel a little bad.

His tail twitches as he leaps onto my bed.

"I wouldn't lie there if I were you." Those sheets are a biohazard at this point.

My familiar takes one whiff of them and dives back off the mattress. He stalks over to his own bed and plops down, giving me a mean look.

"What?" I say defensively. "I warned you that I would have boys over."

His tail gives an agitated thump.

I open my mouth—why am I defending myself to an overgrown cat?—when my phone buzzes from where it must've fallen on the floor at some point last night.

I snatch it up, then groan when I see the caller ID.

*MOM*

I'm pretty uneager to talk to her so soon after I got railed within an inch of my life.

I answer anyway. "Hi Mo—"

"Selene Imogen Bowers," my mom says, her voice shrill, "how *dare* you not tell me what's been going on! I heard you were arrested—" Her voice breaks. In the background, I hear my father soothing her.

The two of them are still in Europe on their months' long vacation. I'd hoped the distance was enough to avoid this conversation altogether, but apparently not.

"Mom, it was a mistake," I say, trying to placate her. "I was released literally hours later. I didn't want to call and worry you."

"Worry me? Worry me!" she says, and I can't tell whether she's outraged or panicked. "I am *your mother*, I carried you inside me for nine months, then lovingly raised you for eighteen years. I have earned the right to worry about you." In a gentler, more hurt voice, she says, "I thought you knew you could tell me anything."

"Mom, I was…confused. And someone framed me for murder."

There's a sickening silence on the other side of the line. Then, "Ben, book us the next available flight home."

"Mom, I'm fine." I really do feel fine. I just don't know how to make her believe that.

"Fine?" She laughs disbelievingly. "Stop *lying* to me. First the fucking plane crash, now arrested for murder? None of that's *fine*. What the fuck is going on over there? This sounds like someone laid a big fucking curse on you."

About that…

"Mom, stop saying *fuck*," I say.

"Don't tell me what to fucking do. *I'm* the mother here."

202

She breathes heavily for several seconds, then clears her throat. "I had to hear the news of your arrest from Donna, that insufferable witch. She called to check on me and see how I was doing now that my daughter was a convict."

I make a face at the term. "Convict?" I echo. "That's being a bit dramatic."

"I get to be dramatic too! And cuss—and worry!"

In the background, "Liv, please, it's all right."

"Don't fucking try to calm me down, Ben!"

It's quiet for several seconds as my mom catches her breath. I can imagine her magenta-colored magic filling the space around her as it sometimes does when she's upset.

"Mom…" Suddenly, my throat thickens, and I want to tell her everything that's happened to me just as I used to do in the past. There's so much I don't feel I can tell her over the phone—my strange relationship with Memnon, my recovered memories, my ancient past, and the fact that I'm trying to sleuth out what's happening with the witches on campus.

But I can talk about the ongoing murders and my mistaken involvement, so a little reluctantly, I do. I let what I can of the truth pour out of me.

By the time I'm done, my mom is no longer panicked. Instead, a troubled silence stretches on.

"Selene," she finally says, "it's not safe there on campus. Come home. Your dad and I will book the next available flight and arrive there as soon as we can."

Moving back in with my parents is honestly an even worse option than living with Memnon. I love them, I do, but to go from the coven I worked so hard to join to being back in my parents' house without any sort of future plans sounds hellish.

"Mom, I'm not going home. You can cut your trip short and see that I'm fine, or you can stay and enjoy the rest of the trip that you and Dad planned for literal years and trust that I'll be okay. But no matter what, I'm not leaving. I worked too hard to be here."

The silence is long and drawn out. I think my mom is realizing she cannot actually strong-arm me into leaving Henbane.

"Text me—daily," she says finally, her words hard. "Even if it's just 'I'm alive.' If you can do that...I will trust your word."

"I can do that," I say solemnly.

I hear her swallow. "Okay. Okay." I can picture her nodding to herself, her hand pressed to her forehead. "Then I will trust—" Her voice breaks. "I will trust you to be safe, but you must be safe, if not for yourself then for me. Please."

"I'll be safe," I promise, my throat raspy as it wells with emotion.

"And if anything happens, anything at all, you let me know, and I'll be there in an instant."

I nod, even though she can't see me.

"Trust your instincts," she continues. "If something doesn't feel right, it likely *isn't* right. I love you, sweet girl."

"I love you too, Mom," I say.

"Love you, Booger!" my dad shouts from the background.

"Ugh, *Dad*." I hear him laugh in the distance. "I love you too. Now both of you go do something fun, like stare at piles of rocks someone stacked together centuries ago."

"All right, but be careful," my mom warns again.

"I will," I promise.

"Okay," she says, only sounding half convinced. "Love you, bye!"

"Bye." I sigh and toss my phone aside, lying on my back.

What a fucking day the last twenty-four hours have been.

I continue to lie there, my body and mind exhausted. Need a shower. And food and…

My stomach drops when I realize all last night and this morning, Memnon came in me. Even now, I can feel the evidence of it.

For a moment, my head is screaming.

*Selene? Memnon says down our bond, noticing my panic.*

I slow my breathing.

*What is it? he presses.*

*Everything's fine, Memnon.*

*You seem to only say that when things are not fine.*

I peel myself off the floor. *They will be,* I say, and then I close off communication with him.

I drag my creaky body downstairs, determined to cook up some birth control spell in the kitchen. I'm pretty sure someone's pinned that potion on one of the walls in there.

The witches I pass look equally haggard, some of them still wearing last night's costumes—what remains of them at least. Others lie passed out in the common rooms—there's a knot of naked witches lying together in the library, the remnants of last night's orgy.

As soon as I duck into the spell kitchen, I nearly cry in relief. Someone has set out a tray of deep blue potions in tiny corked bottles, each of them neatly labeled.

*Contraceptive Potion.*

A tag attached to each vial says *To be taken after intercourse.*

I unstopper one and drink it then and there. *Taking no chances.* I have no problem with children—I nearly had one when I was Roxilana. But as *Selene,* I simply do not want any for the foreseeable future.

I grab another potion vial for Sybil, then leave the spell kitchen and head to her room. It's only once I step inside and see her made bed and the costume options she laid out for me on top of it that I realize she hasn't been back.

*She's still with Sawyer.*

My heart drops when I remember her and Mai and Olga. All of them left with shifters. And if their nights were anything like mine...

Setting the contraceptive potion on Sybil's desk, I rush back to my room and snatch up my phone. I scroll to Sybil's number, my heart beating a mile a minute, and call my best friend.

It rings once...twice...

Please be okay. Please be ok—

"Ugh, you heathen," Sybil groggily croaks on the other end of the line. "Why are you calling me? And what time is it?"

I exhale, my entire body relaxing at her voice. She sounds grumpy but otherwise fine.

"It's noon-ish, I think," I say, "Where are you?"

"Um—"

I hear the low tones of a man's voice in the background.

"Is that Sawyer?" I ask.

"What's up, Selene?" I hear him call out.

"I didn't know he knew my name."

"You're my best friend," Sybil says. "Of course he knows your name." She yawns. "And I'm at his place. Goddess, what was in that witch's brew? It hit me like a freight train." More to herself than to me, she adds, "I think I need to ice my vagina."

I let out a small, semihysterical laugh at the reminder

that I did a lot of bad things with a bad man and I am regret incarnate.

It was a one-time thing, I remind myself all over again.

"Did you know that was going to happen with the witch's brew?" I ask, not quite accusing. Sybil had insinuated the celebrations were wild when she mentioned ripping through her last costume.

She gives an awful laugh. "Not to that extent I didn't." After a moment, Sybil adds, "I'm sorry about last night. You were trying to tell me you didn't want to be on shifter territory, and I didn't listen and then…"

And then it was too late.

"We were all really drunk," I say. It's the closest I can come to accepting the apology.

After a moment, she says, "Did you and Kane…"

Goddess, she missed that part of the evening.

"No. No, I…uh…got together with someone else."

*Legs over my shoulders.*

"Who?" she demands.

I stare at my feet, biting the inside of my cheek.

*On your hands and knees.*

"Who?" she presses.

*You're going to call me* husband *or* soul mate. *Anything else gets punished.*

"Who do you think?" I say hoarsely.

Now it's Sybil's turn to be quiet.

She doesn't know about the binding spell forged between me and Memnon, I realize. Or how the sorcerer is helping me solve the open mysteries on campus. All she knows is that he screwed me over and I hate his guts.

"Are you judging me?" I ask.

Another pause. "No."

"You *are* judging me," I say. I don't know why that makes me feel a little hurt. I've given Sybil every reason to hate Memnon's guts on my behalf. She's just being a loyal friend.

"No. Okay, well, maybe a little. But, Selene, Kane was literally right there. How did you fumble it for that asshole?"

My throat works. "It was the Sacred Seven, and I was afraid of getting bitten."

"So instead you got together with the dude whose house you burned down." She doesn't even try to hide her judgment now.

I wince.

"Just tell me the sex was worth it."

I let out a laugh that might be a sob. "It was worth it."

Sybil whistles. "Damn, that good? I need to look into boning my enemy..."

In the background, I hear "No, you don't," followed by the sounds of kissing and Sybil's laughter.

"How are you?" I ask as delicately as I can.

"You mean, am I a wolf witch?" she asks.

In the distance, I hear Sawyer mutter something.

"You can breathe, Selene. I haven't been bitten." She turns her mouth away from the phone as though addressing Sawyer. "*Yet.*"

I frown. Does my friend *want* to be turned? We've never actually had a serious conversation on this subject, and I just assumed she was having fun and not taking anything too seriously. But maybe I misjudged the whole thing.

Sybil's voice returns to the phone. "I'll have to get back before curfew."

Oh, crap, that's right.

"By the way," Sybil continues, "Olga definitely got down with at least two shifters..."

She keeps talking, but I'm still lingering on the mention of curfew, because tonight I might have to break it. I have a meeting with the lycanthropes I have to make.

# CHAPTER 20

**I don't want to do this,** *I think as I step out onto the back* patio of the residence hall, Nero at my side. *I really, really don't want to do this.*

After the way I left things with Kane, I'm dreading our reunion. However, the lycanthropes showed me loyalty when no one else did. I owe it to them to show up, despite the messy situation with my former crush.

Still, I'm bringing my emotional support panther to bolster my courage.

I force myself to head toward the Everwoods. Even though there's still over an hour left until curfew, I see several older witches casting wards at the tree line.

When I reach the edge of the forest, one of these witches, whose iron-gray hair is twisted into a bun at the nape of her neck, calls out. "These wards go into effect at six o'clock sharp. Make sure you're back by then."

I pause. "What will happen if I cross after six?" I don't know how long this meeting will take.

The witch gives me an arch look. "Is the threat of a violent death not convincing enough for you?" she asks tartly.

"Um..."

"It's spelled to note each trespasser's identity," she adds.

Oh. That doesn't sound too awful. Then again, that's probably how I get my name placed right back on the Politia's suspect list.

*Going to have to ask a shifter for a ride back to my house.* At least then if I'm dropped off and it pings some other erected ward at, say, Henbane's main entrance, it will cause less scrutiny than one on the edge of the Everwoods.

Once Nero and I enter the forest, our surroundings grow unnervingly quiet.

I weave between trees, stepping over bits of discarded costumes. In the light of day, it looks particularly bleak.

I cut across the pumpkin-lined path. Today the lanterns hover a little lower in the air; a few of them have fallen to the ground altogether, their spells worn off. All of it has that post-holiday melancholy. The fun's been had, and now life is expected to go back to normal. The campus-wide curfew isn't helping, and I wonder how it's affecting the Day of the Dead celebrations happening today.

I've nearly gotten my nerves under control when I finally make it to the thin, luminous blue line that marks the boundary between witch and shifter territory. At the sight of it, my dread instantly reforms.

I place a hand on Nero's head. "Do you want to come the rest of the way with me, or do you want to go hunt?" I ask.

Nero gives me a look that I think says *I know you're a fucking chicken, lady.* But maybe I'm just reading into things.

Nero presses himself more firmly against my side, making his decision clear.

I take a deep breath and nod. "That's—that's really sweet of you."

I force myself to make my way to the line. Once I'm there, I wait. The forest feels entirely abandoned. One minute goes by. Then two. Three, four...

I shift my weight.

Kane told me to meet him at the boundary marker, but maybe I was supposed to go to a different section of it. Or maybe after last night, Kane decided to stand me up.

I get a cowardly thrill at the idea of retreating back to my room and burying myself under my newly washed blankets.

The thought has no sooner crossed my mind than I hear the crunch of pine needles. From the shadowy depths of the woods ahead, I make out a large form.

I see the sandy-blond hair and the angular cut of the man's face.

It's Kane.

My stomach knots itself up.

Judging from the stern set of his features, he appears even less thrilled to be here than I am.

And now I'm vividly recalling all the cringiest parts of last night and wishing I still had the ability to forget such memories.

"Hi, Kane." I give him a dopey little wave.

He doesn't wave back.

Nero leans into me again, and I return my hand to his head, my heart hammering away.

Kane is almost to me, his eyes briefly dropping to my familiar before coming back to mine.

Should I apologize about last night? Should I mention it at all? Or should I—

Kane's nostrils flare. "You smell like him," he says in greeting. He looks openly disgusted.

All right, I guess we're fucking talking about it.

"Is that a problem?" I ask, ignoring the way my cheeks heat.

"He's the man who *stalked you*. Not to mention he threw me out of the third story of your house. Why would you choose that monster over me?"

Because...

*I stroke his hair back, drops of my blood and tears hitting his armor.*

*"This is not how we end," I whisper. "We are eternal."*

*Something dark and resolute moves through me.*

*We are eternal.*

*If we cannot have this life, then we shall have another.*

"Listen, Kane, I told you last night I was meeting with somebody else. You and your pack were still observing the Sacred Seven, and I didn't want to be there."

"Then why were you there?"

"I was drunkenly wandering with my friends. I didn't realize until it was too late we'd made it onto your pack's territory."

Kane still looks angry, and his eyes are a bit heartbroken.

I search his features. "Why are you acting like I owe you something?"

"Because I fucking *like* you, Selene. A lot. And I thought you liked me too."

I hear the edge of a growl in his voice.

At the sound, Nero begins to growl himself, and when I run my hand down his back, his hackles are raised.

"It's all right," I murmur to Nero, even as I give Kane a hard look. "Kane, we're not dating, and for better or for worse, that monster I was with happens to be my soul mate."

"About that—when were you going to tell me you had a mate?" Kane demands. "Or did your magic conveniently erase that memory too?"

I flinch from the accusation.

Anger rises up in me. "Actually, Kane, I *did* fucking forget I had a soul mate, and the only reason I do remember is because right before I was arrested the night of the full moon, Memnon ripped away the spell blocking my memories." I wasn't planning on admitting this, but screw it. "He did so against my will, and yes, our engagement was also forced." I glare at the shifter. "I was never deliberately deceitful to you."

Kane's own anger has died down a bit, and I can see the frayed edges of his hurt in his eyes. "Then why are you with him?" he asks softly.

"Who says I'm with him?" I demand. "Sex doesn't equal love or a relationship. I assumed you were aware of that, considering how our own friendship began."

Kane's jaw clenches, but he doesn't say anything. Instead, he wordlessly turns and starts heading back into the woods. Aggression is still pouring off him, and I swear his arms look a little furrier than they did a minute ago.

"C'mon," he says over his shoulder. "We're going to be late."

I share an annoyed look with my familiar—at least I'd like to think we share a moment of mutual annoyance. Nero might've been looking at me just because he was bored, but I'm going to assume it's because Kane is huffy.

The three of us walk for several minutes in silence before Kane says, "You can remember your past now?"

I scowl at him. "Yes."

"What's that like?"

"Painfully normal," I say, "except for the past-life memories." Those are anything but.

Now Kane turns fully around, scrutinizing me. "Memnon was telling the truth last night? You two are some ancient couple?" The shifter doesn't appear as skeptical as most would, but then the supernatural world is full of all sorts of impossible things. The idea of some past-life romance isn't inconceivable.

"Yeah," I say softly. "He was."

"Hmm" is all Kane replies before turning around once more.

The lycan continues to walk ahead of me, and I sense his emotions are somewhat turbulent, so it's a relief when the trees part and I catch sight of the massive cabin I partied in not too long ago. The very one where I first got together with Kane.

Only now, there are cars parked on the gravel drive in front of it and a few people milling on the porch.

Kane finally stops and waits for me and Nero to catch up.

When we get to him, the shifter clears his throat. "This is how the evening is going to go," he says softly, "You'll meet the pack, they'll ask a few questions of you, and at the end of it all, you'll be formally recognized as a friend of the pack." Whatever bitterness Kane might personally harbor toward me, it's wiped free from his voice as he speaks.

"How many people are inside?" I ask, glancing again at

the cabin. The shifters out front have now noticed us, and they're avidly watching my exchange with Kane.

"Almost everyone who is able to make the meeting will be inside," he says. "This is a big deal," he adds.

I dip my head, even as my nerves spike. I don't know what I'm doing here. This is terrifying, and I've already pissed off the one shifter I'm closest to. I don't want to be the center of anything that the pack considers a *big deal*.

I sense Kane's gaze on me.

"I can hear your heartbeat," he says quietly. "You don't need to be nervous. Forget the shit between us. You saved one of my pack mates. You have the gratitude of me and everyone else in that building."

I swallow and nod, and then, almost shyly, I look at him and force a smile. "Thanks," I say softly. I pet my familiar's dark fur, drawing in a few stabilizing breaths. "Is Nero going to be a problem?" I ask offhandedly.

Kane gives the creature a speculative look. "I guess we'll find out."

And with that extremely unreassuring answer, we head for the cabin.

———————

Nero is, in fact, a problem.

That becomes massively clear seconds after the three of us step into the house.

The vast living room is filled with dozens—if not hundreds—of shifters. Most sit in foldable seats that have been brought in, though others stand along the edges of the room, packed in as close as they can get. At the sound of our entrance, they look over at me, Kane, and Nero.

For a second or two, all is well. But then, from around me, low vocalizations rumble from the shifters nearest us.

"It's all right," Kane reassures the crowd. "The panther is her familiar. His name is Nero."

Kane glances at me, like he expects me to speak.

Okay, right. Public speaking. I'm a badass witch who has defied death to be here. Talking to a crowd doesn't scare me one bit.

"Yeah, Nero. His name is Nero," I echo woodenly. My hands are beginning to shake. "He's really the sweetest cat."

Nero takes the room in with steady, unblinking eyes. He doesn't look like the sweetest cat. His body is tense and rigid, and that stillness that I associate with hunting has fallen around him.

The shifters must sense it as well because, if anything, the growls in the room only grow louder.

I really, really want my panther by my side right now. He makes me feel safe and steady. But he seems to be drawing out these shifter's instincts, so—

I crouch down in front of Nero and try my hardest to ignore the people around us.

"I know you wanted to be here for me," I say softly, "but your safety is more important to me. Everyone in this house is my friend," I reassure him. "I will be okay," I promise.

I can't read his expression, but his tail flicks like he's considering my words.

"You can head back to our room or remain out in the woods near Henbane. I'll be fine, and I'll call to you if anything changes."

Nero butts his head against my shoulder then, rubbing himself against my side. I don't know if he's being affectionate or marking me just to make it clear where we all stand, but I smooth my hands down his sides and give his forehead a kiss.

Rising to my feet, I open the door and let my familiar out. "Stay safe," I call after him.

His only response is to twitch his tail, like my concern is annoying. I guess if I were an apex predator, I might be annoyed too if a puny human fussed over me.

I close the door behind him and turn back to the room.

And…everyone is looking at me. Crap, they probably heard every last word I spoke too.

Before I can panic about it, Kane puts his hand on my lower back and steers me down the makeshift aisle in the middle of the room toward a chair set at the far end of it. Unlike the other foldable chairs, this one faces the audience.

My breath hitches.

"It's okay," Kane whispers to me. "Like you said to Nero, we're friends here."

I draw in a deep breath, ignoring my growing queasiness. When we're nearly to my seat, an adolescent girl steps away from the nearby wall and approaches me.

My brows come together as I take in her familiar features before recognition sets in.

"Cara?" I say tentatively.

She nods, and suddenly we're hugging, and I can feel her shaking in my arms as she sobs a little against me.

"Thank you," she whispers. "Thank you."

I hug her tighter and nod. I don't really know what to say except "I couldn't leave you." Not to those supernaturals.

Eventually, she pulls away to take me in.

"I wasn't sure I'd ever see you again," I admit, my eyes roving over her face.

The last time I laid eyes on her, she'd been mostly

unconscious. To see her now, healthy and whole, is… indescribable.

She reaches out and wipes away wetness from my cheek. That's when I realize I'm crying. Her touch is a familiar sort of gesture, one you'd do with someone you're close to. I feel the barest hint then of what it means to be pack. The affection, the care, the bonds between members, bonds that have nothing to do with spells but instead with love and loyalty.

"I had to meet you," she says. "I didn't…" Her throat works. "I didn't remember much from that night. I thought I dreamed you up." She gives my forearms a squeeze, then backs away. With a final smile, Cara retreats to the nearby wall.

Kane is still there, waiting a short distance away. When I catch his eye, he nods to the seat set out for me. I glance at it, then blow out a breath, my heart beginning to pick up again. It doesn't help my nerves that everyone can hear it.

Reluctantly, I sit down and let my eyes wander across the full room. The air around the lycans shimmers a little like a heat wave, and I feel my own instincts screaming at me that I'm in a den of predators.

Kane sits down in an empty chair in the first row across from me, next to several older men and women.

One of those older individuals—a ruggedly handsome man with caramel-colored skin who looks to be somewhere in his late forties—now speaks.

"Selene Bowers, welcome to the Marin Pack."

I nod, smiling tightly.

"I'm Vincent Vilanova, alpha and leader of the Marin Pack, and I have heard quite a lot about you since you rescued Cara a couple of weeks ago."

I give another tight smile, trying to smother my instincts,

which still fully believe I'm surrounded by wolves, not people.

"I assume Kane filled you in on why you're here."

My gaze darts to my former crush, and I nod again.

"Good, good," Vincent says, glancing at the crowd. "I've spoken at length with my pack, but I will fill everyone in again so that we're all on the same page," he says, turning more fully to face the room. "Selene Bowers is a witch attending Henbane Coven. Kane Halloway attended Peel Academy with her a couple of years ago, and the two were friends."

Um, more like he starred in all my teenage fantasies while (I assumed) he had no idea I existed.

But whatever. We were *friends*.

"A couple of weeks ago, Selene saved Cara Gutierrez from a binding ceremony that would've given another supernatural complete power over Cara's free will. Such things are called forced bonds."

My gaze slides to Cara just as the girl dips her head and stares at her feet.

"Kamal, who found Selene and Cara just inside our boundary line, said that Cara was unconscious and smelled of toxins, and Selene was bloody and badly injured."

I chew the inside of my lip and try not to fidget as I feel the room collectively scrutinize me. It's one thing to have lived through that night, another to hear it laid bare before an audience.

"We've all seen other indications that something sinister is happening on coven land. Lots of late-night movement, sightings of a seemingly living creature that doesn't have a pulse or carry a scent."

I start at that description. Could he be talking about that clay creature I destroyed that night?

"And of course the murders—murders that Selene here was considered a prime suspect in up until a few days ago."

I feel my cheeks heat. I thought being praised in front of a crowd was uncomfortable; turns out that's nothing compared to having to sit here while my dirty laundry is aired out to an avid audience.

Vincent continues. "Evidence indicates Selene was framed, which means the true killer is still out there, likely still hunting witches. This is all happening in our backyard. It's important to me—to many of us—that those supernaturals who put their lives at risk to protect our pack mates are extended our protection, especially at a time like this, when their own kind are under threat."

The Marin Pack alpha turns to me, and I think this might be it—Vincent will announce the pack's friendship and the meeting will be over. I might even be able to scurry back to Henbane before curfew.

Instead, he says, "Selene, we would love to hear what you have to share about the night you saved Cara. Would you be willing to tell us about what happened?"

Right. Shit. Sitting up here and staring out at the crowd, I nearly forgot that this was the main thing they wanted to hear about from me.

"Of course." I take a deep breath, collecting my thoughts, but Vincent holds up a finger.

"One moment, Selene." He steps over to the massive, unlit fireplace behind me and grabs a vial resting on the mantel. A moment later, he shows it to me.

My stomach drops the moment I see the shimmery green liquid.

"This is a truth potion," Vincent says, telling me what I already know. "Would you be willing to drink this before answering our questions?"

I hesitate.

*They don't trust witches,* I tell myself, *but they want to pledge their loyalty to me. I simply have to prove I'm worthy of it.* But if I drink the potion, I will be compelled to tell the truth. I don't have too many secrets, but Memnon's warning still echoes in my head.

*Don't share what we've been talking about with anyone else.*

I bite my inner cheek and nod. "I'll drink it," I say, taking the potion from the pack alpha.

I'll just have to watch what I say.

Removing the cork, I bring the vial to my lips and tip it back.

It tastes like shit. Well, shit and rotten apples. I think someone attempted to flavor it as an afterthought, but they clearly sucked at it.

Almost immediately, I feel the press of magic; it coats my tongue like syrup, and as it makes its way down my throat, I feel it tug on my vocal cords. I grimace as the aftertaste lingers on my tongue.

Vincent steps forward and takes the empty container from me. I see him flinch a little as he catches a whiff of the stuff.

"Thank you," he says quietly. Louder, he says, "Can you tell us everything you remember about the night you saved Cara?"

I squeeze my hands together and take a deep breath. "It began because I needed a job…"

———

I tell the lycanthropes the entire story as best I can. And the truth serum must be strong, because even though they only asked about the night itself, I fill them in on everything—my memory loss, how I was approached by Kasey, and why I needed the money so bad.

I mention the clay creature that brought Cara in and the dark rites that I interrupted when I broke the circle and snatched the shifter away. I go into the minutiae of our escape through the persecution tunnels and out across the forest. I even admit my worry that I killed someone in the crossfire.

It's a shameful confession, but no one in the room looks horrified. If anything, I see a level of respect from the faces I look at. I guess to lycans, who value pack loyalty and whose wolves drive them to kill creatures all the time, taking a life to protect another is the ultimate show of devotion.

I end with the dim recollection of the lycanthrope who collected Cara from me as I wove in and out of consciousness.

When I finish speaking, the room is quiet. My own magic sifts out through my palms, curling protectively around my midsection and over my shoulders. I feel split open in the worst way.

Finally, a soft, feminine voice says, "We thank you."

Another, gruffer voice adds, "We thank you."

Then another voice and another and another, until the whole room seems to be thanking me.

I glance at Cara, whose cheeks are wet. She gives me a soft smile, and I see her lips move. *We thank you.*

I bow my head as my own eyes prick. I've done so many things wrong and earned so much ire along the way that the compliments are unexpected and deeply moving.

Once it grows quiet again, someone else speaks up.

"You carried Cara the entire way," a female shifter says, sounding impressed. Her eyes slide over me. "And you did this without the strength of a shifter."

"I did use magic," I say.

"You must be very powerful."

I cringe at the word. "I had help," I deflect.

"Help?" someone else from the crowd says. There's a note of skepticism there.

Shit.

There was one single thing I hadn't mentioned during my conversation. *Memnon*. Trying to explain the ancient warlord would only complicate things, so I omitted him.

Or I tried to at least.

"I...have a soul mate," I confess. "We can share power through a bond we were born with. The night I fled with Cara he sensed I was in danger, and he gave me some of his magic."

The room is deathly quiet.

"Who is this man?" a deep, rumbling voice questions, and they sound distrustful.

I guess I get it. The Marin Pack extended friendship to me, but if I have a soul mate, that relationship could affect this friendship pact.

"He's..." Ah. How to put this without freaking everyone out? "A sorcerer."

All at once, murmuring breaks out. Sorcerers aren't exactly known for their shiny reputations. There are whole dynasties of them scattered throughout the world, and the more powerful they are, the more dangerous they tend to be.

"He's the one who came and took care of me after I delivered Cara to your pack." I don't know why I'm trying to defend the man. He's smeared his own good name. But

I also don't think of him the same way I do most other sorcerers.

Maybe because villain or not, he's mine. And maybe because once upon a time, he gave me the whole world.

"Do you trust him?" someone else asks.

He had my absolute loyalty when I was Roxilana, but as Selene, he's fucked me over a few times.

I don't know what the truth potion is going to pull from my lips until I speak. "He's loyal to no one but me."

Kane's voice cuts through the room. "Tell them how."

I glance sharply at the shifter. At my *friend*.

His expression is stern and unbending. "Tell them how you've made him loyal to you. They deserve to know what you confessed to me last night."

Again, there are a few scattered murmurs from around the room.

Kane set me up for this.

My heart pounds harder as the truth serum is pulling at my windpipe, readying its own sort of answer.

The forged bond between Memnon and me is the one thing I really, really don't want to share. The more people who know about it, the more people might exploit it.

*I will have to butcher a lot more people to keep them from coming after you.*

My hands begin to tremble. "He is bound by magic to serve me."

There are a few scattered gasps, and I hear a low growl start up, one that seems to catch and spread across the room.

"The same way Cara was nearly bound to another?" someone asks.

"*No*." The serum permits the answer because the context matters. "Memnon offered to bind himself to me

225

to earn back my trust. It is not a forced bond between us but a *forged* one."

"Why would a man who is already your mate do such a thing?"

At the word *mate*, I see Kane glance down.

I assess the rest of the room, wondering if the truth serum will be enough for them to believe my next words.

"Memnon isn't just any sorcerer." The words come out tentatively. "He's an ancient one who happens to be my long-lost soul mate. There's lots of complicated details that I could overshare about that situation, but basically for the last couple of months, he believed I betrayed him, so as revenge, he framed me for the murders of the witches found on Henbane's campus. When he discovered I didn't betray him, he offered the bond as a type of"—I search for the right word—"restitution."

Silence. Absolute fucking silence.

"If your mate really did what you said he did," a shifter finally asks, "how do we know *he* didn't kill those women?"

I squeeze my hands together. "He confessed his innocence to me while under a truth spell of his own."

More murmuring.

"Why isn't he here?" a woman calls out. "We should hear this from him as well."

This evening feels like it's spun wildly off course. I knew I'd be retelling the events that unfolded with Cara, but I didn't expect the truth potion or the informal inquisition I'm now getting. And I definitely didn't expect to get Memnon involved. The thought of him in this room, politely answering questions for the lycans, is laughable. He'd sooner gut them all.

"Even if you wanted him here," I say, "he answers to no one."

Vincent gives me an intense look. "No one—except you."

# CHAPTER 21

*I spend another thirty minutes answering more follow-up* questions, and my tongue trips over itself as I try to explain various aspects of the same few topics—the night of the spell circle, the witch murders, and Memnon.

Eventually the questions peter out until there are none left. I stare at the room as several long seconds tick by.

Vincent stands. "Thank you for coming here and speaking to us about all this, Selene." He turns to face his pack. "Now we vote."

Wait, there's a *vote* for this? One I have to sit in on?

I slide a panicked look to Kane, but his eyes are on his alpha.

"A simple majority will determine whether Selene becomes a friend of the pack. By a show of hands, who is in favor of her?"

My heart races as most of the room raises their hands. I exhale.

"And those against?"

Only a few hands rise into the air.

Vincent turns to me. "By the laws of lycans and men, I formally welcome you, Selene Bowers, as a friend of the Marin Pack."

Howls go up across the space, the sound raising my gooseflesh. Instinct is screaming at me to flee, but my magic comes alive at the noise. It spills out of me, moving about the room and weaving in between shifters.

I meet Kane's lupine gaze. Though there's a hard set to his jaw, he smiles at me, then howls along with the rest of them.

Only once the noise dies down do the lycans rise. One by one, they come up and greet me, giving me a hug and rubbing their cheeks against mine. It happens over and over, the entire pack marking me with their scents as they recognize me as their own.

It's not the weirdest thing I've ever experienced, but it's definitely not your normal fucking Wednesday either.

After the last shifter has embraced and marked me, drinks and food are brought out, and the wolves begin to mingle. Before I can so much as attempt to slip away, I'm whisked into a conversation with an older lycanthrope woman who likes to crochet scarves and doilies, then I'm speaking to a bear of a man with a bushy, strawberry-blond beard and kind eyes who insists that Nero is welcome to hunt on their land.

Then I'm chatting with younger female shifters who are looking at me with round, admiring eyes, and I feel entirely like an imposter.

On and on the conversations go until Kane grabs my free hand and physically hauls me away from his pack mates. He doesn't release his hold until he's led me out the rear of the house and onto a secluded back porch.

Night has already fallen out here. Frogs and insects call out from the darkness, and it's such a shift from the high-energy conversations inside that my body relaxes.

Kane closes the door behind us, and the noise inside quiets to a dull background murmur.

"I thought you might need a break," he says by way of explanation.

I give a shaky laugh, my breath misting. "I did. Thank you."

Kane smiles tightly. "I love my pack mates—would give my life for them—but they can be a lot." He moves over to the pine railing, leaning on it.

For a moment, I stare after him, my breath hitching. I'm unsure where the two of us are at or where the relationship goes from here.

"Relax, Selene," he says, not bothering to turn around. "I'm not going to bite you. That's what you've been worried about, right?"

Maybe I thanked Kane too soon. This conversation is already harder than any of the ones I had inside.

"Do you love him?" he asks.

Memnon, he means.

I step up to the railing next to him and lean against it. "I did once."

"Once," he echoes. His gaze returns to me. "But not anymore."

I lift a shoulder. "He's my soul mate—but no, I don't." If I did, the binding spell Memnon invoked would break.

"You don't have to be with an asshole just because your magic is joined," Kane says.

"I'm not with him," I remind Kane. "Last night was …

just sex." I try to ignore the fact that it was the most searing, erotic sex I've had in this life.

"Just sex," Kane echoes, his voice bitter. "Tell me, if he hadn't shown up, would you have spent the night with me? Would you have had *just sex* with me?"

I open my mouth, but I genuinely have no idea what in the seven hells I'm supposed to say.

"You were worried about me biting you," he continues. His eyes drop to my neck before returning to mine. "Was that it?"

I remember how it felt kissing him last night. *Wrong, wrong, wrong.*

"That was partly it," I say, hoping to avoid discussing all the ways my bond betrays me when I'm with people other than Memnon.

"Would that really have been so bad? Would *I* have been so bad?"

I frown, flustered by this entire conversation. "Kane, I'm sorry if I unlocked some secret insecurity—"

He laughs hollowly at that. "An insecurity? Selene, I'm all but *begging* you to actually consider me instead of the menace who thinks you belong to him. This isn't me being insecure. This is me wanting you and wanting you to want me back the way you did a few weeks ago."

I want that version of me back too. I stare at the dark sky. "Kane, my life is a mess. *I'm* a mess. I don't know what you see in me, but you've picked the wrong girl."

"What I see in you?" Again, he laughs, but this time, the sound has a pained edge to it. "You saved my pack mate— you nearly died doing so. You are hilarious and a fucking good time when you cut loose. You're honorable, beautiful, and powerful." His eyes drop to my neck again.

I'm barely breathing. Intuition is telling me to back away from the shifter, but I'm also caught up in his words.

He reaches out and touches the pulse at my throat. "Would it really be so bad?" he says again. His gaze flicks to me, and his wolf is in his eyes. It looks...hungry.

I go still the way I imagine hares do when they face down a predator.

"You're not serious, are you?" I breathe. I can't tell, but intuition is still insisting I back away.

"I could claim you. Right here, right now," he says, his eyes fixed on my throat. "I would make sure it didn't hurt."

Holy Goddess.

I force myself to turn more fully to face him, startled at the proposition. I search his features. "You hardly know me."

He draws his attention up to my eyes. "There is an understanding shifters have with their wolves that mates are a matter of instinct. My wolf likes you—he has since the moment you healed him."

"I'm already mates with someone else," I say.

"You are with a monster," Kane says. "One who was happy enough to destroy your life when it suited him."

Sort of. I mean, shit pulled an Uno reverse real quick.

"If I claimed you," he continues, "then I would have an equal right to be your mate."

I place a hand over the juncture between my neck and shoulder and shake my head. "Kane, I don't want that."

His eyes are lupine when he takes a step toward me. There was barely any distance between us before; he's fully in my space now.

"Are you sure?" he says, his voice unnaturally low. "Imagine what it would be like to be tied to someone who wants you, loves you."

I *do* know what that's like. That's never been the problem. For all Memnon's flaws, he's always loved me.

This is…a lot. And if my life was different—simpler—I might happily bare my neck for Kane and go along with this.

But things aren't simple.

"I think," I say, carefully picking my words, "if it's loyalty your pack holds in high regard, then you're going to understand that I *can't* be with you like that."

Kane flinches as if I struck him, and I feel like I'm carving my own heart out with a dull kitchen knife.

"I have a soul mate," I continue. "One who is legitimately terrible, but he's…*mine*." I laid claim to him in my mind earlier today, but the sentiment rings even truer now that I've spoken it out loud. "Long ago, I gave my life for a spell strong enough to be with him again. To be here, in this life, trying to figure it out with him, and I owe it to who I was to—"

I choke, the rest of the words falling away as sharp, burning pain blooms from my side.

"Selene?" Kane says, alarmed.

I grip my ribcage against the sizzling pain, grinding my teeth together to keep from screaming.

"What's wrong?" the shifter says, reaching for me.

"My side," I gasp out.

Kane gently pries my hands away and lifts my shirt. The skin beneath is smooth, unblemished. I neither sense nor see any malicious magic, but it hurts like someone has shoved a hot poker into it.

What in the seven hells is going on?

"There's nothing there," Kane says.

As he speaks, another wave of pain comes. My back arches, and I fall into the shifter.

"Selene!" Kane wraps his arms around me, a note of panic in his voice. "Tell me what's wrong." His voice deepens as his wolf enters it. "Is this a curse?"

*Selene!* Memnon bellows down our bond. *Where are you?*

The bond—the bond, of course. The pain isn't my own; it's coming from my bond.

Kane's still talking to me, but I'm no longer listening.

*Memnon!* I shout. *Memnon!* What's happening to him? The pain is unbearable, and I'm only feeling an echo of it.

*What's happening?* Memnon demands, echoing my thoughts. *Are you all right?*

Am *I* all right? Why would Memnon be asking that if he's the one hurt?

I suck in a sharp breath when I realize who I'm actually feeling.

"Nero."

My familiar is being attacked.

# CHAPTER 22

*I slip down my connection with my panther and into his* mind, right as he's snarling.

He pounces on someone, the action making his side scream. The metallic tang of blood coats my mouth—*his* mouth—as he sinks his teeth into their neck, then rips out their throat.

Vaguely, I'm aware that my actual knees have buckled and Kane's fully holding me up. I'm shocked by the violence, but I did recently give Nero permission to maim and kill anyone who tries to hurt him.

Even as his victim collapses beneath him, others close in. There's one, two, three, four, five—

A curse strikes my flank, interrupting my count of the assailants, and I yowl at the blistering pain.

I snap back into my own head with a sharp inhale.

*No, no, no.*

I scramble out of Kane's arms.

"Selene, what's going on?"

"My familiar is being attacked."

In one fluid movement, I hop over the wood railing, my magic seamlessly assisting me, and I dash toward the trees.

"*Selene!*" Kane calls after me. "*Fuck.*"

I hear the door to the cabin open behind me and Kane shouting to his pack mates, but it's all background static as far as I'm concerned. Even the explosive pain that's spreading across my torso isn't enough to deter me.

Terror is eclipsing everything but my need to save Nero.

*SELENE, WHAT IS WRONG?* Memnon's voice booms across our bond.

*Nero,* I sob. *Supernaturals have cornered Nero, and they're hurting him.*

On the other end of the cord that links me to the sorcerer, I sense him go very quiet and very cold.

*Where is he?*

*The Everwoods.*

*I'm coming.* It's a vow and a threat.

Even that, however, might not be enough.

By then, it might be too late. *I* might be too late.

Oh Goddess, oh Goddess.

I flood my connection to Nero with as much power as I possibly can. I don't know that it will do anything for him like it would for me, but it's the best solution my panic-laced mind can come up with.

"*Find my panther,*" I command my magic in Sarmatian.

A ribbon of it snakes out of me, weaving through the trees in the same direction my intuition has already been leading me. I run as fast as my legs can carry me, uncaring about my ragged breathing. Even my power is well-honed for once, fluidly catching me when I trip over a fallen branch and helping me right myself before I hit the earth.

Familiars are tied to their supernatural, the magical bond lengthening and strengthening their lives. But they can be killed. It's been known to happen.

At that petrifying thought, I send more magic down my bond with Nero and force my legs to go faster, even as my lungs scream and my body feels like it's incinerating itself from the inside out.

Far away, a chorus of howls fills up the night air. Unlike earlier, there's no mistaking these sounds. They're war cries.

I nearly lose my footing. The lycanthropes are coming to my aid. Despite turning Kane down, he summoned them. I sob a little as I run.

A sharp, slashing pain blooms in my stomach, this one much deeper than the others, and I nearly trip over my own feet at the onslaught of it.

I slip into Nero's head for a split second, but it's long enough to realize that he's been mortally injured.

I choke on a scream.

*No.*

Before he was Nero, he was Ferox. Same soul, different bodies. When I found him in Rome, I made a vow to cherish and protect the panther for the rest of my life.

I intended to keep that promise. I *will* keep that promise.

*Hold on, Nero,* I tell him. *I'll be there soon.*

My head is too panicked for a fancy spell. All I manage is a simple one—

*Make me swift as the wind,* I silently command my magic.

I've been sprinting, but now my pace picks up, straining my muscles and tendons to the brink of their capacity. I feel the wind at my back and on my face, and it feels as though I could melt into it, as though we are one. I blow past the boundary line marking the shifters' territory from the witches', following the ribbon of my magic.

I must be getting close.

I peer through Nero's eyes once more, trying to focus over the debilitating pain and the chill that's filling my familiar's body.

There are at least five supernaturals, witches if I had to guess. Two of them look vaguely familiar, but it's hard to tell. Cat eyes see things differently, and the night cloaks so much. But I sense there are two others who are lying on the ground. The smell of their blood tinges the air.

A couple of the supernaturals are peering beyond Nero, looking for me.

"Any sign of the witch?"

"No, but she's coming. You can see the line of her magic. She knows her familiar is hurt."

"Fuck her, *I'm* hurt."

As they squabble, I return to my own mind and funnel more power down my bond. They likely hurt my familiar to lure me out.

Wind is whipping through my hair, and tears are slipping out the corners of my eyes, but beneath my grief and fear, violence rises in me, ancient and eager. I can feel the edge of it staining my power as my magic gathers in my palms. Those witches are fucking *marked*.

Up ahead, the trail of my magic comes to an abrupt end. I can't see my familiar, but I do notice the witches around him. A few magical orbs hover in the sky above them, illuminating their forms.

"There she is."

I don't know which person announces it, but I'm already dragging my arm back, my power coalescing in my palm.

"*Explode*," I command.

And then I throw it.

*BOOM!*

Magic and fire detonate in the air, blowing back the circle of witches, revealing the slumped shape of my familiar.

The pain that lances through me at the sight of him nearly brings me to my knees.

*Make them pay.* Memnon's voice is icy, wrathful.

More magic floods down my arm and into my palm.

"*Explode*." I throw it at the witches, uncaring that it might blow limbs apart.

My power detonates just above them, throwing the witches farther from my familiar. Several of them scream, and fire has broken out on one of them. I see the woman frantically try to put it out.

The rage that surges through my blood is otherworldly. There's a hungry, sinister part of me that needs to end each one of them slowly, but the moment my eyes return to Nero, it dissolves away.

My familiar lies unmoving on the ground. In the darkness, I can just make out the sheen of blood matting his fur.

I can't breathe over the pain—both physical and emotional—choking the life out of me.

I close the last of the distance between us and fall to Nero's side, my knees landing in a pool of cooling blood. At first glance, my panther looks dead. He's too motionless. But when I slip down our bond and into his head, I can feel him still there. That's the extent of my reassurance, however, because an instant later, I feel the full weight of his pain. It's more than agony; it's death throes.

I bite back a sob.

"You're not dying on me. *Vekahi*." *Heal*. I whisper the Sarmatian word, pressing a hand against his blood-matted fur. My magic soaks into his body, thick like honey.

It's difficult to sense what it's repairing, but I think…I think that bad wound, the one that should've done him in, is healing. Maybe I'm just being overly hopeful.

I run a hand over his cheek, and he makes a soft huffing noise.

"It's okay, big guy," I reassure him. "I've got you. You're not dying."

My hand continues down his back, only stopping when my fingers catch on a piece of paper…and a nailhead that pins it to my familiar.

They literally nailed a note into Nero's skin.

My hands begin to tremble as my power vibrates in me. I'm seeing red—red like blood, red like pain, *red like wrath*.

Before I can act on it, I hear a whisper. Seconds later, a spell hits my back, searing through the cloth and sizzling my skin. Another curse quickly follows, slicing into my shoulder.

I grunt, slumping forward over Nero, my magic still healing him.

My attacker murmurs again, the incantation too low to hear, and I brace myself, using my body as a shield. The curse grazes the side of my temple. Pain bursts from behind my eyes, and for several seconds, I can see nothing—no red vision, no mutilated familiar, nothing.

Slowly, my sight returns, but there's little true relief when the hits continue. Most land on my lower back, carving into my skin and scalding my flesh.

*Selene!* Memnon bellows.

*I'm fine.*

*I fucking* hate *that word,* the sorcerer spits out. *Hold fast, fierce queen. I'm nearly there.*

Blood is dripping from many, many wounds. For a moment, I don't know where I am, *when* I am. This feels like old battles and ruthless enemies.

I draw in an unsteady breath, my hands slipping from Nero, my fingers digging into the blood-soaked soil as the hits continue to rain on me.

*Vengeance.* The word whispers in my ear—now in English, now in Latin, now in Sarmatian.

There are primordial things deep beneath the ground. Things that hunger for blood and chaos. Things I once made a pact with.

*You can have my help again,* the deep earth whispers.

This is the part of cursework and blood magic they don't talk about in the coven—how the darkness sometimes speaks with you if you wake it. If you beckon it.

*"Wi'manvus sisapsa bowad bodit, dubtup san est iv'tav'ap,"* I say slowly. *Devour my spilled blood, feast on my pain.* My hands tighten around the wet earth. *"Do ligohutnutsa batwad wuvknusava xu onut pesasava va'ukudapsa kav sanvasa." Tear into these witches, and let them feel my wrath.*

Along my skin, I hear the hiss of boiling blood and I smell the acrid, burnt edge of it.

Whoever was listening to my plea, they answered. Power races up from the earth, into my palms. No sooner has it entered my system, however, than it pours back out of me, the cast curse streaming toward my assailants.

My magic strikes them so hard they're blown back by the force of it. Seconds later, their screams start up, agonized and terrified.

I rise, my body feeling like one open, festering wound. I

push the pain away, staring down the witches. One of them is already back on her feet. Another two are rising. The others are still screaming on the ground, curling in on themselves.

I glare at them, this growing, seething anger demanding I stop hearts and snap necks.

"Run!" one of the witches shouts.

Those who can run begin to flee into the forest, but the orbs of light above them now bob along overhead like their own personal spotlights. It makes them easy targets.

One of the remaining women is bleeding. Without thinking, I let my power reach for that blood. I've done this so many times in the deep past that it's second nature. Power roars through my veins. It feels tainted with my own darkness.

Right now, I don't care.

I don't speak. I don't form a spell. I simply drag my fingers through the air, my intention forming itself into my magic. I can see oily black streaks in the pale orange magic as the curses barrel across the forest and strike the fleeing witches. I see each of them go down, their cries echoing in the night air.

There are still two witches lying nearby.

They attacked my familiar. They tried to end his life.

Moving over to the witch nearest me, I place my boot on her neck.

I don't know whether it's Memnon's power or my own, but my hair is rippling as my magic gathers. I can feel old, dark things in the ground, things that reach and claw for the surface.

I lift my chin even as I stare down at the witch, her freckled face illuminated by her blue witch's orb above us.

*I recognize her*, I realize with a start. She lives on my floor.

I've shared meals with her, passed by her in the communal bathrooms. She's an acquaintance. It makes this situation so much worse.

"The earth hungers for your life," I say softly, almost in a trance. "Give me one reason why I shouldn't let it eat you alive."

As I speak, the soil shifts beneath the witch, as though it's already eager to get a taste.

The woman lifts her hands, and I can see pale turquoise magic gathering there. All it takes is a little push of my magic, and the ground shifts, dragging the witch's arms into its dark embrace.

The witch cries out, struggling now against both me and the earth. But her hands are pinned, and the more she struggles, the deeper she sinks into the earth.

I dig my heel into her throat. "Why were you attacking my familiar?"

She chokes out a scream, fighting against me.

"Why?" I press.

When she says nothing again, I funnel my magic into the earth, letting a little more of it swallow her up.

The witch makes a strangled noise before gasping out, "I...can't...talk about it."

I frown down at her. Lauren, the instructor, said something similar when Memnon questioned her.

"She wants you," she adds, which is about the least helpful piece of information she could give me. I already know this—people are leaving me threatening notes and attacking my familiar. What I want to know is—

"Who?"

"*Lia*," she finally chokes out.

# CHAPTER 23

**Lia.** *I remember that name. It's the same woman who's been* coordinating the spell circles and forcibly binding witches.

A burst of magic hisses through the air. The moment it hits the ground, it explodes, throwing me off the witch and into a nearby tree trunk. I grunt as all my cursed wounds scream.

Another spell hits me, this one carving open my chest. I gasp as blood spills from me.

"Fuck you." The witch who strides up to me is petite, with cropped, curly black hair.

"Yasmin?" I say softly.

Only last night, we'd been drinking and chatting together. I considered her a friend. And last I saw of her, she had made plans to hunt down the fae rider.

I can't reconcile that woman with this one, who helped torture an animal.

"Help!" the half-buried witch calls out.

While I bleed out, Yasmin turns from me and pulls the other witch from the ground.

I begin to stand, my magic gathering. Yasmin glares at me as she helps the other witch to her feet, then lobs another curse at me. I don't dodge quick enough, and the spell hits me in the forehead, knocking me out.

---

*My queen. My queen, you must wake.*

I rouse at the panic-laced notes of Memnon's voice.

I blink, and Memnon's dark form takes shape in front of me. I stare at him for a moment, searching his gaze. Pain muddles my thoughts. I'm cold. Tired.

His hands cup my cheeks, and his eyes glow.

I shiver. The chilly night feels like it's burrowed itself in my bones.

Abruptly, the air around me warms, and I'm certain Memnon is responsible for it. Beneath his palms, magic seeps into me, drifting through my body and driving out the cold. As it moves through me, it stitches together torn flesh.

I look dazedly around.

*Nero. Where's Nero?*

*He's alive, my queen,* Memnon says. There is heartbreak in those burning eyes. *But you are battle-battered.* He says this lightly, using the same tone he takes with badly wounded soldiers.

*I'm fine,* I insist, trying to get up. Only now that adrenaline and outrage aren't fueling me, my body has given out almost entirely.

Memnon's thumb strokes my cheek from where he cups it. *You've lost a lot of blood. Too much. You need to rest.*

*I can't.* My eyes move to the dark forest where the witches fled. Where Yasmin—

His gaze follows mine.

Memnon turns back to me. "Where are they?" His voice carries a dark, lethal note to it.

The witches, he means.

"They ran," I say hoarsely.

"I'll find them," he says menacingly. I remember that menace in all its horrific glory. The fields of dead soldiers, the blood he sometimes wore like a second skin.

Memnon rises, the shadows catching on that scar of his. But it's his eyes that are the most sinister. They still glow like dying embers, and though I know it's only his magic that makes his irises smolder like that, the effect is downright villainous.

"Stay here," he says. With that, he turns and disappears into the Everwoods.

For several seconds, all I hear are my own ragged breaths. My eyes scan the darkness until I see the slumped form of Nero.

I make a small sound, forcing myself up. Every muscle protests.

*I told you not to move*, Memnon chastises down our bond. He must've sensed my pain.

*I'm the one who gets to be bossy*, I say, dragging myself to my familiar.

I let out a shaky sob when I see the state he's in. Despite my earlier magic, my panther's wounds are still open and still sluggishly bleeding. I can sense oily magic churning inside him. Whatever curses they placed on him, they haven't evaporated away yet.

*Memnon!* I all but cry out down our bond. *Come back. I...I think I'm losing Nero.*

———————

"*Bind the flesh. Mend what has been torn and broken. Heal the wounds within. Make Nero whole once more.*" I incant the spell for the third time since I fell to my familiar's side, pouring my heart and what's left of my magic into it. The pale orange plumes of my power sink into his body just as they have the last two times.

His wounds heal for a few moments before my spell gets no further. I want to scream, but the sound keeps getting trapped beneath this knot of fear in my throat.

The forest has gone unnervingly quiet. It's just me and my helpless grief. I'm losing my familiar, and there's nothing I can do.

I pet Nero softly, my touch light. "*Though the pain exists, you shall no longer feel it,*" I whisper.

My panther nudges my hand, his body relaxing just a touch. I begin to sob then, bowing my head over him.

"I'm sorry, so sorry, Nero. I never meant for this to happen." I should've been more cautious with him. It's easy enough for me to be brave in the face of threats, but my familiar is another matter altogether. He's a true weakness of mine, and the witches who attacked him know that.

*Yasmin* knows that. I cry a little harder, even as my vision darkens at the edges and a shiver racks my body.

Memnon's strong, warm hand falls on my shoulder. "Save your tears, little witch. You are not losing anyone tonight."

I glance up at him, my heart giving a hopeful stutter, as the sorcerer scoops up an unconscious Nero and settles the big cat over his shoulder.

I'm about to stand when Memnon bends down and scoops me up in his other arm.

"If you think I'm going to let you walk in the state you're in, you'd better start revisiting those old memories of ours," he says, striding into the forest.

I lean my head tiredly on his shoulder, not bothering to fight him or revisit those old memories.

*Thank you for coming,* I say down our bond. Distantly I'm aware that I must be in bad shape to be, of all things, *thanking* Memnon.

Memnon's mood darkens. *I got here too late.*

*Maybe for the battle,* I say, *but not for me and Nero.*

My gaze drifts to my panther's dark form. At least I hope so.

*Will he be okay?* I ask. I'm holding my breath, terrified of Memnon's answer.

The sorcerer glances down at me, his eyes no longer glowing. "Ferox didn't survive the Roman arena and the many battles on the steppe only to be cut down by a few hasty curses. He has your magic running through his veins, sustaining him when his own body cannot. He will be okay, little witch. I swear it."

The last of my tension leaves me.

*I'm holding you to that,* est xsaya, I whisper down our bond.

Memnon stiffens at the title, then tightens his hold on me.

It must be incredibly difficult to carry both me and Nero, but Memnon doesn't complain and doesn't slow as he moves through the woods.

I stare into the darkness, wondering about the witches

248

who attacked my familiar. Surely the wards activated at curfew would've caught their identities.

For a few seconds, I'm hopeful that the coven might be able to deal with these threats all on its own. But then I remember the persecution tunnels running beneath the campus. I doubt they were warded, and it's likely the witches who attacked Nero used those to get to the woods unnoticed.

In the distance, a forlorn howl goes up, and I remember all over again how the evening started.

The wolves never came. I thought after I heard those earlier howls that they might. Instead, I had to fend off Nero's attackers on my own, mere hours after the wolves pledged their loyalty. I don't know why that wounds me. It really shouldn't. At the end of the day, I am not a shifter, I am a witch, and no amount of friendship changes that.

Memnon enters Last Rites, Henbane's cemetery. It still bears a few remnants of our Samhain gathering—a melted candle here and there, a few scattered flowers lovingly left on tombstones, an empty potion vial someone left behind.

The sorcerer moves between the headstones, making his way to a particularly large crypt with the phases of the moon carved into its façade.

"What are we doing here?" I ask.

Memnon gives me a curious look. "I thought you would've remembered how we used to travel, *est amage.*"

"By horse?" I say, confounded.

He gives me a secretive smile. "By *ley line.*"

The dreaded ley line. I almost forgot.

Memnon steps up to the massive crypt and releases his power, forcing the stone doorway to open. The slab swings inward, scraping against the ground as it goes.

Of course the portal entrance onto a ley line couldn't be

out in the open. Of course we have to go inside a *tomb* to access it.

While ley lines stretch across the entire world, you can't open these magical roads just anywhere. There are portals onto them, and almost all these portals are located in sacrosanct places like temples and churches, stone circles and cemeteries.

Memnon moves to enter the crypt.

"*Wait*," I caution. "It might be warded." Then again, it might be too late if Memnon already crossed it once to get here.

"There was a partially disintegrated ward when I arrived," the sorcerer says, "but I broke what was left of it. There's nothing else barring our way."

With that, Memnon carries me and Nero inside. Once we enter, candles light, and they reveal a chamber bare of coffins and urns, bones and plaques. Aside from the candles themselves, there's nothing in here at all except for a thin column of space that seems to bend the light a little differently. The ley line entrance.

"Have you traveled along one of these in this life?" Memnon asks.

I shake my head against him.

"Then hold on tight."

I wrap my arms around Memnon's neck, ignoring the way the movement tugs at my wounds.

"Ready?" he asks.

"Yeah," I breathe.

With that, he steps through.

———

I nearly vomit as my surroundings smear together. The

tunnel bends and warps the dark forest around us, the outside world rushing past as Memnon walks along the ley line. These magical roads are little wrinkles in reality, areas where space and time don't follow normal rules. It means you can cross the world—you can even cross into *other* worlds—in seconds. Unfortunately, you can also get lost on these roads.

Fae are masters at crossing them, humans not so much. I never truly learned how to travel them as Roxilana. Instead, I bargained with the magic of these ley lines, giving it gifts in exchange for its assistance. Memnon, on the other hand, did learn. Eislyn taught him.

I hold on tightly to Memnon, breathing slowly so I don't retch.

He only takes a handful of steps before exiting the ley line. Our blurred surroundings sharpen into more shadowy forest that looks identical to the Everwoods.

"Where are we?"

"Nearly home," Memnon says, striding through the woods.

"You mean to *your* house," I correct him tiredly.

He's quiet, contemplative, at that, and I don't know what to make of the mood. I'm so used to Memnon being pushy and conniving and angry with me, it's unsettling to see this side of him. It's the side I remember from long ago, but even then, it was always offset by his thirst for war.

We step out of the forest and onto a street, and Memnon leads us down it.

Up ahead, lampposts partially illuminate a massive house. There looks to be tarps on the roof, and whole segments of the house are nothing more than exposed wood or bare drywall.Despite its half-finished state, a warm, inviting glow comes from within.

"Is this the house I burned down?" I ask as we approach it. Between the darkness and the fire damage, I hardly recognize it.

"It is." Amusement drips from his voice.

I pull away a little and take him in. "You sound proud of that fact."

"I *am*." Memnon glances at me. A tendril of his magic slips out then, the strand of it curling against my cheek. "Your ferocity is attractive, Empress, even when it's focused on me."

"You are unhinged," I say, but my words lack bite.

Memnon lets out a self-assured laugh. "We make a particularly terrifying pair," he admits, heading up the driveway of the house.

My stomach flutters at the idea of us as a unit before pushing the thought away. My gaze goes to Nero—wounded, agonized Nero. My panther's eyes are shut, and his body is still limp. One glance into his mind and it's clear he's temporarily unconscious.

Memnon has been so reassuring that Nero will be okay that I've let down my guard. But now my guard is back up, and my earlier panic has returned.

The sorcerer's magic unfurls ahead of us, and the front door swings open, and the lights inside flick on. Memnon strides straight into the house, heading toward the living room as the door swings shut behind us.

I peer curiously at his house. The walls bear no signs that they were incinerated not so long ago, but there's still a faint scent of smoke that clings to the space, as though it's soaked into the very bones of this structure. A couple of the walls are bare panels of drywall, and the ceiling above us is partially gone, exposing wood beams and some electrical wiring. All in all, however, it could be much worse.

"How did you fix this place so quickly?" I ask. I don't even see scorch marks on the remaining walls or the floor.

"Magic and money," Memnon admits. "It's still very much a work in progress."

A plush dog bed lies in the living room, next to a couch that looks new. Memnon sets me down on the couch, then carefully lays Nero out onto the dog bed.

My familiar doesn't so much as stir.

It's that lack of reaction that breaks whatever was keeping me together. I move off the couch and toward my familiar. Immediately, my eyesight darkens, and my legs fold.

I must black out, at least for a few moments, because when I blink my eyes, Memnon is holding me upright.

"No sudden movements, sweet mate," he says. "You're still badly injured." Gently, he lowers me to the floor next to Nero, then squats in front of me. He gives me a stern look. "I will tend to Nero first, because I can sense your insistence, but you're *not* going to move. When I'm done with him, you're going to let me treat your wounds too. Deal?"

If he is capable of healing Nero, I'll agree to just about anything.

"Deal," I say softly.

Memnon nods, then pivots away from me and settles himself in front of Nero.

The night hid many of the big cat's wounds from me, but under the bright lights of Memnon's living room, it's easy to see the extent of the damage. His belly and flank have been repeatedly sliced into, and the flesh around the cuts looks bubbled and mangled. Despite all my earlier spell-casting, the wounds still weep blood, along with a tar-black substance I recognize as dark magic. I can feel an echo of my familiar's pain, and it seizes up my chest, making me draw in shallow breaths.

Memnon pets Nero as he looks him over, and the big cat licks what he can of the sorcerer's arm. The sight has me biting back a sob.

"The curses he was struck with are still in him, preventing him from healing," Memnon finally says.

Cursework is a complicated art. The Romans used to love curses, but it was Memnon's paternal side, the Moche people of South America, who were truly skilled at cursework. Particularly the royal family. Memnon's father taught it to him, and now, when my soul mate closes his eyes and speaks low, the old Mochica language rolls over me like a lullaby, though I understand little of it.

The indigo magic that leaves Memnon's hands and enters Nero is luminous. I watch it disappear beneath Nero's matted fur, then wait.

Within seconds, oily magic starts to pour out of Nero's festering wounds as Memnon's magic purges it from my familiar's body. As it leaves, it begins to sizzle away. The process takes minutes, but it feels like a small eternity.

Once the last of the dark magic leaves Nero's body, Memnon spends minutes more healing the big panther. The sliced muscle and sinew reform, the bubbled flesh smooths out, and the skin seals itself up until Nero is whole again.

I slip into the panther's mind, just briefly, and I can sense his renewed vitality. His body is still sore, and he's very weak, but he'll be all right.

I retreat back into my own head, shuddering out a breath.

"You did it," I say to Memnon. "You saved him." Disbelief coats my words.

I knew my mate could do it, yet there had been a time earlier tonight when I was certain I was about to lose my familiar.

Memnon turns to me, his eyes dropping to my cheeks. He reaches out and wipes away a couple of tears I hadn't realized I'd shed. "You would've figured it out too, *est amage*," he says quietly.

I catch his wrist and brush a kiss against his knuckles, then press his hand to my cheek. "Thank you," I say sincerely.

Memnon's gaze flitters all over my face before he inclines his head. "Nero's lost a lot of blood, so don't be worried if he sleeps longer than usual or he's a bit tired for another day or so. I will set out a flank of lamb and some water for him in a little bit so he'll have something to eat when he wakes."

Memnon turns to me. "Now," he says, and his tone changes. "Let me see your wounds."

I glance down at my shredded shirt. Beneath the torn material, I can make out lines of scabs. It's a strange sight, almost as though I have tiger stripes, only these were made by spells, then cauterized when I offered my blood to the entity beneath the earth. There's a deeper cut on my belly, and I know my back must be a mess; it took the brunt of the hits. I can feel more dried blood on my face and hairline from the final curse Yasmin threw at me.

Memnon runs his fingers lightly over my skin. Again I hear him murmur in Mochica.

His magic moves like a lover across my flesh, and the way it ripples right now looks like the surface of the ocean. It sinks into my body, and every injury it touches heats. To my shock and horror, beads of black, oily magic push through my wounds.

I hadn't realized some of the curses that struck me earlier were still lingering inside me.

I watch the oily magic burn away into vapor, then nothing at all.

"I used dark magic," I admit softly. I chew the inside of my cheek. It's not the first time I've done so either. I used it when I fought Memnon the night of the dance, and I used it the night of the spell circle. I hadn't realized it, and I definitely hadn't meant to, but it's become a habit.

Fuck, it's been a habit since *before* this life.

Memnon glances up from my skin. "You used your gods-given power to retaliate against those who harmed your familiar. It was justified."

It did seem justified, but it doesn't make me feel better about using it.

The sorcerer must sense my lingering unease because he adds, "We have both used such magic many, many times. It is…tainted, but powerful."

I peer at Memnon, my eyes lingering on his scar. "What do you think it's tainted with?" I ask, fearing the answer. I've heard all the stories about dark magic, the most famous of which is the Law of Three—using it will curse you three times as badly as the original act. But mostly, supernaturals don't speak of dark magic. And now that I've used it a few times, I'm starting to worry.

Memnon shakes his head, his eyes dropping to the last of the curse as it dissolves away. "I don't know."

After a pause, I admit, "I heard a voice."

Memnon's sharp gaze flicks to mine. "What sort of voice?"

I open my mouth, but then I shake my head, at a loss for words. "I don't know. It might have been many voices, but it spoke to me." I don't mention that this likely was the same entity that granted my final spell as Roxilana, nor do I mention that it lent me power tonight. "I don't know what to make of it."

The sorcerer looks concerned as his eyes search mine. He turns back to my arm, watching his magic as it sinks into my skin.

"Have you ever heard of anything like it?" I ask.

After a moment, Memnon nods. "My father called them the Hungering Ones. He told me they were malevolent and formidable deities. They have a taste for power and enjoy nothing more than blood-soaked earth. I've always ignored the voices when they've called out to me. If you hear them again, *est amage*, you should too." He holds my gaze, his eyes steady. "There are things even kings and queens should not meddle with."

Unfortunately, I think it's too late for that.

# CHAPTER 24

*Once the dark magic is out of my system, Memnon sets to* work healing me. His hands press against my stomach, his magic moving through every limb.

"You were with the shifters tonight," he states.

I swallow delicately, already knowing I'm going to hate the conversation.

"How is it that on the very night you met with an entire pack, you and your familiar manage to get severely injured?"

Memnon makes it sound like they were involved.

"It wasn't their fault," I say. "Nero and the shifters didn't get along, so my panther left the meeting to hunt in the woods. It was there that the witches cornered him."

"The lycans must've been aware of the attack—I heard their howls. Why weren't they there fighting off the witches?" Memnon says.

Down our bond, I feel the breadth of his anger.

There's only one explanation that makes sense to me, not that it makes me feel any less wounded.

"Shifters cannot cross into witch territory without permission," I say.

Memnon scowls. "That pup crossed easily enough the night I found him in your bed weeks ago."

I give Memnon a look. "His name is Kane, and I gave him permission then."

"And you didn't tonight?" Memnon presses. "I would assume that permission was implied."

I open my mouth to argue, but nothing comes out. In fact, the longer I muse on what he's saying, the more uneasy I feel. I am a friend of the pack, but where was that friendship thirty minutes ago?

The sorcerer continues. "It seems to me that *Kane* and the rest of his pack are so worried about following the rules that they let evil slip through their fingers in the name of them." Memnon leans forward as the last of my wounds pull together under his magic. "Call me a monster, call me a devil, but you and I both know I will fucking *shatter* the rules for you." He stares at me fervently. "Always for you."

My gaze dips to his lips as my pulse begins to race. Memnon's right; for all his faults, he would do anything, give anything, for me. And at one point in time, I did the same for him. That's why the two of us exist at all in this future—I sold my last life to some buried god for the chance to sit here in this room with him now.

The air feels thick with tension as the moment draws on.

Memnon leans back on his haunches then, breaking the tension as he removes his hands from my stomach.

"Your wounds are all healed, *est amage*, though like Nero, you'll be a little lightheaded from blood loss. You'll need to take it easy."

My eyes flitter around the room. I'm staying here tonight,

I realize. I guess it was assumed from the moment Memnon carted Nero and me away from the forest, but only now is it truly setting in. I'm *staying* here, after a measly few days back at my residence hall.

The defeat stings a lot less than I thought it would.

I go to stand, and the edges of my vision darken.

Memnon is at my side in an instant.

"I'm fine."

The sorcerer gives a malevolent laugh. "I'm understanding that phrase better and better every time you use it."

I give him a weary look. "I just want a hot shower."

"You'll likely pass out from the heat," he says, looking apologetic.

"Then I'll have a hot bath," I say.

"You might still pass out."

I want to growl my frustration. "Then come in with me and make sure I don't."

Memnon's eyes widen.

Exhausted though I am, I nearly laugh. For a scheming sorcerer, he looks awfully surprised.

*That's a command*, I add. My skin itches with the feel of dirt and dried blood, and now that I've seen the dark magic ooze out of me, I need to scrub away the memory of it too.

"All right, Empress," he says, his expression unreadable.

Memnon helps me down the hallway and into his bathroom. I hadn't realized how fatigued I am, but I need the help. Even with his arm around me, I'm still breathing heavily by the time the two of us get there.

"Shower or bath?" he asks, still holding me.

Both the tub and the glass shower stall could easily fit us both.

"Which would be easier for you?"

He shakes his head. "Doesn't matter what I want. Shower or bath?"

"I like showers better—"

Memnon's magic slips past the glass door of the shower and turns the spigot on.

"—but I'm not sure how long I want to stand," I confess.

"Then you can sit in the shower, or I can hold you."

I glance up at him, feeling unusually vulnerable. I don't know why. Memnon has fought alongside me, he's been inside me, he's seen me naked and tended to me. None of it is new. No part of *us* is new.

"Okay," I agree.

Memnon's blue magic encircles us, peeling away our ruined clothes. I hear my phone thump to the floor, along with the soft sounds of my shredded jeans and shirt.

"Wait," I say, bending down to grab the phone while several of Memnon's daggers clatter to the floor alongside his clothes.

I straighten and hastily text my mom *I'm alive* before dropping the device back to the tiled floor. I don't need her fretting about me on top of everything else right now.

The sorcerer's magic pulls the shower door open, and he helps me in. Immediately the shower spray rinses away the most obvious grime that's on me, and Goddess but does it feel good. Under the heat of the spray, my muscles loosen.

I swivel around, leaning against the stone wall of the shower stall, and take in Memnon. He stands close, ready to catch me if I fall. The water has already hit his hair and speckled his face. Rivulets of it trail down his sculpted chest, and my eyes follow their path, taking in the tattoos that I used to doodle into my notebooks—bits of him that my mind never forgot.

"Don't look at me like that," he breathes, grabbing a nearby bar of soap and rolling it between his hands.

"Like what?" I say dazedly, leaning more heavily against the wall.

"Like you want a repeat of last night."

The heat is making me dizzy. "You don't?" I ask.

"Fuck," he curses under his breath. Louder, he says, "Of course I do. But not when you're half dead and delirious from blood loss."

"I'm not delirious," I say, even as I sway.

Memnon steps into the last of my personal space and takes one of my arms. He focuses on scrubbing up and down it. "You are," he insists. "Besides," he adds, moving to my other arm, "I got the impression I was in your bed yesterday because of a potion and nothing more."

I frown, not liking how my reasons sound coming out of his lips. Especially not after Memnon helped me this evening. I hadn't commanded him to come, and I didn't need some fancy friendship pact for him to show up. It's just what Memnon does for me, what he's always done for me.

He continues washing my body, the strokes of his hands decidedly not sexual, even as they move over my torso.

"It's annoying when you're honorable," I say.

He grabs more soap, then kneels down to wash my legs. "Why is that?"

The steam is getting to me. I feel lightheaded, nauseous.

"It makes it harder to hate you," I confess.

Memnon glances up from where he kneels, the water slicking his hair back. I reach out for his face just as I sway again.

"*Selene—*"

262

My vision darkens. When it clears again, I'm in the sorcerer's arms, and the water is cooling.

"Did I pass out?" I ask, my torso pressed against his. I'm about eye level with his pecs, and I get an intimate view of the dragon tattoo over his heart.

"I caught you," he says, keeping me upright.

I draw my gaze up, meeting his eyes. His hands stay on me, and though I don't necessarily need the continued support, I don't move out of his embrace. I think we're both fooling ourselves about how weak I am until I begin to shiver.

"Shit." Memnon uses one hand to pull me in closer to him and the other to nudge up the temperature until it's lukewarm.

Still, my shivers don't fully abate.

"I want to get you out of here," he says, frowning. "You're still lightheaded."

His fretting is disarming.

"Just a little longer," I insist. I still feel like I have dirt in my hair and dark magic on my skin. I press my cheek against his chest. "I trust you to keep me safe."

I can't see his face, but his hold tightens on me.

Without letting me go, he reaches for a bottle of shampoo and puts a little on his hand. Indigo magic flows out of him, wrapping around my midsection and holding me up so he can scrub my hair with both hands.

I stare up at him. The two of us are caught between hate and love, and we've found a tentative alliance right in between the two. Memnon is doing everything he can to prevent me from hating him again, and I'm doing what I can to not topple headfirst into caring about him.

He tilts my head back to wash off the shampoo.

"Did you see who was attacking Nero?" he asks.

I close my eyes, my nausea rising again at the memory.

"They were all witches, I think. Two of them…" My voice catches. I open my eyes. "Two of them live in my house at Henbane."

Memnon's eyes are sharp as he watches me.

"One of them told me that Lia was looking for me."

The sorcerer's expression darkens, growing cold and determined.

"I think these witches might've been working for her, but I don't know," I finish.

It's quiet for several seconds.

"Do you know the names of these witches?" Memnon finally asks. A chilling ruthlessness has entered his voice.

I hesitate.

"I only know one of their names, and only her first name—Yasmin."

Memnon's features smooth, turning placid. That expression is more terrifying than his anger. It's the face he wears as a warlord.

"Memnon, I don't want you to hurt her," I say.

His eyes begin to glow a little as his magic wells. "She sought to kill your familiar. She hurt you. It's too late for her, *est amage*. She is borrowing air at this point."

"She's a coven sister, and she might be involved in something against her will," I say.

"*I don't care.*" It's truly that simple for him too. Yasmin hurt me, so now she must die.

"You won't hurt her," I order.

The sorcerer's jaw tightens, and his eyes glow brighter. "Fine." He bites the word out, and to give him credit, he uses it exactly as I have been using it—to cover an obvious lie.

I reach out and turn off the water, thoroughly worn out by the evening. Memnon uses his magic to call a towel to him. He wraps it around me as another floats over and fits itself around his waist.

The tension in the room once again is thick enough to slice into, only now it's fueled by frustration, not chemistry. Memnon isn't used to truly being hemmed in. It seems the bond he forged with me is finally getting to him.

I've barely finished drying when the sorcerer's magic whisks away our towels. He scoops me up then and carries me to the bed, setting me gently on the mattress and tucking me in.

"Do you want something to sleep in?" he asks.

My eyes are already closing. I'm beyond caring. "This is fine." It's not like he hasn't already seen everything.

Memnon moves away from the bed, toward his closet, stalking around the room like a caged animal. It barely registers until he exits the room altogether.

*Memnon*, I call tiredly down our bond.

*Yes, little witch?*

*Where did you go?* I ask.

*I'm letting you sleep.*

*Oh.*

Several seconds go by, and I think I drift a little, only to wake feeling agitated.

*Memnon?*

*Yes?*

I can't be sure, but he sounds a little amused.

*Will you…come back?*

The other side of the bond is quiet, but a minute later,

Memnon returns to the room wearing only a low-slung pair of sweats. He stands just inside the doorway for several seconds.

I'm half-asleep when I reach for him.

It seems to take another small eternity before he moves to me and takes my hand, threading his fingers between mine.

I blink sleepily at him.

*Will you stay with me until I fall asleep?* I want to ask him for more, but I'm not brave enough.

Memnon uses his other hand to run his knuckles over my cheek.

*Of course, Empress.*

He releases my hand and gets on the bed then. I flip over, curling my body toward his.

"Good night, wife," he murmurs.

"*Former* wife," I whisper, correcting him.

"*Future* wife," he corrects me.

Sleep presses in, pulling me under. I'm too tired to argue further.

The last thing I sense before I fall asleep is Memnon's hand running over my wet hair and this sharp, almost agonized love trickling into me from our bond.

---

Sometime in the middle of the night, I feel the brush of fingers against my hair.

*I need to take care of a few things,* est amage. *I will be back soon.*

But perhaps Memnon's words were just a dream, because when I wake, he's there, pressing kisses to my skin. Against my throat, at the juncture of my neck and shoulder, and down my arm.

I should push him away, but my bond is singing, and the kisses feel like wish fulfillment.

*Good morning, future wife,* he says when he notices me waking, propping himself on a forearm. He's still above the sheets, and I don't know why, but that is disappointing to me. Which is absurd.

*I forbid you from calling me that,* I say, brushing my tangled hair back from my face.

*Good morning, fiancée,* he corrects.

*That too.*

*Good morning, my vicious queen who demands the blood of our enemies.*

I smile.

Another kiss to my shoulder. *You liked that one,* he says, noticing.

*You know, you're my enemy too,* I remind him.

*Then punish me,* he demands.

I part my lips, unsure what to say, when a sound like nails on a chalkboard saves me from having to answer. It comes from the other side of the closed bedroom door.

*SCRIIIITCH. SCRIIIITCH.*

There's only one creature who makes that noise.

"Nero!" I say excitedly. I didn't think my panther would be up for a while still. But at the sound of his claws, my heart nearly leaps from my chest.

Before I can scramble out of bed, Memnon's indigo magic reaches out and opens the door.

Nero walks in silently, and once I see him, I slide out of Memnon's bed and rush over to my panther, only belatedly realizing I'm still very naked and a little dizzy. I wrap my arms around Nero anyway, who leans into my embrace, nuzzling against my cheek, then giving it an abrasive lick.

"How dare you almost die on me," I whisper, squeezing him tighter.

He rubs his head against me again, then pulls away. At first, I think it's because he's only so touchy-feely with his emotions, but then he pads over to the far side of the bed, where Memnon is, and he places his head on the edge of it.

The sorcerer's eyes crinkle at the corners, and Memnon reaches out and rubs Nero's head. "You're a true warrior," the sorcerer says gruffly. "You owe me no thanks for healing you."

Ah, fuck. This man is definitely going to make me fall for him.

Memnon glances at me, a small smile on his lips. *That's my deepest hope, my queen.*

# CHAPTER 25

***"You cannot go back to Henbane,"*** **Memnon says.**

The two of us are in the sorcerer's kitchen.

Memnon is currently shirtless, his back to me as he cooks bacon on the stove. I forgot how good of a cook he is; it was one of his hobbies way back when.

"I'm sorry, what?" I say, my eyebrows rising.

He turns from the stove, crossing his arms over his rippling torso. I can hear the crackle and pop of frying bacon, and the oil must be hitting his back, but the sorcerer doesn't move and doesn't flinch.

He lifts his chin. "You cannot stay there."

Without meaning to, my eyes have drifted down his chest, following the flow of his tattoos.

*Stop staring at his pretty muscles.*

"I'll be fine."

"Fine," he echoes, narrowing his gaze.

I have to force myself not to react to that word. We both now know I often use it when things aren't fine.

I brace myself for his retort.

Instead, he says, "Yes, I can believe that. You are fearsome." There's no mockery in his words. "But how about Nero?"

His question is a sucker punch to the stomach.

Nero.

My gaze moves to the woods beyond the window, where my familiar bounded off to ten minutes ago. Even though this is a different patch of forest, one Memnon has insisted is safe, I've still been worried about my panther's well-being ever since he left.

I rub my forehead and take a deep breath.

"Damn it," I mutter.

Memnon's right. Even if I warded my room to within an inch of my life, and even if I was willing to take on whatever skirmishes might come my way…I'm not willing to risk Nero. Not again.

I scowl. "Did you know this would happen?" I ask, perhaps a touch accusingly.

The sorcerer's expression has softened, and his eyes look almost pitying. "Not this specifically. But, *est amage*, we have always had enemies. This is not new or surprising to me."

My eyes drift over his kitchen again. Memnon watches me like a hawk, drinking in my appraisal of his place. The loud pop from the pan rouses him, and he turns back to the stove.

"So somehow separate from all your plotting, I find myself in a position where I have to stay with you," I say to his back, my eyes trailing over the tattoos covering it.

"You don't have to do *anything*," he responds, rotating his head just enough so I can see his scarred profile. "You are a former queen," he reminds me. "You do as you fucking please." He pauses to turn off the burner and move the pan away from the heat. Then he swivels back to me. "But *I* want you here. This is your house. That"—he nods in the direction of the bedroom—"is your room and your bed."

"*Our* bed," I correct. "It would be *our* bed."

Memnon's gaze burns with intensity. "You're the one with the power, Selene. If you don't want me in it, you can command me to sleep anywhere else," he says. "You are the one in control."

It's the illusion of control, nothing more.

"This house and the woods around it are protected, and here, you and Nero will both be safe," Memnon continues. "And in the meantime, we'll work together to find this Lia, and we'll stop her."

Presumably then I'll be able to return to the residence hall.

I take a deep breath. "Okay." I nod. "I'll stay." Just until it's safe for Nero. "I'll still need to go back to campus," I add, "at least some of the time. There are things that I need." Such as my clothes, my notebooks, my laptop, and my textbooks. "And I'm going to continue attending class," I say, lifting my chin a little. I fought hard to be admitted to Henbane. I'm not going to let a few rogue witches ruin it all for me.

Perhaps if the sorcerer were a modern man, he'd find the idea of me going back to campus supremely foolish. But Memnon is a warlord and a king. He has brazenly walked among enemies and would only assume I'd do the same. It's not in his nature—in *any* Sarmatian's nature—to be cowed by an opponent.

The sorcerer crosses the kitchen and stops close enough to tilt my face up to his, his gold rings pressing against my skin. "Fair enough, Selene," he says, taking in my features. "But if you must be among foes, do not give them this tempered, modern treatment. I don't care what compassionate thoughts fill that heart of yours. If someone so much as looks at you wrong, you use your magic, and you aim to kill."

# CHAPTER 26

*Another witch is missing.*

I learn that ten minutes after I arrive on campus, right as I'm settling into my seat in Spellcasting 101.

The news steals the air from my lungs. Could the missing witch be one of Nero's attackers? There was at least one whose throat he ripped out.

Goddess, she had to have died. I try not to panic in my seat as I remember that. What happened to the body? Is it still out there, waiting to be found? Could she have survived? Or is she the missing witch, her body moved sometime in the last twelve hours?

Throughout the lecture, I woodenly take down notes, but I'm not really listening. Instead my mind is turning and turning. There have been murdered witches, and there are now missing witches—Kasey is one of them, and now there's another one. Both disappearances happened right after battles. Could whoever they're working for be cleaning up any evidence? Or could it be...

*I need to take care of a few things,* est amage. *I will be back soon.*

Maybe that wasn't just a dream. Maybe Memnon legitimately left.

I reach out to the sorcerer now. *Did you move any bodies from the forest last night?*

*Is this an intrusive thought, or is this my little witch?* Memnon responds.

I glance heavenward. *Memnon.*

I feel the warmth of his smile down our bond.

*Did I mention that I miss you?*

*Memnon, be serious.*

I can almost feel his next words—*I am serious.*

But he lets them go unspoken. Instead, *I went back and removed any evidence that might be incriminating,* he says evasively.

*Including bodies?*

*I do believe there was a body involved. Maybe even two.*

My stomach turns over. Witches died last night, and while my blood still boils that they tried to kill my familiar, I feel nauseated at the thought of more lives lost.

*Don't,* Memnon says, cutting through my thoughts.

*Don't what?*

*Don't let your guilt obscure the truth. This was a planned attack on your familiar. You and he both defended yourselves against it, and in the process, some of your attackers died. More of them will die if they're foolish enough to take you on again,* he says fervently.

The knot forming in my stomach now loosens. They're words I didn't know I needed to hear.

*Now go be studious. I'll see you at six sharp.*

Abruptly, Memnon pulls away from our link, leaving me to mull over his words.

My pale orange magic hovers around me like a storm cloud as I enter the residence hall after class. I'm braced for a confrontation with Yasmin or that other housemate.

But today, the house is mostly quiet. Only a few witches linger in the common areas, and they aren't either of the witches I'm keeping an eye out for.

I head to my room, my heart sinking when I see Nero's empty bed. Quickly, I pack up what I need and set it by the door. I hate that I'm being forced out of this room.

*This isn't forever*, I promise myself.

I have some time in between now and my next class, and there are a million things I could be doing with the precious time I have left on campus.

I don't end up doing any of them.

Instead, I head down to my house's dining room and through an inconspicuous door that leads to the house's kitchen. Inside are two witches currently on cooking duty. One look at the roster hanging up on the adjacent wall, and I can see that I'll be called to help prep a meal next week.

My power thickens as I take in the witches' faces, but it resettles a little when I realize none of them are the witches from last night.

I breeze past them and head for the metal freezer. Cold air hisses out when I open it. Inside, I see exactly what I was looking for.

"What are you doing?" one of them demands.

I drag out a massive tub of ice cream. "I'm tossing this out. The ice cream has been recalled," I say. "There was a listeria outbreak at the factory where it was made."

"Oh," one of the witches says, looking baffled. The other one eyes me skeptically.

I walk out of there, carrying the industrial-size carton. Once I'm in the dining room, I use my magic to call a spoon to me. And then I head to my house's den.

I sit down cross-legged on the couch, set the carton in my lap, and begin stress eating the shit out of Neapolitan ice cream.

Need to go to class, need to finish the assigned reading, need to finish my spellcasting homework…

My hands itch to write this down in one of my notebooks, but since I left my notebooks in my room, I just manically go over and over my list, trying to sear it into my brain so I don't forget.

Need to double-check that I packed everything I need for…for…

I shove another panicked bite of ice cream into my mouth.

*Tonight.*

The evening looms ominously in my mind. It was one thing to stay with Memnon when Nero and I were hurt. It's another to deliberately choose to stay there. And now that my mind isn't busy taking notes or worrying about missing witches, I have all the time in the world to stress about *living with Memnon.*

I take another massive scoop of ice cream.

One of the witches passing by stops in the doorway of the den. I recognize her as the same witch who, weeks ago, fell asleep on our staircase landing with her fox familiar. I think her name is Rosemary.

"What are you doing with that?" she asks, her tone both curious and accusing as she takes in the industrial-size container of ice cream.

"Obviously, I stole it," I say. A little petty theft seems

like nothing compared to some of the crimes I've witnessed lately.

The witch glances up and down the hall, then heads toward the dining room.

She returns less than a minute later with a spoon.

"Scooch over, Selene," she says, sitting next to me. "I want some too."

My eyebrows rise at the sound of my name—I didn't realize she knew it—but I do make room for her.

"You okay?" she asks as a group of three witches catch sight of us.

"Why wouldn't I be?" I say. Was she one of the witches who attacked me? I reassess her.

Rosemary scoops out a bite from the carton. "No one steals a tub of ice cream and eats it alone without having a supremely shitty day."

I mean technically, I could just really like ice cream and not care about the consequences.

But she's right.

"I'm just…overwhelmed…by things lately," I admit. As I speak, the three witches I noticed earlier now come in, each of them carrying spoons.

Damn it. Now I have to share.

I eye each one of them, relaxing a little when I see that none of them are the witches from last night.

They could've still been out there in the woods. Or they could've been at the spell circle. They could be plotting against me even now.

I hate these thoughts, and I hate that I have to think about them at all. All I've wanted for the last year is to come to Henbane and make friends with other witches. But now

I feel paranoid, like those medieval inquisitors who seemed to find witches in every shadow and demons in every witch.

Rosemary makes an agreeing noise, oblivious to my churning inner monologue.

"If that isn't the Mother's damn truth," she says while the three new witches cram themselves onto the couch.

One of the new witches who sits down on my other side adds, "I've heard that Henbane is seriously considering closing its doors."

I glance at her wide brown eyes, alarmed.

"What?" One of her friends echoes my thoughts. "Where did you hear this?"

"One of our instructors was discussing it with another faculty member when I came in for office hours."

"Why?" Rosemary asks. "No other witches have been killed since the dance."

"But more have gone missing," the witch says, brushing back her curly brown hair before scooping out another bite of ice cream. "Not to mention there are plenty of angry parents set to sue the coven."

Everyone is quiet.

I don't want Henbane to shut down, not after all the effort that it took for me to get accepted and to stay here and make it work. However, it's not like the concerns are fabricated.

More witches step into the room, some of them with spoons, some of them asking to borrow their coven sisters' utensils.

I'm starting to feel agitated by the swarm of them when I catch sight of Sybil at the threshold of the den, her owl Merlin perched on her shoulder.

She must see the growing panic in my eyes because she

smirks before she cuts through the room and the cluster of witches around me.

"All right, snack time's over for you," Sybil says, grabbing my hand and pulling me off the couch. Another witch catches the half-eaten carton of ice cream with her magic before it hits the floor.

Taking my spoon from my hand, Sybil gives it to another witch who needs one, then steers me out of the den and up to her room. As soon as the door shuts behind her, she leans against it.

"Okay," she says. "Where the fuck have you been?" At her tone, Merlin flaps his wings before resettling. "And don't give me some bullshit answer. Kane called me frantic last night, asking me if you made it home okay, and when I checked, you weren't here."

As she speaks, her lilac magic sifts out of her, a clear sign of her agitation. It weaves through my own power, which still hovers around me.

I swallow. "Last night was bad, Sybil," I admit. "Someone tried to kill Nero."

Horror washes over her features. "What?" she says softly.

I tell her everything, from meeting with the shifters to the attack to going home with Memnon. And I know I'm distrustful of witches overall, and maybe that should extend to Sybil, but honestly, I need someone besides Memnon to trust.

My friend glances heavenward, letting out a ragged breath. "I hate that this is becoming normal for us. You disappearing and me worrying that you're hurt or worse." She doesn't voice what *worse* is, though we both know what she means.

Dead.

She continues, "And now it's witches who are after you, witches we *know*, and Memnon who's the good guy?" Sybil shakes her head, the action jostling her owl a little. "What parallel universe are we in?"

I glance down at my hands, my emotions a tangled mess. "I don't know. I *did* hate him. I...I do still..." I squeeze my hands into fists. "Fuck, I don't know. He saved Nero, and he's been good to me. I know he doesn't deserve a second chance but—"

"Listen, Selene," Sybil cuts in, "you do what makes you happy. Personally, given all the disappearances, it's probably safer for you that you're off campus. If you happen to hate-fuck the guy along the way, more power to you. He seems like he's a ride."

"Sybil!" I give her a push, and she cackles, falling back on her bed while Merlin flies to his perch above Sybil's headboard.

"Just be sure to brew lots of contraceptive potions," she adds. "One sorcerer is more than enough."

# CHAPTER 27

*My packed bags are sitting just inside the spell kitchen as I* work on the final task I want to complete before I return to Memnon's house. Namely, making a protective amulet for Nero. Or at least I'm trying to make one.

Spellwork is a painstaking, intricate business. It's easy enough for a witch to press their intention into their power as they cast it out, but the actual crafting of a spell, one that draws magic mostly from external things, is like weaving a tapestry. There are lots of moving parts. But if done correctly, the protective talisman is like a mobile ward, one whose strength can grow over time.

Despite the fact that the last time I tried to make an amulet it was a disaster, I'm determined to get it right, for Nero's sake.

I glance down at the grimoire open on the counter.

*Thrice by thrice thorn of rose*

What the fuck is *thrice*? I know I'm a witch and this sounds like my jam, but there are some old-as-shit terms that even I don't understand.

One quick internet search and okay, *thrice* means three, which I guess I should've assumed.

So thrice by thrice…three by three—nine. Maiden, Mother, and Crone, they could've just said nine.

I'm bitching under my breath as I grab the roses I'd already gathered from the residence hall's greenhouse. When most spells call for roses, they want the petals or the pressed oil from them. Not this one. This one calls for the thorns.

Quickly, I begin to snap them off the stem, counting them out as I go. I'm removing my ninth one when—

"Fuck," I curse. One of the thorns cradled in my palm has lodged itself in my flesh. I snap off the final thorn and toss eight of the nine into the boiling cauldron. The ninth one I pry from my palm, grimacing as it comes away bloody.

I hold it over the cauldron, transfixed by that red liquid. I've already used blood magic—dark magic. I've felt the alluring, forbidden press of it, and I've heard dark voices calling to me when I've used it.

I should rinse my hands and grab another thorn, one free of blood.

Instead, still under trance, I release the one in my hand, letting it fall into the cauldron. It hisses the moment it makes contact, and shimmering smoke wafts up from the potion.

I blink a few times, then take a shaky breath. Well, guess that decides that.

I move on to the last ingredient, heading to the other side of the kitchen to grab the jar labeled *Toad Legs (ethically harvested under the full moon)*—whatever *that* means—and pull one out, throwing it into the brew.

I eye the appendage bobbing in the bubbling cauldron, wondering how frog legs—ethically harvested or not—fit into dark magic. Where is the line drawn? Witches don't really say, and I have a prickly, uncomfortable feeling this falls into that gray area where it's only okay until somebody in the future says it isn't.

*Oh well, I'm probably already thoroughly fucked.*

*Thoroughly fucked?* Memnon's voice is sin given sound. *Oh no, little witch, you haven't even* begun *to experience what it means to be thoroughly fucked.*

I press a hand to my head. *No one invited you into the conversation,* I say, holding back the thought that only days ago, Memnon *did* very thoroughly fuck me.

*The conversation?* Memnon echoes. *Who else are you talking to? Please don't tell me you've involved the panther in this.*

*Memnon.*

I feel him grin, and in response, my entire body seems to come alive. Lately, the sorcerer has been...cheeky. And Goddess help me, I think I like it.

*I'll see you soon, Empress.*

Crap, that's right. The mounted cuckoo clock in the spell kitchen says I have ten minutes, though it could be wrong—magic makes the thing finicky.

Hurriedly, I clean up my spot on the counter, then stir the pot.

The grimoire lists an incantation as the final step. I lift a hand over the cauldron and read it off: "*Mortal hearts full of woe and ire, see not my form if thou dost conspire. Turn thine eyes away from me, protect my body and blessed be.*"

A flare of light brightens the mixture, and I see all the solid ingredients dissolve into the liquid.

From my pocket, I pull out a soft leather cord I found

in one of the drawers of the spell kitchen. On it, I strung an old quartz pendant I used to wear. Now I dip the cord, stone first, into the potion, making sure all of it is submerged. When I pull it out, the soft luster of my pale orange magic coats the pendant and cord before sinking into the objects. I can sense the ward taking hold.

I did it. I made my first successful amulet.

Once the ward has completely set, I tuck the newly made amulet into my pocket.

For the first time since Nero was attacked last night, I breathe easy.

Now to meet with Memnon.

# CHAPTER 28

***My soul mate drives up on a gleaming motorcycle, his dark***
hair billowing in the wind, no helmet in sight.

Hell's bells.

"What is that?" I ask from the pavement in front of my
residence hall, my bags at my feet.

He raises an eyebrow, then glances at the motorcycle
between his legs before looking back at me again. "You're
the modern woman. I imagine you already know."

"You want *me* to ride on that thing?" The roads around
here are winding, mountainous, and often pitted. Many
lack guardrails, and the drops from them can be steep. The
thought of taking those turns on a motorcycle sends a shiver
down my spine.

Memnon swings himself off his seat. "You sound mighty
judgmental for a woman who has no vehicle."

"Considering you *stole yours*, I think I have a right to be."

"You scared, little witch?" Memnon asks, eyeing me.

"No," I say quickly. Too quickly.

A sinful smile blooms across his face. "You *are*."

Maybe it's his tall stature. Maybe it's the outfit, a simple black shirt and black fatigues tucked into combat boots, which seems to display every damnably beautiful inch of him and showcase his dangerous nature. Or maybe it's his face, with his annoyingly high cheekbones and those wicked lips. But he takes my breath away. He looks like something mythical and forgotten.

He steps in close. "I'll keep you safe, Selene," he says roughly. "You know that."

I think I've stepped closer to him, lured in by that magnetic pull he has.

His gaze draws up to my residence hall. "Or we could stay here, maybe have a little dinner. You could introduce me to your coven sisters, and I could read their minds one by one." His expression grows cold, cruel. "It could be a game—see how many witches survive the evening."

Memnon looks half-convinced of his own plan when he steps past me and starts up the walkway to my house.

Shit—he isn't serious, is he?

I rush after him. "Wait. Wait a goddess-damned minute," I say, grabbing him by the wrist. "So long as you have a helmet for me, I'll ride on your death machine."

It does, after all, beat staying here among my enemies.

———

The drive is terrifying.

Memnon lives a few miles south of the coven, and the main road from Henbane to his house is especially winding.

Despite Memnon's magic, which wraps around our waists and holds me in place, I cling to Memnon like my life depends on it. Down our bond, I can feel his amusement and the glow of his affection.

I'm glad he's enjoying this. That makes *one* of us.

When we arrive at Memnon's house, I nearly weep with relief. My limbs feel boneless from tensing for so long.

I slide off the motorcycle and remove the helmet Memnon did end up having with him.

Above the tree line, the sun is setting, but it's not the sky that takes my breath away. Outside the sorcerer's house, dozens of lanterns float above us, the flickering flames within them giving the place a ghoulish, magical ambiance.

Using a pinch of magic, Memnon grabs my bags from the tiny storage compartment on his stolen death bike—

*Steel horse*, he corrects me.

—and he comes up to my side.

"Did you do this for me?" I ask, pointing to the lanterns.

His eyes flick over my face, then he nods.

"Why?" I ask.

"I wanted to bring a little of the magic of your coven here," he admits.

I frown as my heart skips a little.

Movement at the corner of my eye has me tearing my attention away from the house.

Relief washes over me when I see my familiar loping toward us. I get down on one knee and catch Nero in my arms, the weight of him nearly bowling me backward.

"I missed you," I whisper, holding him tightly as he rubs his head against the side of mine.

It's unnatural to be so far from my familiar. All day, there was this persistent tug at the back of my mind, like I forgot an important memory. I've been so used to that feeling that

I didn't realize until now that it was because Nero and I were parted.

"I have something for you," I say.

My panther watches me, probably hopeful it's food. Instead, I pull out the cord.

"This is warded to protect you so you'll be safe while you're out hunting." Honestly, I should've done this much sooner.

Nero's ears flick back, and I think...I think he's insulted.

"It *isn't* a collar. It's a protective amulet."

He lets out a small, displeased sound.

Grumpy bastard.

"It's for your safety," I say.

Memnon steps up behind me. "Wear it for Selene's sake, and I will give you a fresh cut of venison as soon as we get inside."

Nero's tail twitches with irritation, but he lowers his head and allows me to tie the protective amulet around his neck.

I give Memnon a look over my shoulder, partly annoyed but mostly grateful that his bribe worked.

"This is only a temporary solution," I promise.

As soon as it's secured, Nero heads toward the house, tail still twitching with his agitation.

*He'll get over it.* Memnon says down our bond. *Now, come,* est amage. *Let's get you settled.*

---

My eyebrows lift when I catch my first glimpse inside Memnon's house. Clusters of pillar candles line every available surface—shelves, side tables, even the floor in some locations—their wax dripping all over the place.

Fifty dollars says I'm going to accidentally knock one of them over and start another fire in this house.

There's a whisper-soft sound that accompanies hundreds of tiny flames burning through wicks, and it draws my magic up to the surface of my skin. I reach out as I pass a cluster of candles, running my fingers through the flames.

The front door clicks closed behind me, and I hear Memnon set down my bags. When I glance back at him, he's watching me carefully; his head is tilted just a little, gauging my reaction.

"Are these more witchy details for me to appreciate?" I ask.

"No," he says, coming to me. He moves to my front and continues to peer at my face, his smoky amber eyes shining in the dim light. "I simply wanted to remember the way firelight danced on your face."

He continues to gaze at me, and his expression makes my heart skip. He used to look at me like this all the time. I didn't know it was something I missed until this very moment. Unthinkingly, I take a step toward him, my eyes dropping to his lips.

What would happen if I decided we could be something other than enemies—or even something besides allies with benefits? What if I gave in to my deepest hidden wants the way witches are encouraged to do?

The thought is too tantalizing to pass up, especially when Memnon is right here, waiting for me to do something.

Very carefully, very deliberately, I wrap my hand around his neck, drawing his face down to mine. His eyes burn bright as I lean in and press a kiss to his lips, enjoying a brief taste of him.

His hands move to my arms, but already I'm slipping out of his reach.

I'm playing a dangerous game with this man. I know it, and I can see evidence of it—there's a calculating edge to my soul mate's expression, one that makes my pulse thrill. He's looking at me like he's sighted prey.

Thanks to the forged bond between us, I'm also completely in control. One word from me and I can change the entire flow of this evening.

I could get drunk on this sort of power. And I just might.

---

While Memnon makes good on his promise to Nero and gets the panther his slab of meat, I quickly send my mom my nightly proof-of-life text, this time along with a photo of me blowing her a kiss. Then I wander into the house's dining room. The sight before me stops me in my tracks.

The long, carved oak table in front of me is laden with platters of food. Grapes spill from bowls, cheeses sit next to thickly cut slices of bread, and a whole-ass roasted chicken glistens on a platter.

A thin, glittering plume of Memnon's magic covers the space. I run my hand through the magic, watching with no little awe as it shifts, moving toward me as though I'm a lodestone.

I've seen this spell many times before—it's a laughably mundane one. A spell for freshness—to keep meat warm, bread soft and moist, produce crisp, and dairy from souring.

Memnon enters the room then, moving to the other side of the table where he tracks my movements over more candlelight.

As I play with his magic, the spell dissipates, my touch

enough to break it. Between the flickering candlelight, the deep shadows, and the heavily laden table, I'm reminded of that final dinner, right before we were betrayed.

But I cannot think of it without remembering how it ended. I can still hear the pounding footsteps of the Roman soldiers closing in on me that night. I can still see the bloody bodies of Memnon's mother and sister. Their bones have been ground to dust, their lives just a ghost of a memory. Civilizations have come and gone, and the world has forgotten.

All that's left is us. Just us.

I push away the bleak thought.

"This looks like it was a lot of work," I say softly.

"It isn't work if it gives you pleasure," Memnon replies. There it is, my soul mate's resurrected hobby. It makes me strangely happy to know he's found it again.

I pull out the chair in front of me and sit down, noting the alcohol he's already poured for me. "Plying me with wine, *est xsaya*?" I tease. His eyes flash at the title. "And when I'm not legally old enough to drink? *Very* bold of you."

Memnon arches a brow, taking a seat across from me. "You were drinking spiced wine since you were a child."

That's Roxilana he's referring to.

"But if you wish to refrain…" He lifts a shoulder.

I take the wineglass and drink a swallow. My eyebrows rise at the taste. It's thinner than what I'm used to and flavored with honey and cinnamon.

Once more, the past overcomes me. I can feel the thick press of summer air, the sharp stench of the Roman streets, the desperate dream to leave. Then campfires and creaking wooden wagons and sweaty bodies that smell like horsehair and wild grass. The past is all right there, so close I swear I could step into it.

But as quickly as the memories come, they're gone again, leaving only an ache in their wake.

The skin around Memnon's eyes crinkles with mirth. "The flavor is not quite as...*pungent* as it once was—"

I laugh, because fuck, that's *right*. Some of the wines we once drank had additives like pepper and coriander—even chalk and sea water—in them. The past was wild, man.

"Do you miss it?" Memnon asks after a moment, and he must be reading my thoughts.

Right now?

"Maybe a little," I admit. "But the past is gone," I add.

"Not for us," Memnon says, reverting to Sarmatian. "The past is alive in us. You and I are eternal, my queen."

I stare at him, caught in his gaze. I don't want to keep looking at him—I feel like he can see too much—but I can't seem to look away either.

It begins to rain, the sound pitter-pattering on the tarp above the exposed wood ceiling.

My eyes move up to it.

"You might get wet tonight, *est amage*, but not from the rain."

My gaze snaps back to Memnon, and my core tightens. I have a retort already loaded on my tongue, but just as soon as it comes to me, I swallow it back down.

I don't want to flirt or tease or bicker with Memnon. I don't want to be *playful* at all right now. I'm feeling nostalgic and bittersweet in this room where the past is still alive.

A phone vibrates, pulling me out of the moment. I think it's mine, but then Memnon is pulling his own device out of his pocket. He glances at the number, then tucks it back away without answering.

"Who's calling you?" I ask, curious. I feel some unnameable emotion at the idea of Memnon having a whole other side of his life that I'm not privy to.

"You could be privy to it," he responds.

"Get out of my head."

"I would follow your orders if I could, Empress, but it's you, not me, who's broadcasting those pretty thoughts. As for the call," he continues, "that's the mage I work for."

The one who believes he's bonded Memnon to him.

I raise my eyebrows. "You're not going to answer?"

"If I do, he'll likely give me a command that will take me from you, and, *est amage*, I don't want that."

I'm caught in his gaze again, and we're in Rome, we're on the plains of the Pontic steppe, we're in Bosporus. It all comes rushing back—the feeling that I'm on some precipice, waiting to jump. Waiting to fall.

"What *do* you want?" I ask.

"You know what I want," he challenges. "It's the one thing I've wanted since I first woke."

*Me*, I think he means.

Yet he's just sitting there, waiting. As though *I'm* supposed to come to *him*.

I feel a rising restlessness in me.

*You could*, a small voice inside me says. *You could do anything you want. Anything at all. You could even give in to those deep, hidden desires. You're in control.*

My magic snaps out of me, half in agitation, half in eagerness, blowing out all the candles and leaving us in darkness. I didn't consciously choose to extinguish the last of the light, yet once it's gone, I don't try to relight the candles. Instead,

I flick my wrist, and platters careen into each other as my power sweeps them away from the middle of the table.

In the darkness, I stand, then I step onto the table. I don't entirely know what I'm doing, but my magic is rushing through my veins, and my bond is beckoning me closer. The wood creaks beneath my weight as I cross it. I step down, right into Memnon's lap.

"Is this what you want?" I ask, placing my hands lightly on his shoulders.

The sorcerer's hands come to rest on my hips. "*Yes*," he breathes, his eyes glinting in the darkness. The rain patters above us, making the space feel particularly intimate. "But you don't need to concern yourself with what I want. What do *you* want?"

This is a trap, one expertly set. It's too late for me to care.

"I want you," I whisper into the darkness.

I lean forward, and my lips meet his. The kiss I give him is rough, resentful. I don't want to want him, but I do.

Memnon grabs a fistful of my hair, tugging on it just as roughly as he kisses me back. *Then you shall have me.*

Memnon's hands return to my hips, and he stands, lifting me with him. I assume he's going to set me on the edge of the table, but instead, he carries me out of the dining room.

The rest of the house is still illuminated by the burning candles. We pass Nero, who's gnawing on the bone Memnon gave him with his meat, and we head toward the back of the house. As we go, my power snuffs out candles one by one, banishing the light from this house. I don't mean to do it, but my magic is enjoying acting out tonight.

I'm too busy kissing Memnon to much care.

There are no candles in my mate's bedroom. The only light comes from the moon and the streetlamps outside. I begrudgingly appreciate that the sorcerer didn't assume his plan would lead back here.

I'm still kissing him when he sits down on the bed, keeping me perched in his lap. We've done this a thousand times before, and Memnon is usually stripping away my clothes by now and spreading my legs apart.

But not tonight.

Tonight he's reserved, which only seems to further draw out this wild, restless aspect of my magic. Ropes of my power reach out, mostly to caress Memnon in the darkness but also to knock shit about. As my magic moves around us, it also forms a few witch orbs, the pale orange light floating up near the ceiling.

Ever since Memnon forged the bond between us, he has seemed somewhat reluctant to be with me.

The sorcerer reaches out and tucks a stray strand of my hair. Judging by the way he looks at me, I can tell he heard that last thought.

"You believe that I've manipulated you into everything. And I have. For weeks, I have. I don't want you to believe that when I'm inside you, I've manipulated you into that as well. That's the one line I chose to never cross, even when I was angry and wrathful toward you. And I still refuse to cross it until you are sure of me. So for now, when it comes to sex, you'll have to lead."

Again I feel my earlier agitation, along with my growing desire. "I could command you to lead."

"You could. You would still be leading."

I disentangle myself, if only to put a little distance between us. I can't think when I'm so close to him.

I assumed this was a trap, one meant to lure me in. But

maybe it's not. Maybe the only trap is my own conflicting emotions.

I want Memnon. I have wanted him for a while. And I'm tired of fighting it, but I'm scared of setting aside my bitterness, of letting go of my animosity. I'm not entirely sure I'm ready for that.

As I back away from the bed, my eyes snag on a black duffel bag with an iron chain hanging partially out of it.

*Not a chain*, I realize.

Manacles.

I raise an eyebrow and look at Memnon. "What are those for?" I ask.

His mouth curves into a wicked smile from where he watches me on the edge of the bed. "Don't ask questions you don't want answers to, *est amage*."

"Have you been using them on people?" I ask, moving over to the bag and picking the manacles up.

Memnon rises from the mattress and moves to my side. "Would you like to chat about that right now, Empress? I can promise you the evening will go in a much different direction."

Memnon is standing far too close.

I don't know what possesses me, but I glance at his wrist, then clamp one of the cuffs over it. With a heavy click, it snaps into place.

Memnon raises an eyebrow. "Should I be worried?"

With a clink, I cuff his other wrist. Memnon doesn't even bother fighting me.

"You wanted me to lead. Don't regret it now." I get a perverse thrill out of seeing this man's wrists chained together.

Memnon glances down at his bound hands. "Then I am

your prisoner." When his eyes meet mine, there's so much goddess-damned intensity in them. Intensity...and *challenge*. As though he doesn't believe I'll do anything with the power I have over him.

I grab the chain and use it to drag his upper body downward.

Once he's close enough, I stand on my tippy-toes and brush a kiss along his lips.

I hear his deep, supremely satisfied exhale.

"You're slippery," I whisper against his mouth.

"Then you'd better keep your eyes on me," he says.

As soon as the kiss ends, I tug on the manacles and lead the sorcerer back to his bed.

Memnon follows, playing the part of obedient prisoner. I give him a careful look, one that he returns innocently enough. I don't buy it. Not for an instant. However, having this dangerous man cuffed before me and at my mercy emboldens me.

"Lie on the bed."

The sorcerer gives me a long look—one I can't quite meet—as he climbs onto the mattress. Between his searing stare and his bound hands, Memnon's movements should be clumsy. But he moves with the same feline grace Nero does.

His bed has a beautifully carved headboard depicting flowers and animals not so different from the Sarmatian art I was used to seeing when I lived with Memnon long ago. There are open spaces between each carved animal and flower, and it sparks an idea.

I slip away to Memnon's closet, the orbs of light trailing behind me. Inside it, I step up to his inset dresser and pull open several drawers until I find what I'm looking for. Nestled in neat rows are several rolled-up leather belts. I grab one of them and return to the bed, the soft light following after me.

Memnon waits for me, curiosity brimming in his eyes as he lounges back against his mattress. I don't think he knows what I'm about to do.

I move over to him and straddle his torso. He barely has time to react to my sudden presence when I grasp his manacles and force his arms to lift over his head. Pressing the chain against the headboard, I slide the belt through both the metal restraints and the holes in the wooden bedframe. With a little help from my magic, I buckle the leather strap.

"You're being awfully quiet while I work," I say, glancing down at him.

*I'd rather wait to see what you have in store for me before I start begging,* he whispers in my mind.

"Begging sounds nice."

Memnon stares at me for several beats until a slow smile spreads across his features.

"Please, don't hurt me. I have money." He rattles his chains a little for effect.

Is he being...playful?

I let out a disbelieving laugh. "*That* is your attempt at begging?" I laugh again. "You make a *terrible* captive."

"On the contrary, I think you'll find that I'm very agreeable. I'm eager to do your bidding."

I clasp Memnon's face in my hands, taking perverse pleasure in how his body stills beneath me. "I see what you're doing, trying to be disarming," I say.

"Is it working?"

My gaze drops to his lips, and after a moment, I lean in and take them.

The kiss is answer enough. The truth is, I have no

defenses against playful Memnon. I barely had defenses against him when he was an asshole.

I feel him smile against me.

In response, I nip his lower lip, and the sorcerer groans into my mouth. He leans forward and the chains rattle, presumably as he tries to reach for me. He lets out a frustrated noise, and it's my turn to smile midkiss.

I stretch my body out along his.

*I like you like this*, I say. *All trussed up.*

I move away from Memnon's mouth and pepper kisses down his throat. I'm soon stopped by the collar of his shirt.

I place a hand to the material and whisper a spell. "*With a slice and a tear, leave Memnon's torso bare.*"

The fabric beneath my hand parts from sleeve to neck and collar to hem until the shirt altogether falls away. The spell only partially rips apart Memnon's pants and whatever lies beneath, the material shifting under my thighs as it slips off him. I can feel the hard press of his cock trapped between us, and it makes my core clench. Yet the rest of his pant legs remains intact, my spell only extending as far as the bottom of his torso.

My eyes linger on Memnon's chest. His tattoos seem to jump out in the soft light. His dragon emblem, his hunting and battle conquests, even the marks that indicate he's a king. I run my fingers over these beloved tattoos, nostalgia and want rising in me.

Beneath me, I sense the sorcerer notice my mood shift—he's so fucking observant. So I duck my head and resume trailing kisses down Memnon's torso, pausing to nip at one of his rolling pecs.

He groans again, and it's so goddess-damned sexy.

The sheathed dagger he always has on him is now resting

in the tatters of his clothes. I pause in my ministrations to grab it and slide the blade out. It gleams in the light.

Even though I'm holding the weapon over him, Memnon doesn't so much as tense. He really is a terrible captive.

"Is this where you stab me and free yourself once and for all?" he says in Sarmatian. "Because," he continues slowly, his eyes smoldering, "I promise you, if you don't, I will work to tie you so fucking tight to me you won't eventually know where you end and I begin."

"So dramatic," I whisper. "Maybe I just want to play with your knife."

I swivel around, repositioning myself so my back is to him. Before Memnon can continue to wonder what I'm thinking, I bring the knife down, sawing the blade through what remains of his pants.

The material makes a satisfying ripping noise.

I lean over, cutting open one entire pant leg, then the other. While I work, tendrils of my magic reach for his boots of their own accord, unlacing them, then tugging them off along with his socks underneath.

Once I cut away the last of the material, my pulse quickens. He's completely naked, and I'm still fully dressed. The thought has barely crossed my mind when my power, again of its own accord, begins to undo the laces of my Doc Martens. It then continues up my legs, tendrils of the sunset-orange magic reaching for the buttons of my pants.

One of the first lessons witches learn about magic is that it is semi-sentient. We can control it, but it can just as easily control us. As I watch my power undo the top button of my own pants, a command I did *not* give it, I think that maybe tonight I'm seeing a little of that.

I swing myself off Memnon and leave the bed, as though moving might help me escape my own magic. It doesn't.

With my back to the sorcerer, I toss Memnon's dagger aside, the metal clattering against the floorboards as I'm helped out of my pants by my power. I've only just gripped the hem of my shirt when my power lifts it over my head, my hair cascading back to my shoulders. Already it's unclasping my bra, and it helps me wiggle out of my panties. There's nothing sexy or drawn out about any of this, yet even without looking, I can feel Memnon's gaze on me like a touch.

*Beautiful*, I hear his mind whisper.

I want to laugh. He's smooth and self-assured while I'm tripping through the motions, trying to stay one step ahead of my magic and act like I'm still in control when I no longer feel like it. Even tying him up and stripping him naked no longer eclipses this feeling welling up in me.

I'm nervous.

I may have memories of doing this in another life, I may have even drunkenly done this with the sorcerer in *this* one, but this time, there's no alcohol or *espiritus* to blunt my nerves.

"*Selene.*"

My shoulders tense at the sound of his voice, which is somehow tender and intimate and *knowing*. I don't know how it's knowing—unless he's been eavesdropping on this entire inner dialogue.

"Come here, little mate," Memnon says, his voice gruff. "I am tied up and yours to do with as you please."

I draw a deep breath and turn to Memnon. It takes so much to let him look his fill at my naked body. And he does. He looks and looks, swears under his breath, and looks some more.

Eventually, his gaze moves to my face, pausing on my cheeks, where I can feel the hot rush of blood staining my skin.

"You're embarrassed," he says, surprised. Never mind that he's lying naked and chained to the bed. "We've done this many times."

"It's not that," I say as one of my orbs of light dips in close before bobbing back up above us.

*What is it?* he says down our bond.

But the answer is right there.

Casual intimacy is fun and easy for me. *This* is something else. Not even the lightly kinky aspects of it can hide the fact that this entire night, I've been seeing Memnon differently. I've pursued him not as some drunken mistake but because I wanted to touch something real and deep.

And that's terrifying when it comes to the sorcerer. The moment Memnon's greedy, devouring eyes recognize I'm no longer keeping it casual, he will be all in, pressing his advantage. And like he said, he'll continue to tie himself closer and closer to me in every way that he can.

I should walk out of the room right now. There's a couch to sleep on, and there are other unexplored rooms to this house that likely have beds. We can still keep this relationship carefully contained.

The damnable truth of it is that I want my mate. I want him so badly my skin throbs from it and my magic is acting out to make it happen.

So I return to the bed, climbing on like nothing was ever amiss. Once more, I straddle Memnon, though I'm having trouble meeting his face. My eyes would much rather take in all the lines of his tattoos.

But I do force my gaze up. "I can do anything to you, *est xsaya*?" I ask. It's not really a question of whether I literally can. He's already given me that power over him. It's a question of whether he's okay with it.

"Anything," he agrees fervently. "I am yours."

He is right there, his face so close, his heart laid bare before me.

The look has me feeling shy and skittish all over again, and only my deep-seated desire to be close to him keeps me from backing down.

*You're in control*, I remind myself.

I move down his body and grasp his cock. He's already rock-hard, and I'm intimidated all over again by how large he is, which is silly. Leaning over it, I take the head of him into my mouth.

Memnon hisses, the chains rattling as he nearly rises off the bed.

"*Gods*, Selene."

I swirl my tongue over the head of him, pumping my fist up and down his shaft. The sorcerer's muscles have gone taut with tension, and when I take him deeper, those manacles clink together again.

"Fucking witchcraft, that mouth of yours…" he mutters, making me smile around him. He groans when he feels the action. "Only do that again, my queen, if you want me to come in your mouth. I have no resistance to those smiles."

Much as I'd enjoy bringing him to release this way, I'm not ready to be done with him yet. So I let my grin fall away, and I work him until his hips are bucking and he's whispering praises in Sarmatian, his head flung back against the pillow.

Only then, once I've gotten my fill of him, do I move, releasing his shaft so that I can straddle his hips. I rise up on my knees and position his cock at my opening. The head of it skims between my folds.

Memnon groans as his eyes fix on that point of contact. His gaze rises to mine, and my earlier insecurities are gone.

*This* is right. Finally, it's right.

Slowly, I sink down on him. The headboard creaks as Memnon strains to stay still, letting me control the pace.

"Intoxicating witch," he breathes, "you're a vision."

As is he, bound beneath me, though I don't say this. I'm too busy enjoying the sensation of my core stretching around him.

"Gods, yes, my queen," he says, reverting to Sarmatian. "You take me so well."

I feel myself tighten around him, and he hisses out a breath, his hips reflexively jerking up against mine. I moan as he buries the last of himself in me, and I'm unprepared for the overwhelming feeling of having him fully seated in me.

I lean forward, breathing through the sharp, tight sensation.

Memnon gazes down the line of his body at me. "Are you all right?" he says, concern wrinkling his brow.

*Your massive dick almost killed me, but I'm fine.*

I don't mean to actually pass that thought along, but then I see his features relax a little. The corners of Memnon's mouth quirk. *Wait for your orgasm. If it doesn't deliver you to the gods for a moment or two, then I'll have to do it over again.*

The painful tightness dissolves away as my body adjusts

to him, and I grind against Memnon a little, testing out whether I'm good.

His manacles clink again, and I see his arms strain against the bonds as he throws his head back for a moment, exhaling a ragged breath. "This is the sweetest torment, little witch."

The sight of him truly at my mercy now emboldens me. I place a hand on his chest and lift myself off his cock until only the tip remains in me. Then I sink back down.

Again the chains rattle and Memnon's muscles strain. I *like* that reaction.

I do it again and again and again.

Memnon groans. "My lovely, wicked mate. I was wrong earlier. This is *simply* torment."

"Good," I say. "You deserve to be tormented." I find a rhythm and stick to it. The sorcerer's hips move in time with mine, meeting me thrust for thrust until I'm gasping and moaning.

I look at the sorcerer's face, and my heart feels like it's caving in, and my lungs can't quite draw in enough air.

I cup the side of his face. *Beloved.* I remember when he was beloved by me. I can feel the emotion right there, waiting to sweep back in.

He doesn't have to be my enemy. He doesn't have to even be just my friend. We could have what we once did.

I lean forward and kiss Memnon again, my hand moving from his cheek. I'm torn. So torn. I want to let go. I'm scared to do so. I'm not sure I'll have a choice soon.

The manacles clang and the headboard knocks against the wall, and then I feel Memnon's arms wrap around me even as he continues to kiss me.

I flick my eyes to the headboard, where the now empty manacles hang limply against Memnon's belt.

"I'm sorry, *est amage*," he breathes, breaking off the kiss. "I wanted to be a good captive, I did. But after two thousand years apart, I have grown greedy."

With that, he flips us so I'm beneath him, and now he's setting the pace, his cock driving into me harder and harder, the action making slick, wet sounds.

I gasp out a breath, not just because the change in tempo is rapidly driving me toward an orgasm. Pinned beneath him like this, I'm not in control. Not unless I command him, and my heart's not interested in that.

Instead, I stare up at him, feeling lighter than air, afraid I might fall. Terrified he'll notice and make it happen.

So I force my eyes away and rake my nails up his back, focusing my attention on where the two of us are joined.

"Love your pussy most when it's stretched around me like this," he says. "I can feel it fluttering."

Memnon grinds himself against me, swiveling his hips in a figure eight motion.

I gasp at the sensation, nearly going boneless.

When I meet his eyes, he flashes me a wicked look. "There are perks to my knowing your body as well as I do."

*You can let go*, a small voice inside me says. *He will catch you.*

*Don't fall,* another voice cautions. *Once you do, there will be no going back.*

*Let go.*

*Hold on.*

*Fall.*

*Don't.*

I grasp Memnon's ass, my nails digging in as I brace myself, each thrust throwing me closer and closer to the edge.

"Tell me to stop and I will stop," he says, unaware of my thoughts. "Bound or not, I'm still your captive." He means it too. I see that.

But I can't tell him to stop. Not when each stroke feels like a slice of heaven.

So instead, I stare at him as I climb and climb and—

My nails dig in. "*Memnon*."

That's all I manage to get out before my orgasm *shatters* through me. Memnon watches me as I come, his strokes relentless, his eyes greedily drinking in my expression.

I stare into those smoky amber eyes, locked in whatever spell he's cast. Or maybe this is the magic of our bond—the one fate made for us.

*Fall. Don't. Fall.*

Memnon comes then, his body crashing against mine again and again and again.

His orgasm seems endless, and his expression is the definition of bliss. His eyes never leave mine, even after his climax has rolled through him.

My heart thunders.

Will either of us know when the bond between us is broken? Will we sense it? I want to give him a command, just to check. But then he'll know I'm checking the bond, and he'll quickly put together just how close I am to falling for him. I don't want him to know. I still have my sliver of control, and I want to wield it until it disintegrates away.

Memnon slows, studying me as he pulls out, a slight frown marring his lips, as though he senses the undercurrents of my thoughts. But then the expression is wiped free from his face, and I have no idea whether I imagined it all.

Before I get the chance to flee, the sorcerer gathers me to him, and…it's nice. Really nice.

Maybe I'll just lie here for a little while…

*The shackles were fun, Empress.*

They were.

*Too bad they didn't hold you,* I say. *Where am I going to sleep tonight?* I don't know why I ask. He's already given me this bed, this room. But now he's in it, and our bodies are cooling, and this situation feels hasty.

*Right here, in my arms.*

There's no hesitation to his words, just a shit ton of kingly authority. It's pretty ballsy, considering I'm the one with the commands. At least I think I can still command him.

But his arms feel nice. No, *better* than nice—they feel like home, even if I'm loath to admit it.

*How long are you planning on holding me?* I ask.

*As long as I can get away with.*

Warmth suffuses me. Damn this man.

For several minutes, the two of us lie there, Memnon playing with my hair and me tracing his tattoos. I nearly put myself in a trance, following those flowing, curving lines.

"What's the strangest thing about the modern world?" I ask him.

"There are many strange things about this world," he says smoothly, as though the question isn't completely out of the blue. "Cars, computers, phones, television. There is such precision to even common things, and there are so many choices—gods, the choices. There's also the ease of existence. Things that once took hours you can now buy instantly and cheaply."

"Is any of it off-putting?" I ask.

"It is *all* off-putting."

"You wouldn't know it," I say softly. This is a man who electronically deposited money into my account, who drove me in his car, then his motorcycle, and who is holding down a job, even if it is for the supernatural mafia. A man who has some grasp on modern fashion, and who now speaks English flawlessly.

"I have spent whole weeks mining people's minds for information on this modern world so that I might not fall prey to it," he confesses.

I try not to think of what that must've looked like and how many people's heads he must've pried into.

"Do you regret being here, in the modern world?"

"If you had asked me before I saw your memories, I would've said *yes*," Memnon answers. "Now, however, I know truly what you did. You, Roxilana, bought us a future when there was none, and you paid for it with your life. We no longer have armies or palaces, but we exist, little witch. You go by a different name and speak a different tongue and wear different clothes, but you are still my soul mate and my queen."

*And you are still my king.* I almost say it, but I bite back the sentiment.

"I do have a family," I say instead.

That was one of my deepest agonies in my past life— losing them. And it is something I took for granted up until my memories returned to me.

Memnon's face lights with interest. "Your family," he says, as though it's only now clicking. "They were in your photo albums." Despite seeing their pictures, it seems as though he's only now putting together what that actually means to me. "I haven't met them," he says, and there's true regret in his voice.

I nearly laugh. Of course he hasn't met him.

"You've been too busy making yourself my enemy to get the chance to meet your future in-laws."

I realize my mistake immediately.

Unfortunately, so does Memnon.

"My future in-laws?" His voice is dripping with delight.

I cannot even *explain* the slip of the tongue.

"I can," Memnon says, listening in to my thoughts. "You rode me better than I ride horses. Of course you want more."

*Goddess above.* I cover his mouth. "You are never to speak another lewd comment that involves me and horses."

"Forever?" he asks solemnly, his response muffled by my hand.

"Forever and ever and ever," I say, feeling a perplexing combination of relief and disappointment that the command seems to take.

"Aw, damn, soul mate," he says, dragging my hand away. "Now you've just given me a challenge too good to pass up."

He moves down my body.

"What is the challenge? And what are you doing?"

The sorcerer keeps lowering himself, the tips of his hair brushing against my skin. It's not until he's settled himself between my thighs and spread them apart that I become aware of what he intends to do.

"It's dirty down there!" I say, attempting to close my legs.

He easily catches them and moves them one by one over his shoulders.

"Take the order back, and I won't horrify your delicate senses."

"I take it back! You can say lewd things all you want."

"Thank you, mate."

And then he leans in and kisses my pussy anyway.

I'm about to screech like an owl when he pulls away,

laughing. "All right, fine, keep me away from your pussy."
He rests his head on my pubic bone. "But I do want to meet
my future wife's parents."

I groan and cover my eyes with my hand. "Please never
again bring my parents up when you're about to eat me out."

Down our bond, I can feel his pleasure, and I'm pretty
sure it's because I didn't fight him on the issue of marriage.

*He knows you're crumbling.*

"Does this mean I get to feast on you after all?" he says.

"Memnon," I groan.

"Never mind." He moves up my body, draping himself
over me. "When do I get to meet them?" he asks, brushing
my hair away from my face.

I'm too distracted by the new yet familiar feel of his
weight on me to answer. Despite our size difference, we fit
together like puzzle pieces.

He brushes a finger over my lower lip, then leans in and
kisses me. "When?" he presses.

My parents. Right. "They're away at the moment,
playing tourist around Europe, but once they return home,
maybe..." I trail off, unsure of exactly what I want to
say—unsure of exactly what I want.

"*Yes,*" Memnon says, and I hear the eagerness in his
response. "I would like that."

Warmth blossoms at his response. I feel incandescent
with it.

The sorcerer shifts against me, and I feel his hardening
length brush against my leg.

*Where in the Goddess's name do you get this stamina?*

*Magic and two millennia of yearning,* he says.

He begins kissing my upper arm and shoulder, his hand

moving to cup my sex. "Now open those thighs, my pretty mate. We have a long night ahead of us."

———————

He doesn't give me much peace.

If his cock isn't in me, then it's his mouth or his fingers, and none of my earlier squeamishness does much to change that. The only breaks are when he uses his magic to float our dinner into the room and feed it to me or the brief spurts of sleep we have between rounds.

When we had sex on Samhain, I assumed our fervor was driven by the witch's brew. But there's a feverishness in us both that drives us to come together again and again throughout the night.

At some point before dawn, I feel Memnon's fingers trail over my cheek, and then the soft brush of his lips.

"My heart is filled to bursting," he murmurs.

I reach for him, though I am tired and sore. Rather than letting me reel him in, he takes my hand and kisses my knuckles.

"I have to go, but I will be back as soon as possible. Be well and sleep deeply, my queen."

His hand slides from mine, and then he's gone.

I wake some time later, the sun low in the sky. There's a warm body pressed against my back.

Immediately, my heart begins to hammer, and I flip over, excited and nervous to see Memnon. But it's not Memnon taking up space on the bed. It's Nero.

The moment I shift, my massive familiar leans his head back toward me, silently asking for attention.

I rub under his chin. "Look at you," I say fondly. "Sneaking onto the bed at the first opportunity."

The big cat looks mighty pleased with himself.

I pet him a little longer, then attack his face with kisses until, affronted by the gross display of affection, my panther rolls away.

Oh, to be a cat.

I slip out of Memnon's bed, my body satisfyingly sore. I'm also stark naked, I smell like sex and sweat, and I need another birth-control potion.

Fuck, if I'm doing this regularly, I'll need to stockpile the stuff or else get a human prescription.

I shower, then change. Memnon still hasn't returned by the time I'm fully dressed, and I have thirty minutes until my first class of the day begins.

I'm not missing it.

I'm about to call a car when I wander into the foyer and my eyes land on a side table. A set of car keys rests there.

*What do you want?* Memnon had asked me last night.

Well, sir, today I want the car.

# CHAPTER 29

*When Nero and I arrive on Henbane campus, we're greeted* with the sound of anguished howls.

Stepping away from Memnon's car, I stare out across the grassy lawn, toward the tree line behind Morgana Hall and Cauldron Hall. Nero comes to my side, his ears perked.

Something is obviously happening.

The baleful howls continue as I head to Cauldron Hall, its stone façade looking particularly ominous against the overcast sky. My skin prickles. I haven't checked on the wolves since Nero was attacked. Perhaps I should've.

A witch with warm brown skin and curly black hair passes me, and I stop her.

"Do you know what's going on?" I ask, nodding toward the tree line beyond the campus buildings.

The witch pauses, her hooded brown eyes flittering over me and Nero.

"You haven't heard?" she asks. "A lycanthrope has been killed."

Immediately, I call Kane. The phone rings and rings, but he doesn't answer. I try again, and then a third time.

Nothing.

Fuck.

Of course Kane's not answering. He's out in the woods with the rest of his pack, mourning the shifter they lost.

I call once more and leave a hasty message, and then reluctantly, I head into Wards.

I sit there among my peers, listen to the lecture, and I diligently take notes, but the excitement that normally suffuses this class is lost on me. It feels pointless, so goddess-damned pointless to be here, when all around us supernaturals are being preyed on.

Perhaps this latest death is unrelated to the murders. Perhaps the dead shifter got gored by a deer or shot by some trigger-happy human who wandered onto the wrong patch of wilderness. Perhaps it was a mere accident or a more mundane misfortune.

I don't know for sure until shortly after class lets out.

My phone buzzes in my pocket as I head down the stone steps of Cauldron Hall. I snatch it up before the second ring.

"Hello?" I answer, ducking as someone's bat familiar zips past my head.

"Selene?" Kane says. His voice is unnaturally low and gravelly. In the background, the grief-filled howls are amplified, the noise punctuated by whimpers and sobs.

"I heard the news. I'm so sorry, Kane," I say.

The other end of the line is quiet, and part of me is sure Kane's shifted and I'm now speaking to a wolf.

"Miranda was ripped apart," he finally says, "just like the witches on your side of the woods." It's silent for another long moment, then he adds, "Her body carried the stink of something unnatural..." Kane's voice disintegrates into a growl.

I take that in, wondering how much time I have to talk with the lycanthrope before he gives in to his shift.

"I'm sorry," I say again, though the sentiment rings hollow. What is an apology in the face of a life cut horrifyingly short? "Do you or your pack mates need anything?" I ask. I don't know that I have anything of substance to offer, but the rest of my peers and I have dealt with these deaths several times already.

The other end of the line is quiet again.

"The last time we spoke in person, you admitted that Memnon moves the bodies," Kane eventually says.

My stomach drops.

"My pack would like to meet with him so that he might answer for this."

———

After the call ends, I sit down on a random patch of grass in front of Henbane's main buildings, Nero flopping down beside me.

I idly coax a small daisy to grow from the soil. As its stalk rises and a flower unfurls, I sit with my thoughts. Worry, doubt, and dread all knot together.

*Memnon?*

I feel the brush of Memnon's pleasure, though beneath it, I sense...strain.

Est amage...*your voice is sweeter than wine after conquest.* Despite his words, his voice sounds tight, thready.

A light, fluttery feeling blossoms in my stomach. It has no business being there, given the current circumstances.

*Did you move another body?*

*They found the shifter already? Perhaps…* Again, his voice sounds strained.

I frown, and the daisy beneath my palm wilts a little.

*Are you okay?* I ask.

*Is my fiancée worried about my well-being?* he teases.

I look skyward even as I suppress a smile. *Forget I asked.*

*Never. I'm collecting your slipups.*

Maiden, Mother, and Crone.

*Please don't.* I don't even bother trying to deny that they are in fact slipups.

I feel the brush of his mirth, though there's still that nagging sensation beneath it.

*You're really okay?* I ask.

Again I feel his pleasure. *Sweet mate, I'm fine. Were you reaching out just to ask about the body?*

The one he all but confirmed he moved.

*The shifters want to speak with you about their dead pack mate,* I say. *And…I told them you would.*

Memnon groans.

I draw in a deep breath. *We're meeting Kane and his pack at five o'clock tonight to discuss it.*

The moment I mention Kane, there's a shift in Memnon's energy.

*I'll pick you up at four thirty in front of your house. I can't wait to fuck with the wolves.*

*Memnon.*

*I'm kidding, Empress. I'll only fuck with Kane.*

Tonight's going to be a long night.

# CHAPTER 30

*I've just sent my mom her daily text and started reading up* about contraceptive spells on the steps of the residence hall when Memnon tears through the front gates of Henbane on his motorcycle. Once again he's not wearing a helmet, and my worry rises.

Ugh, I'm worried about him. I have it bad. And that's saying nothing about that annoying, happy warmth pooling in my belly at the sight of him.

I tuck my phone away, sparing a glance at Nero, who is busy trying—and failing—to catch a butterfly with his teeth. My familiar has forgotten for a moment that he's supposed to be a proud, majestic creature.

Memnon pulls into a parking spot near where I parked his car and cuts the engine, grimacing as he swings himself off his seat. As soon as he sees me, his previous expression is wiped clean, and his gaze deepens. I get the distinct impression he's vividly remembering our night together.

Or maybe that's just me.

Memnon comes over to me then, his shoulders set a little rigidly, his stride a little stiff. A spark of unease moves through me, even as he takes me by the chin and presses an ardent kiss to my lips.

I guess we're greeting by way of kissing now.

More warmth pools in my belly. Ugh, but I like that too.

My arms go around him to pull him closer to me when I feel wetness at his back. His shirt is drenched.

"Is this…" I'm about to say *sweat* when the sorcerer sags a little in my arms.

Seven hells.

"*Memnon?*" I say, alarmed.

He locks his knees, straightening back up. "I'm fine. Just a little dizzy."

I move my hand away from his back, sucking in a breath when I see the blood smeared all over it.

"You're hurt." I mean for it to be accusing, but my tone comes out soft and concerned. Fuck, I *am* concerned.

"It is nothing to worry about," Memnon says as he winces.

"I'll decide that for myself," I say, trying to think over the pounding of my heart. "Why didn't you heal yourself?"

He sways, the movement so subtle I might not have noticed it if he were someone less familiar to me.

"I was ordered not to," he admits.

So this was some punishment he was supposed to bear out.

My brows draw together. "But you only answer to me," I say, not following.

He nods in agreement, and now I'm *really* not following.

"Couldn't you have healed yourself?" I ask slowly. "Or at least taken away your own pain?"

319

"I am a Sarmatian king, born of a warrior queen, raised from birth to fight—"

"Okay, okay, I get it. Sorry I asked." Memnon is apparently only practical when it comes to my injuries.

I press a hand lightly to his back and incant in Sarmatian, "*Banish the pain to the far corners of the world.*"

Thick plumes of my magic spread out beneath my palm, moving across the expanse of his back before sinking in.

Memnon gives me an arch look, like he disapproves of what I'm doing.

"Arguing is useless. I'm not going to let you walk around in pain just because you can bear it."

Memnon's bourbon eyes flicker, then soften. He's a hard man, and I know from memory that he hates being fussed over. I also know nothing leveled him like when I took care of him in the past.

Even now, I can feel a whisper of adoration down our bond.

I look him over again. "I'm not leaving you like this." I maneuver myself so that I'm wedged under his arm.

"Selene—"

"Arguing really is useless," I remind him. "If you resist, I'll simply command you to follow me."

He huffs but lets me gingerly wrap my arm around his back. With a little help from my magic, I lead Memnon toward my house. Nero reluctantly leaves the butterfly, trailing after us.

Once we're at the front door, the Medusa door knocker comes to life.

"Memnon the Indomitable, king of nomads, smiter of armies, what business do you have here?"

The knocker's never done this before. Someone must

have refreshed the house's wards. Sure enough, when I focus on the air above the threshold, I make out the glinting edges of the ward's magical, silver writing.

"He's with me." I grab the handle and shove the door open.

I force the sorcerer through the ward, the spell resisting him for only a moment before it lets him pass. I hold the door open long enough for my shadowy familiar to slip in as well.

The foyer smells like someone's opened a portal to hell, the smell of sulfur thick in the air.

"Sorry! Sorry!" a witch in the spell kitchen shouts. "I fucked up!"

"Dude, were you trying to summon an imp?" says another witch in the kitchen.

Their conversation drifts away as I drag Memnon to the library on my right. Despite the chatter in the rest of the house, no one is in here at the moment, affording us a sliver of privacy.

The wall sconces buzz and the light flickers precariously as I lead Memnon deep into the room so that we're hidden by aisles of books. I stop us at a scarlet couch.

"Sit," I command, "and lean forward."

*My beloved queen,* Memnon protests, even as he does what I say, *this is not necessary.*

"I disagree," I reply as I follow him down to the couch. My heart has been beating a mile a minute since I discovered his injury. I don't think I'll be capable of relaxing until I'm sure he is okay.

Nero sits down next to Memnon's legs, leaning against them for support. I see my sorcerer place a hand on the panther's head, and a lump forms in my throat. Nero genuinely cares for Memnon, and Memnon genuinely cares for him.

I force my gaze to return to my mate's back. My teeth scour my lower lip as I stare at his drenched black shirt. It's so wet it clings to his back. *That's all blood.*

I reach for the hem of it, then hesitate.

I'm…afraid.

"You don't have to do this," Memnon says over his shoulder.

"No one is compelling me to do anything," I say brusquely. "I…want to help."

I feel a burst of—of *love* from Memnon's side of the bond. I don't let myself linger on it, though I badly want to.

Instead, I draw in a fortifying breath, then grab the hem of his shirt. I peel it slowly away from his skin, hissing in a breath at the sight before me.

Crisscrossing his back are strips of open wounds, the skin split and jagged. There are over a dozen of them, each one oozing blood and a black, oily substance.

Seven hells. The wounds are cursed.

"How long ago did this happen?" I ask, trying to understand the extent of the damage.

Already my magic pours out of me, thick clouds of it settling over his injuries. The frayed edges of his skin reach for each other, but the dark magic forces them apart just as quickly.

"Hours," Memnon says.

"You were commanded not to heal yourself?" I ask, my mind racing to remember the curse-breaking spell Memnon used on me.

He nods reluctantly.

So Patrick, the mage he was supposedly bonded

to, must've ordered the punishment. But it was an order Memnon didn't need to follow. The forced bond between him and the mage is entirely fabricated; Memnon has never been under its sway.

I set my remaining questions aside for the moment.

I glance around at the shelves and shelves of books. Any one of them might have instructions on curse breaking. And if I enter the little room at the back of the library, I'll have access to many, many grimoires that might have the spell I need.

It feels like a waste of time trying to chase the right spell down when the sorcerer here already knows one.

"I need help breaking the curse on my own," I say softly. "Will you remind me of the incantation you used?" It feels funny to ask for his help when he refused to heal himself.

But he answers readily enough. *"Tirub xeqeqoyaq yaqub evritiwuwa yasnnichis, puqamubyaqpi chiqmachibmi."*

I extend my hand over his back, gathering my magic. The buzzing from the sconces grows louder, and the lights flicker more intensely as I recite the curse-breaking spell.

My magic spreads across his back once more, but this time, it doesn't bother healing the wounds at all. Instead, an alarming amount of the black, tarry substance coating his wounds now oozes from them. The moment it's expelled from his body, it begins to bubble and hiss away, dissolving into an oily smoke that dissipates into the air.

"What do the words of the spell mean?" I ask softly as my magic works.

*"Begone poisoned death that corrupts my spirit. With love I destroy you."*

I muse on that as the last of the dark magic burns away.

Once I'm sure the spell is finished, I lick my dry lips, inspecting the wounds. They look clean.

"I think it worked," I say softly.

"I had no doubt," Memnon says, still leaning forward and idly petting Nero's head. My panther closes his eyes, reveling in the touch.

"I'm going to finish healing you," I say, letting my magic spill from me. This doesn't take an incantation. My power wants to heal him, the soft plumes of it rolling over his back and sinking into his flesh. It begins stitching muscle and skin together, his torn tattoos beginning to reform.

My gaze crawls up his back to what I can see of his profile and his wavy, blood-speckled hair.

I cannot seem to help myself—I reach out and run my fingers through that black hair. Belatedly, I realize this is a caress. I'm caressing this man.

My heart stumbles over itself as Memnon leans into the touch, and I have a moment of déjà vu—we have done this many times before. This is muscle memory as much as anything else, and for some reason, that makes my heart ache all the more.

I withdraw my hand and refocus my attention on his wounds.

*How did this happen?* I ask down our bond. I don't dare voice the question out loud while I can still hear my coven sisters in the distance. I can't forget that here in this house, I'm at least partially among enemies.

*Shortly after the murdered shifter was found today, the mage I worked for, Patrick, and his employees were called in before Luca Fortuna. We were all punished for negligence and sloppy work, and Patrick was...disposed of.*

So this was retaliation for the bodies in the woods, bodies that Patrick ordered Memnon to move.

From everything Memnon's told me, it seems blatantly clear that he's the one staging these victims. It doesn't seem like it would've been hard for Patrick to prove Memnon's guilt. But the mage didn't do that. Instead he died, and Memnon was punished alongside his colleagues as though no one knew who the culprit was.

This is a dangerous sort of game Memnon is playing. He's clearly manipulating many minds to hide what he's doing. But this is a multimillion-dollar criminal organization he's messing with. Luck and strategy can only last so long.

*Why did you move the body?* I ask. It made sense before, when he was framing me. It doesn't make sense now.

*We're working to bring down the murderers,* Memnon reminds me. *The killers aren't just people. They're a kingdom. A seemingly untouchable one. They're not so different from Rome, really. The first step in defeating such a kingdom is undermining their power.*

*You don't have to put yourself at risk for this—for me. I don't want that.*

*Make no mistake, Empress. I enjoy doing this. I feel like the king I once was.*

Spoken to me while his back is a mass of injuries and he's faint from blood loss.

But Memnon could've healed himself or else altered minds to prevent his punishment in the first place. He didn't. I need to remember that.

*If Patrick is dead, then why would you still pretend to follow his command?* I ask as my eyes linger on his healing injuries. Most of them have closed, the new skin pink.

*Juliana Fortuna commanded it. I was forced to bond to her, along with the rest of Patrick's former bonds.*

I go still. From what Memnon previously told me, Juliana is a daughter of Luca Fortuna, the head of Ensanguine Enterprises, a.k.a. the Fortuna crime ring. If this binding was as public as it sounds, then—

*Is the bond—*

*Real?* Memnon finishes. *Gods, it nearly was, but no. I managed to avoid it. Barely. But Juliana and everyone else there believes it is.*

I exhale, my body going slack with my relief.

*I'll meet with her tomorrow,* Memnon continues. *I still haven't been able to get close enough to either her or Luca to physically see into their minds, but now that I'm under Juliana's control, I'll have more opportunities. Once I'm able to peer at their thoughts, I'll understand why the murders are happening—and I can then perhaps alter their minds and stop them.*

Or he'll kill them, but he doesn't say that.

Suddenly, I feel weary. So weary. I should be thrilled. Finally, the pieces are falling into place, and Memnon has all but admitted he might actually be able to stop the murders.

But when I asked for his help, I was fueled by anger and resentment and my own sort of revenge. Now, I can feel two thousand years of fear creeping up my spine.

*Memnon, the last time you took on an empire like this, it ended badly for us.*

He turns on the couch to look at me fully, and his hand goes to my cheek. *This isn't Rome. It will be different.*

I search his eyes. There's a feeling knotted in my chest, an echo of the pain I felt the night I discovered him in that sarcophagus, hopelessly out of reach.

*I can't lose you again.* I'm horrified when I realize I've pushed the words down our bond.

Memnon's eyes go soft, too soft, and if I were standing, my knees would weaken at the sight.

*My queen, since I woke, I have desperately dreamed you might say such a thing. That you might feel a shadow of what I feel for you. But you do not need to worry,* he continues. *I'd sooner burn every last remnant of the Fortuna dynasty than let something come between us. You won't lose me, I swear it to you.*

That's not truly something he can promise me, but I tuck the vow away anyway.

I glance at his back. The last of his lashes are nothing more than faded lines. Even those are slowly darkening to match the rest of his bronze-toned skin. I release a little more of my power, this time to lift the blood from Memnon's shirt, his skin, and his hair, and then my own. The red liquid vanishes in seconds, and it appears as though he weren't hurt to begin with.

I tug the hem of his shirt down, covering his back. "You're going to have to make up an excuse to your shitty new boss about why your back is healed—or you can just snap her neck as you do most people who annoy you."

Memnon gives me an amused smirk, his eyes twinkling. "Is my soul mate growing vicious? I do approve."

Before I get a chance to respond, Memnon stands, pulling me to my feet. He cups my face.

His eyes glitter. "*Thank you*, Empress," he says.

I take a deep breath and nod. "Of course."

His expression turns amused. "Now let's go meet these wolves."

# CHAPTER 31

**When Memnon and I drive up to the cabin on shifter terri-**
tory, the place is unsettlingly quiet. There are cars parked
outside it, but there's not a soul around, nor do I hear the
bereaved howls that cut through the air earlier.

Memnon and I get out of the car, shutting the doors
behind us.

"You sure there's a meeting tonight?" Memnon asks.

No sooner has he spoken than the cabin's front door
opens, and Kane comes out. I catch a glimpse of the room
inside, and I notice the solemn, silent crowd.

It might be quiet here, but there's a crowd inside.

Kane's eyes are red-rimmed as he closes the door and
approaches us. "I didn't think you were coming," he says.

We're more than twenty minutes late.

"I had to drop Nero off somewhere safe," I say, forcing
myself not to think too hard about my familiar, who's likely
stalking some cute, fluffy forest creature in the woods behind
Memnon's place.

*He's safe*, the sorcerer reassures me.

"How is he doing?" Kane asks.

Plumes of Memnon's magic unfurl out of him then, a clear sign his agitation is rising.

"He's okay," I say softly.

"I'm sorry we didn't come," Kane says. "Our alpha forbade us from crossing—"

"*Kane*," Memnon cuts in.

Just the tone of the sorcerer's voice has the lycan tensing. I can hear low rumbling from Kane, like he chafes at the power in Memnon's voice.

"Enough," my mate says. "Your apology is an insult. This whole meeting is an insult."

Hell's spells, here we go.

A menacing growl rumbles deep in Kane's chest. "How dare you—"

Memnon steps in close, his eyes beginning to glow. "Yes, I dare. You and your pack left my mate to be attacked. They were outnumbered, and when I found them bloody and brutalized in the woods, they were alone. Why were they alone?"

Kane's growl has deepened, and his eyes have shifted. "We cannot cross—"

"You failed her. All of you failed her. And now you have the audacity to use your useless friendship with her to call me in—"

"Is everything all right out here?" Vincent, the Marin Pack alpha, stands on the front porch. Despite his easy words, his body looks tense and his translucent magic is thick in the air around him.

Memnon's cruel gaze flicks up to the lycan. My mate looks ready to unleash on him as well.

"Everything is fine," I call out while Kane's growl dies down a little. "We were just getting ready to come in."

*Please, Memnon,* I say down our bond, *can we get through this without you resorting to violence?*

The sorcerer glances at me, and his glowing eyes dim and soften, until all that anger is banked. *If that's what you wish, est amage, then yes, I will try to control my visceral need to punish each one of these dogs.*

"All right," Vincent calls out. "We're all ready in here." With that, the shifter re-enters the cabin, leaving me, Kane, and Memnon alone once more.

My mate nods to the cabin. "This meeting cannot involve everyone," he says to Kane.

"This is how our pack does things." Kane's growl continues to rattle between his words, and his voice is low and rough. "We are all entitled to know about what killed our pack mate." There's so much fire and anguish rolling off him.

Memnon slips his hands into his pockets, and to the unknowing eye, he is all poised confidence. But his body sways just a little, and I remember that he lost a lot of blood by the time he got to me. "I don't care about what you think you're entitled to or how your pack handles its shit. If you want me to go in there and explain how it is I came across your pack mate's body, then you're going to need to limit your fucking audience."

Kane's growl deepens, and his lips curl back, revealing partially shifted teeth.

*Oh, for fuck's sake.*

"Kane, I won't make Memnon go in there and explain the situation unless you can do this for us," I say, trusting Memnon's reasons for this demand. I imagine this has something to do with limiting the number of people who know what we do.

Kane takes several deep breaths, and slowly, the growling quiets and his teeth grow blunt. "Fine," the shifter bites out, "but no one's going to like it."

———————

Uproar.

That's what we're met with when the shifters pour out of the cabin ten minutes later and Kane escorts us in.

The group of lycanthropes is no longer quiet, now that whatever they believed was going to happen no longer is. I hear sobs and growls among them as we pass into the building. Some of the ones who so openly welcomed me last time are now glaring at me.

They want blood. I can all but sense their lust for it. They thought they were going to get it tonight, either from what Memnon might reveal or from Memnon himself.

"Everyone," Vincent, the Marin Pack alpha, calls from the back of the room to those who still remain inside, "you will get answers. Be calm. Once we have heard what our friend and her mate have to say, we shall share what news we can. They have indicated that their information is sensitive in nature and that, for the overall good of the pack, it must only be given to a few trusted ears."

Kane leads us to his alpha.

When he intercepts us, Vincent nods to me, then Memnon, his expression grim. "Vincent," he says, extending his hand, "alpha of the Marin Pack."

My mate takes it and gives it a shake. "Memnon," he says, leaving it at that. The sorcerer has sheathed his earlier anger, but I can still see it glinting in his eyes.

"Nice to meet you," Vincent says, even as a few nearby wolves growl. "We don't need to wait for the last of the pack to exit. We have a sufficiently secluded room. This way."

Memnon and I are brought to a soundproof room, one that's small and clearly meant for only a dozen or so people to fit inside. I see a transparent green ward glittering across the threshold, though I cannot tell what it's for.

Memnon's magic unfurls as he enters the room, his indigo power moving over the walls and floor of the space. After a moment, I realize he's erecting his own ward, this one likely to protect his interests, whatever those may be.

A single long table runs the length of the room, and mounted on one of the walls is a whiteboard.

"Please, take a seat anywhere," Vincent says.

Memnon sits at the far end of the table, lounging in one of the proffered seats like an indolent king. I take a seat next to him and watch as the rest file in.

First is Vincent, followed by a willowy woman with golden-brown skin and a halo of tight corkscrew curls framing her face. I sense that she's quick to laugh, but right now her features are hard, and her glimmering brown eyes are sharp. Behind her is Kane, who comes to sit directly on my other side, his sandy-blond hair mussed, probably from running his hand through it so many times.

Last to enter is an old woman with light-brown skin, wide cheekbones, and a waterfall of wrinkles across her face. Her thick white hair is wrapped in a braided bun at the nape of her neck.

She closes the door, and she and the remaining shifters take their seats across from me.

"I trust you both already know Kane, the alpha who will take over for me once I retire," Vincent says, gesturing to my old crush. "But as for the others, next to me is Irene, my beta and the second in command," he says, indicating the willowy woman next to him. "And this is Apani," he says, gesturing to the white-haired shifter, "our pack elder. They are here as they are the most crucial members who help run the pack and guide the decisions we make."

I nod to them. "Nice to meet you," I say.

Memnon does nothing more than idly watch the shifters, like they're tonight's entertainment, and they're boring him.

I can feel the tension in the room mounting.

"Memnon," Vincent says, and I can already tell he's choosing his words carefully, "your mate is a friend of our pack, and naturally, that friendship should extend to you—"

There's a *but* coming. I can feel it.

Memnon watches the alpha, looking amused, like he knows he's the villain and is remorseless about it.

"—but you framed your mate for murder, and you are responsible for moving the bodies of murdered supernaturals." The alpha's words grow hoarse and gravelly as his composure slips.

Memnon nods. "Yes," he agrees. "I did, and I am."

I see Irene's hand fist, and next to me, Kane radiates tension. Only Apani, the pack elder, remains placid.

"We want you to explain yourself," Vincent says.

Memnon leans back in his seat. "Perhaps I will, after you explain why you left my mate to fight off half a dozen attackers on her own, right after she met with you."

I'm caught between annoyance and a strange sort of pride that Memnon is so adamant about holding these shifters accountable for not coming to my aid. Vincent rolls his shoulders as Irene and Kane begin to growl. "We are forbidden from entering coven lands—"

"And would you have entered them if it were a shifter being attacked?" Memnon presses.

Vincent's expression grows grim.

*Yes.* We all know his answer is *yes*. I wasn't worth breaking whatever delicate truce witches and lycans have made for themselves, but a shifter would be worth it.

Vincent turns his attention to me. "Truly, Selene, on behalf of the entire pack, we are sorry. We were not trying to abandon you. We want to hunt down these monsters as much as you do. I made the decision to not cross boundary lines in the hope that you would bring your familiar back to our land, where we could properly protect you both, just like you did with Cara."

The room falls quiet, and I think I'm supposed to do something, so I nod.

After a long moment, Vincent returns his attention to Memnon. "Now, I don't want to keep either of you here tonight. I'm sure you both have plans.

"Memnon," he says, "would you be willing to answer a few questions we have about our—" he hesitates, "murdered pack mate?"

Memnon's gaze narrows, even as his mouth curves up at the corners. "The only person I explain myself to is my mate." His eyes flick to me, and they gentle. "But if *you* want me to tell them the truth," he says, directing his words to me, "then I will."

I stare at him while the rest of the room waits. The sorcerer was right when he pointed out that the pack hasn't been very friendly to me since the last time I visited them. However, they were the ones who extended their help to me when no one else would. For that alone, I'm willing to help.

"I do want that," I finally say.

The sorcerer's eyes roam over my features, then he straightens in his seat. "All right," he says, his eyes sweeping over the room. "I will tell you what no one else besides Selene knows. But because this information is confidential, I need something from you all."

Irene and Kane both begin to growl, and Vincent's face hardens.

"A truth spell will do."

The growls don't stop, and maybe it's seeing Memnon hurt earlier or how he advocated for me only minutes ago, but a protectiveness toward him rises up in me.

"You have your pack. I have my mate," I say. "I am innately loyal to him—even when I don't wish to be. And friend of the pack or not, I won't ask Memnon to tell you a single piece of information if you cannot do this one thing—an act that your pack asked of me only days ago."

Memnon stiffens next to me, and I feel his eyes on my face. Through our bond, his emotions are hard to make out, but I gather that he didn't expect the show of loyalty from me.

I didn't entirely expect it either.

The growls die down until the room is painfully quiet. Vincent is grimacing, and Kane is looking at me like maybe he doesn't know me.

"Do it." This comes from Apani. Her eyes move to mine, looking more wolfish than human. "This girl saved one of our own and nearly died doing so. She has earned our trust and friendship. We can allow her to ask for ours as well."

The alpha glances first at Apani, then at Kane and his beta.

Finally, he agrees. "All right, we'll do it."

———————

Placing four adult shifters under a truth spell is no small thing, and I sense that Memnon is relishing every second of it.

"*Only the truth shall leave these lips until my questions are answered*," the sorcerer incants.

The shifters cannot see Memnon's indigo magic as it moves toward them, but I see Vincent scowl and Irene flinch as the magical smoke slides up their nostrils and down through their mouths, and I know they must sense the spell as it takes hold.

Once the magic settles, Irene says, "Now what?"

"Now, you answer a few of my questions. If you're not compromised, then you can ask me whatever you please."

"Compromised?" Kane echoes, but Memnon doesn't elaborate.

None of the shifters look particularly pleased. Tonight Memnon was the one who was supposed to answer questions, not them.

But Vincent clears his throat and threads his hands together on the table in front of him.

"Let's get this over with then," he says.

Memnon's gaze moves over the group. "Have any of you been magically bonded in your life?"

Three nos ring out. The single yes comes from Vincent.

I raise my eyebrows. *That's* interesting.

"Was it against your will?" Memnon asks.

"My wife is a witch." Vincent bites out the words. "It was part of our marital vows."

A bit hypocritical of the Marin Pack to have come down so hard on my own forged bond when this entire time, their leader had one of his own.

"Was it against your will?" Memnon presses.

"*No*," Vincent growls out.

Memnon's gaze sweeps back over the room. "Have any of you worked for Ensanguine Enterprises or the Fortuna family at any point in your life?"

Four nos ring out.

The sorcerer settles back in his seat. "My questions are answered."

The only hint that the last of Memnon's truth spells has dissolved away is the faint blue sheen that leaves the lycans' lips a moment later. It happens so quickly it looks like a trick of the eye.

Vincent reaches into his pocket and pulls out a stoppered vial of emerald-green liquid. Truth potion.

"Now that's over with, I trust you will grant us the same favor we granted you."

Rather than answering, Memnon's magic reaches out and lifts the potion from where it rests and floats it over to the sorcerer's hand. He unstoppers the small vial and drinks it down.

He corks the empty bottle and sets it in front of him.

Vincent's gaze focuses on that vial for a moment, before it then lifts to Memnon. "Will you now tell us what you can of the murders?"

Memnon gives the alpha another narrow-eyed look, then begins. "I recently came to work for the Fortuna family..."

My mate tells the shifters mostly what he told me. How

the criminal organization is run by a dynasty of sorcerers and the main players of it—Luca, the family patriarch, his wife, Annalee, and his children, Leonard, Juliana, and Sophia. How up until today, his job consisted of making bodies disappear, which was how he came into possession of the murder victims. How he doesn't know who killed them, only that they appeared to come from the Equinox Building.

The sorcerer even discusses how he initially staged the bodies because he wanted to frame me for murder, and how this last body was meant purely to make the Fortunas sweat. He ends with how he's now being transferred to a different branch of the organization and likely won't have access to further bodies.

When Memnon finally finishes telling them what he knows, Vincent frowns, looking the sorcerer over. "How have you gotten away with this?"

"I have an...aptitude."

"Tell us about this aptitude," Irene says.

Memnon leans his forearms against the table, his eyes glinting. "I can read minds, lift information stored in them, and manipulate thoughts and memories."

The lycanthropes, Kane included, go preternaturally still.

"Have you read ours?" the beta finally asks.

Memnon cocks his head, and he has that look in his eye, like he's a cat toying with his prey. "What does it matter?"

A growl starts up across the table.

"He hasn't," I say to stop the fight before it can begin. I would've seen Memnon's magic at work if he had.

The sorcerer eases back in his seat, a carefree grin on his face. I think he enjoys unsettling these shifters.

The freak.

"His ability to manipulate minds means that he's been

able to gain access to their thoughts and make them misre-member events or forget them entirely," I say. "That's why he hasn't been caught." *Yet.* I hate that the word tacks itself on in my head.

"Do you know why or how these supernaturals are being killed?" Irene asks.

"No. That's what Selene and I are trying to figure out," Memnon says.

"It must be a supernatural who has access to dark magic," I say. "A sorcerer, a witch, a necromancer—someone who can perform these sorts of spells."

Memnon stands. "That is all I know and all I have to share."

"We have more questions," Vincent insists.

Rather than looking at Vincent, Memnon glances down at me, waiting for me to choose—let him leave or make him answer more of the shifter's questions.

I rise, my chair scraping back. "That's it for now," I say. "I'll reach out to Kane if anything else comes up."

The lycans must hear how my heart pounds, defending Memnon, standing with him. I cannot decide if I'm being supremely loyal or supremely foolish.

Likely both.

The shifters watch us leave, all of them still seated. I sense that the moment the door shuts behind me and Memnon, they will have an entire second meeting to dissect what they've learned.

Memnon must sense this as well because as I reach for the door, his magic slips past me and holds it shut.

The sorcerer turns to the room. "What I have told you is confidential. The Fortunas have eyes and ears everywhere, and I'm certain there must be at least one pack mate who is compromised."

I sense indignation from the group still seated, but before they can get a word in, Memnon continues.

"I know you trust your pack with your life, but you cannot trust them with this until we know more."

"That is not our way," Vincent says.

Magic sifts out of Memnon. "Then I will erase all that I've told you from each of your minds, and we will leave."

Four growls start up. I see fur begin to sprout along Kane's arms.

Packs, apparently, do not take kindly to threats.

"If you tell the wrong shifter, and they tell someone else involved with the Fortunas, then I will be exposed," he says. "And if *I'm* exposed, a lot of people will die." Memnon doesn't clarify that he's the one who will be doing the killing, but I'm aware of it. "That will be blood on *your* heads."

The growls ratchet up at the accusation.

Memnon continues. "Selene wants to bring the murderers to justice, and I am oath bound to make sure that happens," he says. "I believe that's what you want too. So make an exception, and keep this information confidential. Otherwise, you're simply in my way."

Vincent's eyes move between me and the sorcerer, debating, debating.

Finally, he says, "If you keep us informed, we will keep this confidential."

The sorcerer dips his head, and his magic moves from the door. "Then we have an arrangement." He grabs the knob and pulls the door open for me. To the rest of the room, he says, "We'll see you soon."

# CHAPTER 32

***Living with Memnon is going to prove to be my doom.***

That's all I can think the next day, after another raging night of sex. I'm pretty sure the sorcerer's goal is to screw me into loving him, and it's working. Or at least I think I'm developing an unhealthy addiction to it.

I don't even try to leave his bed until he's called away to meet with Juliana.

I shower, change, then I pack my messenger bag, eager to get some work done back on campus. Nero comes up to me, clearly interested in going wherever I'm going.

I kneel down in front of him and pet his head. "I can't take you with me today," I say, the words cleaving my heart in two.

Nero stares up at me, and for once, he doesn't look like a panther annoyed with my very existence. He looks like a loyal friend who knows he's getting left behind.

"I'm sorry," I say softly. I don't want to leave him, but I

haven't worked up the courage to let the panther back into the Everwoods.

The way Nero nudges his head into my chest, as though he's insistent on staying close to me, makes me want to cry.

"I know it's supremely unfair," I say, "but I can't risk you getting hurt—not after what happened. At least here, you can wander and hunt in the woods without fear of someone attacking you."

He doesn't look like he cares about that, but he's also done begging. Nero turns from me, whacking my cheek with a flick of his tail before heading toward an open window at the back of the living room.

Without giving me another glance, he hops through it and heads out for the woods beyond.

I stay kneeling there for another second, torn. I could just stay in Memnon's empty house. It is the weekend after all. I could busy myself inspecting every corner of this place, then read the books he's stocked his bookshelf with. I could wait—for Memnon to return, for Nero to come back, for the weekend to end and classes to start up again.

But I have assignments that require the use of my house's spell kitchen, and perhaps more importantly, I need to work on that birth control potion or else find out if the house keeps any on hand. I haven't taken anything since the day after Samhain, and we've had rounds of sex since then.

So even feeling like the world's worst pet owner, I leave Memnon's house, using his car to return to Henbane.

And then I get to work.

---

By the end of the day, my assignments are done and I've even brewed a contraceptive potion. Or at least I tried.

I hold the beaker of potion up, worrying my lower lip. It's a murky brownish-purple, rather than the deep-blue I remember from after Samhain.

To drink it or not to drink it?

Will it even *work*?

A group of witches pass by the spell kitchen, and I glance up, momentarily distracted as they pass the doorway. Part of me is still bracing to see Yasmin or the other girl I recognized the night they attacked Nero, but I haven't seen them in the days since the attack, and I don't see them now.

I return my attention to the potion I brewed. There's no way I'm drinking this. I dump the thing down the sink.

I'll try again tomorrow. Until then, I should find Sybil and see if she has any contraceptive potion I can use until I sort myself out.

Briskly, I clean up my things, then head out of the kitchen and up the stairs, ignoring the faint scents of dinner.

Outside, the sky is a luminous deep-blue, and the lampposts speckling the campus flicker to life.

I hadn't realized how long I'd been working. I pull my phone from my pocket.

6:44 p.m.

Shit.

It's way past curfew.

*You've broken curfew before,* I reassure myself. *What is one more day?*

But when it happened before, I had my reasons. Now, I merely lost track of time.

Setting aside my worries about curfew for a moment, I send my mother a quick text—*I'm still kicking!*—then tuck my phone away and step off the second floor of the house, heading down the hall.

When I get to my best friend's room, I open the door and step inside.

Sybil is busy typing away on her laptop, but when she hears me, she glances up.

"Selene!" Sybil's face blooms into a smile. "I didn't realize you were here. I was going to grab dinner in a few minutes. Want to join?"

"Oh." I hadn't even considered it. But I've already broken curfew. What's the harm in lingering a little longer?

"I would *love* to come to dinner with you," I say to Sybil.

"Yay!" she says.

I reach down my bond to Memnon. *I'll be out late tonight. Don't wait up.*

It feels weird checking in like this, as though I'm somehow answerable to him. But Goddess forbid the man worries about me. Heads might literally roll.

From the other side of the bond I feel Memnon's warmth. *Hello, Empress, I've been missing you,* he says, and damn him, but I get butterflies at his words. After a moment, he adds, *I might also be late. I'm now involved in a whole new arm of the organization and, Selene, I have so much to tell you.*

My breath catches. Memnon has clearly learned something new, something that will probably shed light on the murders. It's also clearly meant to entice me to return to his house.

*I'll see you later then,* I say.

*Stay safe,* Memnon says. *And kill anyone who crosses you.*

Not going to address that.

I pull away from the connection in time for Sybil to come up to my side. Her eyes flick over me. "You were talking to Memnon just now, weren't you?"

"Yeah."

"Well, what did you two chat about?" she says.

"That I'll be staying late here."

My friend's expression brightens. "That means you can come to the bonfire."

"The bonfire?" I echo.

"It's a small party happening at the beach. I assumed you wouldn't be able to come because you've been cautious and staying with Memnon, and I didn't want to make you feel bad for missing out."

I make a face, annoyance flaring in me. Just because shitty people exist in the world doesn't mean I need to stop living.

Caution be damned. I am not prey, and I'm not about to start acting like it.

Setting my jaw, I say, "I would *love* to go to the bonfire tonight."

---

Two hours later, Sybil and I step onto the back patio of the residence hall, the two of us wearing dresses, tights, and combat boots. Sybil slathered a store's worth of gold glitter around my eyes and hers, and honestly, it is cute as shit.

Resting near an overgrown love-lies-bleeding bush are two brooms. There's nothing particularly special about them, except that they look old and handmade, their bristles uneven and their handles worn with age.

I side-eye Sybil. "You're not thinking…"

"*Yes.* We're going to fly to the party! The wards for curfew apparently don't extend higher than the buildings on campus, so if we fly above them we can get past them unnoticed."

My lips part. "But…I haven't learned how to fly."

"No one taught you half the spells you regularly use. You just wing it."

I have a 62 percent success rate with winging it—which means I'm only a little likely to eat shit flying this thing.

And you know what? Caution. Be. Damned. I grab one of the brooms.

"It's second nature," Sybil adds, grasping the other broom. "See, watch. *With air I lift, with wind I fly. Keep me airborne in the sky.*" Once she finishes the incantation, the broom rises up and levels out. Sybil swings a leg over it, her dress hiking up with the action.

I turn to the remaining broom, a thrill running through me. Sybil's right. I *can* do this.

I open my mouth to incant in Sarmatian when I hesitate. It's one thing for my best friend to know there's this ancient side to me, and it's another to openly display it. So at the last moment, I slap a spell together.

"*Broom, fly high and carry me far.*" Shit, what rhymes with *far*? "*Steer me onward toward the star...sss.*"

My broom leaps upward, and I have to throw myself on it.

Sybil snickers. "Goddess, you may have gotten your memories back, but your spells still suck."

I adjust myself on my broom, a thrill running through me when it levels out next to hers. "Your dad didn't think so last time I saw him."

She cackles from where she sits. "Fuck you, Selene. What did my dad ever do to you?"

I shift my weight as the broom floats slowly up. Seriously, why are flying brooms still a thing? There is literally no room for my ass cheeks on this thing.

"Better question is what *didn't* he do—"

Sybil screams and clutches her ears. "Don't end that sentence."

Now it's my turn to cackle.

Sybil brings her hands back to her broom and throws me a look. "Bet your *fiancé* wouldn't like hearing you talk about other men like that."

I lift a shoulder. "He'd probably just spank me. I think I'd enjoy that. I might even call him 'Daddy,' just like I did your—"

Another scream, and then Sybil's off, racing ahead of me. Which leaves me to figure out how to follow her.

Most magic is intuitive. It knows what its caster wants; spells just help funnel and fine-tune that intention. So I envision myself following after my best friend.

I've no sooner willed it than my broom shoots forward, propelled onward by my magic and my shitty spell. And maybe it's that shitty spell that causes it to bank sharply upward.

I use every last ounce of my upper-body strength to hold on as it rapidly ascends. Once I'm far above the buildings on the coven's campus, the broom levels out, and I exhale.

Holy Goddess, I'm flying.

Beneath me, the lamps of Henbane Coven glow softly, casting the campus in soft, warm light. To my right, I can see Cauldron Hall. Behind that, I see Beldame Library and the domed roof of the Lunar Observatory. And with a quick glance over my left shoulder, I catch sight of the illuminated conservatory. It all looks particularly magical at night.

Ahead of me I can barely make out Sybil's dark form before she's swallowed up by a cloud. I follow her, the wind whipping my hair behind me.

The cloud envelops me a moment later, and for a

heart-stopping few seconds, I can't see anything beyond swathes of mist. But then I break through to the other side of it, and the sight before me is…unreal.

There's a blanket of pale clouds beneath me, and the moon and stars hang above me, gleaming like gems.

"Hey, freak!" Sybil calls out from ahead of me. She's come to a stop, her broom hovering in the sky. "Incredible, isn't it?"

I nod, not trusting my voice.

"We're almost there. Follow me!" With that, she takes off again, her broom arcing back down into the cloud cover.

I will my magic to follow hers and begin my descent. Not for the first time, I stare in awe after Sybil. I thought I was throwing caution to the wind, but it's my friend who is downright fearless.

That point is only further driven home when I cut through the clouds once more. The experience isn't as jarring as it was a minute ago, but as soon as I clear the clouds, I can see the ground far, far below me.

Fuck, why is it so *far*?

But it's a rhetorical question. The coastal mountains that Henbane is nestled among descend rapidly, ending right at the ocean. Most of the coastline here is inaccessible since it's bordered by the sides of these mountains. But every so often, there's a crescent-shaped section of beach, which is perfect for intimate parties, such as the one I can see below me, illuminated by a bonfire and several orbs of light.

It's hard to see much beyond that, however, because a hazy cloud of magic hangs over the party, partially cloaking the supernaturals below it.

Ahead of me, Sybil drives her broom straight for the magical cloud. I can hear her peals of laughter as she cuts straight through the gathering, and I can imagine her parting the crowd of partygoers and possibly colliding with a few of them.

Yeah, I'm not going to do that.

Instead, I steer my broom toward the ocean beyond the party.

Under the moonlight, the water looks like glass, and the closer I get to it, the greater the urge to touch it. I lower my broom until I'm no more than a couple of feet above the sea's rippling surface, the waves looking inky in the night. I tuck my legs in close to my broom and lean down and reach out, dragging my fingertips across the top of the ocean.

The water is icy cold, and moving as fast as I am, the sea sprays against me. I laugh at the sensation, something primal stirring in me. I'm still a ways from shore, and if I fell into the water, I'd probably have to use more magic to get out of the situation, but I'm not afraid of the possibility.

This is what it means to be a witch.

I lift my hand from the water and rise a little higher as the water swells, then crests into waves the nearer to shore I get. I fly over the churning surf, then will the broom to slow as, beneath me, sand replaces sea. Once I hit dry sand, the broom comes to a stop, and I hop off, walking over to the edge of the party. A dozen other brooms lean against the rocky cliffside that borders it, and I leave mine among them.

I use a wordless spell to dry my skin and clothes. My nose and hands are numb from the cold, but I don't bother wasting more power on heating them up. It's nothing that a bonfire and booze can't fix.

On the far side of the party a group of musicians play the fiddle, the harp, and the flute.

I walk over to the cluster of witches and mages and

shifters mingling around the fire. Among them is Kane. My stomach drops at the sight of him. I hadn't realized he would be here. I nearly duck when he turns his head my way.

I move deeper into the group, my eyes drinking in faces. I can't help but search the crowd for Nero's attackers. I don't know that they're here or what I'll do if I do see them, but—

"Selene!"

I turn at the sound of my name, thinking it's Sybil.

Instead, I take in wild-haired Olga. I'm used to seeing the witch with her Ledger of Last Words tucked under her arm. But for the second time this week, the book is out of sight. Instead, my coven sister holds two drinks in her hands.

"I haven't seen you since Samhain!" she says, looking genuinely happy to see me. "So good to see you. Here." She thrusts one of her drinks at me. "Want this? I got it for Mai, but now I can't find her."

"Oh," I say, taking the drink reflexively, "thanks. I can't find Sybil either, so that makes two of us." I glance down at the drink. "Does this have any *espiritus* in it?" I ask.

I'm still traumatized by the last time I drank the stuff.

"Not sure, if I'm being completely honest. A shifter was handing the drinks out. Why?" she asks.

I make a face. "Samhain was...an experience," I say. "I ended up spending the night screwing my nemesis." It feels weird calling Memnon that. My *nemesis*. Wrong somehow. Lately, he's been something else entirely.

"Oooh, sounds threatening and *very* hot," Olga says. "Well, cheers to making love in war." She clinks her cup with mine, then downs her drink.

Tonight, the witch has put on makeup, and her wild hair looks more windblown than frizzy. All done up, Olga is stunning. One would hardly know that she's unnervingly obsessed with people's final words.

Olga finishes off her drink and breathes in the briny air. "Mmm…tonight smells like a night for reaping. I bet I'll get another entry in my book."

And there it is. Her witchiness making itself known.

I grimace at the glee in Olga's voice and take a reluctant sip of my drink, which tastes like cranberries, cheap vodka, and spices meant to cover up said cheapness. But it lacks the bittersweet edge of witch's brew, and I relax a little.

Sybil finds us then, slinging her arms around my neck and Olga's. A bit of her drink sloshes onto Olga's shirt.

"What's up, witches?" she says, nuzzling my cheek, her lilac magic twining around my head before drifting up into the air above us.

Behind Sybil are Mai and another witch whose name I'm pretty sure is Cordelia. They move over to join our group.

Sybil glances at my cup. "How about you? You've hardly had any of your drink."

"She's worried if she drinks it, she's going to screw her archnemesis again," Olga adds helpfully.

I throw Olga an annoyed look, taking another deliberate swallow of my drink.

Out of the corner of my eye, I see Kane glance over sharply.

Fuck me. He must've heard that.

"Oh, archnemesis is it?" Sybil says, raising her eyebrows as she drops her arms and squeezes in between me and Olga. "We *definitely* wouldn't want you to make the same mistake twice," she says, knowing full well that I've made that mistake more than twice now.

Hell's spells, that reminds me—I still have to ask her about the birth control potion.

I feel the press of a broad chest behind me, then an arm snakes around my midsection.

"We need to talk." Kane's voice is soft against my ear.

My heart leaps at the touch even as my stomach twists. I don't want to talk to Kane. Not really. It was fine when things with him were simple, but now they're messy. *We're* messy.

I take another long swallow of my drink.

"Ohhh, her fiancé is not going to like how handsy you're being," Sybil says.

Kane doesn't let me go, and I stare down at his arm, unsure whether the embrace is bothering me or not.

"I don't remember having to answer to him," Kane says smoothly. "He can fuck himself for all I care."

"I don't think he needs to. Not when he's got your girl here to fulfill all his dark, *depraved* needs."

"Fucking Furies, Sybil," I say. This is her getting me back for the dad comments earlier.

Kane's grip on me tightens, and I feel rather than hear a low, possessive growl vibrate in his chest.

My best friend looks delighted, and the witches around us watch all this avidly.

I turn in Kane's arms and push him back, out of the group.

"I'll be right back," I tell them over my shoulder.

"Take your time!" Sybil says, waggling her eyebrows.

To Kane, I say, "Get your shit together. You and I are just friends, and she is just teasing."

"About your sex life."

I lift a shoulder. "And?"

He grimaces, and I feel our different worlds colliding. Witches tend to be very sex positive. We like the act of coming together; it goes hand in hand with our magic, and it's part of our ethos to celebrate it. It's even incorporated into some of our rituals, such as Beltane.

Shifters, on the other hand, seem a bit more territorial about who they fuck and how they flaunt it.

Kane shakes his head and pulls me aside. I sway a little at the action, and the lycanthrope frowns. "You okay, Bowers?"

"What? Me?" I point to myself. "I'm *fine*."

Kane scrutinizes me for another second, then moves on. "I wanted to apologize to you again. For not helping you when your familiar was hurt."

Bile rises at the memory. Don't want to talk about this. Don't want to remember that night.

I have another swallow of my drink.

"I should've ignored my alpha's orders," he continues. "I could...hear the screams. I knew something was happening. All the shifters out there could." Kane's throat bobs, and he ducks his head, toeing a clump of sand. "I had admitted I liked you, and I didn't help. I didn't take care of you as I should've."

"I don't *want* to be taken care of." If I did, I would be sitting prettily in Memnon's home, waiting on him to arrive.

Kane's and my true differences creep up on me then. How we view intimacy, how we view relationships. A casual fling with Kane might've worked out, but anything more would've stifled me.

I don't answer to anyone, not even Memnon. Memnon knows that. Fuck, Memnon *likes* that aspect of me. He's been all too eager to goad me into my own power.

I drink down a good portion of my alcohol then, wanting

to be anywhere other than right here in this conversation with Kane.

"Selene, are you listening?" Kane says.

I glance up too quickly from my drink, realizing the shifter has been talking. Shit, maybe he has been asking me about Nero.

I sway a little, and my drink slips from my hands, the last of it spilling onto the sand.

Kane frowns, eyeing me up and down. "How drunk are you?"

I shake my head, swaying more as I reach down to grab my empty cup. "I'm not drunk. I haven't even had one full glass."

The lycanthrope's brow furrows. He steps in close and leans into my neck, breathing me in.

"*Kane,*" I say, pushing him back.

"You smell off."

"What is that supposed to mean?" I say, laughing semihysterically. "You don't know me well enough to know what I smell like."

Behind us, one of the other shifters whistles and gestures that they're getting ready to leave.

Kane nods to the shifter, then his gaze flicks over me. "My pack is getting ready to leave. I want you to come with us." Though it's a suggestion, there's a thread of his power in his voice. I'm not a lycanthrope, but even I am compelled by the order in it.

I raise my eyebrows at him. "Are you trying to assert your *dominance* over me?" I say skeptically, a wisp of anger rising in me.

His features harden. "Yes," he says. "And you can like it or not, but, Selene, I'm not backing down on this. The last time I let you go, both you and your familiar got hurt. I won't make the same mistake again."

I stare at him for a moment. "This is all because I *smell* funny?"

He presses his lips together, then slightly dips his head. *Yes.*

I want to laugh; the whole situation is beyond absurd. But the man is obviously serious, and I have no doubt he means what he says.

Which means I have three options: One, go along with what he says like a good little witch. Two, stand my ground and go toe-to-toe with an alpha werewolf. Or three, run.

I am a powerful witch, daughter of those who shaped the world and bent it to their will. I have a legacy to uphold.

Which I'll do on another day.

I turn on my heel and dash away. I also nearly face plant three steps into my getaway sprint.

Alcohol and sand do not mix well.

I flail, then right myself and book it, using a pinch of my magic to spur me onward and help my balance.

Behind me, Kane growls, the sound full of annoyance and maybe a little possessive promise. Then he's chasing after me.

I manage to run a total of maybe ten steps before his arms wrap around my waist and he swings me over his shoulder, causing my skirt to ride up. Only a quick spurt of my magic prevents the whole party from seeing my ass.

A group of nearby witches and mages whoop and catcall at us.

"I'm done playing," Kane growls into my ear, ignoring the attention we're receiving. "We're going."

I see red.

*Who's offended you,* est amage*?*

*You stay out of this.*

*I fear for the person who crossed you,* Memnon says a little too gleefully for the sentiment to be genuine. *Also, the eyes are a great place to attack first.*

I'm not interested in Kane's eyes.

To Kane, I say, "I will curse your dick to shrivel up and fall off if you don't put me down."

"That's more than a little disturbing," Kane says, "but you and I both know that I won't be cowed by a threat."

Before I can respond—or gather my magic—Kane presses his nose into my side and gives me another sniff. "You still don't smell right," he says.

I want to scream. Instead, my power rolls off me in agitated waves.

The lycan must sense it, because he says, "Don't make a scene."

*Going to murder him. Going to enjoy it too.*

"Says the man who's *kidnapping* me," I hiss out. I *bet* he doesn't want a scene. Makes him look bad.

"I'm not *kidnapping* you," he says. "I'm—" His words are interrupted when another shifter comes up to him, asking about fuck knows what.

Across the party, I catch sight of Sybil, who mouths *Are you okay?*

*No,* I respond.

Immediately, she shoves her drink at someone and begins walking toward us, determination in her eyes.

Before she can do anything, however, I reach my arm out toward the cliffside, where over a dozen brooms rest.

"*Come to me,*" I order in Sarmatian, flicking a bit of magic out. I feel like a drunk Jedi as I call out to one of the brooms.

The alcohol is blunting a bit of my power, because for a second, the broom I focus on does nothing more than tremble where it leans against the sheer rock. But then, a little sluggishly, it peels itself from the wall and cuts through the crowd, knocking supernaturals aside.

The broom lands in my hands.

Success.

Kane glances over his shoulder.

"*Fly us home,*" I command the broom.

It jerks forward, pulling me with it.

Kane curses as I slip through his grip. It's not my proudest moment, scrambling to drag myself onto the wooden handle and away from Kane's determined hold.

I've just gotten myself firmly on it when the broom launches forward, and now I am cutting through the party, bowling people over.

"Sorry! Sorry!" I call out as I go.

Kane strides after me, but Sybil's magic is pouring out across the beach, likely to stop the shifter from getting any closer to me. My heart swells; she's such a fucking amazing friend.

"Selene!" Kane bellows, his lupine eyes glinting when I glance back at him.

So much for not causing a scene.

I will the broom to rotate around so I can face the lycan head on.

"Screw you, Kane!" My voice rings out. "*No one orders a witch around.*"

The crowd around me must agree because, despite running into several of them, I hear whoops and cheers.

My broom lifts higher into the sky, above the reach of Kane and everyone else there, and then I'm zipping away.

For one exhilarating minute, I enjoy the absolute victory of besting the determined lycan.

Then I realize one huge, glaring error—I spelled my broom to fly *home*. I don't *want* to go home. I simply wanted to get away from Kane.

I'm about to order my broom to turn around when a gust of wind blows my broom sideways and nearly unseats me. When I right myself, the world spins.

I blink several times, trying to clear my sight, but the world is still spinning, and my broom is still climbing higher and higher into the air. I'm now fifty feet or so above the ground and very, very intoxicated. Impossibly so.

I grip the broom handle tightly, feeling nauseated.

I had less than one full drink. Even if the vodka was really strong, it shouldn't affect me this intensely. Not unless—

*Unless it was spiked.*

Devil's dick. Did someone *spike* my drink? Or Olga's drink, since she gave it to me? Did *she* do it?

Fuck, Kane must've been right after all to worry about me, even if he went about it in the most atrocious way possible.

I call on my power. "*Lower me to the ground*," I command in Sarmatian.

My magic comes out of me in sluggish spurts, but rather than lowering, my broom jerks beneath my grip, nearly throwing me off.

"Seven hells," I curse, righting myself.

It bounces again, and my body tips sideways. As I tip, the world spins.

Shit, shit, shit.

I desperately wrap my arms and legs around the broom as

I'm fully unseated, clinging to the underside of my airborne broom.

This is fucking unfortunate.

I glance over my shoulder only to see the earth passing by fifty feet below me. My broom bounces again and again and again, eventually dislodging my feet. I'm too terrified to yelp out as my legs slip off the broom, leaving me hanging from it by my hands.

My surroundings are blurring past me faster than my eyes can follow, and my stomach churns. I pinch my eyes shut, just to make the world stop moving.

"Lower us to the ground!" I shout the command.

*Selene?* Memnon's voice cuts in. *Are you...in the sky?*

He must've overheard some of my thoughts.

*Not for much longer.*

My magic seems to trip over my command, weakly pulling at the broom. In response, the broom pauses in midair, then it begins to simply fall, taking me along with it.

*What does that mean?* The alarm in his voice pairs well with the screaming in my head.

Blessedly and through no attempt on my part, the broom seems to remember it's enchanted to fly. Abruptly, it stops falling and levels out.

I grit my teeth as the action yanks at my shoulder joints, but it's my hands I'm worried about. My palms have slickened with sweat, and my grip is sliding off the wooden handle, and fuck, fuck, fuck—

"*Seal my hands to this broom!*" I command in Sarmatian, channeling my power down my arms and into my palms.

Despite invoking the dead language and funneling my magic to my hands, nothing happens. My power doesn't leave my flesh, and the incantation doesn't take root.

The spell fails entirely.

*I'm coming!* Memnon says. *Just hold on.*

But holding on is the one thing I can no longer do.

My fingers slip off the sweat-slickened handle, and I fall.

# CHAPTER 33

**Selene. Selene.**

*Selene!*

*Damn all the gods... Roxilana, answer me, my love!*

I sigh out a breath, a pinch of pain blooming at the action, and I blink.

*Memnon?* I say, my brows coming together.

*Thank the fucking stars. Are you hurt? I'm coming for you. Just keep speaking to me.*

I blink again, staring at the cloudy night sky above me, which still appears to spin. Am I hurt? There's something warm and wet at my back, and it's hard to breathe...

I move a little, and *holy mother goddess.* Agony radiates from *everywhere.*

*Yes*, I gasp down our bond, choking back a sob that might further jostle my body. *I'm hurt. I think...I think I fell.*

It comes back to me then, the terrifying broom ride, the loss of magic, *the fall.*

I must've blacked out on impact, but now, unfortunately,

I'm awake—as is my pain. White-hot sparks of it radiate from my legs. One leg in particular feels exposed, as though if the wind picked up, even its light caress would send shooting pains through me.

I have old memories of open wounds. I know the sensation of my insides kissing the air.

*Assess yourself, est amage. Tell me what is injured.*

I lift my head and glance down the line of my body. It takes several extra seconds to stop my surroundings from spinning. In the dim light, I can make out a white bone sticking out from the mess of my left leg. I bite back a whimper.

It's hard to tell in the darkness, but my right leg looks twisted at all the wrong angles. And my back…

I pinch my eyes shut and swallow down my rising sickness.

*Legs are broken. One is…it's a compound fracture—I can see my bone.*

Between the pain and the knowledge, I nearly retch, and the only thing that stops me is the sinking awareness that I cannot move. I'm already lying in a pool of what I'm pretty sure is my own blood. I don't want to add vomit to the mix.

*Should've just gone with Kane,* I think despairingly.

*I don't know what the fuck the shifter has to do with any of this,* Memnon says darkly, *but I will make sure to skin the dog alive and mount his pelt to my wall at the first chance I get.*

*This wasn't…his fault…*

Unless *he* spiked my drink of course, but I find that incredibly unlikely. That's the sort of shady, cowardly shit alphas fight *against*.

*Never mind about Kane,* Memnon commands. *I'm going to press my magic into you. Take what you need, and heal yourself as best you can. I'm tracking you right now. I'll be there soon.*

*How are you tracking me?* I ask dazedly.

*Heal those wounds,* he says gently. *Then I'll tell you.*

Focusing inward, I reach out and try to grab hold of Memnon's magic. Maybe it's the pain, or maybe it's something else, but even grasping it proves to be more difficult than usual. And when I try to shape his power into a spell, it doesn't respond to my will the way it has in the past.

My breath is coming in faster and faster pants, which is setting my chest ablaze. Broken rib? Punctured lung? Internal bleeding?

I drag my attention away from the pain and focus on my own coiled power. It's there, living inside me, but now, it's as though I can no longer channel it.

I cry out in frustration and pain.

*It's not working.*

*What's not working?* Memnon demands.

*My magic—and yours. I can't use either of them to heal myself.*

*You...can't use it?* He sounds as though the thought is inconceivable.

Two thousand years ago, when supernaturals were not nearly so unified and our magic not so specialized, something like this *was* largely inconceivable.

*Someone...drugged me...I think.*

His fury breaks through our connection, that someone would dare do this to me.

*I swear to you,* est amage, *once you are safe, I will find them, and they will pay.*

I think of Olga, who gave me the drink. Olga, who I hadn't suspected a thing from. I pinch my eyes shut to keep from crying. I wasn't supposed to trust my coven sisters, but I did.

*I was a fool,* I admit. *I trusted someone I shouldn't have.*

Somewhere in the distance, a car drives by. I'm near a road. That's…that's good, I guess.

*Trusting people doesn't make you a fool. Just an optimist. It's one of the things I love most fiercely about who you are in this life. The world hasn't broken your faith yet.*

*Yet.*

I think that's the key word. Because every violent altercation whittles it away little by little.

*That might be one of the kindest things you've ever said to me,* I say.

*Pain is dulling your memory, my love.*

My heart pangs at the endearment. *Don't call me that.*

*Fine,* he says. *Then how about my fierce queen, my exquisite mate, mother of my future children.*

I grimace. *Definitely not that last one.* Need to get my hands on some contraceptive potion to make it so.

*You're giving me so much ammunition to use against you the next time I'm teasing your pussy.*

*Memnon,* I say, horrified. I know he's saying this to distract me from the pain, but crap, it's working a little too well. *You wouldn't* dare *use that against me.*

I feel his amusement, though it's tinged with worry. *If only I were an honorable man…*

*Memnon!*

In the distance, another engine rumbles on the road. It sounds like it's moving slowly, and instead of zooming by the grassy hill I'm on, it slows, then idles.

I hear a door creak open, then the heavy tread of feet against the roadside gravel.

*Is that you, Memnon?*

*I'm not there yet.*

Fuck.

*Someone is,* I say.

And the odds of them being a good Samaritan are vanishingly small.

On the other end of the bond, I feel Memnon's alarm. Then it's gone, pulled back so quickly that the sorcerer must be deliberately shielding it from me.

*Do you have any weapons on you?* he asks. This is something he used to make sure Roxilana had on her.

*No,* I say softly.

He shields me from whatever reaction he has to that news.

Meanwhile, the stranger below me is climbing up the mountainous incline, wild grass crunching beneath their shoes.

*Call on your magic again,* Memnon orders me, sounding like the warlord he once was. While there's no compulsion in his voice, I'm bending to the order without question.

I reach for my power, even as those footsteps draw near. It's there, swirling beneath my skin, but I am utterly disconnected from it. And despite magic being semi-sentient, it's showed no interest in healing me all on its own.

*It's still not working,* I say to Memnon. I try to suppress my growing panic.

*Hold fast, Empress. I'm coming.*

There is nothing I can do *but* hold fast. I have no usable magic, no weapon, and no mobility.

Wait—

I wiggle my fingers and test my arms. They both feel pretty banged up, but my right arm can move okay if I hold the rest of my body very still.

Cautiously, I grope around for anything I might use to defend myself with. Even the slight movements of my arm tug at my side, and I have to bite my lower lip to smother a cry. But my fingers brush a rock partially embedded in the soil. I dig my nails into the earth to work it free.

The action causes the grass to rustle, and I have no magic to mask the sound. I almost give up then in favor of staying quiet and still.

*If they've come this far for you, they're going to find you,* I remind myself.

So I yank on the rock until I pry it free. It's no bigger than my palm, but it's rough and has a sharp side to it.

Good enough.

Now the only thing to do is lie in wait.

Those ominous footsteps make their way over to where I lie on the coastal hillside, drawn to me like I'm a beacon. When I first catch sight of the figure, all I can make out is a dark, hooded shape.

It steps in closer, and I get a glimpse of a humanoid face and a pair of unseeing eyes.

I jolt in surprise.

*I thought I had annihilated you back in the Everwoods.*

The clay creature, the one I shattered apart with a spell only a few weeks ago, is whole once more, and now it's returned for me.

# CHAPTER 34

*For several seconds, the creature stares down at me, and I'm* curious what it's thinking—if it even *can* think. That head of its was hollow when I crushed it beneath my foot.

Maybe it'll do the same thing to me, stomp my face into oblivion now that our roles are reversed.

Eventually, it bends down, its hands reaching for my body.

I wait until it's close enough, and then I lunge forward, swinging the stone in my hand, a pained cry ripping from my throat as the action makes my injuries scream. As soon as the stone connects with the monster's cheek, I hear the sound of pottery breaking.

The creature rears back a little, but that's the extent of its reaction. Then it's reaching for me again.

My torso is on fire, but I pull my arm back and swing a second time, aiming for the being's wrist.

The appendage snaps off a split second before the creature's other arm comes around me and drags up.

Seven hells, *the pain!*

It's everywhere—my ribs, my legs, my back and neck. Clouding my vision and ripping me open anew.

The monster grips me as best it can, crushing my torso to its and heightening my agony. Then it begins to walk.

A ragged scream bubbles up as my broken legs drag against the ground, the agony overwhelming. The darkness at the edges of my vision now swarms in and blessedly, I black out.

*Selene!* Memnon bellows down our bond. *Selene! Answer me, please, my queen!* Thick, coagulated fear presses in with his words.

I barely have time to register it when the agony returns.

*I can feel your pain!* Memnon continues. *What's happening? Abducted...there's a creature...*

Bile rises faster than I can stop it, and I just have time to turn my head away from the creature dragging me to retch.

The monster doesn't slow, and my broken, bloody legs trail over the hillside, the wild grass we pass sticking to my open wounds, the sensation making me vomit again.

*Hold on, my fierce queen.*

I don't think I get a fucking choice about that. I have to endure this, whether I like it or not.

I think I'm sobbing, writhing. I feel like the pain is consuming me. And maybe it is because the night darkens once more...and then it swallows me up entirely.

---

*PAIN!*

I wake to it. I am engulfed *in* it. Perhaps I'm dead. Perhaps I've gone to hell and I'm bathing in its fiery halls.

I force my heavy eyelids to open. I'm swaying, spinning, slipping as the world moves.

Am I still flying?

But no, there's a drop ceiling above me and something cupping my back and thighs.

A chair, I realize.

I try to move my arms, but they're restrained at my back, the angle of it pinching my shoulder blades.

My mangled legs droop from the chair, and the position I'm now in places so much pressure on them, the pain is relentless.

*Think I'm going to retch again...* Even my thoughts come sluggishly.

*Selene!*

My eyes flutter closed to stop the room from spinning, and I swallow down my rising sickness.

*Memnon?* I say dazedly.

*I'm right here,* he says. *Stay with me.*

"Look who I've found," says a feminine voice in front of me, drawing my attention away from my mate. "A broken little witch lost in the woods."

That voice sounds vaguely familiar.

I'm about to open my eyes when something presses into my wounded leg.

I scream, then I do lean over and vomit as the fiery agony consumes me.

Down my bond I can hear Memnon bellowing my name.

"*Look at me,*" the voice commands, and there's magic woven into the order.

My face is forced back to the woman speaking. She has rich brown hair and soft, Bambi eyes that give her face an air of innocence. The woman is lovely—lovely and familiar, and maybe I could place her if my body weren't bathed in agony and whatever drug I've been given.

"Do you remember me?" she asks, echoing my thoughts. "Because *I* remember *you*."

My leg makes a wet sucking noise as she removes her finger, the digit now bloody.

I shriek from both pain and horror.

*SELENE!* Memnon's voice booms in my head. *Whatever is happening, stay with me,* he pleads.

*Can't...talk...*

"Towel," she orders, reaching out a hand.

From the shadows, the humanoid creature steps forward, its face and hands whole once more. In one of those hands, it holds a white cloth, which it gives to the woman.

She takes it without looking at the monster, meticulously wiping the blood from her finger before tossing it aside.

It's all so practiced. The readied towel, the chair, the bindings, her steady, sure, *familiar* presence.

I notice now what I didn't before: She commands the creature, just as the high priestess commanded the creature the night of the spell circle. *That's* who this is. The high priestess.

My eyes snap back to the woman too fast, and the room spins.

"Did you think you'd never see me again?" she asks.

I try to sharpen my mind, because this is important, but the pain and the blood loss and whatever I've been drugged with disorient everything.

This must be what the high priestess gave the shifter girl, Cara, before she tried to bond her. It must affect our magic.

"Ever since that night, I've been looking for you," she says.

*She wants you,* one of the witches who attacked Nero had warned me.

*Who?* I'd asked.

*Lia.*

I stare at the high priestess, putting a name to her face. Lia. More than surprise, I feel…dread.

She's bonded at least one witch—Lauren, the instructor Memnon questioned—and she nearly bonded Cara. And then those witches who attacked Nero, perhaps some—if not all—of them were bonded to this woman. Probably against their will.

And now I'm here, drugged and injured and restrained and very, very vulnerable.

"You cost me more than just a single girl," Lia says. "You cost me *six*. And all for what, your naive belief in honor? Justice? Where was your moral superiority when you killed my girls? The ones who lay dead in the woods. Did you know they were as innocent as the shifter you saved?"

My stomach turns on itself as she stares me down.

Lia leans forward, placing her hands on my thighs. I lock my jaw against the pain, tears pricking my eyes. "Do you feel superior now?" When I don't respond, she digs in her fingers and shakes one of my broken legs, and my vision darkens. "*Answer me.*"

*Selene!* Memnon's voice is alarmed. *Whatever is happening, I am here. I am always here with you.*

I cannot respond to my mate's sentiment. Not when I'm sucking air through my nose, trying not to scream or retch.

Once I think I can answer Lia, I whisper, "*No.*"

The woman stares at me, her face pitiless. She must see something that placates her, because her expression smooths out.

371

"First things first," Lia says. "Let's deal with these wounds."

I clench my jaw and steel myself for whatever she intends.

"*Bones reseal, flesh be stitched. Sinew mend, and wounds be fixed.*"

Thick, plum-colored magic flows out of her and pours over me in waves. It sinks into my skin, warming my body as it begins repairing injuries. Whatever I expected, it wasn't a healing spell.

Not that the spell is particularly kind.

My legs jerk sharply, Lia's power resetting them roughly. I lean over the side of the chair and heave, sweat and a couple of rogue tears dripping from my face. Her magic jostles my ribs, and it's so much pain, too much—

A wail escapes my throat. But the pain crests for only moments. Then it recedes into something more manageable as her magic fixes the worst of my injuries.

I sit there panting, sweaty strands of my hair sticking to my face. I want to ask Lia why she's healing me, but I have a horrible feeling I'm going to find out soon enough.

As the pain lifts, so too does some of my disorientation. I'm still bone-weary, but the room no longer spins, and I can truly focus on the woman in front of me.

Once my body is all put back together, her magic dissipates from the room.

"You have been betrayed by your friends, Selene Bowers," Lia says. "Just as you will soon betray others on my behalf. You won't get a choice. None of you do." She pushes away from me and stands. "Most of the time, I don't give a shit about the lives of my witches," Lia says, backing up. "But you? You've pissed me off. So I'm going to enjoy using you."

She turns from me, toward the monster.

"Creature, round up six witches or mages." Her attention returns to me when she adds, "One for every person Selene has cost me."

The monster mechanically walks to a door behind Lia, then exits the room.

Lia reaches for her side and unsheathes a small blade. I stare at the gleaming steel, aware of what she intends to do next.

*Memnon, I hate to be the damsel in distress, but I could really use you right now.*

From the other end of our bond, I feel Memnon's impotent rage. *I'm sorry, sweet mate. I'm coming. Until then, mark our enemies. I vow to you their deaths will be slow.*

By the time he reaches me, it might be too late.

"Normally, I like to do this at the coven with my bonded witches," Lia says, tapping the blade against her palm. "There's food and drinks and a small celebration. It's civilized and fun." She saunters toward my chair. "This will not be fun. I can't even say how civilized it will be. You *will* hate me, that I'll make sure of, but by then, you will be committed to me entirely," Lia says.

A chill slides down my back at her words and the certainty in her eyes. I'd been too drugged and hurt earlier to feel real fear. But now it drips into my system.

I frantically reach for my magic again as she closes in on me. I can grab onto a few sluggish tendrils of it, but when I try to push it out, I sense only a thin stream leaving my hand, melting into the air mere seconds after I release it.

Fuck.

My legs aren't tied to the chair, probably because they were twisted up too badly earlier. Her mistake. As soon as

Lia's within reach, I pull a leg back and kick her hard in the thigh.

She stumbles, nearly dropping her blade.

"*Bitch*." Her magic swarms me, wrapping around my throat and choking me while magically binding my ankles to the chair. "I'm going to make you do *awful* things," she vows. "Things you'll abhor. Things that will make you want to crawl from your very skin."

Terror congeals in my blood.

I reach for my magic again, but it's useless.

*Take my power,* Memnon says, pushing his own through.

*It hasn't been working,* I say despondently.

*Try again anyway,* he commands, a desperate edge to his voice.

When I coax his magic toward my center, it moves into me readily enough. The comfort of having this part of Memnon with me, inside me, takes the edge off my fear.

His magic swirls around my own power, mixing the two together, and when I direct Memnon's magic down my arms, it goes where I call it, as though eager to please me. It even manages to drag my own magic along with it. But both of them stall at my palms. Not even a wisp leaves me this time.

*Nothing still,* I tell Memnon.

I only sense the barest breath of the sorcerer's fear before he locks the emotion away. In its place is more power. He funnels it down our bond as though it might make up for the magical blockages.

*Can you move?* Memnon asks. *Can you get hold of a weapon?*

My attention is ripped from him when the door behind Lia opens, and six individuals enter, followed by the clay creature.

*Something's happening,* I say. *I can't talk.*

I pull away from the bond as I study the newcomers. None of them wear masks like the last spell circle Lia presided over, and most of them are men with hard, unforgiving faces. I don't recognize the two women in the group. They look older than most of the witches I go to school with.

There's a flatness to all these supernaturals' eyes, and intuitively, I know none of them will rescue me as I did Cara.

"I'm going to perform a binding," Lia announces.

The group of six don't speak, but they begin to remove their shoes and socks, setting them to the side of the room. Once they're barefoot, they form a circle around me, with Lia at its head. The seven of them grasp hands, and then Lia begins to incant in Latin.

*"I call on old magic and the darkness from deep beneath our feet. Lend us your power for tonight's spellcasting. Our circle calls forth your magic."*

The hairs along my arms rise as I feel the spell circle form and the magical current rush around me from one arm to the next.

Only once the circle has been formed does Lia join me in the middle of the circle. Dagger still in hand, she raises her arms and her blade above her head.

*"I call on the darkness and the old, hungry gods who will bear witness to my deeds,"* she incants in Latin.

The words are the same ones she used at the last spell circle. Only now, I sense those old, hungry gods somewhere deep beneath my feet in a way I didn't a month ago. Their eyes are focused on Lia and me.

*We will watch,* they seem to whisper.

Lia lowers her arms, then presses the tip of her dagger to the tan skin of her forearm. Slowly, she drags the blade down, a line of blood welling as she goes. "You remember this part from the spell circle, don't you?" she says to me as she works.

Around us, the other supernaturals are silent.

I *do* remember this part of the ritual, only when she did it last, the wound she made was on her sternum.

*Memnon,* I say uncertainly, reaching down our bond once more. My gaze is fixed to that line of blood.

*What do you need from me, Empress?*

I need for him to be here, but I cannot will him to come any faster than he already is, so I stay silent.

Lia moves around to the back of my chair and cuts away my bindings.

Before I can take a swing at her, her magic is there, restraining my arms. She grabs one of my hands and pries it free of her magical restraints.

Lia extends my arm out and slices her blade down my skin, parting the delicate flesh.

*Memnon!* I cry out now. *Memnon!*

*"With blood I bind, with bone I break—"*

*No, no, no!*

She grabs my cut forearm and presses her own bloody one to mine, her expression determined.

*WHAT IS HAPPENING?*

I struggle against Lia. *She's placing a binding spell on me!* I cry.

The other end of our bond goes still as death.

Then Memnon's magic is flooding my system—an ocean of it pouring into me. Normally I have to reach for it to pull it through the bond, but it's as though the sorcerer himself is shoving it all out.

With his magic comes warmth, devotion, *love*. I'm tired and weak, but I grasp what I can of his power and my own, and I funnel every bit of it down my arms and out my hands. A sluggish plume of orange and indigo magic releases, though it does nothing more than push Lia back a little. It's not even enough to break her hold on me. I can still feel her blood mingling with mine.

Maiden, Mother, and Crone, this cannot be happening.

"*Only through death shall I at last forsake.*"

I scream as a new, intrusive bond forces its way through me, the magic slicing into my body.

"*What I command, you shall obey. Your will is mine till your dying day.*"

The pain of this bond is searing, but maybe that's because, unlike the others, this one isn't consensual.

It lodges itself behind my sternum, and its roots seem to burrow into my bones. My cheeks are wet, and I realize I'm still screaming. My throat is ragged from the sound.

For a moment, I feel Memnon right there, as close as he can be through the bond.

It's quiet on his end, but from that silence comes...

*Rage. Apoplectic rage.*

So much rage. Enough to kill an army ten times over.

Beneath my sorrow and horror, I can sense the same determination that helped him fell kingdoms.

*I am coming,* he says again, but his voice is entirely different. Cold. Wrathful. *They'll pay.*

---

"Leave us." Lia says, dismissing the group of supernaturals without tearing her eyes from me.

The six individuals release their hands and wordlessly file out of the room. There's not a single sound except for my ragged sobs, and I think I might hate these supernaturals as much as I do Lia. They cannot all be as evil as she is, yet they participated in such an act.

Maybe they're bonded just as I am.

The thought draws another ragged cry out of me.

Once the door clicks shut behind them, Lia's magical hold on me loosens. Without it pinning me in place, I sink off the chair and onto the cold concrete floor.

My cries trail off, but I'm now heaving in breaths as I bow my head.

Lia steps up to me. I can see the pointed tips of her heels.

"My, my, you *are* a powerful witch. No one warned me about that. They all said you were weak, *forgetful*. An easy target but a poor asset." She taps the toe of one of her shoes against the bare floor. "And what is this?" She looks at me, but her eyes are unfocused. She tilts her head. "Another bond?" She frowns. "*Two* bonds?"

The fact that she can sense *any* bonds besides hers is horrifying.

She takes me by the jaw and tilts my head up. "I cannot allow them to exist." There's a gleeful gleam in her eyes. "That would complicate things. Your first true task once I release you tonight will be to sever each of those bonds the first chance you get."

I press a hand to my sternum as her malevolent power digs in, and I begin to heave, over and over, as it forces its intentions upon me.

Memnon could survive such an assault, but sweet, cranky Nero, who's waiting for me even now…

I heave again.

*No, no, no.*

Plum-colored magic spills from Lia, giving her an ominous backdrop. "Let's go over the basics. You will *never* harm me," she commands, the order slipping straight down the bond and into me. "You will do everything in your power to protect and serve me."

My fingers dig into the skin over my sternum. I can *feel* Lia in me just as I can Memnon. But where Memnon's magical presence is familiar and comforting, Lia's magical imprint feels like a violation.

She comes over to me then and places a hand on my head. I want to knock it away, but one of her commands activates and stops me.

I grind my teeth together, my body bowed beneath her touch.

Her deep purple magic trickles over me, then into me, and I'm powerless to stop it. But as it slips down my throat and into my body, I feel it driving out the effects of the drug in my system. I can feel my own magic swarm me again, and my control over it sharpens.

"I imagine that feels better, doesn't it?" she asks from above me.

I press my lips together.

"Answer me."

"*Yes,*" I hiss out.

Her hand slides from my head. "Why don't we have a demonstration of what it means to be bonded to me?"

I hear the click of her heels as she moves away from me.

"Bow to me."

It's not even a choice. Her power forces my body to obey. I bend forward at the waist, my arms stretching out in front of me. I press my palms into the cold concrete.

"Now crawl over and kiss my feet."

*This is a nightmare,* I think as I move across the floor to her.

Finally I understand her motives for healing me. If I were still injured, I would be incapable of doing these degrading acts. Lia obviously knows there's more than one way to hurt someone.

I press a kiss to the top of each foot, every fiber of me rejecting this moment. Lia yanks her leg back, out of my reach, and kicks my face, sending me sprawling backward.

I taste blood in my mouth as my head cracks against the concrete.

"Thank me for hurting you."

I can hear the glee in her voice. This evil motherfucker.

"Thank you for hurting me." The words are pried from my throat.

Out of the corner of my eye, I see Lia smile, her eyes narrowed. "Get up."

My legs position themselves under me, and I rise.

"That's better," she says, assessing me.

I try to lunge at her, but that same insidious magic moves through me, seizing up my muscles before I can do more than lean forward. She doesn't even notice.

She glances to the corner of the room, where the clay monster waits in the shadows.

"Creature, come here."

I tense as I watch it approach. On its forehead is that same archaic word I saw the night of the spell circle. I couldn't remember it's name or meaning then, because I thought it was Aramaic. But it's not. There's another language that shares the same alphabet as Aramaic—Hebrew.

The Hebrew word I'm looking at is *emet*.

*Truth.*

It was one of a few hundred words I learned of Hebrew before my first life was cut short. The sight of it now pricks my skin. This is ancient magic at play.

When the creature gets to her, Lia reaches out and touches its cheek tenderly. "Though I have many bonds," she says, "I don't have a familiar. My creature here is the closest thing that comes to one."

It's literally a glorified pot.

She continues to creepily stroke its skin. "Selene, you are not to defend yourself against it."

I'm not to—*what?* My gaze sharpens, moving between the two figures.

"Creature, hurt her."

The fuck?

The massive monster strides toward me, and I stumble back, calling on my magic.

To my shock, it comes to me. But the moment I try to direct it at the monster, my magic halts, bound by Lia's command.

Shit.

The creature grabs me by the throat and throws me across the room. I crash into a stack of cardboard boxes shoved near one of the walls, and I grunt at the impact, the boxes rattling as whatever's inside them is shaken.

*I can't defend myself*, I think as I scramble off the boxes as the monster heads toward me once more. That was the command. But it's not immutable. There are *always* workarounds. I should know—I spent years figuring out my own when it came to functioning with memory loss.

Lia's orders have holes I can exploit. She commanded me not to *defend* myself, but leading an attack isn't the same thing.

I gather my magic in my palms.

I might only have one chance at this. I'd better make it count. I level my gaze on the approaching monster.

"*Annihilate.*" I shove my power out at the creature.

It hits it square in the chest—

*BOOM!*

The spell shatters the monster and launches sharp sherds in every direction. I barely have time to throw up a hasty ward before bits of the creature blow back at me.

Across from me, Lia shrieks as hundreds of the sharp fragments drive themselves into her with unnatural force.

This is my opening.

I dash for the exit.

"Stop!" she shouts.

My feet pause midstride, and I want to shriek in frustration. The door out is mere feet from me.

"I *forbid* you from using your magic again tonight," Lia says hoarsely.

My power dries up, receding back into my body.

"Creature," Lia continues as she heals her various wounds, "repair yourself, then attack the witch."

My stomach hollows out, and I try not to panic as I stand there immobilized. I blew the monster into a thousand pieces. Surely it can't come back and hurt me?

But even as I think it, I hear broken bits of pottery scrape across the ground behind me. They clatter as they fit themselves together.

The thing is going to reanimate. Then it will hurt me, and I still cannot defend myself, and I cannot use magic. I might still be able to attack it, but I cannot move my legs.

I hear the thing behind me drag itself to its feet. Its heavy steps have me bracing. Once I see it, I'll try to smash its arms.

Only, it never comes within my line of vision. It stops somewhere close to my back, and the momentary stillness is hellish.

The hit comes seconds later, the monster's heavy fist driving into the side of my skull with so much force I go sprawling.

I can't see through the pain, but then the creature is there, kicking my side.

I grunt as the air is forced out of me.

Another kick, this one sliding me into nearby debris.

It lifts its foot, the bottom of its boot aimed at my head.

"You're not to kill her," Lia instructs calmly from the other side of the room. "Just hurt her—badly."

The monster crouches and takes one of my forearms into its hands, and—

*Snap.* I scream as bones break. Almost mechanically, the monster moves its touch to my upper arm and—

"No, please, no—"

*Snap.*

I scream.

*So much pain!*

*Selene, I am right here.* Memnon sounds heartbroken. *Breathe through it, my fierce queen. I am with you.*

I feel anguish a split second before I realize it's coming through the bond.

"This is just the beginning of the nightmare, Selene,"

Lia says. Her clothing is still bloody and shredded from the sherds that tore through it, and that provides me some cold comfort.

The monster releases my arm and moves down to my leg. Goddess, no...

I lock my jaw as I feel those unforgiving hands take hold of my calf. I'm not going to beg Lia to stop. Not when my pleas will only stoke her perverse enjoyment of this moment. I won't give her that.

She must sense my resolve.

I hear the ominous click of her heels getting closer and closer.

"You think a few broken bones are torture?" she says, stopping next to me. She crouches and threads her fingers through my hair, forcing my head to face hers. "I will have you do things that will make your blood curdle in your veins. Who you sleep with is now *my* choice, and I will make your sex life a horror show. I will make a list of people whom you love, and I will force you to ruin their lives until they curse your name. I will learn your dreams, and I will break them. Through it all, I will make you worship me."

Her words are punctuated by another snap, and I scream and scream, my limbs trembling and worsening the pain.

*Take my power!* Memnon is openly begging.

*Cannot...use it.*

The monster's hands move up to my thigh, and I feel his grip tighten. I swallow my plea, though I can't stop the tears that leak from my eyes or the way my body is shaking from fear and pain. No, no—

*Snap.*

The agony is indescribable. I'm not a person anymore. Just raw pain shaped into a woman.

"Enough, Creature."

The monster releases me and backs away from where I lie. I'm struggling to stay conscious through the agony. It feels like every breath is a challenge.

The chilling clicks of heels draw near. They stop right next to my face.

"Now, Selene, kiss my feet, and thank me for the pain."

I can't. It isn't possible with so many broken bones.

But my body isn't listening. I grind my teeth together so my whimpers don't slip out as I turn my head and brush my lips against the top of Lia's shoe.

Memnon's voice drifts to me across epochs of time. *Sarmatians are the fiercest people in the world. They are trained from birth to ride horses and wield weapons. They must fight in at least one battle before they are allowed to marry. And you are to be their queen... You will wear the riches of my empire, and you will ride astride my horse...and you will show these people that you were made to rule my horde of warriors.*

I cling to the memory. I was once a queen.

"*Thank...you,*" I rasp out.

I fought in battles and ruled a kingdom.

"Good," Lia says.

I gasp out several breaths, my chest heaving.

I will not let this break me.

*I will not let this break me.*

*Spoken like a true queen of warriors,* Memnon says.

I don't know if he heard my earlier memory, but I sob now, clinging to his words like they can keep out the evil happening in this room.

*The gods gave me the fiercest woman. The fiercest one. I am right here,* est amage. *Right here.*

"Listen closely. This is important," Lia says, as though I'm in any state to remember anything.

Tears track down my cheeks, and my jaw aches from how tightly I'm tensing it.

*Stay with me, Memnon,* I beg, even though he's repeatedly promised as much. I'm afraid of what's coming next.

*I'm not leaving you,* he says. *I will never leave you,* est vexava. *My love.*

I close my eyes and swallow, trying to wrap Memnon's words around me like a blanket.

"You will tell no one that you are bonded to me, nor will you give any hints that you work for me," Lia says. "Even when you are with your family and friends, you will keep my interests in the forefront of your mind. You will do my work discreetly and absolutely."

She continues, "You will find me other witches to bond with. You will look for lonely ones and ones who do not have good family relations. Those who seem promising you will befriend. You will be subtle about this, and you will not let them know about me or my intentions."

My stomach twists at the orders, and I grimace, opening my eyes. This is how Kasey picked me out, and now I'm being forced to perpetuate the cycle.

"You will call me once a week and keep me informed of potential witches as well as what's going on in the coven," Lia says. "I will call you from time to time, and if I do, you will answer. If you see a missed call from me, you will call me back as soon as you can. Once a month, we will have in-person meetings, which will take place either here in the city or in the tunnels beneath the coven. Those meetings will be followed by spell circles—you remember how that goes—and I will expect you to recruit at least one witch per circle."

I want to hurl all over again.

"If at any point I need something from you," she says, "you are to immediately—and discreetly—stop what you're doing and come to me. Got it?"

I don't have the energy to glare at her. I barely have the energy to listen over the pain.

"And," Lia continues, "if you hear anyone asking questions about the recent murders, I want to know about—"

*BOOM!*

A wave of magic ripples across the room, shaking the walls, toppling boxes, and causing more debris to fall from the ruined ceiling. Lia staggers, and my vision darkens as my injuries are jostled. The whole building quakes from the distant explosion.

"What the fuck is happening now?" Lia says.

Despite my pain, I smile.

It's not what but *who*.

Memnon has arrived.

# CHAPTER 35

*I begin to laugh, though it sounds a bit like a sob. I sound like* I've lost it, which maybe I have.

Lia's eyes find mine. "You think this is funny?" She steps on one of my legs, causing me to scream all over again.

From the other end of the bond, Memnon's warmth has iced over, and I feel his cold-blooded wrath.

There are no more words between us. It's more primal than that. All that's left is pain, rage, and vengeance, and it swirls together until I'm not sure what's mine and what's his.

*BOOM!*

The door to the room blows clear off its hinges, flying across the space and crashing into the pile of boxes.

Filling up the open doorway is my mate.

Memnon's eyes are glowing like hot coals, and his hair has lifted from his shoulders, rippling like he's swimming underwater.

I want to sob at the sight of him. As it is, my heart

leaps, and Goddess, the things I'll forgive this man for simply because he showed up.

His eyes immediately find mine, and even distant as they get when his power takes over, I swear they burn brighter.

"*Selene.*" He growls my name possessively.

His gaze scans my broken body, and that rage that whispered down our bond now *consumes* him. Memnon's power burgeons around him, sparks of it lighting up the indigo plumes like it's all a miniature storm cloud.

A split second later, his power is there, slipping down my throat and into me, reaching for my injuries and attempting to heal them from a distance. But because healing usually requires pressing hands to flesh, his magic doesn't do much besides setting my broken bones. The action causes me to scream through my teeth.

*I'm sorry, love.* His voice has an otherworldly edge to it as his magic rides him. Memnon begins striding toward me, likely to finish healing me.

"Don't come any closer," Lia warns.

Memnon pauses, his gaze flicking to the woman.

As soon as he sees her, he stills. "*Juliana.*"

Juliana?

I glance up at who I thought was Lia. Seven hells.

It all comes together fast. *Lia* must be a nickname. As in Ju-*lia*-na.

This isn't just some random witch gone rogue. This is a sorceress and one of the heirs of Ensanguine Enterprises.

Juliana Fortuna.

# CHAPTER 36

*I stare at Juliana Fortuna with new eyes as she takes in* Memnon, whose power is crackling off him. I can practically hear the gears in her head grinding together as she tries to piece together the situation from her end.

"Put your magic away," she finally commands.

I'm sure she's expecting him to do as she says. She believes he's bonded to her after all.

Instead, Memnon continues to stare at her, his expression growing colder and colder as his power gathers.

"You touched my mate."

"Mate?" I hear the surprise in Juliana's voice. "*You're* her bond?"

She glances down at me, reassessing, before returning her gaze to Memnon. I can't move with my injuries, but I imagine she's taking in his glowing eyes and rustling hair.

"Who are you really?" she asks. She must realize she's been played.

"Your executioner." He says it without malice, as though it were simply a fact, and that makes the words truly ominous.

The sorceress murmurs under her breath, drawing her magic in her hands, then she throws a spell at my mate, the thick mass of it streaked through with oily black lines.

Dark magic.

Memnon lifts a hand and *catches* the curse. I've never seen that done. I can hear it sizzling against his flesh as he closes his fist around it. With a final hiss, it snuffs out like a blown candle.

"Creature, attack him!"

The clay monstrosity charges toward Memnon, and its clay lips peel back, revealing sharp gray canines.

Right as it's nearly on Memnon, my mate reaches out and rubs away a portion of the Hebrew word *truth* from the creature's forehead.

All at once, the creature's form stiffens, losing its animation. It falls to the ground, shattering apart, the sound like a clay pot smashing. I stare at what remains of the thing's head. On its forehead, I can just make out what remains of the Hebrew word, which is now missing one letter. What remains reads as a different word entirely.

*Death.*

"Creature, repair yourself!" Juliana commands.

I wait for the bits of dried clay to cobble themselves back together, but they remain where they fell, still and lifeless.

Memnon returns his attention to the sorceress, his magic rapidly folding inward, toward his form.

For the first time, I see a flicker of misgiving in Juliana's eyes, even as they begin to glow—

*BOOM!*

Memnon's magic explodes out of him, ripping through

the room and throwing Juliana and everything else back. The only thing Memnon's magic doesn't touch is me. The hair on my head doesn't so much as stir.

The sorceress coughs as debris falls and dust kicks up. Through the haze, I see a set of glowing eyes as Memnon strides forward.

"There is one thing I hold holy in all this gods-forsaken world," Memnon says, closing in on Juliana. Goose bumps break out along my skin. His voice still has that unsettling otherness to it. "And you hurt her."

The sorceress sits up enough to lob a curse at Memnon. He bats it away like it's a fly, but when it hits the wall behind him, it *melts* a section of drywall.

She throws another and another. He doesn't bother knocking them all away, and he doesn't react at all, even when the curses eat away at his clothes, and bits of his flesh smoke.

"You cannot hurt me," Juliana insists. "I bonded you to me. I remember."

He doesn't respond, but when he bends down and grasps her by the neck, it's clear he can in fact hurt her. His magic closes in on her, the indigo swathes of it stained with dark, oily streaks.

Juliana begins to writhe and scream.

"Selene," she gasps out between cries, "kill him."

I suck in a sharp breath as my broken limbs tense at her command. She had ordered something similar of me earlier—

*Your first true task once I release you tonight will be to sever each of those bonds.*

That command hadn't taken root because she hadn't

released me, but now, *now* her insidious magic is pressing in on me, forcing my body to move.

I cry out as my broken bones are jostled.

*Est amage!*

In response, Juliana's screams intensify, as if Memnon worsened the curse he struck her with.

My body is still trying to pick itself up, broken bones and all. Beyond the pain, there is a different sort of anguish. Horror crawls along my skin at the thought of killing Memnon. I have loathed the man and wished for his demise more than once, but…but somewhere along the way, things between us have changed.

*No.* I fight the compulsion. *I will not do this.*

Sweat begins to bead on my brow as I battle the magic.

*I will not harm my soul mate.*

Just when I'm sure I'll be forced to comply anyway, the command's power over me dissipates, washing away like blood in the rain.

I breathe hard as I lie there on the ground, sweat dripping down my face. Or maybe they're tears.

Some bonds are stronger than others. Not even a forced bond can overpower a fated one.

I stare up at the ceiling. "*That foolish woman doesn't know who we are,*" I say in Sarmatian, my voice shaky. *King, queen. Husband, wife. Ancient lovers, recent enemies. Soul mates.*

Beneath his rage, I feel Memnon's violent pleasure at this acknowledgment.

He reels the writhing sorceress in close. "You made enemies of the wrong people, sorceress." I see his grip visibly tighten.

Juliana's screams have turned into choked sobs. "Please, please," she says hoarsely. She doesn't say what she's begging for. Mercy of some sort. I think she knows she's not going to get it. Not given the circumstances of the evening.

With his free hand, Memnon withdraws his dagger. "I made a promise to my mate," he says softly, "that the moment I found who had hurt her, I would make their deaths slow."

He releases Juliana's throat, and the sorceress falls to her knees. No sooner is she kneeling than Memnon grabs her hair, tilts her head back, and drags his blade across the sorceress's throat.

A line of blood blooms like a crimson necklace, and I startle at the sudden violence.

Juliana cries out, her power flaring, but Memnon's own power snaps out in response, forcing hers back into her body.

She's not dying, I realize. The cut, though it looked wicked, was simply a flesh wound.

Memnon releases her hair and brings the tip of the dagger to his other hand. Swiftly he draws it down his palm. My stomach bottoms out when I begin to suspect what he intends.

He wraps his bloody hand around the sorceress's wounded neck.

"*With blood I bind—*"

"No!" she screams. "No, no! Selene Bowers, I *command* you to stop him."

I clench my teeth as another compulsion takes root and I have to fight it off all over again.

"*With bone I break.*" Memnon begins to smile now, unholy menace in his glowing eyes. "*Only through death shall I at last forsake.*"

What Memnon is doing shouldn't be possible. The amount of magic needed for a forced bond is so massive it requires a spell circle. That's why Lia called in those supernaturals earlier when she bonded me, and it's why she hosted spell circles beneath Henbane Coven. But I can sense the sorcerer's magic relentlessly building anyway.

"*What I command, you shall obey. Your will is mine till your dying day.*"

She screams again, only this time, it's more out of anguish than physical pain.

Holy Goddess. Memnon did it. He bound Juliana's will to his own.

"You will not give Selene Bowers another order, *ever,*" he says. "You will not hurt Selene ever again. You will not hurt me ever. You will not use magic ever. You will stay here on your knees, and you won't speak, and you won't move. You will wait patiently for me." Roughly, he releases the sorceress.

Memnon crosses the room to me, his hair stirring and his eyes burning. His power billows about him as he crunches over the remains of the sorceress's creature. If I were anyone else, I would be terrified.

When he gets to me, he kneels. So much of him is consumed by his power at the moment. I can't see any softness to him. But then his hand presses to my cheek.

Beneath Memnon's touch, his power floods my body, reaching for my broken bones. The healing spell warms me as it moves though my system and mends my injuries.

His thumb strokes my cheek as he gazes down at me.

*I'm sorry,* he says. *For your pain. For not healing you sooner. For coming so late.*

I don't know how I have any more tears in me, but a few more squeeze out.

I lean into his hand. *You came.* That's all I can seem to say.

*I will* always *come,* he vows.

Gradually, my pain ebbs away. I sense it the moment I'm fully healed.

With a sob, I lunge for Memnon, wrapping my arms around him and burying my face in his shoulder. My whole body is shaking violently. Even though my body is healed, it still has some memory of all that's been done to it.

I still sense Memnon's otherness—he's more magic than man at the moment—but his arms close around me, and he holds me tight to him.

*Fierce queen, enduring mate, I've got you. I am yours, forever.*

# CHAPTER 37

*"You don't understand,"* **Juliana says angrily once Memnon** has returned to her and allowed the sorceress to speak once more. "I am the daughter of Luca Fortuna. He *will* make you pay for what you've done."

I sit amid the rubble, my body weary, my clothes in tatters, my mind aching to leave this room where so many horrors have happened.

My mate stares down at Juliana where she still kneels, studying her with those burning eyes.

"I felt it when you snapped Selene's bones one by one," he says. "I felt her pain, and I heard her screams. They will haunt me for all my days. I am not a nice man. I am an evil one—even more so than you and your siblings. Even more than your father. You think you understand pain? Torture? I want you to know that I can be even more creative than you. If you fail to cooperate with me, I will make you break your own bones, one by one."

She looks afraid now.

He crouches in front of her. "Do you want to hear the rest of what I'll do to you? How I will order you to skin yourself alive, how I will make you draw out your own intestines—"

"Stop! *Stop!*"

"Then you will truthfully tell me everything you know about the murders of witches."

"I don't know much about the murders," Juliana begins. "I didn't kill them." She pauses, like that's enough to fulfill Memnon's magical command.

However, after a couple of tense seconds, her throat works and more spills out.

"My father and my brother are the ones who know more. I don't know if they killed the witches themselves or why. I don't want to know so I've never asked."

She stops again, and I see the muscles in her throat strain as Memnon's command still rides her.

*Tell me everything*, he said.

"Each month on the night of the new moon, my sister and I deliver one or two of our bonded supernaturals to my dad and my brother. They're the ones that die."

I don't know what is more shocking: that all the murder victims were previously bonded or that we now know exactly who the killers are.

"This happens every new moon?"

Juliana clenches her jaw, then nods. "At midnight sharp."

"And your father and brother are the only ones who would know what happens to these supernaturals?"

She hesitates. "No," she eventually admits.

"Explain yourself—again, truthfully," Memnon says.

"My father and brother—they get paid for the…the

deaths. Whoever pays them probably also knows what's going on."

"Yet you don't?" Memnon says, looking unconvinced.

"It's the truth," she hisses out.

"How do I get into the Equinox on the night of the new moon?" Memnon asks.

Juliana laughs. I think she's about to tell Memnon that getting in is impossible, but then her throat works.

"You need to be invited as a guest to the midnight auction—we hold those on the new moon as well." After she speaks, she spits at Memnon.

The spittle hits his shirt. "Do that again, and I cut off a finger."

Juliana grimaces. "I hate you."

She begins to turn toward where I'm resting when Memnon catches her face.

"This is between you and me," Memnon says. "You will not look at Selene. You will not speak to her unless spoken to. Or else I get creative *and* I make you answer my questions."

My heart beats faster as Juliana glares at him.

"Now, tell me about this auction," Memnon says. "Is it connected to the murders?"

"No," she says.

"Then what is it for?" he asks.

Juliana fights this answer in particular. Eventually it's ripped from her. "We auction off bonds to supernaturals."

Goddess.

That sounds like a living nightmare.

It could've easily been my fate as well.

"The girls I bond—not all of them go to my father and

brother," Juliana continues. "Most of them are sold, either privately or at these monthly auctions."

For a second, I cannot draw in air. Then, then—

I lean over and gag. There's nothing left to purge from my stomach, but I cannot stop the visceral reaction.

It was horrifying enough when I knew Juliana was forcibly binding witches, but to realize these same women—women I went to school with, women I was friends with—were then being sold off to other supernaturals…

Memnon's magic is unspooling out of him, and through our bond, I sense his rage deepening.

"Do the"—Memnon's lip curls into a grimace—"*buyers* know these supernaturals are already bonded?"

Juliana's gaze has drifted to Memnon's magic, but now she brings her attention back to him.

"My clients believe their intended bonds are willing."

"But they're not," Memnon says flatly.

"Some are." Juliana has the gall to sound defensive. "Some are excited for their new lives."

"No one is fucking excited to be trafficked, Juliana," I say to her.

Juliana twitches, like she's about to turn to me, but Memnon's previous command stops her.

"How does the exchange happen?" Memnon says.

She glares at him. "The buyers pay the money, and we officiate a bond. Once it's complete, my own bond dissolves away, and the new pair move on with their life."

My mind catches on one detail—*her bond dissolves away*. Some of these binding spells, like the one she forced on me, are for life, while others must end the moment a new bond is created.

"Who sets the terms of this auctioned bond—you or the buyer?" Memnon asks.

I don't want to know. This is all so sick.

Juliana hesitates again. "The buyer," she eventually admits.

The terms of *that* forged bond could be anything, anything at all. Even the fabled deals with the devil are technically forged bonds, despite favoring one side over the other. Just like those bonds, these buyers could have some terrible stipulations, and it wouldn't matter. Juliana could make her bonded victims agree to it while they were still under her control.

It's not lost on me that not even the devil does forced bonds. That's how dark this shit has gotten.

I must make some noise. I feel nauseated again. It's too much. Too much pain, too much violence, too much sick, twisted perversion. I have many questions I still want answered, but I don't think I can stomach them tonight.

Memnon glances over at me, his power still consuming him. His eyes look merciless as he takes me in.

"Juliana," my mate says, "you will stay here kneeling, and you will not speak. If you displease me in any way, I will make you remove an appendage."

The sorceress glares at him, but already, the magic has silenced her.

Memnon strides over to me, his blue magic shrouding him.

He kneels next to me and cups my cheek. *I will take care of this. You are safe now, I vow it.*

He presses his palm more firmly against my skin. "*Sleep.*"

Darkness swallows me up.

# CHAPTER 38

*The first thing I notice when I rouse is a sense of weightless-*ness, like a stone has been lifted off my chest.

I blink my eyes open and realize I'm cradled in Memnon's arms, my head nestled against the crook of his neck. My body sways gently as he carries me.

*Fearsome queen. Brave-hearted warrior,* he murmurs down our bond, noticing that I've roused. *You valiantly survived horrors tonight. I could not be prouder.*

*Horrors?* I say groggily.

But then I turn my head just a little and take in a familiar room. There's debris and smashed cardboard boxes and an overturned chair. Immediately, a shiver racks my body.

I fist a bit of Memnon's shirt as I *remember.*

My gaze falls to the center of the room, where a massive pool of blood glistens around a dozen fleshy lumps that my eyes refuse to make sense of.

A hand cups my face, angling my head back to where it had been resting and shielding me from the sight.

*She died slow,* he reassures me.

I swallow thickly. Those lumps...those are Juliana. Or what's left of her at least.

Revulsion claws up my throat. But it's offset by that lightness in my chest. The bond Juliana forced on me...it's gone. I can sense the hollowed-out space where it once was. With her death, it dissolved away.

Memnon did that.

I glance up at him as we exit the room and head down a sterile hallway, my heart suddenly overfull. The sorcerer's eyes are still glowing, and his magic is still churning.

*I won't release my power until I know you're safe*, he admits.

He must be listening to my every thought.

*I am.*

"Stop that," I whisper.

He gazes down at me. *Not until I know you're safe.*

I'm too weak and weary to argue. My limbs throb and I'm still trembling faintly. My stomach feels like it won't ever keep another meal down, and my mind is rebelling against all it's witnessed this evening.

But my heart—gratitude is spilling from it. If not for Memnon, I'd likely still be in that room, enduring who knows what sorts of twisted tortures.

His arms tighten around me, and he brushes a kiss against my temple.

*I will always come for you. I will always fight for you.*

I press my lips together to keep my sad little sob in my throat. I've been whittled down to this soft, weepy thing. I would say I hate it, but right now in the security of Memnon's arms, it feels safe to be vulnerable.

So I let him carry me, not thinking much of anything as we pass one slumped form, then another and another in the hallway. I think my eyes touch on half a dozen people lying motionless on the ground before I notice the lines of blood running from their noses, eyes, and ears.

I don't need to stretch my senses or my magic out to know they're all dead.

*What happened to them?* I ask.

*They were in my way.*

Reflexively, my hand tightens around the fistful of shirt I clutch. Memnon must have done this when he entered the building.

I take it all in as we round a corner and a gust of wind hits us. I glance over at what once must've been the front entrance of the building. Now the double doors and shattered glass shards lie on the ground in the entrance hall, more bodies scattered among them.

Red and blue flashing lights spill across the space, and the gaping opening is filled with a semitransparent ward, the magical wall indigo blue. Several spent bullets lie on the other side of it, and beyond them are police officers crouching behind the open doors of their cruisers, their guns drawn. I squint my eyes as I take in the parked police cars that line the street outside the building.

As soon as the officers catch sight of Memnon, they tense and adjust their stances.

"Set the civilian down, and come out with your hands up," someone on a loudspeaker announces.

*What's going on?* I ask.

*I came for you as fast as I could*, he says apologetically.

It's obviously a bit more complicated than that. There's a whole squadron of armed officers waiting for him, each one ready to violently stop him. He must've badly broken the law to get to me.

Emotion knots in my throat, and I fight back another sob.

I *begged* the sorcerer to come faster. I wondered what was taking him so long. And now guns are being pointed at him because he did his best.

Memnon's grip tightens on me as he stares out at the cops.

Rather than setting me down, his magic rolls out of him like a wave, rushing toward the officers until they are all swallowed up by it. Memnon's power lingers outside for several minutes, but I hear car doors slam shut and the roar of engines as they move away. When it clears, the street outside the building is empty. In the sky above, a helicopter I didn't notice before hangs around, but as I watch, it slowly drifts away.

Memnon's boots crunch on the glass as we cross the room, then pass through his ward.

He gazes down at me, and I sense, behind those glowing eyes, that he's mostly magic and instinct.

*You were brave tonight,* he says down our bond. His hand moves to cradle my head. *But now* rest.

The world goes dark.

---

I jerk awake at the sound of a door slamming.

"Easy, little witch, you're safe," Memnon says from slightly above me.

I blink, taking in the sorcerer still holding me. His hair has settled, and his eyes are now their usual smoky-brown color. They shimmer too brightly, like he might be fighting back tears.

That look has my own heart racing, and my emotions feel too big for my body—or maybe they're his? The bond between us seems extra loud at the moment.

405

I reach a hand up, cupping his face and lightly tracing the edges of his scar.

*Safe...*

It all comes roaring back to me then. The party, the spiked drink, the terrifying broom ride, and my abduction. Then the torture, the endless torture. There had been revelations after that and a harrowing escape, but my mind keeps taking me back to that room and the pain—

"You're safe, my queen." Memnon speaks softly to me in Sarmatian, using the same tone he reserved for skittish horses. "You're not there anymore."

A choked sob escapes my lips as Memnon continues carrying me deeper into the building—

"You're here in our home," he reassures me before my panic can spike. "There are over a hundred wards guarding this house and the land around it. This is not Henbane. No one can get in here. You are safe."

I hadn't realized how much I had tensed up until right then, when I relax.

It's strange on the one hand to be completely uninjured yet to still bear the visceral memory of the pain. My mind is unconvinced I'm healed.

Memnon carries me into the kitchen, setting me down on the island countertop in the center of the space.

I reach for him, but he catches my hands and clasps them together. "I'm getting you water. I won't leave your sight."

I draw in a deep breath, then, licking my dry lips, I nod, maybe too quickly. Water. I'd like water.

Giving me one last meaningful look, Memnon releases my hands and moves toward a cupboard.

While he's grabbing a glass, I hear the scrabble of claws in the next room over. A split second later, Nero bounds into the kitchen, presumably coming in from outside. As soon as he sees me, his pupils dilate. The big cat only pauses a moment before leaping onto the island, nearly bowling me over in the process.

"Nero," Memnon says sharply.

But my familiar has already crawled halfway onto my lap. He lifts his head and presses his snout against the juncture where my jaw meets my neck. If he were a dog, I'm sure I'd now get lavished with licks. Nero being a panther, he nips at my jaw, growling a little.

"Hey—" I say.

"*Nero.*" Memnon's tone has darkened into something dangerous as he comes over with a glass of water.

The panther gives my jaw an abrasive lick, then bumps me with his head.

I slip into my familiar's mind long enough to sense a restless irritation and an edge of relief. At least I think those are the emotions. I do recognize the love beneath it all as he looks at me.

Returning to my own mind, I pet the big cat.

"I'm not going to apologize to you for leaving you here," I say. "You would've gotten hurt had I taken you along."

Just like that, I'm sucked back into that room.

*Your first true task once I release you tonight will be to sever each of those bonds.*

If Nero had been there… A shudder works its way through me, and my body is trembling all over again.

Memnon steps in close and takes my hand, pressing the glass of water into it.

"You're not in that room. You're here, in our kitchen, with your soul mate and your familiar," he says, and again, his eyes glisten as he gazes at me. "We both love you, and we would happily kill and die for you. Now, please, *est amage*, drink the water. You'll feel better."

Again, his words have me relaxing, and I do drink the water in several long gulps. I feel faintly queasy.

Goddess, but this night needs to end. All I want is to pass out pressed against my familiar and my soul mate.

"Then that's what you'll get," Memnon says softly. "Nero, you're sleeping in the bedroom with Selene."

My panther rises up, looking more than a little pleased at that. He hops off the counter and slinks out of the kitchen toward the main bedroom.

Once my familiar is gone, Memnon scoops me back up and begins carrying me once more.

I lean my head against his shoulder. *You can put me down,* I say tiredly.

*You'll have to command it of me,* he says. *Otherwise, that's not happening.*

I'd have to command it of him…

I turn my face into his chest as my face crumbles.

"I'm sorry," I whisper. "So sorry."

He rubs my back. "For what, little witch?" he says, perplexed.

"The bond." My voice breaks. "It's awful, so awful. I'm sorry." I begin to sob. "I *never* should've agreed to it."

My mate's grip tightens on me. "*I* offered *you* the bond," he reminds me as we head down his hallway. "I did so willingly, to repay the debt I owed you. If you hadn't accepted it, I would've never gotten the chance to atone for my mistakes."

His answer doesn't placate me. I felt what it was like to have another's will imposed on me.

"I command you to never take another command from me," I say.

Memnon stares at me steadily for a few seconds.

"*No*," he eventually says.

I raise my eyebrows. "What do you mean *no*?"

Memnon clasps me by the back of my neck and forces me to look at him. "I gave you my power because I did unforgiveable things to the only person I have ever truly loved. And I *like* our forged bond. I can tell I'm earning back your trust, and I get pleasure from serving you. We are soul mates, Empress. You are my heart, and I trust you absolutely with this power you have over me. I will not let you break this bond, just like I didn't let you break the one fate forged between us."

Memnon halts at the threshold to the main bedroom.

"So," he says, "I am asking you, as the man who wants to continue proving himself to you, to take back your last command."

I pull away so I can really see him.

"Fine," I say, making a face. "I take back my previous command." The words taste like ash on my tongue, but as soon as I speak them, Memnon's expression softens.

"Thank you," he says, and he resumes walking once more.

He approaches the bed where Nero is already waiting, and his magic pulls back the sheets.

"I'm dirty," I realize. I'm still covered in blood and grime.

I've barely spoken when the sorcerer's magic spills over me, scouring my body. I feel the sticky bloodstains vanish away, and I can only imagine what else the spell cleaned off.

"Better?" Memnon asks.

I nod.

His power moves to my feet, and it tugs off my boots and socks, and they fall to the floor.

From Memnon's closet, one of his T-shirts floats out, passing over the bed, where Nero tries to nip at it.

Memnon's magic drifts over me once more, and the outfit I wear melts off my body. His power is still hiding my nudity when his shirt slips itself over my head. I reach out to thread my arms through the armholes.

"You look good in my clothes, *est amage*," he says as the shirt settles over my torso and his magic clears. "You always have."

I give him a whisper of a smile, and for the first time tonight, I see Memnon grin. I think it's purely in response to my own smile.

He settles me into the bed, then retreats.

"*Memnon*." I hate how panicked I feel at his absence.

"I need to remove my own clothes."

Right, of course.

I give him that same anxious nod and watch him undress as Nero nestles in close.

I pet my panther, but my entire body stays on edge until Memnon, clad only in a pair of boxer briefs, slips into the bed with me.

I flip onto my side to more fully face Memnon. There's so much I want to say to him, so much I saw, so much Memnon did. I can't seem to put words to any of it at the moment, so I simply take one of his hands and clasp it between mine.

"Thank you," I whisper. I brush a kiss against his knuckles. "*Thank you*."

"Don't thank me," he says softly, searching my face. "I will *always* come for you, and I will *always* fight for you."

He wraps a hand around my clasped ones. "Little witch," he breathes, "please tell me what happened before I found you."

Another shudder works its way through my system.

I *can't.*

"Read my mind." It's a plea, one that would allow me to avoid lingering longer than necessary on what happened this evening. It only registers a few seconds later, when his hands move to my head, that I gave him a command, one he's forced to follow.

I squeeze my eyes shut. "I'm sorry. Read my mind *only* if you want."

"Selene." As Memnon speaks, his magic sifts out of him, the inky blue clouds of it pooling in the air. "Stop apologizing to me."

His power creeps toward me, moving as though it has a mind of its own. I draw in a breath, and as easy as that, the magic slips in, coating my mouth and plunging down my throat.

I brace my hands on his forearms as the night flickers behind my eyes. Bones breaking, screaming, suffocating pain. I swallow down the taste of bile, my body shaking all over again from the memory.

His eyes begin to glow and his hair lifts. That burning gaze finds mine.

"The sorceress is lucky she's dead," he says solemnly.

I tense.

His thumbs stroke the sides of my face, even as his power continues to rage through him. "I will draw our enemies out and break them one by one," he says, his eyes hypnotic. "I won't stop until I make chalices from their skulls and coats from their skin. I will not rest until the *entire* Fortuna clan is nothing but a fucking memory."

These are monstrous promises, but for once, they don't frighten me as they should. The Fortunas have built an entire empire on abusing supernaturals. They deserve the ruthless attentions of someone like Memnon.

I squeeze his forearms, a tear slipping out.

"This," he finishes, "I swear to you."

# CHAPTER 39

***Yesterday, I woke as one person.***

Today, I am another.

I feel a hardness to me, one that wasn't there before. If yesterday I was exposed and vulnerable, today new armor has grown back. The world exists on one side of it, and on the other… The only things that exist within that armor are me and my bonds.

Memnon must notice this change because I've caught him studying me a few times since we've woken up, a curious look on his face, like he's trying to figure me out.

Nero sticks to me like glue.

There are a thousand things the sorcerer and I need to discuss, but right now, all I want is some semblance of normalcy to follow the nightmare of last night.

I pad into the kitchen, opening up cupboards and making myself at home. Since I started living here, cookies and crackers, chips and granola bars have filled up what originally was a bare pantry.

Today, there's cereal.

I raise an eyebrow when I take a long look at the various colorful boxes that were definitely made with kids in mind.

After a moment, I pull out one of them. "Is this what you think of me?" I ask, holding the box up.

Memnon lifts his chin. "Tell me I'm wrong."

I give him a look as I close the pantry door. It's annoying how accurately he has me pegged. My heart might have iced over, but I will always have a soft spot for colorful, oversugared cereal.

"I couldn't buy the one with those round chocolate balls," he adds, grabbing a bowl and spoon. "It looked too much like goat shit," he says, setting the items on the table.

"I've never *once* considered that in my life," I say, watching him move to the refrigerator. Since last night, he's pulled on some loose-fitting pants, but his torso remains gloriously, distractingly bare.

"I will not feed my queen food that's offensive to look at," he says, opening the refrigerator door. "Now sit down and let me serve you."

I cringe at that word. *Serve.*

"I can do it myself," I say, carrying the box of cereal over to the table.

"Believe it or not, my queen, I want to do this." Memnon comes to my side and sets the milk down. "Stop assuming otherwise."

Memnon has me sit there while he pours my cereal, then milk, into my bowl.

I stare down at it. "Who takes care of you?" I ask offhandedly.

"Hmm?" he says. He's already drifting away, moving to the stove where a teapot rests.

I turn away from my breakfast and toward my soul mate. "Who takes care of *you*?" I repeat.

He glances up, meeting my gaze.

The answer is clear.

*No one.*

We used to take care of each other, and he had family and friends and a kingdom to give him whatever he needed. But that's all gone now.

Though my mind still recoils from what happened last night, I force myself to remember the police officers, the dead bodies...

There's a trail of evidence Memnon left behind when he came for me. He saved me from a nightmarish situation, and he might've inadvertently gotten himself into one. And despite his staggering power, not even Memnon is omnipotent.

I feel that armor I woke up with, and I feel our bond within it.

I shake my head as I look at him. "That changes today. From this moment on, *I* also take care of *you*."

This puts me on the wrong side of the law. Shit, it puts me on the wrong side of a lot of things. I don't care.

Memnon gazes at me, and I don't think he breathes. I can feel a sharp, painfully sweet emotion through our bond. I know from experience it's one that cannot be formed into words.

My own emotions get lodged in my throat. I don't want this to be a big deal. I just want this to be the way things are between us: From now on, we take care of each other. It's not just one way.

My magic drifts out of me, a tendril of it reaching for one of the cupboards and withdrawing a bowl. Another rope of it opens a drawer and removes a spoon. Both items float back to the table and clatter onto the spot next to me. My power pushes out a chair.

"Sit," I say. "Come eat with me."

I force down an apology that wants to bubble up at the command. Instead, I grab the cereal box and pour him a bowl of it while he takes a seat.

He grimaces at the colorful cereal, but when his attention moves to me, Memnon looks happy. Really happy. My heart leaps at his reaction.

"What happened to the bodies last night?" I ask as I pour out milk into his cereal. "The ones inside the building?"

Memnon tentatively dips a spoon into his breakfast, looking highly suspicious of the rainbow cereal.

"I left them there," he says. "The Fortunas can clean up their own mess this time."

He scoops up a spoonful of the cereal and brings it to his lips. After a moment's hesitation, he takes a bite.

Immediately, he makes a face, and I can tell he is fighting to get that mouthful down his throat. "What on Api's good earth *is* this?"

Memnon looks like it's personally offended him.

"Cereal."

"I love you, Selene, but this—this is unholy shit."

I smile at that, oddly tickled by his reaction. "Fine. You don't have to eat it."

Memnon pushes the bowl away.

As he's about to stand, I place a hand on his inked forearm. "What about the Politia and the human police? Both are probably looking for you."

He takes my hand and threads his fingers through mine. I stare at our entwined hands, his bronze skin against my paler tone. A thrilling sensation courses through me at the sight.

"They can look. I am not worried about them," he says. Memnon gives my hand a squeeze. "Remember, there is only one law humans ever follow: Might makes right. I don't plan on being dragged away by cops—magical or otherwise."

I'm still worried, and I have to fight the urge to go to him now and wrap myself in his arms, afraid he will slip beyond my reach the way he once did.

"There are, however, a few final things I must take care of today," he says. "I'll be out for a little while."

"You're going back?" I say sharply. There are so many things we haven't even begun to discuss, but at the top of that list is the fact that Memnon probably incriminated himself to his employers. If he goes back...who knows what they'll do to him? There's a chance they're already looking for him.

Memnon gives his head a shake. "No, I'm sure after last night, I've been compromised. Truthfully, I've been preparing to leave the Fortunas' employment long before this. But I need to tie up a few loose ends."

I squeeze his hand harder. "You'll be safe?"

He squeezes it back. "For you, *est amage*, I will be."

———

Memnon and I still haven't spoken about what we learned last night when he takes me via ley line to Henbane. It needs to be discussed, but both of us have other tasks we must handle first.

I've come to the decision that until the new moon, I will stay with Memnon. My own identity could've been compromised last night, and though Juliana is gone, her family and the criminal ring they run are not. Like Memnon, today is mainly about tying up loose ends.

I left my phone, wallet, and keys in my room, and I need to grab them and anything else I might need for the next week. There's also a personal matter I want to deal with.

Memnon and I step off the ley line and into the empty, dark crypt. The candles around us have barely sparked to life when Memnon grabs my arm and reels me back to him.

I have only a moment to look up at him before his mouth crashes into mine. The sorcerer gathers me to him like a man starving for touch, connection.

Reflexively, my lips move against his, but as my mind catches up, I fall into the kiss, just as consumed by it as he is.

Memnon's hands are squeezing my arms, and now they're tangled in my hair as his tongue strokes mine. My own hands have moved to his back, and my nails dig into his flesh. There's a maelstrom of emotions moving between the two of us. My loyalty, his love, these treacherous circumstances that are binding us together.

Not so long ago, I hated Memnon with a passion. Now... now that hate seems to be a very, very distant thing.

Memnon rips his mouth away. "Stay fucking safe today, *est amage*."

It's an easy promise to agree to. Still—

"I will if you will."

"Done."

His eyes drop to my mouth, and as though he cannot help himself, he leans back in and retakes my lips, kissing me with a rough desperation.

"Sweeter than honey," he murmurs against my mouth. He forces himself away, backing up. "I plan on tasting the rest of you tonight," he vows, a searing look in his eyes.

I feel my skin flush.

Even in the dim light he must notice it, because he says, "Love the way you blush, little witch. I hope you do that again when I eat you out like dinner later."

"*Memnon*—" I admonish.

But he's already stepped back onto the ley line and vanished from sight.

# CHAPTER 40

*I enter my residence hall, no longer fearful of the enemies* housed under this roof. I have an ease—and a resolve—I didn't have a day ago.

Inside the house, a row of bags are piled in the foyer, and as I head up the stairs, the witches I pass appear to be packing or speaking in low, somber tones. The atmosphere of the place is strange and unsettling.

I step off the stairs on the fourth floor of the house and head down a wing I haven't much visited. The buzzing lights flicker on and off in their sconces as I pass by room after room, as though the magic itself can sense a shift in me.

As I sidestep yet another pile of bags stacked in the hallway, I begin to wonder if this exodus has to do with Juliana's death. But she couldn't have possibly had so many witches bonded to her, could she?

The hallway at the end of the fourth floor hooks right, and beyond the turn, only two rooms remain, one to my left and one to my right.

The smell of formaldehyde thickens the air, and I feel bad for the witch on the right. It reeks back here.

I approach the door on my left and open it without knocking.

Inside, the first thing I see are shelves and shelves of mason jars, each one containing bits and pieces of zoological anatomy. One jar has eyeballs; another contains toads. I rip my gaze away before I can figure out the rest. Resting on the desk beneath them is a taxidermy cat—one that's in rough shape. A massive vulture perches on the stuffed creature's back, and as I watch, it pecks at the thing.

Well, that answers the question of how the cat got to be in such poor condition.

I don't have time to take in the rest of the room before I hear a gasp.

My gaze moves to the floor, where Olga looks busy putting together a skeleton of some animal.

"Selene?" Her eyes flick over me. "What are you doing here?"

I don't bother with niceties. "I know you gave me a spiked drink last night." I step into the room and close the door behind me. "I wonder if you can guess what happened after that."

She shrinks back. "I don't know what—"

"I fell off my broom, broke a few bones." I say it casually as I step deeper into the room, as though the memory doesn't hurt me. "Then I was collected."

I stare down at her, letting the silence settle a bit.

"I imagine you don't want to know the next part," I say, crouching down in front of her, fully aware I'm being a menace. I don't care. I want her to see the unshed tears in my eyes. I want her to see my horror and my pain. "I was taken to a room, and I was tortured, then bound to a psychopath against my will, then tortured some more."

"I—I don't..."

"I know you were bonded," I say, speaking over her, "and I know you were made to do many things against your will."

Olga blinks a few times, and I see her tears well.

"Juliana—Lia—is dead. If you feel a lightness in your chest, you're not imagining it. Whatever link held you to her, it's gone."

Olga's eyes are wide as she touches her chest. "She's... gone?" the witch whispers.

I nod. "I understand she made you do things, and you didn't have a choice in the matter." I suppress the shiver that wants to work its way through me. "But you do have to atone for what you've done—to me and the other supernaturals you've hurt."

"I didn't *want* to hurt anyone!" she says sharply. It sounds like a line she's been silently telling herself to feel better. I cannot imagine the horrors she's been exposed to before now.

She opens her mouth to say more, but I wave it off. "It doesn't matter. What *does* matter is that we weren't the only supernaturals forced into bonds, and Juliana—or Lia, depending on how you knew her—wasn't the only one making those bonds. The murdered witches found on campus were bonded before their deaths, just like you and me, but something happened to them in their final moments, and I want to know what."

"Why are you telling me this?" she asks.

My eyes scan the morbid decorations of Olga's room. "In your ledger, did you record any of the last words given by the murdered witches?" It's a long shot, but she's obsessed with that thing.

Olga's eyes brighten. "I have two of them—but they are not public knowledge, and I'm not allowed to share those lines."

Oh, so now she wants to be a law-abiding citizen?

I place a hand on her arm and lean in. "I am not one to make threats, Olga, but I had a rough fucking night. So please make an exception for a friend, or I'll start destroying your room one decoration at a time."

Wisps of my pale orange magic drift out and move to her shelves. Her jars rattle and clink as my power descends on them.

"All right, all right!" she says begrudgingly, giving me a disgruntled look. "I'll do it, just this once—to make amends for...last night."

I withdraw my magic as the witch gets up, muttering under her breath as she crosses to her bookcase.

From it, she pulls out her Ledger of Last Words, her fingers lovingly trailing along the spine. It reminds me of how much I adored my own notebooks, back when I relied on them. An aching sense of nostalgia rises in me. I hadn't realized how much I missed paging through them until now.

Olga settles back down on the floor beside me and opens the book. She flips through it, and I catch glimpses of names and dates and quotes—the final words these various individuals spoke before they died.

She stops on a page with a redacted row, the name, date, and quote blotted out entirely with black ink. There's another blacked-out row on the following page as well. I stare at those omissions. I'm sure they hold the key.

A bit of wine-red magic slips out of Olga. She taps a

finger on the open pages of her ledger. "What I'm about to share with you was only shared with me because the Politia hired me on to pull last words from a couple of the bodies."

"They *hired* you?"

"Yeah. Not everyone can coax information from a body. It's a rare gift," she says matter-of-factly.

I mean, I might not use the word *gift* when it requires handling dead bodies, but sure, it's rare.

My attention drifts to her mutilated, stuffed cat. "I... understand."

Olga follows my gaze. "That's Mr. Whiskers. He was my first cat. Odessa is fond of him."

As she speaks, the vulture—Odessa, presumably—pecks at the poor thing again.

I take in the rest of her surroundings. "You really like death, don't you?" My eyes touch on a row of animal skulls resting behind her bed, then linger on a set of mounted shadow boxes that house pinned butterflies.

"It's the ultimate mystery," Olga says. "One even we witches only get a few glimpses of."

With that, she holds her hand over the open book. More of her magic sifts from her palm, small plumes of it billowing out along the surface of the book. When her magic clears, the blotted lines have vanished, and in their place are rows of writing. The first one reads:

*Katherine Thompson | Age 22 | Death Date: September 25, 2023 | Last Word(s): Oh Goddess—[screams]*

I grimace at the entry.

"This next one I find particularly interesting," Olga says,

tapping on the second entry. As soon as I see the name, I have to steel myself. *Charlotte Evensen.*

I knew her, as did Olga, not that she gives any indication of it now.

I don't really want to read the entry. These are no longer just words on the page but the last and likely agonized words of a former friend.

*Charlotte Evensen | Age 20 | Death Date: October 10, 2023 | Last Word(s): Damn you and your kind to the farthest pits of hell. May you rot there.*

*Damn you and your kind?*

I glance at Olga. "What do you think that means?"

Now my coven sister looks particularly animated. "I don't know, but the bodies I saw were mauled. Perhaps we're dealing with a supernatural that is not fully human or one that can shift."

I shiver at that. I've been working hand in hand with the lycanthropes. Could they...?

No, the thought is too twisted to consider. Shifters hold family above all else. They were wrecked when one of their own showed up murdered.

But Charlotte's final words do bring up an aspect of the killings that I'd overlooked—the manner in which they died. Mauled and steeped in dark magic.

What could the Fortunas possibly want with a bunch of gruesomely killed witches? Where's the profit in that sort of death?

Whatever the answer, it will happen again in a week unless Memnon and I can stop it.

# CHAPTER 41

*When I get to my room, my phone is ringing.*

I cross the room and snatch it up from where I left it on my bed.

"Hello?"

"Finally." Kane's voice is unnaturally gruff.

Goblin's tits. I don't want to talk to this man. I haven't even begun to sort through my own tangled emotions toward him after last night.

"What's going on?" he demands.

"What do you mean what's going on?" I say, gathering together the belongings I'm going to need for the next week.

"Memnon is all over the news."

"*What?*"

I rush over to my laptop and wake the device up. As quickly as I can, I log into one of the few supernatural news outlets. On its home page is a grainy photograph of Memnon on the street outside the building I was held in.

The angle makes me think it was taken by a security camera. His eyes are glowing, and his hair is partially lifted. The camera couldn't capture his magic, but it's obvious it must be spread out around him. The headline reads *33 Dead in Largest Magical Attack of the Year: Killer at Large.*

Fuck, fuck, fuck.

"You're just now hearing about this?" Kane says.

"Hmm?" I'm still distracted by the photo. In it, Memnon's scar is hard to see, and his tattoos are entirely obscured. But there are likely more images out there.

"He's in both the magical and nonmagical news." Kane pauses, then adds, "Selene, I've seen at least one picture of him carrying a woman. Tell me that isn't you." His voice has softened. "Tell me after the party, you got home safely—that you've been ignoring my calls purely out of anger."

I draw in a long breath, my heart hammering louder and louder. My gaze returns to the photo.

"Memnon blew his cover saving me," I admit.

"Saving you?" Kane echoes. "What happened to you after you left the party?" In his voice, there's a note of fear.

"I...I don't think I can tell you over the phone."

The line is quiet for a moment.

"Selene, I'm sorry," Kane finally says. At first I think he's apologizing for last night, until he adds, "You're status as friend of the pack will be revoked at the next meeting. We cannot protect the mate of a murderer."

I tighten my grip on the phone.

*It's just you and your bonds. They are the only ones you can trust.*

I push away the thought. What would Roxilana say? Roxilana who lived through the death of her own family, who ruled hard men and women and saw too many battles.

She wouldn't settle.

"Memnon has been officially accused of nothing," I say. "Any assumption of guilt on his part is pure hearsay." I draw in a steadying breath. In a softer tone I add, "Your alpha needs to hear what Memnon and I learned last night."

"Memnon is not welcome—"

"I control Memnon." I ignore the sick twist in my gut that comes with that statement. "I will give him whatever command your alpha would like to feel more at ease, but, Kane, I am asking you, as the future alpha of your pack, to listen to what we have to say." After a moment, I admit, "I think if we want to take these people down, we'll need your pack's help."

We cannot trust the Politia, and we likely still cannot trust the witches. The shifters might be the last line of help either Memnon or I have.

It's quiet for a long time.

Kane sighs. "Okay, Selene," he capitulates. "One last favor for a friend of the pack. Be at the cabin at six p.m. sharp."

The line clicks before I can thank him.

I blow out a breath, then reach down my bond.

*Memnon?* I call out to my mate. *I arranged a meeting with the lycanthropes at six to tell them what we've learned. Before then, I'd like to discuss with you everything we know.*

I feel Memnon's slow smile through our connection, and it makes my lower belly tighten.

*Hello, my queen.*

My pulse races at the sound of his voice.

*I will have to meet you there,* he says apologetically, *but before then let us chat like this and form a battle strategy.*

A battle strategy. I glance at the news article once more and take in Memnon's grainy form. We do need a strategy.

A shiver of anticipation—and maybe a little foreboding—moves through me. It's been two thousand years, but I'm finally starting to feel like the queen I once was.

# CHAPTER 42

***The meeting with the lycanthropes is going poorly.***

It has been since Memnon and I stepped into their soundproof room minutes ago. Every shifter but Kane is openly growling as we take our seats. Even their elder, Apani, appears hostile.

Vincent doesn't bother sitting. Instead, he leans his fists on the table and glares at Memnon, his wolf shining out of his eyes.

"Let me make something absolutely clear: At this point, I don't want to hear what either of you have to say, I'm not interested in working together, and as soon as we take a vote to remove you"—he nods at me—"as a friend of the pack, I am planning on tipping off the Politia that I know who last night's *mass murderer* is."

My clasped hands tremble a little as I sit there and watch the alpha seethe across the table. I'm rusty at reining in my emotions, but next to me, Memnon is making an art of it. He's splayed in his seat, his forefinger rubbing his lower lip, projecting only mild interest in the words being lobbed against us.

"The only reason this meeting is happening at all is because Kane insisted on it."

Kane sits on my other side, just as he did during the last meeting.

I draw in a deep breath and force my frayed nerves to settle. "I appreciate you all coming here nonetheless," I say.

Vincent glares at me.

"You're an honorable man," I say. "But the people who have hurt your pack are not. Nor do they care to play by the rules the rest of us supernaturals try to follow."

"As opposed to your mate?" He nods to Memnon. "Don't give me that bullsh—"

"On Monday, November 13," I cut in, "the night of the new moon, there will be a midnight auction at the Equinox Building in San Francisco. But this is no ordinary auction. Supernaturals will be auctioning off *other* supernaturals. Witches, mages, and likely shifters."

The growls in the room slowly grow quiet, and reluctantly, Vincent takes his seat.

"Specifically," I continue, "what is being auctioned is called a forged bond—a magical bond that connects two supernaturals together, potentially until death. Depending on the terms of this bond, one or both parties can exert control over the other. Despite the sometimes distasteful nature of them, forged bonds are technically legal. However, the supernaturals being auctioned have already secretly been bonded once against their will to force their participation and cooperation in these auctions. This is likely what would've happened to Cara if the forced bond had gone through.

"The Fortuna family then scoops up the profit from

these…sales, and they will continue to do so unless they are stopped."

The silence in the room is almost painful.

"That's not all," I say. "We've discovered the murder victims were themselves bonded to members of the Fortuna crime ring at the time of their deaths. The Fortunas use these bonds to exert absolute control over supernaturals. And like the auction, we know the murders are also happening in the Equinox Building." I take another quick glance at Memnon. "And we have good reason to believe another murder will happen on the night of the auction." Before anyone can ask me how I know this, I add, "For witches and several other supernaturals, the new moon represents not just literal darkness but secrecy, obscurity, mystery, and confusion. It's when witches are likeliest to perform illicit spells and forbidden magic. It's the one night every lunar cycle when dark magic carries the most power."

For a long moment, the room stays quiet.

Finally, Vincent lets out a long sigh and reaches into his pocket. He fishes out two vials of truth serum.

"Before we discuss anything further," the alpha says, "I want you both to drink this so I can confirm the truthfulness of your words."

I bite back a groan, but when he tosses the vial to me, I readily unstopper it and drink the thing down, wincing at the taste.

Memnon catches the vial lobbed at him, but he just stares at it. I can already tell he's going to resist the alpha's commands.

"Memnon."

The sorcerer looks at me, the corner of his mouth curving up. He removes the cork then and holds it up.

"For you and only you," he toasts to me, then he kicks the drink back.

The room is quiet as the potion takes effect. I can feel the magic winding around my windpipe and coating my tongue.

"Is everything you told me about the auction and the murders true?" Vincent asks me.

"To the best of my knowledge, yes," I say.

His gaze shifts to Memnon. "Did she tell the truth?" Vincent asks.

"As she knows it, yes," Memnon says.

"As she knows it," Vincent echoes. "And how do *you* know it?"

Memnon and Vincent stare one another down.

Next to me, Kane rotates, his eyes fixed on my face.

"How did *you* get this information?" he asks me. What he really wants to know is what happened last night.

I blow out a breath, even as my stomach turns over. That earlier strength I felt is slipping...

*You are the strongest person I know,* est amage, Memnon says. *Take your time. I am here.*

I draw a deep breath. "The same woman who tried to bond Cara came for me last night—after the bonfire. Her name is Juliana Fortuna, daughter of Luca Fortuna. She... forced me to bond with her."

The room is unnaturally quiet for several seconds.

"*What?*" Kane finally says. His voice has gone deep and gravelly. "You mean to tell me that if you had left the beach with me, this would not have happened?"

Memnon sits forward a little. "What's this now?" His magic is beginning to unfurl out of him. He hasn't heard about what happened between me and Kane last night *because it wasn't important.* I didn't realize we were going to have a clash over it.

"Are you still bonded to this Juliana?" the alpha cuts in.

"No," Memnon cuts in. "I killed the sorceress."

It's quiet again, and I imagine Vincent, Apani, Kane, and the pack beta, Irene, are all putting together what they might've seen on the news with this information.

Memnon's gaze narrows on Kane. "By then, she had spent a good hour torturing my mate. I bound the woman to me, forced her to give up the information we just shared, and then I gave her the death she deserved."

If I expected the shifters to be horrified by Memnon's implied brutality, I assumed wrong. They all have a slightly feral look about them, but none seem disturbed by the information. If anything, they seem to be reconsidering him.

"An hour?" Kane says, his voice rough. Clearing his throat, he runs a hand over his mouth. "Shit, Selene..." When Kane looks at me again, there is so much pain in his eyes.

I shake my head. "I'm...fine."

*Hate that word*, Memnon says down our bond.

To the rest of the room, I say, "Juliana's death freed a number of supernaturals from their forced bonds, and it's likely some of them will bring this information to the Politia. If you have a pack member working for the authorities, this is how you can verify our story."

The room is quiet, almost thoughtful.

"You're planning on attending the upcoming auction?" Vincent finally asks.

"Yes, we plan on stopping it," Memnon says. My soul mate looks like he's relishing the thought, and why wouldn't he? It's undoubtedly going to get messy and violent, and Memnon was raised for battle.

Kane looks between us, frowning. "Doing so could get you killed. Why don't you just let the Politia handle this? If supernaturals are informing them of these forced bonds like you said, they might go after the sorcerers themselves."

Memnon leans back in his seat. "*If* these newly unbonded supernaturals do report their experiences to the Politia, and *if* the Politia believe them, and *if* the department's pockets are not too weighed down by Fortuna money, then *perhaps* they will go after this crime ring. The stars must align just so for those cursed authorities to do anything."

"The sorcerer has a point, Kane," Vincent says, his eyes flicking to the shifter sitting next to me. "It's not clear the Politia will have enough evidence or time to stop the Fortunas before this auction, especially not when they're likely pooling their resources to hunt down a mass murderer." Vincent's gaze moves pointedly to Memnon.

My mate narrows his eyes at the alpha, but before he can say anything, I cut in. "They're taking my coven sisters." There is a whole previous lifetime of steel in my voice. "And they're taking your pack mates."

Irene growls at my words. "We're aware."

I continue. "I'm not willing to risk another supernatural dying or getting bonded against their will because these monsters care more about money than about human lives."

Vincent clears his throat. "We must discuss this with the entire pack before we make a decision about our involvement in this," the alpha says.

Memnon leans across the table, his entire demeanor going from relaxed to malevolent in two-point-five seconds. "You will *not*."

The alpha growls, his eyes shifting. "Think twice, sorcerer, before you challenge me beneath my own roof."

Memnon's eyes begin to glow. "We've discussed this before. I will not let you put my soul mate at risk because you believe everyone has a right to know this classified information." The alpha's growl only deepens, but now Memnon rises, leaning his hands heavily on the table. "Do you want me to tell you how the sorceress broke my mate's bones one by one? How I *heard* Selene's screams through our bond before I could get there? These are not mild people. You do not have to involve your pack in this business, but you will not risk *mine*."

The air is crackling with tension. What muscles I can see of the alpha's are taut. Something is about to happen unless I put a stop to it.

"Once the sorceress bonded me," I say, interrupting the standoff, "Juliana commanded me to keep our bond a secret. She then ordered me to be loyal to her above all others."

Vincent is still squaring off with Memnon, but the other shifters are listening to me, so I press on.

"So if you want to find the shifters who might be under forced bonds," I continue, "give your pack mates a vial of truth serum and ask each one these questions: One, did you swear an oath to secrecy with someone outside the pack? And two, were you forced to do so against your will?" Vincent has reluctantly torn his gaze from Memnon. He too is now listening to me.

"Exclude any shifters who answer *yes* to those questions from the meeting," I say, "and make sure no information gets back to them. Then make your decision." My gaze moves over Vincent and Irene, Apani and Kane. "As for me and Memnon, you already know our decision. If a fight breaks out, we will defend any shifters present at the auction as well as any other supernaturals there against their will. I hope your pack considers joining us, but if not, then I want to thank you all anyway for considering me a friend of the pack for a time. I will still always consider the Marin Pack friends of mine."

I stand and nod to each lycan. Vincent and Irene stare at me speculatively. Apani dips her head, and Kane—Kane looks heartbroken all over again.

Nothing more to stay, I head for the door. I've barely passed Kane when the shifter catches my wrist.

"Selene."

I stop and turn to him, decidedly ignoring Memnon.

"Swear to me you won't die."

I stare down at him, and though I cannot read his mind, I can practically feel his worry and powerlessness. Kane is hemmed in by the will of his pact. And I think right now, he desperately wants to join the fight, or at least protect me from it.

Memnon's chair scrapes back, then the sorcerer's heavy hand falls on Kane's shoulder.

"You're a good man, Kane," Memnon says, "and your protectiveness will serve you well as a leader one day. Selene cannot make you that promise any more than I can. But I can vow to you this: I will not willingly lead her to her death."

Kane stares at me a moment longer, and I nod.

"It will be okay," I say softly.

It's as close to a promise as I can make, and it might not even be the truth. Because none of this is okay. Not the forced bonds, not the killings, not the auction, and not the upcoming violence.

But there's no going back from what happened last night. Not for Memnon and not for me. The only option for either of us is to stop the Fortunas before they stop us.

And hopefully the shifters decide to help.

# CHAPTER 43

*I drive Memnon's car back to his house while the sorcerer* takes his motorcycle. The sky has been heavy with the scent of rain this whole evening, but it's only once I'm on the winding mountain roads that the heavens open up.

I flick on the wipers and try to force my focus to stay purely on the road.

Unfortunately, it keeps drifting.

*"Did she tell the truth?"* Vincent had asked.

*"As she knows it, yes,"* my mate had replied.

What had he meant by that?

*Memnon?*

I shouldn't be bothering him. Not when he's traveling these same rain-slick roads I am. On a motorcycle. With no helmet.

*Yes, est amage?*

*Forget it,* I say.

*Well, I cannot forget it now, after I've been teased. What is it?*

I adjust my grip on the wheel. Fuck it.

*Tell me something you don't want me to know.*

I ignore the twinge of guilt in my stomach that comes with the command and brace for some horrible truth.

*I think about marrying you all the godsdamned time,* Memnon says down our bond. *I think of ways to work around our arrangement just to make it official sooner. And once you're my wife, I plan on convincing you with gifts and food and mind-blowing sex to stay with me, in our house, forever.*

I rear back in my seat. That...wasn't the confession I was expecting. I assumed he'd tell me some scheme he'd been keeping from me, not serve me his heart on a platter. I'd almost forgotten the unbreakable oath I made to him. But Memnon hasn't.

*You didn't want me to know that?*

*No,* he says. He doesn't explain himself further.

When I pull up the long driveway to Memnon's secluded house, he's already there, standing out in the elements, waiting for me to get to him. The rain mats his hair to his face. Distractedly, he runs a hand through the wet locks, and the sight sets my whole body on fire.

I look at him, and finally, I see him, really see him. He's no longer just some strange menace come to haunt me. He's my soul mate, the man whose mind reached out to mine two thousand years ago when we were both children in the ancient world. He has been my enemy recently, but he has always been my partner.

The truth of it hits me like a blow to the chest, and it's as though I can breathe again for the first time since he reentered my life.

I turn off his car and step out of it.

My gaze moves from him to his motorcycle, then back.

I shut the car door and round the vehicle. "You're

never going to drive that motorcycle again without a helmet," I say.

I see him shiver at the command in my voice.

He twists his lips into a smirk. "And why is that?"

He wants the answer. He's scented the truth.

I stop walking, and the two of us stare at each other.

"Because I care about you. Because you're my soul mate," I say. I've always known it, but now I accept it. I accept *him*. The two of us are connected by an invisible cord of magic. It mingles, his darkness tingeing my power, my light brightening his. "And I claim you as *mine*."

My power flows through me, yearning for one thing, and he's standing in front of me.

Memnon looks at me like I contain the whole world beneath my skin. "*Selene.*" His eyes begin to glow, and thick plumes of his magic flow out of him.

I don't know which one of us moves first, only that we come together as the rain batters down on us.

Memnon's mouth finds mine, even as his eyes still burn like embers. The press of his mouth is desperate, insistent, as though he might coax more truth from it.

I thread my fingers through his hair, reveling in the strange feel of his floating locks.

This is our deepest truth. That time and place can change—even life experiences can change—but we will still come together.

Memnon closes his eyes as though basking in this moment. "How I have longed to hear those words." He presses his forehead to mine. When he opens his eyes, they are that beautiful, complicated brown once more. "I am yours, dear soul mate," he breathes. "Always yours."

He kisses me again, and there's a heady rush.

The leather jacket he wears hangs open, and I push it off his shoulders. It hits the driveway with a wet *plop*.

I need to get closer to him. Need to feel his very essence on me and in me. There's a hurried, almost instinctual rush to this, and I don't know if it's driven by my magic or my repressed feelings.

Perhaps it's a bit of both, because when I reach the hem of his shirt, my magic has beaten me to it. It tugs the garment up, breaking our kiss. Memnon grins devilishly as my power pulls it over his head and casts it aside. Then the sorcerer's hands and his mouth are back on mine.

His chest is deliciously warm, and I step closer into his embrace, savoring his heat and closeness.

He picks me up, wrapping my legs around his hips. My hands are still in his wavy hair, and my magic is moving about us. It's at my back, and though I can't see it, I sense it swarming around Memnon's hands. It tugs at my shirt, then—

*Riiiip*. My power tears the back of my shirt in two. It falls in tatters between us, and I pull away enough to shrug out of it. Memnon uses the moment to cast a silent spell of his own, his magic taking the weight of my body to free his hands.

The sorcerer reaches out, wiping the wet locks of my hair out of my face.

"Hello again, my love. It has been an age." We look at each other, our torsos bare save my bra and his tattoos, and the two of us laugh.

In that moment, there's no division between who I was as Roxilana and who I am as Selene; the past and the present are here, all at once.

"It worked," I say softly. My fingertips graze his face and the puckered skin where his scar is. "I never truly lost you."

He shakes his head. "No, my queen, this is just the beginning."

---

Memnon carries us inside. We're dripping from head to foot, and the sorcerer's shoes are making hilarious squishing noises until one of our spells removes them from his feet. The rest of our clothing gets peeled and ripped away by our power as we move through his foyer, then down the hall to his bedroom, each discarded garment hitting the floor with a wet slap until the two of us are naked.

I shiver in Memnon's arms, my legs locked around his waist. I can feel his erection brush against the curve of my ass.

"I don't need a bed for this," I say.

"I do," Memnon says with too much fervency. He leans into me and nips my lower lip. "There will be time to make love like the heathens we are. But tonight, I want to savor your skin and the look in your eyes. They hold my whole universe in them."

I swallow, growing serious. We've done this many times in the past week, but I've always, always had my guard up. But when I woke this morning, fresh from an evening of hell, all those guards I put in place to keep Memnon out were ripped apart.

The sorcerer's eyes drop to my throat, and he presses a gentle kiss there. "My fierce queen, who battled death to save me, who gave up much so that we could be here in this moment." His gaze flicks over me, and I think he sees that I'm ready for the slow sex he's been promising and all the intimate connection that comes with it. "My exquisite mate, who has been *exceedingly* patient with me."

He lays me out on the bed, then follows me onto it, fitting himself into the space between my thighs.

Despite the patter of rain, the world has grown very, very quiet.

"Let me show you how I love you," he breathes.

He grabs my legs, sliding his hands down my thighs like he can't help but touch me before spreading them obscenely apart.

Memnon dips his mouth to my core. "I promised you I'd feast on your pussy," he says against my sensitive skin, and I moan at the way even that casual brush of his lips sets my nerve endings on fire.

He kisses my pussy then, his tongue slipping inside me briefly.

I arch off the bed, nearly coming undone from that alone.

Memnon groans, leaning his forehead on my pubic bone. "You're *dripping*."

I'm breathing heavily, though he's hardly touched me. I run my hands over his shoulders, reveling in the roll of his muscles.

Memnon dips his head to press a soft kiss to my clit. I nearly yelp at the sensation.

"I hate to break my earlier promise," he says, "but—" Another rough kiss to my clit that sets me alight. Memnon lifts his head, and our eyes meet across the expanse of my body. "I did not imagine you would look at me tonight the way you have been or say the things you've said."

With that, he drags himself up the length of my body until his hips are cradled against mine.

My hands glide up the rippling muscles of his abs, then circle around to his back.

The sorcerer stares down at me. "Don't look away," he says. It's equal parts command and plea.

"Don't *you* look away," I say, turning the command back on him.

"I won't," he vows.

He reaches between us, adjusting himself until his cock is right at my entrance, and I'm about to glance down at where we touch—

"Eyes on me," he reminds me.

I inhale shakily.

Watching my every movement, Memnon shifts his hips and begins to sink inside me.

I suck in a breath as the head of his cock stretches me. The sensation is intoxicating, but I'm still caught up in his face. That face I first saw in Rome all those years ago. It's grown hardened and more rugged since then, but for the first time in this life, I realize it's not *just* a handsome face, it's a beloved one.

That makes my heart pound all the faster.

Once he's fully seated in me, he goes still again, and the two of us remain locked in each other's gaze.

"You can look away now," I say softly. I don't honestly know if my orders hold any power over him.

"I don't want to," he admits.

I don't want to either.

"Please, *est amage*. Explore me," he coaxes softly.

*I'll have to look away,* I admit down our bond.

Memnon runs the tip of his nose down the bridge of my own.

"I don't mind," he breathes against my lips as his cock

moves in and out of me. My eyes flutter a little at the sensation, but his thrusts are slow, measured.

My palms skim up his back, and I feel goose bumps rise along Memnon's skin in their wake. I pause when I touch the seam of an old scar several inches from his armpit. A barbed arrow had embedded itself here, though it happened before we met. This was the day when Memnon's voice first called out down our bond.

My hands continue up until my fingers graze the curling ends of his black hair. I play with a few strands of it. Then, because I cannot help myself, my touch migrates to his scar, tracing it up the side of his face and over to his eye, remembering when I first touched it—

*"This looks like it hurt."*

*His eyes are closed. "It did, but I am grateful for it."*

*"Why is that?" I ask. I cannot imagine being grateful for something so heinous.*

*"Because it made you stroke my skin."*

Down my hands move, to the column of his throat, where the inked image of my panther rests. Then lower, to the pectoral tattoo of a dragon—his family crest. His mother had the same tattoo, as did his sister.

As did I, once, long ago.

I feel his whole body shudder as I run my hands over it, and the sensation somehow heightens the drag of his cock inside me. I ache a little at the absence of my own tattoos and scars. They didn't make the journey through time with me.

My hands move lower, over Memnon's abdomen before they seem to drift of their own accord back to his face.

I hold that face, the two of us watching each other.

"I love you, my Roxi, my Selene," Memnon murmurs.

Deeper he drives himself, though his speed is punishingly slow.

I want to beg him to go faster, but even that would be an order wrapped in a plea, and I'm afraid my order will work—and equally afraid it won't.

The corner of his lip curls as he studies me, and his eyes blaze with intensity. "Your face says what your lips won't."

I jerk a little. Did he just hear my thoughts?

But then he follows with "I will go faster—if you command it."

My heart is now pounding hard for an entirely different reason. I tense, accidentally clenching around his cock.

Memnon hisses out a breath, then laughs, his thrusts still languishingly slow. "You grip me so well, little witch." He bows his head to take one of my breasts in his mouth, teasing my nipple between his teeth. He releases it to lave the other. I never thought my breasts were particularly sensitive, but this man has me seeing the goddess with his tongue.

I moan, grinding myself a little harder against him.

"I love you," he breathes against my skin. "I love you, I love you, I love you. A thousand lives wouldn't be enough with you, but I have to content myself with just this one."

He pulls away from my breasts to gaze down at me. And once again, we're back to staring at each other.

"Command me, my queen. I am yours," he says as he thrusts into me.

I stroke his cheek. "You are mine, *est xsaya*, but I won't command you." Not right now at least.

He smiles at me, the expression softening his entire face but most especially his eyes.

*Fine, do not command me. I shall simply anticipate your desires.*

He leans in and kisses me, his strokes quickening, the exquisite friction setting my whole body on fire.

I gasp, my fingers moving to his back, where they dig in.

He's pumping into me, all his massive muscles rippling and bunching with the action.

I writhe beneath him, caught in his relentless pace. If before he was able to keep his strokes slow and shallow enough to tantalize me, now his pace is almost too much. He's too much.

*I am going to give you the world, Empress*, he vows, his voice lethally soft in my mind. *It's already begun.*

I don't know if Memnon meant for me to hear those words, so I ignore them as my hips meet his, my body hurtling toward an orgasm.

My gaze drifts down to where I can see the lower part of his thick shaft sliding in and out—

"Eyes on me."

My gaze snaps to his.

There's no magic in this moment save for the deeper, richer power that links the two of us together.

I stare at him. My past, my present.

My future.

His eyes blaze.

I think he heard that.

Rather than being mortified at the thought, it along with his rough, merciless thrusts sends me right over the edge.

My lips part as my orgasm shatters through me.

Memnon's pupils go wide. "Gods, I feel you…" His fingers dig into my hair, then he's spilling into me, his gaze pinned to mine.

His climax echoes down our bond, stretching out my own. And still, the two of us continue gazing at each other, as though we truly haven't seen each other for two thousand years.

We only break eye contact once Memnon slips out of me and gathers me in his arms. Tonight, even this feels sacred. I don't know what's happening to my heart, but I'm not nearly as terrified as I should be.

Memnon's hand drifts to my stomach, his fingers idly stroking the skin there. For some reason, this touch—his hand on my stomach—will forever harken back to the child we briefly had, then lost with everything else.

"I am sorry," he begins.

"What?" I say, bewildered.

"I will *never* stop apologizing to you. My faith in you faltered when I woke in that tomb, and my faithlessness drove me to hurt you in ways I cannot take back. So I will apologize to you, my soul mate—my dearest and best friend. Again and again and again. Until you are sick of it. Because even once this bond between us breaks, my debt to you will not be paid. It won't be until I draw my last breath and you and I meet the gods who made us."

I place my hand on his cheek and lift my head to take him in. From the bond, I feel his yearning. I think I know what he wants.

"Are you wondering if the forged bond is still there?"

After a moment's hesitation, he nods.

Only one way to find out.

"Tell me another secret you don't want me to know."

"I picked out a ring," Memnon admits. He blinks, then—"Fuck, I really wasn't planning on sharing that."

He has an engagement ring. My heart is beating loudly. Memnon really is ready to marry me at the first opportunity.

I see a flash of dismay cross his features.

"You are mine," I whisper, grasping his hand and threading my fingers through his.

He closes his eyes as a shiver courses through him. When he opens them again, they briefly glow with his magic.

"You are mine," I repeat. "You are *mine*. My eternal mate." It is not a declaration of love, but it doesn't matter.

He smiles then, so big it threatens to split his face in two.

I grin back at him, feeling light, giddy. This damn giddiness.

Memnon's emotions are pouring down our bond. I've made the man incandescently happy.

Memnon leans forward and kisses me. Against my lips, he whispers, "I am yours, *forever*."

# CHAPTER 44

*I assumed that spending my days holed up with Memnon* would make the time move at an unnervingly slow rate, but between strategizing and reacquainting myself with Memnon, the days fall away one by one.

I continue sending my parents daily texts letting them know I'm alive, I fill Sybil in on my absence at Henbane, and I let myself actually enjoy a period of time when no one is actively trying to harm me or my familiar.

Well, perhaps they *are* actively trying, but Memnon has successfully warded this place against our enemies.

The news still focuses heavily on the killings in San Francisco and the mass murderer on the loose, and there is precious little about the Fortuna empire, aside from a brief mention of a donation the Fortunas made to the Bay Area Politia.

Whatever whistleblowing might be happening by the supernaturals freed from Juliana's influence, none of it is being broadcast. There's also no mention of Juliana herself or her untimely death—there isn't even a simple obituary. It's as though her death never happened.

I cannot know the Fortunas' reasons for such secrecy, but it's clear that whatever they are, they place them in higher regard than publicizing their grief.

Halfway through the week, Kane sends me a series of texts:

Fourteen shifters have forced bonds. They've been quarantined away from the pack.

From what we know, the Politia has gathered a few testimonies from supernaturals who were bonded to Juliana, but they don't have enough evidence to make arrests, nor do they have enough probable cause to involve themselves in the upcoming auction.

I hadn't been holding out for the Politia's help, but it's still a punch to the gut to hear how they'll do nothing. The two final texts from Kane, however, make up for it.

The rest of my pack voted, and the decision was unanimous.

We'll be there.

Relief floods my system. Memnon and I will have help. I don't focus too much on the fact that Kane doesn't suggest we meet up and exchange notes, nor do he or his pack seem interested in joint strategizing. Their help will be entirely separate from us.

It's better than nothing.

During the week, I resume using my notebooks, and it's like reacquainting myself with an old friend. Though I no longer need my journals to assist my memory, I now fill the pages with notes and pictures of the Equinox Building, the murder victims, the auction event, and finally, the Fortuna family themselves.

When the day of the new moon rolls around, I find myself lounging in Memnon's bed and studying these photos of the family behind this whole mess.

There's Juliana, with her dark brown hair and doe eyes. On the next page is her sister, Sophia. Her hair is a little lighter than her sister's, and her face is a little broader. I haven't met her, but from what I've heard, she's just as awful as Juliana.

On the following page is Leonard, the brother of the two sorceresses. He's handsome, but there's a cruel edge to his expression that makes my gut churn with unease. I haven't met him either, but in my bones, I sense he's the worst, and he's the one most closely involved with the murders.

Well, him and his father. Luca Fortuna has black hair that has gone gray at his temples, and honestly, the guy has really great skin. How is this guy sixty? Is this some drinking-the-blood-of-innocents shit?

I stare at the family. Aside from Leonard's slightly cruel edge, they look like normal people. I hate that. I hate that evil can look entirely benign. I wonder what their worries are, what their cares are. I wonder how they love and how they mourn the death of Juliana. I wonder what that looks like for them. How they grieve. I assumed it would be showy, but so far, it seems as though they're trying to cover it up.

My phone rings, interrupting my thoughts. I pull it out, ready to ignore it, when I see the caller. *Kane.*

"Hello—"

"*Selene.*" The voice that sobs out my name isn't Kane's. It's—

"Sybil?" I straighten up in the bed. "Are you okay? What are you doing with Kane's phone?"

A curl of Memnon's magic floats in from the kitchen, where he's been cooking something since he left my side.

"It's a long story," she says hoarsely. "And yes, I'm fine—more than fine, finally. I'm—I'm—Sawyer bit me."

"*What?*" I scramble out of the bed, my notebook entirely forgotten. I don't know where I'm going or what I intend to do, but I'm ready to jump to her aid the moment she gives the word.

At my tone, more of Memnon's power floats over to me, the indigo magic wrapping protectively around my torso.

I hear the sorcerer's strides as he heads to the room, clearly ready to check on me.

Do I congratulate her? Do I gauge her mood? Is this a happy occasion, or—

She begins to cry.

"I will kill him," I say as Memnon enters the room.

"Whose life are we ending?" the sorcerer says. He crosses the room and grabs his dagger and sheath from the bedside table, clearly ready to charge into battle with me.

"No, you won't," Sybil says. "Sawyer *saved* my life—and he might've saved yours as well," my friend says.

I go still at her words, a chill skittering up my back.

"Listen to me, Selene. There's a crime family, the Fortunas." Sybil gasps. "Fuck, I really can speak on it."

Goosebumps break out across my skin hearing the Fortuna name cross her lips.

She starts crying again, and she's trying to talk through her sobs. "I can't…the bite…broke it…"

My hand is trembling, and I feel like I'm squeezing the life out of my phone. "Sybil, please, breathe. I promise, I'm listening."

"Sawyer bit me, and it broke a bond that had been forced on me."

My lungs aren't working. I can't seem to breathe.

"Where are you right now?" I ask.

"I'm in the Everwoods. I needed a little privacy to talk—I haven't been able to tell Sawyer about this." She hesitates. "This call can't be long. Now that I'm bonded, Sawyer…he's not really letting me out of his sight…" Her voice changes, and she sounds less traumatized and more exhilarated. Like she might enjoy that possessiveness. "I barely managed to convince him to let me use Kane's phone instead of his—that's how intense the bond is. But I didn't think you would answer a stranger's number."

She's right. I probably would've ignored the call and never heard any of this. I shift my weight from foot to foot.

*Congratulations*, I mean to tell her. It seems like that word should fit somewhere into this conversation. After all, Sybil bonded herself to someone she cares about, and in the process, she freed herself from a terrible fate.

"Please get out of those woods and go back to Sawyer and the rest of the pack," I beg her instead. My gut is churning.

Memnon glances at me as he arms himself. I can tell he's holding back a lot of questions. His magic has almost entirely encapsulated my body, like it can shield me from the horrors my best friend is telling me.

"Okay." She takes a deep breath. "Okay. But, Selene, S-Sophia—the fucking monster who bonded me—she has been looking for you and Memnon since we last spoke." She begins sobbing again. "I had to break my phone to avoid her calls, but now I'm worried that she's—she's—"

I think I might be ill. "You think she's after you too," I say.

I can feel my own tears slipping down my cheeks.

"Yes," she whispers. "She knows you're my best friend."

Fuck.

"Please, ward yourself and get back to the pack, immediately."

"I will," she promises. "But I wanted to let you know that you might not see me for a while. Between this and learning how to shift...I don't know how long it will be," she confesses. "I'm going to have to tell Sawyer every-thing—" Her voice breaks off, and I can sense my best friend's emotions crumbling. "I'm so sorry for being an absent friend lately," she says hoarsely. "And a shitty one. There are so many things I tried to shield you from before now. Just please know I tried my b—"

*BOOM!*

My friend screams over the line.

"*Sybil!*" I shriek.

*What is going on?* Memnon says down our bond, his expression concerned.

I'm openly weeping now. My best friend put herself in danger to protect me.

"Sybil!" I cry out again. "Please answer me."

I can hear voices and scuffling.

"Did you really think you could hide from me?" a woman says.

In the background, Sybil screams.

"And look who it is." The voice grows louder. "Hello, Selene. Sybil has told me a lot about you."

Fear seizes up my windpipe.

I've been so preoccupied with the possibility that the bad guys were coming for me that it didn't cross my mind that they might instead come for Sybil.

*Memnon, the Fortunas have my best friend.* My horror is drowning out every other thought.

I put the phone on speaker and lay it on the bed while Memnon comes closer.

"Sophia?"

"Listen, I'm going to be direct," Sophia, presumably, says. "Sybil is going to die tonight."

In the background, I hear Sybil scream again.

My magic rushes out of me, uselessly spreading across the room.

"Unless, of course, you come retrieve her," she says.

"What do you—"

"Come to the lobby of the Equinox at ten till midnight," she interjects. "Not earlier, not later."

I can hear the staccato beat of my heart. "Promise you won't harm her."

"Hmm...no. See you at midnight."

*Click.*

The line goes dead.

An angry scream forces its way up my throat. Before I can release it, Memnon is there.

He settles his hands on my shoulders. His indigo magic surrounds us on all sides.

"Look at me," he says.

I raise my face to take him in. His eyes are eager, and his expression is resolute.

"We have gone to battle before, *est amage*." He gives my shoulders a squeeze. "We have faced worse foes. We *will* save her. I *vow* this to you."

# CHAPTER 45

*That evening, I stare out at the twinkling city lights of the* bay from the window in Memnon's bedroom. Somewhere amid all that glitter and glare, my best friend is being held by a murderous, violent family.

Nero is at my side, staring into the dark expanse as though he might be able to see her as well.

My mind is on fire, and my heart is screaming. I'm supposed to be composed, and maybe outwardly I am, but I have lost my focus.

This isn't what I wished for when I offered up my life two thousand years ago. I hadn't wanted more of what plagued my past.

I sense Memnon leave the en suite bathroom, where he's been getting ready, and enter the bedroom. He's as silent as my panther as he crosses over to me.

The sorcerer wraps an arm around my midsection, his body heat warming my back. "Are you ready?"

I turn in his arms and study him. The sharp cut of his

jaw, his curving lips. Those glittering, calculating eyes and the thick, dark hair that frames his face. Memnon's wearing a tux, and he's just as viciously beautiful in it as he was at the Samhain Ball.

"No," I admit, though he must already know that. I haven't tried to poke through his closet yet to see if there's something suitable for a midnight auction slash rescue mission.

Despite the pressing need to find my friend, a different sort of terror is gripping me at the moment.

I feel like I'm only just beginning to rediscover my mate. And tonight...tonight it feels as though it could all be taken away.

Memnon leans down. A hair's-breadth from my lips, he whispers, "It will be okay."

He closes the last of the space between us and brushes his lips against mine. It's a love note of a kiss, and I hate it. It's too sentimental, too wistful. It makes my fears scream louder and my courage grow quiet.

"Harder." I breathe out the demand against his lips. "Kiss me harder."

And Memnon does. He still *must*. Whatever I feel for him, it is soft and pliant and deepening, but it's not quite love.

Not yet.

For a few moments, there are no murders and no dangerous battle plans. There's nothing but the crisp press of my mate's suit against my chest and his demanding mouth against my own.

But once he pulls away it all comes roaring back.

The Equinox. The auction. Sybil.

Fuck.

Fuck, fuck, fuck.

"Settle your fears, *est amage*," he says. "They will only sabotage you in battle."

I draw in a steadying breath and nod.

Memnon touches my cheek. "I got you something."

Before I have a chance to react, he retreats to his closet. When he returns, it's with a long, crimson silk dress and a pair of matching heels. The dress itself has slits up the sides and a choker-like collar. Gold detailing runs along its edges. It's beautiful, and the color and detailing are very, very Sarmatian.

"They are," Memnon agrees, hearing the stray thought. "It's fitting to remember our origins on a night like tonight," he says. "We have toppled armies and slain enemies for each other. We are bold, wicked creatures, *est amage*."

Only weeks ago, I would've scoffed at the sentiment, but Memnon is right. We are bold. We are wicked.

Hesitantly, I reach out, rubbing the fabric of the evening gown between my fingers.

"Thank you," I say softly. "These are…perfect." And the gift itself is thoughtful. *He's* thoughtful.

Taking the items from Memnon, I disappear into the bathroom and dress. Once I've donned the outfit, I lean against the counter, letting my magic drift out to style my hair before I touch my makeup bag. Normally I would do this with Sybil. She was the one who always insisted on getting dressed up. Going through the motions now without her only serves to remind me that she's in a bad situation, that she has been all day.

I drag on red lipstick, and I make myself think of it as war paint. *We'll get you out, Sybil.*

When I leave the bathroom, Memnon is sitting on the

edge of the bed, a black bag open at his feet. He glances up, and his entire expression shifts at the sight of me.

"*Selene.*" His eyes move to mine. "You are so godsdamned lovely."

A pang of nostalgia seeps into me from the bond, along with an emotion that feels like wish fulfillment.

I smooth a hand over the silk self-consciously.

Memnon rises from the bed and comes to me then and kisses me like I might slip through his fingers.

He pulls away. "I got you something else as well."

I raise my eyebrows. "There's *more*?"

He gives me a conspiratorial look as he backs away. "Don't you remember, Empress? There's always more when it comes to you."

The sorcerer retreats to that open duffel bag, and I follow him over, watching curiously as he pulls out two sheathed daggers, Velcro straps wrapped around them.

My eyebrows hike all the way up. "You got me a pair of daggers?"

"My wrathful queen needs a good set of blades when facing down enemies." Returning to me, Memnon kneels at my feet. "May I?" he says, gesturing to my legs.

I nod, and he unravels one of the Velcro straps. Lifting a heeled foot, he slips one of the thigh sheaths up my leg, settling it right at the apex of my limb. He tightens and adjusts it until it's sitting comfortably against me and the weapon lies smoothly against my skin.

Memnon reaches for the other blade and sheath. "I'm still getting used to the sight of modern dresses," he says as he works, "and I have to admit there is something *very* provocative about them." He lifts my skirt high enough to slide the other sheath on. "Particularly when they hide weapons." After he secures my second blade, he sits back on his haunches. "Now, show me how easily my pretty, deadly wife can pull a dagger on an enemy."

I've never worn a thigh sheath, nor have I played with blades in this life, but I manage to smoothly reach into the slit of my dress and withdraw one in a matter of seconds. It's light and delicate, long enough to hit internal organs but thin enough to easily wield.

I press the blade up to Memnon's throat.

"*Good.*" His smoky eyes gleam. "And the other?"

Without looking away from him, I unsheathe it, crossing this second dagger over the first so that Memnon's neck is scissored between the two.

The grin he gives me is downright evil. "*Very* good."

I withdraw the blades from his throat, tucking them back in their sheaths, and breathe down my unease. It's been a long time since I touched a weapon in earnest. My muscles remember the movements, but my mind snags on the thought of using them.

The sorcerer's expression grows serious. "Remember, these are violent, dangerous people," he says, catching my stray thought. "Use those blades the moment you need them—if, of course, you need them."

Memnon's eyes gleam, and wisps of his magic are escaping his skin. I know he's thinking of ending all these people himself. I can feel the call to war roaring across our bond. The warlord is finally back to battle.

"Ready?" he asks.

I draw in a deep breath, the weight of the daggers comforting. "Ready."

# CHAPTER 46

***The Equinox is a huge, deep-green skyscraper, its glittering*** outer walls made from reflective glass.

*The Fortuna family owns the entire building?* I ask down our bond, aghast as I take in the staggering structure.

*Every inch,* Memnon says, giving my hand a squeeze.

I glance over at him only to see empty space. A split second later, a man in a business suit bumps against what looks like thin air, stumbling a little on the congested sidewalk. The man looks around, then glares at the woman in front of us before moving on.

Memnon and I have both placed enchantments on ourselves that make us invisible. It takes a lot of power, but it's a simple enough spell—one that bends the light to hide you. I used it before when I had to bring Nero through a couple of airports, but this version of the spell is a lot more sophisticated.

We continue onward, toward the Equinox Building,

sidestepping other pedestrians where we can. The two of us left Memnon's car in a parking garage a block back.

*Beware*, Memnon says. *The building is crawling with guards, security cameras, and wards.*

I'm not worried about the first two issues, especially being essentially invisible at the moment. It's the third one that might be tricky.

*What sorts of wards?* I ask. There are wards that can confuse the mind so you wander in circles, wards that form impenetrable walls, wards that make you irrationally scared, wards that will slingshot you ten feet back if you touch them.

*From what I learned when I picked up bodies here,* Memnon says, *the spells change frequently, so the Fortunas' enemies can never be sure what they're dealing with.*

Considering we're now the enemies in question, that's not exactly what I was hoping to hear.

*Besides wards, remind me again what else can we expect?* I say. We've been over this several times, but now that adrenaline is surging through my veins, my thoughts have scattered.

*There will likely be guards posted around the perimeter of the building, especially since they're expecting you,* Memnon says. *I will take care of any of them we run into.*

For once, I'm grateful that Memnon isn't squeamish about violence. I try not to think about the fact that I still am.

We get to the stoplight across from the Equinox and wait for the light to change.

*If these enchantments fall,* Memnon says, *it will only be a matter of time before they see us. And once that happens, things will unfold quickly.*

I swallow. This is the part of the plan that truly terrifies me. We aren't heading through the lobby like Sophia demanded. I have to force away my worries over what Sybil might endure for this breach in plan.

The light changes to green, and Memnon and I cross the street, the sound of cars and horns blaring.

*If both murders and illegal auctions are happening inside this building, then it will be a fortress, one that is safe for the Fortunas and their clients but not for us,* Memnon says.

Which means that the only way out is to stop the Fortunas first, along with anyone who works with them.

As soon as we step onto the city block where the Equinox Building is located, I feel the tug of the first ward against my skin. I glance up and see the faint edges of the glittering spell, the spindly threads of this one a raspberry color. It looks like nothing more than a shimmery spiderweb, the strands of it faint.

I hear a gasp from a woman behind me. When I turn to look at the middle-aged woman, her eyes are wide.

*Our illusion is gone,* Memnon says down our bond.

Fuck.

The first ward apparently strips enchantments.

The woman hurries away, and the flow of pedestrian traffic continues on around us, the rest of the crowd indifferent to the fact that two people manifested out of thin air.

*Should we redo the spell?* I ask Memnon.

My mate attempts to, his magic spiraling out of him, but the enchantment only forms for an instant before dissipating again. It looks like the ward won't allow illusions at all.

So we have no choice.

We walk down the block to the Equinox parking garage entrance, which gapes like a mouth. My skin pricks; I don't see any cameras nor any obvious guards, but that doesn't mean anything. The Fortunas might already know I'm on their city block.

I reach into the armhole of my dress and pull out my phone from where I've tucked it in my cleavage. I check the time.

*11:39 p.m.*

I have eleven minutes until I'm expected to show up at the front lobby and twenty-one minutes until the auction— and likely Sybil's murder—is to begin.

My heart thunders as I slip the phone back into my gown. I peer into the shadowy garage entrance, noticing that at the base of the decline into it, another ward shimmers. The semitransparent spell stretches from floor to ceiling like a makeshift wall. The color on this one is more obvious than most high-level wards, and in this case, it's dual toned—a burnt orange in some places and a blue-green in others. Clearly, two separate supernaturals made this ward together, and their magic didn't mesh well.

Memnon and I step up to it, and I look for any streaks of black that might indicate someone attached a curse to it, but I don't see anything. Intuition is telling me this is just a basic ward, the kind that lets some people in and keeps others out.

Tentatively, I lift my hand and release the barest plume of power. I watch the pale orange hue of it cross the ward unimpeded.

I think if it allows my magic to pass, it will also let *me* pass.

*I think it's safe,* I say. Or safe enough at least.

*Once we go through,* Memnon cautions, *it truly begins.*

The plan to retrieve Sybil is this: Get to the lowest floor of the building, the one closest to the earth. That's where the dark magic will have the strongest pull, so it's the likeliest place Sybil will be if they intend to kill her. Fight the bad guys, save my friend. That's what it really boils down to.

I touch the hilts of my new daggers through the soft silk of my dress and stare at the looming garage beyond. *I'm ready.*

Memnon's rising excitement trickles through our bond. *Then lead on, my queen.*

With that, I step through the ward. The magic skims along my skin, but there's no resistance.

*Thump.*

I turn at the dull sound of a body hitting a wall. Memnon still stands on the other side of the ward, his hand splayed across it and his power fanning out over the magical wall's surface.

Well, fuck. One of us can enter but the other cannot. We hadn't anticipated this.

I try to step back to him, but this time, the ward bars me from returning. Witches' tits, the ward has trapped me inside.

Memnon studies the magical wall separating us.

*I can shatter this one, but once I do, the Fortunas will be aware of it, and the fighting will likely begin.*

He doesn't sound upset about that prospect.

I run my teeth along my lower lip. I don't think we have time for a fight, not if I want to find Sybil before midnight.

*Can you give me a three-minute head start?* I say.

The sorcerer hesitates. *You were never meant to go in there alone,* he says. *We don't know what's waiting for us.*

I sense his conflicted emotions down our bond. He believes in my strength more than anyone else, but he's also fanatic about my safety.

I feel the sands of the hourglass counting down.

*I'll be okay for three minutes,* I tell him.

*Death can come in an instant,* Memnon says. *I've watched you nearly die before,* est amage, *after I brought you into battle.* A muscle in his jaw jumps. *You are powerful and more than capable, but…that memory is always there, at the back of my mind. And it's there right now.*

I place my hand against his splayed one. *You trained me how to fight a long time ago. The lessons are still there. I will be okay.*

The words are supposed to be reassuring, but if anything, Memnon only looks like he has more to lose now.

He clenches his jaw, then nods. *Two minutes,* he amends. *That's all I'm giving you before I break this ward down and come after you.*

Two minutes.

I nod and swivel around, scanning the space for the elevators.

*Wait,* est amage.

I pause, turning back.

Memnon's gaze is fierce. *Cities can burn and centuries can pass and none of it means anything to me without you. So stay safe, my queen. And remember—stab first, ask questions later.*

A feeling rises in me. *I love—*

His eyes flash.

The rest of the sentence snags in my throat.

*I'll be safe,* I say instead.

Then I turn and run.

# CHAPTER 47

**Not even thirty seconds have gone by before I hear a sound** like shattering glass. I glance around me at the various parked cars when a wave of magic throws me forward. I catch myself on a concrete pylon.

*What was that?* I ask Memnon.

*The sound of me changing my mind.*

Fuck, did he knock out the ward already?

*You were supposed to give me a two-minute head start.* It was a paltry enough amount of time as it was.

*Yes, but then I decided I'm not going to let my queen face our foes alone.*

*Memnon. We had a moment there and everything.*

Memnon jogs over to my side, his shoes clicking against the ground. *It was a good moment too,* he agrees.

The pound of footfalls heading our way interrupts our exchange.

*Hide,* Memnon commands me, using a tone of voice he only reserves for battle.

Without thinking, I duck behind a nearby car.

I narrow my gaze at the sorcerer, who still stands out in the open. *Did you have to use that tone on me?*

*It was effective. I wonder what would happen if we tried it in the bedroom...*

*I'd get violent,* I say.

*Well now, consider me intrigued.*

Memnon's magic billows out of him before I have a chance to respond. I hear two bodies fall.

*It's clear, Selene.*

I step out just as he's bending over two fallen guards, his magic flowing over their faces. It's likely he's altering their memories.

Memnon straightens, then juts his chin ahead of us. *Elevators are that way.*

The parking garage is unnervingly quiet as the two of us head toward them. Aside from those two guards, no one else has come to see why one of the Equinox's outer wards was broken. That can't be accidental, can it?

When I catch sight of the elevators, I tense. In front of them is another ward, this one a translucent crimson color filled with row after row of curling glyphs. This ward isn't even trying to blend in. It's meant to scare off trespassers.

*What do you think this one does?*

Memnon tilts his head to the side. *I don't know, but there's some dark magic involved in it.* He points to a streak of black.

I step closer, studying the lines of what must be a curse.

Memnon reaches out and touches it.

*Son of a swine,* he curses in Sarmatian, his hand recoiling. I watch in horror as the skin along the back of his hand splits from the tip of his finger up to his wrist. The lines of the wound spread, branching out along the initial slice as they crawl up his forearm.

I catch his arm, my magic rushing out of my palm. "*Begone poisoned death that corrupts the spirit.*" The incantation comes out in English, not its original Mochica, but I say the spell with conviction. "*With love, I destroy you.*"

As I watch, the curse disintegrates, the oily magic burning away until all that's left is a line of bilious smoke. My magic lingers for several more seconds, resealing the cuts and healing the open wounds.

When I look up, Memnon is staring wondrously at my lips.

*You remembered the curse-breaking spell,* he says.

*I've got a decent memory now.*

Abruptly, he leans forward and kisses me. *Thank you.*

I've only just tasted his lips when he pulls away.

*Brace yourself.*

He turns from me, and I only catch the spark of power in his eyes before he slams his fist into the crimson ward.

*CRACK!*

The ward shatters, the energy from it throwing me back. Memnon catches my arm and saves me from falling.

Two wards broken. If the Fortunas hadn't been aware of an attack tonight, now they surely are.

*We'd better move fast,* the sorcerer says down our bond.

The two of us head to the elevators, and I slap the down button.

I gather my magic as I wait, sure that once the doors open, supernaturals are going to pour out of it. But when it dings open, it is ominously empty. There are no people, no wards—nothing at all beyond gleaming metallic walls and another set of doors at the back of the elevator.

*This is too easy,* I say.

*Hmm,* Memnon muses.

For the first time tonight, I sense the sorcerer's misgivings.

*Ready yourself, Empress. Our enemies know we're here, and they're waiting for us.*

With that, Memnon strides into the elevator.

I hesitate only a split second longer, mentally preparing myself for whatever battle lies beyond these doors. Then I gather my courage and follow Memnon in.

The elevator is spacious and elegant, but once the doors close, I feel like I'm trapped in a coffin.

I stare at the floor numbers, eager to be out of this box. There are sixty-two numbered floors, plus some levels marked L and G and P that for the sake of time I have to assume are not of interest to us. Then there are the subterranean floors. Naturally, the building can't just have one basement, it has to have *three.* I panic and hit the buttons for them all.

Memnon arches a brow at me.

*I've...got a plan.*

The corner of his lip twitches. *I have no doubt.*

The elevator dings without ever moving, and the doors reopen, revealing floor B1, a.k.a., the parking garage.

From our bond, I feel Memnon's amusement. *Incredible plan.*

*If you have a better one, I'm all ears.* I pull out my phone as the doors close, checking the time.

*11:44 p.m.*

Six minutes until I'm to show up at the lobby. Sixteen minutes until midnight. My legs begin to tremble as I put the phone away and the elevator descends to B2.

*Steady, my queen. We'll get them.*

*Do you think there will be any more wards? We haven't come across—*

Darkness steals the last of my thoughts and my consciousness along with it. I don't feel it when I hit the floor.

# CHAPTER 48

*"I'll be damned. We got them both."*

I make a noise as I blink my eyes open. My cheek is pressed to cold marble, and the room is sideways, but I can see several sets of suit-clad legs.

Before I can rise onto my knees, I feel someone's boot connect with the back of my head. I grunt as pain explodes behind my eyes, dulling my vision, and I fall back to the floor.

Behind me, I hear a scream.

"Stay down," a masculine voice growls at me, "or we'll make you."

Somewhere beyond my back, I can hear soft sobbing.

The man who kicked me now moves away, his boots squeaking against the floor. "I assumed you'd be happy you wouldn't have to die tonight," he taunts the crying woman.

*Sybil.*

I lift my head and turn it, uncaring that I might receive another hit to the head for the action.

The hit doesn't come, and the first thing I see is my friend, flanked by several burly men who are currently talking quietly to one another. At least I *think* that's Sybil.

Horror drips down my spine as I take her in. Both of her eyes are bruised and swollen nearly shut, and her body is bloody. She's still sobbing, her entire body quaking.

"Sybil…" I whisper, reaching for her.

Sybil glances up at me, then shakes her head frantically, her gaze moving briefly to one of the men standing guard. The man glances her way, and she shrinks back, her shoulders curling in on herself.

Was he the one who gave her those bruises? He's a dead man.

Ignoring her warning, my power leaves my palm, aimed at the guard in question. It's only moved about a foot from me when it fans out across an invisible wall.

What the—?

I sit up a little more, and that's when I notice the hastily made chalk circle drawn around me, clearly made to contain me and my power inside.

I reach out a finger to the edge of the chalk, but instead of touching the powdery substance, I feel the bottom of the circle's transparent wall.

I'm trapped.

My attention moves past the invisible barrier to the rest of the room. Everything in me goes still when I see a massive, slumped form just beyond my feet, trapped in his own chalk circle.

I make a low, aggrieved sound. All I can see of him from this angle is his wavy black hair and his broad back. He lies there, unmoving.

*Memnon? Are you all right?*

I wait for some sort of response, but the bond between us is idle. I let out another noise, and the guard who kicked me scowls down at me, taking a step in my direction.

"Leave it, Dain," one of the other guards says. "Sophia is already on her way, and she wants the girl terrified, not beaten."

*Memnon, wake up!* I push what magic I can down our bond.

Nothing.

I can still feel the eyes of the guard, Dain, on me. "Sophia wants the girl terrified?"

*For the love of your gods,* est xsaya, *wake up!* I command.

On the other side of our connection, I feel his awareness flicker, and his body stirs a little.

"I can give her terrified," Dain says darkly.

Sybil cowers as he passes her, and I swear I see my friend's nails elongate before quickly retracting. Dain stops at the edge of the chalk circle encasing my mate. He assesses Memnon curiously before lifting a buffed black shoe as though preparing to kick the back of the sorcerer's skull.

*Memnon!*

My power flares out of me and fills the spell circle as Dain's leg snaps out.

Faster than I can follow, Memnon rolls onto his back and catches Dain's boot in his hands. With a jerk of his arms, he twists Dain's leg.

*Snap.*

Dain screams as bone breaks, and he topples into the circle.

One of the other guards rushes after Dain, who Memnon now has by the head. My mate twists hard to the right—

*Snap.*

Sybil screams as the lifeless body of Dain slumps against Memnon, partway in, partway out of the spell circle.

The sorcerer is already angling the body to try to get some part of it to smudge the chalk and break the circle when one of the guards grabs onto Dain's legs.

In the distance, I hear an elevator ding, followed by the click of heels, but I hardly pay it much attention.

I rise to my feet, placing my palms on the translucent walls of my cage as I watch my mate play tug-of-war with a corpse.

*Est amage, are you all right?* Memnon asks down our bond. His concern is so at odds with the merciless way he's handling what's left of Dain.

*Now that you're awake, yes.*

*You honor me,* Memnon says.

"What the fuck is happening here?" Sophia's voice echoes from the hallway beyond Memnon. A moment later, she enters the room, two more guards in suits flanking her.

Her eyes fall to Memnon, Dain, and the guard tussling with my mate.

She lifts an arm toward my mate. "*Sleep.*" The spell hits the sorcerer square in the face, and I cry out as he falls back against the invisible wall of his cage, his eyes closed.

The other guard stumbles back with the lifeless body of Dain.

"You fucking fool," Sophia spits out at him. "Do you realize this is a *sorcerer* we have trapped? Had I not shown up when I did, you'd be dead and my family's chance at revenge would've been squandered." Her magic is unspooling out of her with her anger. "Get the hell off the ground, and take the girl"—she gestures to Sybil—"upstairs to the auction room."

Sybil wails at the order, and I cry out along with her.

The guard drops Dain and hustles over to Sybil, roughly grabbing my friend by the arm and prying her from the two remaining guards posted on either side of her. Sybil begins to shriek and flail. Fur sprouts from her skin before retreating back into her.

"You will not shift," the sorceress commands, "nor will you fight back."

Sybil cries out brokenly, a shiver racking her body as the order does something to her. The fact that Sophia's words worked at all means my friend must be bonded to her again.

A hopeless sort of fury rises in me. Sybil had done so much to escape this woman and all for what, a day or two of freedom?

I slam my fist against the wall of the spell circle as I watch the guard drag my sobbing friend away.

The action catches Sophia's eye, and she turns to me briefly. "Ah, yes, Selene. You made it. Just in time, too." She follows my gaze to where I'm looking at Sybil. "Oh, don't worry about her. I am a woman of my word, and I did promise that if you came, your friend's life would be spared." She flashes me a smile that's more cruel than sweet. "So I shall spare it." Sophia calls out to the retreating guard. "Make sure you first ensure the girl is healed and then get her appropriately dressed for the auction. She needs to look enticing, not like she's been mauled by wolves." Sophia gives me a conspiratorial look. "Though I hear she's into that sort of thing these days."

Sybil begins to shriek anew, and the sorceress stands there, listening to her cries, while the elevator dings in the distance. They continue until the doors hiss closed, and my friend is whisked away.

My cheeks are wet when Sophia turns her attention to Memnon's sleeping form. She tilts her head, studying him briefly.

"Funny to think that the man who killed my"—Sophia's voice catches—"so many of our men," she corrects, "could look so vulnerable. What a waste," she muses, seemingly to herself. To the guards who flank her, Sophia says, "Take the sorcerer to my brother immediately. Even though our captive is under spelled sleep, use extreme caution—he could wake at any point. I don't need to remind you that he killed dozens of people the last time he wasn't happy."

*Memnon!* I call out to him. *Memnon, wake up!* I push as much command as I can into those words, hoping that the bond might force him awake. But the sorcerer doesn't stir as the guards break the chalk circle and grab him. One of them must be a mage because I see his red-orange magic pool around Memnon as the two heft my mate up by the arms.

*Please, Memnon,* I beg, *wake up.*

He still doesn't stir.

The two guards cart the sorcerer away, the tips of my mate's shoes squeaking as they drag across the marble.

"What is your brother going to do to him?" My voice comes out as a whisper.

"The same thing my father plans to do to you," Sophia says. She tilts her head. "I hear you've been trying to solve the murders." She gives me another cruel smile. "Congratulations. You're about to." She lifts a hand. "*Sleep.*"

# CHAPTER 49

***When I wake, I'm slumped between two guards who each*** have me by the arms. My feet drag uselessly behind me.

I lift my head and blink away the spelled sleep as we approach two ominous maroon doors with fancy golden handles. At the sight of them, a bolt of fear runs down my spine. I know intuitively that beyond them is the secret behind the murders, the mystery that not even Memnon has been able to figure out. I can feel the wrongness of whatever lies beyond.

I struggle against the guards' hold, my magic surging up. I gather it in my hands—

"*Sleep*." Royal purple magic billows into my face, and the world goes dark again.

———————

The sharp bite of pain right over my heart wakes me. I can feel warm blood welling from the wound when suddenly

I'm tossed forward onto cold concrete, my body skidding across it.

I groan, blinking my eyes and trying to focus.

Another sleep spell.

I roll onto my back, and the movement causes the skin over my heart to sting. Absently I touch it, and my fingers come away bloody.

A hoarse, masculine voice begins speaking in Latin, their tone low. "*By water and flame, earth and sky, I invoke the elements.*"

Behind me, I can hear the sound of sand being poured from a bag.

What in the seven hells is going on?

I press my hands to the concrete floor and sit up. The room is dimly lit by several sets of wrought iron chandeliers, the warm glow of their lights illuminating the black walls of the cavernous room. Besides the light itself, there are precious few things in the room, save for the two men in front of me and the one coming around from my back.

The older of the two wears a brown tweed suit, his wiry white hair sticking up here and there around his head. He looks like an academic, with the exception of his eyes, which seem to dance darkly here in the dim light.

Next to him—

I freeze at the sight of the man whose face I've repeatedly stared at over the last week. His hair is a little whiter at the temples than in his picture, and his skin is perhaps not quite as enviable, but Luca Fortuna is still an arresting sight.

In his hands, he cradles a leather-bound grimoire, a fairly wicked one if the oily black smoke wafting off it is any indication.

He pauses his incantation, his eyes fixed on the individual

pouring the sand along a clockwise arc. I glance at the man in question. He wears a suit, a thick bag in his hands.

It's not sand he's pouring, I realize as the man completes the arc and empties out the last of the bag's contents, but *salt*.

Horror dawns. It's another fucking spell circle. One he just finished drawing while I sat here getting my bearings.

I lunge for the curving line of salt.

*"Bind this circle so that nothing may escape."* Luca rushes out the last of the incantation.

The blood on my fingers sizzles as it touches the salt, and the lights above me flicker as the physical walls of the spell circle rise, trapping me inside.

Fuck.

My pulse is beginning to pound in my ears.

I back up, my eyes moving from the men to the space within the circle. I realize the concrete I'm standing on is *stained*, and it smells like antiseptic and...

Blood.

My insides wither when I realize this is where all the other witches died. This is where *I* will die, unless I can escape this cursed circle.

I feel three sets of eyes on me. The suited guard gives me a flat look, like he's seen too much and cannot summon the energy to care. The elderly scholar—or whoever he is—stares at me intently, his head cocked.

But it's Luca, Luca Fortuna, whose attention seizes me. There's a bitter glee to his expression.

"Selene Bowers," he says, eyeing me up and down. "I know your name, and I know you were one of the last to see my Li—" He cuts himself off, though I'm positive he was about to say his daughter's name.

The scholar watches the two of us quizzically, looking

back and forth, while the suit-clad guard quietly exits the room.

"I don't make it a habit to learn the names of the witches I need," Luca continues, drawing my attention back to him, "but you mean something to that fucking *dead* man, Memnon. If any part of him still lives once Leonard is finished with him, then I will make sure he knows about your last moments, and I will savor his pain."

My heart nearly stops at his words. *Memnon.* I haven't heard a thing from him since we were parted.

Frantically, I reach out across our bond, but other than the warmth of his life force, there's no spark of awareness. He must still be asleep.

*Wake up, Memnon,* I command him, unsure if consciousness is better, given our circumstances.

But whatever spell my mate is under, it's too powerful for even my words to penetrate.

The scholar glances between me and Luca, looking a little uneasy at the topic of my impending death and how Luca might savor it. But he doesn't appear surprised. The man clearly knows that whatever is about to happen, I'm not supposed to survive it. He knows it, and he's not trying to stop it at all.

As though he can't help himself, Luca steps in close to the circle's edge, his gaze fixed to mine.

"I don't have to hope your death will be slow and painful," Luca says so softly only I can hear it. "Because I *know* it will be. That is the only comfort I get, knowing I gave my Lia some measure of justice."

My eyes drop to the grimoire in Luca's hands. As I watch, more oily dark magic curls and smokes off it.

I suck in a sharp breath as I remember the bloody bodies, the dark magic that coated the victims' butchered remains.

It suddenly strikes me. *The book is not a grimoire.*

Though the cover in Luca's arms bears no title, this book has one. There's only one tome that comes steeped in that much unholy magic.

*The Book of the Damned.*

I look at Luca with dawning horror. "You're summoning demons."

# CHAPTER 50

**Holy Goddess. Demons.**

Those ravaged bodies out in the woods were the work of demons.

That's my fate and Memnon's unless I can escape this fucking spell circle.

*Memnon!* I call out to him, more desperate than ever. *Wake up!* I nearly weep out the command.

But the other end of the bond stays placid. The sorcerer is still asleep.

My mind races. I have minutes until midnight to figure out some sort of game plan.

Unfortunately, I don't know much about demons. They've always been slotted in with the dark magic shit that witches aren't supposed to trifle with. Not reading about them has probably fucked me over.

"Why are you summoning demons?" I ask.

Luca tilts his head. "We're not simply summoning them," the sorcerer admits. "We're *binding* them."

"Binding them?" I echo. Even as I say it, the Fortunas' entire industry becomes clear, and my blood runs cold.

They're in the business of trafficking supernaturals. I assumed that was limited to those of us who were of this realm, but it's clearly not. They're moving demons too.

My eyes touch briefly on the somewhat anxious-looking scholar. That...that must be Luca's client, the one who is buying this demon's bond.

"If this is about binding demons," I say slowly, returning my attention to Luca, "then what do you need me for?"

"Demons are different from mortals," Luca replies, backing up. "They need to feed once they come here if they wish to remain." His eyes skate over my form. "They *like* the young ones in particular. Something about their innocence and vitality makes them taste richer, sweeter. We use that to get the demons to bond."

I vividly recall the body of Charlotte Evensen. It had been badly mutilated, and all her organs had been removed...

No, *eaten.*

Nausea rolls through me.

I glance down at the cut on my own chest, the bloody wound making much more sense now. Like throwing bleeding bait overboard in hopes it will lure in a shark.

I force my rising terror down.

*Focus.*

I'm not going to die tonight. Not like this.

On impulse, I reach for my heels and remove them, tossing one then the other aside so I can be light on my feet. I try not to grimace as the chill from the floor seeps into my skin.

Next, I turn to the walls of my prison. Spell circles like

this one, which has been activated in blood, are notoriously hard for anyone but the spellcaster to undo.

However, at the end of the day, a spell circle is nothing more than a really strong ward. Wards themselves are essentially giant tapestries, and like tapestries, they can be unraveled if one knows where to pull.

I look for the telltale magical signature, but if it's there, it's just as translucent as the rest of the circle's walls.

Luca glances down at a fancy gold watch on his wrist. "It's about time we begin." he says to the older man. "Are you ready, Jacques?"

"Yes," Jacques replies, his eyes alight with excitement.

"Good," Luca says. With a final, heavy look at me, the sorcerer begins incanting in Latin again.

"*From the infernal fires of hell, I call forth Asmodeth, devourer of the damned, reveler of the anguished. Curse weaver and soul eater. Rise within the circle I have cast.*"

The air smokes, then sizzles. Noxious plumes rise from the ground. Rather than dissipating into the air, it begins to shape itself into the form of a man.

Fuck, fuck, *fuck.*

The curling black smoke coalesces.

On the other end of my bond, I feel the spark of awareness.

*Selene!* Memnon bellows down our bond. It's his first thought.

*Memnon, forget about me. They're summoning demons,* I rush out. *We're about to fight for our lives.*

It's quiet for a long, pensive moment. *How do you know this?* he finally asks.

*I'm trapped in a demon-summoning circle.* After a moment, I add, *Aren't you?*

Rather than answering, the floor begins to tremble, and I can feel the burn of Memnon's rapidly growing rage.

*Memnon, do not give whoever is there with you another reason to knock you out,* I beg him. *I will be all right. Stay safe. I need to go.*

I pull away before he can say more, and I ready my magic. For this fight, I'll need all my attention to remain on my opponent.

The demon is now less dark smoke and more flesh and bone, the magic solidifying into body parts. I study the creature's features as they take shape.

I've heard that some demons are truly hideous looking, with forked serpent tongues, razor-sharp teeth, and slitted noses, but this one looks like a man, and a handsome one at that—if you can get past his sharp claws, the horizontal pupils at the centers of his eyes, and the wicked horns that curve away from his face. He's also as naked as the day he was born—or formed or damned or however the hell demons are created.

"Asmodeth," Luca says, "I offer this witch to you as a sign of my good will."

The demon takes a step toward me, his nostrils flaring.

"But be warned. It comes at a price. With the first swallow of her blood, you bind your body and will to Jacques Allard. You will roam the earth, deathless and unchanging for the span of this mortal's lifetime. Upon Jacques's death, the bond shall be severed, and you shall return to the Underworld.

"You have until the rise of the sun to make your decision, or else you shall be banished back to the fiery realm from whence you came."

Asmodeth turns from me and levels a look at the men standing there. "I want a *soul*. Only that will do."

"You shall only get a body," Luca says smoothly.

Asmodeth's laughter fills the space, raising the hairs at the nape of my neck. "Insolent human. Do you have any concept of who I am?"

As he speaks, his head keeps drifting in my direction, and his nostrils continue to flare, like he's distracted by the smell of me.

Because he wants to eat me.

Fuck, do I attack him? Do I let this play out? Do I and the demon enter into an unholy pact where we become reluctant allies?

That last one sounds good, except again, *he wants to eat me*.

"Of course I know who you are," Luca says. "It's all laid out in this book. The legions you command, the damned you oversee. You can go back to it all at first light, or you can bind yourself to this mage next to me and see your first true sunrise in one hundred and seven years."

Asmodeth stares at Luca and Jacques for a long moment. Then, slowly, the demon turns to me.

Fuck. I think he's made his decision.

I shift my weight, drawing my magic close. The demon's eyes dip to the cut along my chest, and his pupils grow wide.

Asmodeth snarls, then he lunges for me. I dive to the side, banging hard against the invisible barrier.

I barely have time to pivot before the demon is charging again. And again I dive out of the way, only just escaping the attack.

The action is futile. There's nowhere to go. The circle can't be more than twenty feet in diameter. I can keep this up for another few minutes, but I'm going to stumble eventually, and the beast will get me. He's practically vibrating with need.

I form my magic in my hand.

"*Explode*," I whisper, lobbing the spell at him.

*BOOM!*

It detonates before it even reaches Asmodeth, blowing the demon into the air. He slams against the curved walls of the spell circle, then falls to the ground. His shoulder is mildly cut up, but for the most part, he looks unharmed.

Jacques has crept near the edge of the circle, his eyes rapt as he watches me and Asmodeth.

"Do not get close," Luca warns. "If you smudge the salt, the demon can escape unbonded, and if any part of you crosses the barrier, you can be dragged in, and the demon gets a free meal."

I draw together my power as, across from me, Asmodeth rises.

"*Annihilate.*" The curse hisses out of me, hitting him square in the chest.

The demon grunts as he staggers back, but the spell that should have blown him to bits seems to sink into him.

Asmodeth laughs. "I am made of curses, witch. They do not harm me. They *fuel* me."

That bit of information would've been helpful a while ago.

From the other side of my bond, I feel a burst of pain.

*Memnon!*

I hear him laugh across our connection. *I am fine,* est amage. *Just fighting a worthy opponent. Hold fast, and give these creatures hell.*

While I'm half-distracted, the demon rushes me, his

claws extended. His body slams into mine, taking us both to the ground.

Shit. I go for one of my daggers, but the weapon is pinned beneath the silk dress, and the silk dress is pinned beneath the demon.

I grunt as Asmodeth presses his face into my wound. His wet tongue licks up the slit of the cut, and ugh, that is so fucking gross.

He groans. "Haven't tasted flesh in a long time."

Beneath us, the ground trembles.

"He did it," Jacques says way too eagerly. "The demon tasted her."

"Congratulations," Luca murmurs. "He's agreed to the bond. Now we simply wait for him to finish."

Finish *me*, they mean.

Asmodeth's lips curl back to reveal *two* rows of sharp teeth. The sight is frightening, terrible.

*You too are a dark, deadly thing*, I remind myself. I gave myself to that earth for two millennia, and now I can easily draw power from it.

Here, deep in the bowels of the earth, at midnight of the new moon, the magic beneath the ground is especially potent. I press my hands to the cold floor, reaching for the buried power, siphoning it up from the earth. My palms prick as magic seeps into my flesh, then my bloodstream. It gathers like a storm in my veins.

*Mistress of old*, something far beneath me whispers, *we've tasted your blood and bones before...*

The demon pauses, his head cocking to the side.

"The Old Ones speak to you? *And* they've tasted you?" His eyes flit over my body. "How very interesting." He casually swipes out, his claws cleanly slicing through my dress and the skin beneath.

I jerk, swallowing my scream as my blood wells.

"I don't often meet curious mortals," he says. "A pity you have to die. I will enjoy feasting on you though." Asmodeth leans forward, his teeth and tongue hot on my injured flesh.

I draw my power together, and all at once, I shove my hands and my power at him. "*Get off me.*"

Clouds of my orange magic blow the demon back clear across the spell circle. I hear the smack of flesh as his body hits the ground.

I force myself to my feet, but just as quickly as I rise, Asmodeth does as well. A low, demonic growl rises from him, and when he glances at me, his eyes flash red.

I raise a hand. "*Stop,*" I command in Sarmatian, my power rushing out of me.

The demon freezes in place, his body going still beneath my spell. It holds for mere seconds before Asmodeth breaks through it, then barrels toward me once more.

I draw more power from beneath the soles of my feet.

*Empress,* the voices below hiss out, *amage…mistress… queen…how we hunger…*

"*Explode.*" I cast the spell at the demon, aware it will hardly affect him.

*BOOM!*

It detonates against his shoulder, throwing him against the wall of the spell circle for a moment.

Blood drips down my torso, but I'm too focused on Asmodeth to heal myself. My hand hovers over my thigh, where my dagger rests hidden.

*In battle, you cannot solely rely on magic to save you.* Memnon told me that long ago.

I will myself to believe it as Asmodeth closes in on me. I draw in a breath, growing calm as the demon reaches me. This time, I don't cast a spell, and I don't dive away. I let Asmodeth crash into me, slamming my body against the walls of the circle.

If the demon is surprised by my sudden lack of fight, he doesn't stop to question it. His mouth opens, and his lips peel back, his gaze fixed on my throat.

All at once, he lunges for it.

*Now.*

I withdraw my dagger, and just as those sharp canines close around my neck, I sink my blade into his throat.

Asmodeth lets out an unholy cry, releasing my bloody neck. I yank the dagger out, and black blood spatters onto my dress and skin. Once more, I slam the blade into his throat.

The demon shrieks, then falls from me, my dagger making a wet noise as it exits the wound. Asmodeth hits the ground hard, and as he lies there, he weakly places a clawed hand against his neck. Blood rapidly spills out from between his fingers.

The whole building trembles, and someone somewhere is shitting their pants right now that they underestimated my mate.

I breathe heavily as I stare down at Asmodeth. I don't believe demons can be killed, merely sent back to the Underworld.

I round on the demon's body. Though every fiber of my being is screaming at me to run from this creature, I move to straddle him, my dagger still loosely held in my hands.

Weakly, he swipes at me, his claws parting my flesh like a

knife through butter. The pain bursts to life along my arms and torso, but I ignore it, raising my dagger.

I bring it down sharply, letting my magic guide my movements. The thin blade cleanly slides between Asmodeth's ribs and impales his heart.

The demon's scream echoes through the room, the sound terrifying and not of this world.

I draw on both my own blood and the demon's, the crimson liquid burning up as my power devours it. And then I call on the magic beneath the earth, pulling it into me.

*We give you power. Give us something in return.*

I ignore the voices and cobble together a spell.

"*From blood and air, to rock and flame.*" As I incant, I fold my power into the words. "*I banish you back from whence you came.*"

My magic detonates, filling the space in a massive cloud of pale orange plumes. I can't see anything, but it doesn't matter, I can feel my magic pressing in on the demon.

"I assure you," Luca says somewhere beyond the circle, "she cannot send the creature back."

*Old queen, forgotten queen...*the voices murmur.

Harder and harder, my power tightens on the demon. I see the plumes of it push and push against the demon bleeding out.

Asmodeth tries to fight the magic, but he's lost so much blood, and my power holds him fast.

My body trembles as I continue to exert force, pressing, pressing. I scream at the energy it takes, my limbs beginning to tremble as my power strains.

All at once, there's a *pop*, then Asmodeth is gone.

I'm breathing hard as I kneel on the now empty ground, which is scrubbed clean of all the black blood that pooled on it a moment ago. I can hear the steady drip of my own bleeding wounds. Aside from that, the room is deathly silent.

Eventually, Jacques says, "You said she couldn't send the demon back!"

"That's...never happened before." Luca clears his throat. "It doesn't matter. We can try summoning Asmodeth once more...though he might be too weak to make the journey. I have another demon in mind that might be perfect." He begins flipping through the pages of *The Book of the Damned*.

I glare at the pair of them and gather my magic.

I'm too angry and too impatient to study this spell circle for some exploitable weakness. I want out now.

I rise from the floor and draw on my magic remorselessly. One of the most basic aspects of a spell circle is that power moves in two directions along them: clockwise for creation, counterclockwise for destruction.

My blood continues to drip from the wounds on my chest, but for what I intend, I know intuitively that I need more. I drag the knife I still hold across my wrist and let my blood flow freely.

This whole time, I've been pretending to be something wholesome when being wholesome meant denying *this* part of me.

I let the blood drip down my fisted hand to the ground, my bare feet stepping over the droplets as I begin to walk in a counterclockwise motion.

"*To the gods that dwell beneath my feet,*" I call out in Sarmatian, "*give me power, and I will give you blood.*" My voice sounds deeper, stronger, surer as I speak.

I sense something beneath me moving toward my offering. The blood on the floor evaporates, and thick, smoky plumes of my orange magic rise up, streaked with veins of inky black. Dark magic.

Distantly, I'm aware that my power is falling on the wrong side of good and evil. But too much of me thrills at the thick ropes of power I drag up from the earth. It's so much more magic than what the ground usually offers up.

*We hunger for more, mistress...more blood. We have missed the taste of you...*

I let my blood continue to fall as I pace the perimeter of the circle. "*From air, I breathe. With fire, I burn. From water, I drink. To earth, all shall return.*"

Blood magic is destructive magic, and I drag that destruction along with every step I take. It batters at the ward, and I sense the walls that entrap me weakening. The ground begins to tremble, but this time, Memnon isn't responsible for it.

"*Sky above, spirits below, my blood you take.*" The coven was a match; this is an inferno. "*This ward unmake.*" My gaze falls to Luca. "*This spell I break.*"

*BOOM!*

Power floods out of me, shattering the walls of the spell circle. It sweeps across the room, blowing the salt away and throwing the men backward.

I stand there, wounded and bloodstained, as my magic retreats into me, clearing the air.

*Fearsome mate, I felt that,* Memnon says down our bond. I swear I hear the sorcerer's low laugh. *The Fortunas made a mistake trying to capture a true Sarmatian queen. I hope you make them pay for it.*

*I am.* With that, I pull away from our connection. I grip my dagger tightly and stride forward, the pads of my feet stepping on all those old, nearly forgotten bloodstains. Magic still lingers in those stains, stale and fetid but there nonetheless. I pull it into me, and the stains hiss as they simmer away.

This power came from the blood of my coven sisters, my mage brothers, and my lycan friends—them and perhaps other innocent supernaturals who were forced to give up their lives. It's wrong to form another's pain into power, but these individuals have already suffered. I won't let it be for nothing.

Both Luca and Jacques are pushing themselves up from where they've fallen.

I draw together my magic—

Luca incants beneath his breath, and a split-second later, a curse hits me in the abdomen. The magic impales my torso as though it were a stake.

I stagger, choking on the pain, then fall.

*SELENE!* Memnon roars. The building shakes violently.

Luca drags himself the rest of the way up from the ground, his arm still outstretched. Tucked under his other arm is the hateful *Book of the Damned*. It still smokes, that acrid power wafting off it.

"Fucking cunt," he spits out. "You think you can best me? In my own home? I haven't survived all these years on might alone…"

He continues speaking, but I stop listening when I sense those beings in the ground beneath me. They clamor close, lured in by my spilled blood.

They can have it.

"*Take my blood but spare my life,*" I whisper. "*Feast instead on Luca Fortuna and Jacques Allard.*"

My blood sinks into the floor, drawn down by the creatures beneath me.

A moment later, the ground trembles, and a crack forms

beneath my legs. It slithers forward, breaking concrete and heading right for Luca. Another crack branches from it, moving toward Jacques.

As soon as the crack reaches him, it widens to a fissure. The building creaks under the pressure.

"Fuck!" Jacques curses as one of his legs falls through the growing opening. The earth continues to shake as he attempts to pull his leg from the hole. He's almost gotten himself out of the fissure when the ground beneath his hands and upper torso falls away. His body is swallowed into the earth, and the last thing I hear is his echoing cry.

"What in God's name have you done?" Luca shouts as the other crack follows him across the room.

I'd love to answer, but the crack beneath me now widens. I drag myself away, crying out a little as the pain in my stomach darkens my vision.

The earth shakes again, and the floor beneath the sorcerer crumbles away. Luca drops *The Book of the Damned* to lunge for solid ground, but it too gives way under his body. His hands manage to catch the lip of the concrete floor, exposed rebar jutting out from it.

Luca's eyes meet mine for an instant, and I see true terror in his eyes. Then the concrete lip he holds onto collapses, and the sorcerer falls.

He's barely disappeared from sight when the ground begins to seal back up, the building shrieking and swaying as it does so.

Above me, the lights in the chandeliers flicker.

*Rejoin us, Empress. Your blood tastes better when it comes with your flesh...*

As the voices speak, the floor beneath my own legs disintegrates.

Oh *fuck*.

It feels like a direct portal to the Underworld has been ripped open beneath my feet.

I scramble to get to more solid ground, crying out as the movement tugs at my injuries. More of the ground falls away beneath my stomach, and I swallow my fear as my bloodied hands grip the smooth, chilled concrete for dear life. I struggle to pull myself farther out of the hole, but my muscles are shaking, and my strength is waning, and every time I move, I feel like I'm tearing through a bit more of my innards.

I don't know why I'm fighting this. If these gods that dwell beneath the earth want me, I'll have to live in the sky to truly stop them.

At the thought, my grip loosens, and I slide a little deeper into the fissure.

*Don't you dare stop fighting.* Memnon's voice rings out down our bond.

The double doors blow open, and my soul mate strides in, his magic billowing around him like churning storm clouds. His hair is stirring, and his eyes glow the faintest amount. He himself looks thoroughly torn up. His tux is in shreds, and claw marks run along his forearms, legs, and back. He even has a gruesome set running along the underside of his jaw.

I make a small sound at the state he's in, and the noise draws his eyes to mine. The moment he sees me, his magic barrels across the room. It molds itself around my body and drags me forward, out of the chasm.

I scream as the movement jostles my innards.

"*Selene!*" Memnon roars.

I can no longer see him, not when his magic surrounds me. But then, I feel his hands on me.

He murmurs a quick spell, and my pain vanishes. An instant later, he pulls me into his arms, sitting back on his haunches to hold me, his hand moving to my abdominal wound.

Before he can press a healing spell against it, the ground shudders again, dislodging his grip on my stomach and sliding the two of us forward. It feels as though the earth itself is trying to pitch us into the massive crack Memnon just dragged me out of.

*Mistress…join us as you once did…*

My eyes move to the dark opening down, down in the deep earth, and I grit my teeth.

"No," I say.

Memnon gives me a curious look before following my gaze. He studies the fissure for several seconds, then returns his attention to me.

*You've been speaking to the Hungering Ones, haven't you?* he says down our bond.

*They didn't seem so bad when I was facing down a demon,* I admit wearily.

*It seems they've acquired a taste for powerful witches.*

Memnon lifts his eyes from mine. To the chasm in the earth, he says in Sarmatian, "Old gods below, you *cannot* have Selene. She is mine. Honor your oaths, and take my blood as an offering of peace."

The sorcerer unsheathes the blade strapped to his side. In one sharp motion, he cuts his forearm and lets the blood pour onto the ground.

The shaking slows, then eventually stops altogether.

The room grows very, very quiet, save for the drip of Memnon's blood.

My eyes meet my mate's eyes, feeling exposed. "Thank you." Whatever those voices are, they are boogeymen.

The glow in his eyes fades back to brown. "*Est amage*, you do not need to thank me for things that come with being your soul mate. We pull each other back from the edge."

He wipes his blade and returns it to its sheath.

Memnon's gaze drops to my stomach and my mess of a wound. He makes an agonized sound. "*Est amage.*"

Memnon's hand covers my injury once more, his fingers splayed out across it, and I can feel the lick of his magic as it seeps in, the tingling warmth spreading through my flesh. He murmurs the Mochica curse-breaking spell, and I sense some inner darkness release and flitter away with it.

"As much as I love your ferocity, I cannot stand this part of it," Memnon admits. His words are punctuated by the uncomfortable tugging sensation as his healing spell takes root and my innards reform. "Where is the demon?" Memnon asks.

"Where he belongs," I say.

A smile curves his lips, and he tilts his head so he can see me better. "That's my queen." His eyes sweep over the mess of the room. "I notice the spell circle you mentioned is gone as well."

"I really don't like being trapped."

Memnon laughs, the sound light and joyful. It's at odds with the oppressive magic that saturates the very walls of this room.

"Of course you don't," he says mirthfully. "You are a Sarmatian queen, made to roam the boundless, open plains of the steppe. Your soul is made of vaster stuff." He pulls his hand away from my midsection, studying the pink, newly formed skin. My mate lets out a shuddering breath. "How does your stomach feel?"

"Fine," I say dismissively, staring up at his face. I don't care about my stomach at the moment.

I grab the tattered lapels of his tux and drag him to me. His lips meet mine, and we're kissing each other feverishly, as though the world is ending. It's bruising, desperate. We are in Rome, we are in Bosporus, we are on the Eurasian steppe, and we are here.

We are eternal.

I feel my heart...*give in.*

I gasp into his mouth at the sensation.

Immediately, Memnon pulls away, his eyes returning to my former injury. He places a hand back on the skin and presses his power into me.

I grab his wrist. "It's okay. *I'm* okay," I say softly.

My scary, violent sorcerer takes a deep breath. "Little witch, there will always be a part of me that fears your mortality, and right now...I just want to hold you for a little longer."

So the two of us stay there for another minute, Memnon holding me against him. I lightly grasp Memnon's forearm and press a wordless healing spell into his skin. Almost immediately, the claw marks begin to seal up. I watch them mend, now knowing the creature that inflicted them.

"How did you get rid of your demon?" I ask.

"I beheaded the first and second. The third one, I stabbed in the heart."

"You faced *three* demons?" I say, my voice hushed. One was hard enough.

"Leonard was determined to kill me off."

I stiffen. "What happened to him?"

"Dead. He bled out from a nicked artery." Memnon's voice grows cold. "It was too quick and too clean for a monster like him."

I shiver as I think about those old bloodstains on the floor.

There's still one Fortuna left, and—shit, *Sybil*.

I stand too quickly, then sway a little.

"Easy, Empress," Memnon says, rising up.

"We need to save my friend."

He groans—*groans*! "Must you make me act honorably?"

"Memnon!"

There's a gleam in his eyes. "I tease." He reaches for my hand. "Let's go save your friend."

# CHAPTER 51

***When we get to the auction floor, pandemonium.***

The entire room is one seething, churning mass of aggression.

Lycanthropes swarm the place—many of them in their animal form—along with the guests from the midnight auction. Those individuals still wear glittering gowns and pressed suits. And everywhere my eyes fall, supernaturals are fighting.

The only people who are absent, it appears, are Politia officers. Go figure. I'm sure they'll show up soon enough, given the carnage.

Blood decorates the walls and floors and even a few of the circular tables that fill the room. Not twenty feet away, I see the body of a man with his throat ripped out, and several more bodies lie slumped over the linen-covered tables or on the floor.

I scan the room, looking for Sybil and any other super-naturals who might've been captives, but it's hard to make sense of the tangle of people. I don't see anyone who looks like a captive, and I can only hope the lycans have already evacuated those supernaturals from the building.

Memnon strides forward into the mayhem, his hair beginning to rise. His eyes are fixed on a woman to our left. Her hair is now unbound and her dress is ripped, but it's easy enough to recognize Sophia Fortuna from the haughty set of her chin and the glow of her eyes. A small army of guards encircles her, and she fights from behind them, lobbing spells at the lycans closing in on her. I hear one wolf yelp as a curse lands and its fur catches fire.

*This sorceress tried to take you from me*, Memnon says, unsheathing his dagger. *I cannot let her live.* His thoughts are as simple as that, now that his power has consumed him.

Whatever plan the two of us might've formed to locate Sybil, it's just crumbled to dust in the wake of this battle.

Memnon strides forward and as soon as he hits the melee, he *unleashes* himself. The sorcerer spins and lunges, cutting through the fighters, stabbing and slicing when he needs to. He makes it look like a dance. What an awful thing, to think of killing as a dance, but there is a mesmerizing quality to it, even as blood arcs. The entire time, his attention remains riveted to Sophia, who hasn't noticed him yet.

I take a step back, eager to search all sixty-some floors of this building if I have to, to find my friend. I'm about to turn when a cascade of pale blond hair catches my eye. It triggers some old, unpleasant emotion, and reflexively, my gaze moves to the individual's ears, their *pointed* ears, then their eyes, which are the color of meadow-sweet grass, the hue too rich for human irises.

It's *not* possible…

I'm staring at a ghost, one who haunts my old memories.

She's the fairy who nearly abducted my soul mate two *thousand* years ago.

Eislyn.

My magic immediately rises. She should've been long dead. Even the fae have expiration dates. How is she alive? And what the fuck is she doing here, in San Francisco, *in this very building*?

My power is unspooling out of me the longer I stare at her.

I feel her eyes catch mine, and I see her falter. And now she's the one looking at me as though *I'm* the ghost. Did she not know I was here, alive?

Then her gaze moves like a magnet to Memnon. I realize belatedly that she'd been staring at him before she saw me.

Her expression is both fearful and covetous as she takes in my soul mate. Possessiveness rises in me at the look, along with the pressing need to end the fairy before she can be a threat to him once more.

I sense the moment Memnon sees her. He's nearly upon Sophia when he halts. For several seconds, he stands there, completely still, his head turned in Eislyn's direction.

Then, all at once, Memnon's power *consumes* him. His hair almost violently rises, and sparks crackle in the plumes of his magic.

This is the woman who killed his sister, his mother, his loyal brothers in arms. She's the one who whispered into his traitorous friend's ear and brokered a sinister agreement with Rome. She is the one who cursed Memnon to a hundred years of sleep so she might entrap him. And she is the one who set a Roman legion on me and all but killed me that fateful evening.

Memnon *detonates*.

His power rips across the room, flinging tables and chairs and people across the space. Only my soul mate and I remain standing.

Memnon strides forward toward the fallen figure of Eislyn, more rays of his power lashing out around his form. His magic looks like a thunderstorm that's descended on the room. The billowing power catches supernaturals in its grip and lifts them into the air.

They scream and thrash, but only for a few moments. Then something sweeps through the roiling mass of magic, and the supernaturals caught up in it grow docile.

I stare at their glazed eyes as they hang from Memnon's smoky power.

"Eislyn, what are you doing here?" he bellows, his magic wrapping around her torso. "Were you too wicked to be accepted into hell?"

I can feel his hate and anger filling him like poison. This is more than just regular power usage. This is the kind that eats away at the conscience, and Memnon already has so little of it left.

"Neither you nor I believe in hell, old king." Eislyn's voice is as soft as the wind and as melodic as birdsong.

My mate slowly prowls toward the fairy, who's caught in the matrix of Memnon's magic. Unlike the other supernaturals in the room, Eislyn's eyes are wide and a touch frightened, but they're not glazed over. If anything, they're sharp with focus. She stares at him like she's hanging on to his every word.

"Two thousand years, I was forced to sleep, all to escape your curse," Memnon continues. "I didn't expect to see you *alive*. How I burn, knowing you walked under the sun and *lived* while I rotted away. But then again, if you hadn't lived, you wouldn't be here in my clutches."

*Snap.*

A bone breaks somewhere in the room, then the lifeless body of Sophia Fortuna falls to the ground, her corpse smacking into a table on its way down, her neck bent at an odd angle. Hours ago, she was next to untouchable. Now, she's dead, killed in an instant.

"Did you know I would be here, or was it merely a happy coincidence?" Memnon demands.

Eislyn's lips part. "I thought I imagined you," she says softly.

*Snap.*

*Snap. Snap. Snap.* One by one, men and women in suits and gowns fall to the floor, dead.

What had he told me about a sorcerer's power the night of the Samhain Ball?

*The stronger the magic we cast, the less we can control who that magic touches.*

Memnon can't control his power. Not when it consumes him like this.

Eislyn watches him wondrously. "You are just as vicious as I remember," she says.

She blinks, then after a moment, she raises her hand to Memnon's magic, which holds her like a vise.

She murmurs something to the indigo magic, and to my shock, it loosens its hold on her. A set of wings unfurl at her back.

"I don't think so, Eislyn," Memnon says, using his power to barricade the exits.

She turns in midair. "We will speak again, warlord. But not tonight." She flicks her wrist, dropping her arm down, and it's as though she dragged the light down with her. The room fills with darkness.

"*Eislyn!*" Memnon bellows.

*Snap, snap, snap.*

Fuck. There are definitely enemies in Memnon's clutches, but there are plenty of shifters trapped in the plumes of his power as well. As the bodies hit the floor, I force my power out, beating back the darkness.

Slowly it lifts, revealing a room full of bespelled supernaturals and an angry sorcerer but no Eislyn.

Memnon roars at her absence, and through our bond, I can feel more of the sorcerer's bloodthirsty power slip its leash.

Now it's swirling around the supernaturals above us. To my horror, I make out Kane, his face expressionless as he hangs there in Memnon's magic. My eyes move over the trapped supernaturals until I see Irene, the Marin Pack beta, floating in the air. I even see Cara, sweet Cara, who must've felt compelled to come and save other shifters from a fate she escaped.

I'm the only one at this point besides Memnon himself who hasn't been swept up in his power. And given how much magic the sorcerer is drawing on, that could change at any moment.

"Memnon!" I shout. "Please, release the captives!"

He doesn't release them. He doesn't even register that he's heard me.

*Snap, snap.*

Two more supernaturals fall, these two old men in suits.

"Memnon!" I cry out desperately.

When he turns to me, his eyes burn like embers, and

his hair has lifted up and around his face. He takes me in, though his eyes appear unseeing.

*For you, mate,* he says. *All this is for you.*

*It's not for me. You're hurting our allies, my friends!*

He stares back at me.

*Snap.*

Another body falls, this one a middle-aged woman in a magenta dress. So far the deaths have all been auction guests, but it's only a matter of time before my mate kills someone truly innocent.

*You wanted to stop these terrible people,* he says. *We are stopping them.*

*Memnon, please.* A tear slips down my cheek as I start toward him. *I'm begging you!*

*They cannot hurt you, my queen. I will not let them. No one will hurt you ever again. Our fates will not be repeated.* He turns away from me.

*Snap, snap, snap, snap—*

"*Est xsaya!*" The ancient words rip from my throat. "*Stop!*" I shriek. "For me. For us. Stop before I must use my magic and stop you myself."

My soul mate falters. Slowly, he rotates to face me.

His eyes are still glowing, and they still appear unseeing.

He studies me for a long moment.

"It didn't work," he finally says, taking me in. "Your command didn't work."

I halt in my tracks, and the two of us stare at each other across the auction hall. Above us, his magic begins to lower its hostages to the ground.

"You *love* me," Memnon breathes.

I blink, and another tear rolls down my cheek. His glowing eyes flicker as he watches that tear. His gaze returns to mine, and he begins to stride across the room, his expression growing purposeful. The sorcerer's magic pushes aside chairs and tables as he goes.

Memnon's power finally releases the supernaturals, and the indigo magic leaves them to swirl around us like a vortex, hiding me and the sorcerer from the rest of the room.

"You love me," Memnon repeats, daring me to deny it. His gaze still burns with his power.

Another tear slips out.

"I do." I give him a shaky smile. "I love you." I always have. I just managed to bury it for a while. He's my friend, my monster, my one-time enemy and lover.

There's no more tightly wielded control. I'm free-falling.

Memnon closes the last of the distance, his eyes dimming to their normal smoky amber, and his hair lowers to the nape of his neck. But though his magic has waned, the intensity of his expression has not.

He brushes his knuckles over my cheekbone. "*Te amo in aeternum*," he says softly in Latin. His eyes search my face as though trying to commit this moment to memory.

Memnon leans in and kisses me, the stroke of his lips desperate. I reach for him, my hands cupping his face. I feel a tear drip onto my hand, and I realize he's shaking, his whole body trembling.

"A love like ours defies everything," he breathes against my lips. "I am yours forever."

---

The Politia do eventually come, though by then, the fight itself is long over.

Initially, I expect the supernaturals in the room to point fingers at Memnon, who held them all hostage for a time.

Instead, the shifters seem to focus their wrath on the auction guests, and those individuals in evening wear seem to be defensively arguing back. I don't think any of them recall that they were held captive by a raging sorcerer.

Once it becomes clear the officers want to detain everyone in the room for hours longer, my soul mate alters a few minds so the two of us can slip away and find Sybil.

Memnon and I find her sitting on the sidewalk outside the Equinox Building, near a line of ambulances with flashing lights. Sybil's nestled between Sawyer's thighs, an emergency blanket covering her, and her new mate is murmuring something to her and holding her close. It's startlingly tender.

"Sybil," I say softly, stepping away from Memnon. I pull the suit jacket he placed on me tighter around myself, trying to keep out the chill of the evening.

My friend glances up, and a small noise escapes her lips when she sees me. Shucking off her blanket, she rises to her feet, and then the two of us are moving toward each other.

We meet somewhere in the middle, and I sweep her into a hug. My best friend immediately begins to bawl in my arms.

"I thought—thought you w-were dead," she chokes out.

I laugh a little as a few tears trickle out of my own eyes. "You can't kill me that easily."

I pull back, brushing her hair away from her face so I can see her better. Her earlier wounds are gone, but there are shadows in her eyes, things that not even magic can heal.

"We survived," I whisper.

Her face crumples, and she nods, gripping me tighter.

My hands move to her upper arms, and I give them a

squeeze. "Thank you," I say softly, "for trying to protect me for so long. You are the best damn friend there ever was."

Sybil's sobs only grow louder, and I pull her back in for another hug.

The two of us hold each other for several minutes.

"Sybil." Sawyer's voice is low, rumbly, as he approaches us. "The car is here." He lays a hand on my friend's shoulder and runs his thumb over a patch of skin that causes a full-body shiver to course through Sybil. "We need to get you back. It's not safe for you to be out here before you have mastered your shifts."

What's this now?

Sybil looks horrified as she pulls away from me. "I would never…" But as she speaks, her body spasms a little.

Sawyer steps in a little closer, and he makes a soft rumbling sound that causes my friend to relax. "Of course you wouldn't. I would make sure both you and your best friend were safe."

My eyes move between the two of them, and only now do I realize that the sweet embrace Memnon and I saw between Sybil and Sawyer a moment ago might've been more than just simple physical contact. Sawyer might've been containing her in case she accidentally shifted.

My best friend's chin trembles, and I hate how fragile she appears. "Selene." Her voice is hoarse with emotion. "The pack is going to keep me sequestered away until the next Sacred Seven. Apparently, this first month for witches can be…difficult." Tears well in her eyes, and she looks scared. Everything she endured today couldn't have helped that.

But the pack Sawyer is a part of is good, and I know they will take care of my friend until I can see her again. The weeks will go by in a blink of an eye, I reassure myself.

I tuck a stray lock of hair behind her ear. "You're a badass. You'll do great. I'm sure of it."

Sybil's eyes flit over my tattered dress and the puckered flesh of my forearms. "You're okay?" she asks tentatively.

I nod and give her a tight smile. "I'm fine."

She frowns but then forces out her own smile. "I'm so relieved." She swallows, and her eyes are welling again. "You should go home, Selene," she says, her voice hoarse with emotion. "It's freezing out here. We can talk more later." As she speaks, Sawyer begins to gently steer her away from me and toward a car parked behind the ambulances.

"I'm holding you to that," I call out after her.

I stand there, watching as Sybil and Sawyer head toward their waiting ride. Memnon comes to my side then, one of his arms draping comfortingly around my shoulders.

"Hey, Selene," Sybil calls out over her shoulder. She pauses to turn back to me. "Seven other supernaturals were saved from bonds tonight. *You* did that. Not the Politia, not even the shifters. *You.* I hope you know how proud I am to be your friend." She flashes me a shaky smile and another tear leaks from my face. "Now get out of here, you freak," she says fondly, "before you catch your death."

# CHAPTER 52

***The next morning, I wake to hands on my thighs. Those*** fingers dig into my skin.

*Good morning, fiancée.*

Memnon punctuates the words with a searing kiss to my clit, and I wake with a gasp. I nearly rise off the bed.

Memnon smiles against my sensitive flesh.

"I've decided, *est amage*, that as your husband, I'm going to make you come on my tongue at least once a day—maybe twice."

"What?" I say dazedly. Last night returns to me then, but Memnon's touch quickly eclipses the memories.

I begin to sit up, but the sorcerer pushes my torso back down, hauling my hips up closer to him.

"And since you can no longer command me," he continues, "I'm going to control the pace of your orgasms, starting right now."

Before I can respond or even come to grips with the fact

that Memnon is holding my legs and ass like I'm his favorite teddy bear, the sorcerer kisses my clit again.

I cry out, my hands threading into his hair.

Memnon single-mindedly sucks on my clit, his tongue stroking the overly sensitive knot of flesh again and again.

The feeling is overwhelming.

Sensation is rising in me, and my core clenches uselessly.

"*Memnon!*" I sob out.

*Est xsaya*, he corrects. *Say it, and you'll get something besides just my mouth on your clit.*

"*Est xsaya*," I gasp out, hoping for a brief respite from the almost unbearable amount of stimulation coming from that nerve bundle between my thighs.

"Good woman."

Again, I feel him smile against me, and his mouth moves down from my clit. If I thought, however, I'd get a break from the intense sensation, I assumed wrong. Memnon's magic merely replaces his tongue, and it's just as cunning, the blue power circling that knot of nerves again and again.

The sorcerer's tongue circles my core before dipping inside.

He groans. "Missed the taste of your pussy."

I'm writhing beneath him. I throw my head back. "Need you inside me." It's less a demand and more a plea.

"No," he breathes against my skin. "Next time I come, you'll be wearing white and I'll be your husband."

My breath hitches. Our unbreakable oath to marry— now that I've fallen for Memnon, it's been enacted once more.

"But right now," he continues, "you'll come for me against my face like the good little witch you are."

Maybe it's Memnon's confidence, or maybe I'm quite suggestible, or maybe I'm finally overwhelmed by sensation, but all it takes is another searing kiss of his and my orgasm shatters through me.

I cry out as I come, my fingers tightening in Memnon's hair. I feel his grin as he greedily continues to eat me out through the aftershocks of my climax…and then beyond.

"Why aren't you stopping?" I nearly weep the words out when it becomes clear he won't.

*There's one more thing we're going to do every day,* he says down our bond as he feasts on me. *I'm going to tell you I love you more than life itself, and you're going to tell me those three magic words as well, starting today. And if you don't,* he continues, *then I'll simply eat you out until you do.*

*You are such a bastard.*

He laughs against my pussy, causing me to cry out.

*Yes,* he agrees wholeheartedly. *I am.*

I gaze down the line of my body toward Memnon's bowed head. "Look at me," I command.

There's no power behind the order, but still, my mate lifts his head, and his eyes meet mine.

"I love you, Memnon. I love you so much. And you don't need to hold any part of me hostage to get me to say it. *I love you.*"

His bourbon eyes glitter as he bathes in my words. Finally, he releases my hips, and they drop limply down to the bed.

As I stare at him, I feel a tightness in my chest. I rub my sternum, but the pressure doesn't go away.

Memnon notices.

"The magic from our unbreakable oath is taking root again," he says softly. The sorcerer moves up my body. "I feel it too." He dips his head and presses a kiss against my sternum. "Do you remember what that means?" he asks.

It feels like my heart has lodged itself in my throat. "It means," I say softly, "we're getting married today."

# CHAPTER 53

*Memnon leaves the room to make us coffee and tea and—judg-*ing by the sound of the gas burner igniting to life—a surprise breakfast. I feel like the emotions in me are too light and expansive to be contained beneath my skin.

So this is love.

I let out a happy little laugh that probably sounds like I've lost it just as Nero prowls into the room then unceremoniously hops onto the bed.

I take his furry face into my hands. "Can you believe I'm getting married?" My stomach flutters at the thought. *Flutters!*

Nero gives me a look that says *Yeah, no shit, lady, no one's surprised.*

But I am caught off-guard in the best way possible. This oath was loathsome to me when I first made it, but now... now I feel oddly thrilled. I was married to Memnon once. He was an incredible husband then.

He will be an incredible husband again.

My phone buzzes from the nightstand, dragging me from my thoughts. I release Nero, who immediately proceeds to clean his face where I touched him, and I grab the phone. On the screen is a text from Kane.

Suddenly, all of last night slams back into me. The demon, the auction, the fight, Eislyn.

Selene, we need to talk in person.

Another text follows the first.

Now.

I sit up in bed, gathering the sheets to me.

It's about Memnon.

My heart drops.
Why? I text back, my pulse beginning to rise.
I wait impatiently for him to respond.

You asked me to stick my neck out for you a week ago.
I'm asking you to give me your time.

Fine, I reply. Come to my place in thirty minutes.
I glance past Nero to where the sorcerer disappeared down the hallway. I can hear him humming some old Sarmatian song beneath his breath.

*Memnon,* I reach out down our bond. *I have to go to my residence hall to grab a few things for…later today.*

Rather than answering, Memnon pads back down the hallway, leaning against the doorframe to his bedroom. He wears only a pair of low-slung joggers, and the sight of his muscular, inked torso makes my knees go weak. A corner of his mouth is curled up into a soft smile.

His smoky amber eyes glitter as he takes me in. He's looking at me with so much longing it makes my chest ache.

"Don't be gone long, little witch," he says. "I have a surprise for you before we say our vows."

My heart beats a little harder.

This better be fucking good, Kane.

# CHAPTER 54

*Though I haven't been to my residence hall in a week, it's as* though nothing at all has changed—with the exception, perhaps, of the solitude. The house is much quieter and emptier than before. At first I simply assume that's because the two beings that made this place feel full—Sybil and Nero—are not currently here, but then I realize there's no cawing, screeching sounds from the various familiars that live here, nor are there any loud cackles from coven sisters. The murmured conversations I do hear are subdued. The house still smells, however, like comfort food. Today, it's cinnamon rolls.

I drop my things off in my room and head downstairs to grab one when someone bangs the ever-loving shit out of our front door.

One guess who that might be.

I retrace my steps to the foyer and open the door. Standing on the other side of it is Kane.

"What are you doing trying to knock down my door like you're the Big Bad Wolf?" I say.

He gives me a look. "That's not funny."

It's a *little* funny, but I keep that to myself. Last night obviously made everybody lose their sense of humor.

Despite the chill in the air, Kane wears only a tank top, jogging shorts, and tennis shoes. His sandy blond hair looks windblown.

"Did you *run* here?" I ask, holding the door open for him to come in.

The lycanthrope steps inside, his body rolling like a wolf on the prowl.

"Did you know?" he demands.

My heart beats loudly. There are a number of sensitive topics I know about that I likely shouldn't.

"Know what?" I say innocently enough. A moment later, I hold up a hand. "Wait. I'm not ready to have this conversation until I get some breakfast in me." Namely coffee.

"*Selene*," Kane protests, an impatient growl rumbling in his throat.

I give him an amused look. "That growl might've worked on me before I met a demon." I grab his hand. "Come on."

I feel his surprise at the touch, then his own grip tightens on mine. I can't see his face, but the alpha who bristles under others' orders now lets me lead him into my house's dining hall.

"You met a demon?" Kane echoes.

"Just for a little bit," I say evasively. That's an entire separate conversation, one that will likely ruin my appetite.

In my house's dining hall, fresh fruit sits out next to a tray of glistening cinnamon rolls, the frosting still dripping down them.

I release the shifter's hand to grab two plates. Ignoring the fruit altogether, I dish out a cinnamon roll for each of us, then hand Kane the plates.

"Go sit down," I say, nodding to one of the tables in the empty room behind us. "Also, do you like coffee or tea?"

"Christ, Selene, I just want to talk."

My sternum throbs, constricting a little tighter. The unbreakable oath I made to Memnon is starting to become uncomfortable.

"Listen, Kane, last night was rough, and I need some semblance of normal at the moment, so please go sit the fuck down while I brew you something."

He growls at the order.

"*Go.*" I give him a push.

He growls again but reluctantly heads to one of the wooden tables.

I grab two colorful mugs stacked next to a coffee maker and fill each of them up with steaming coffee. On a whim, I add cream to both. No clue if Kane even likes coffee or cream, but I'm beyond caring.

Coffees in hand, I head over to the table where Kane waits, looking very much like a caged wolf. His leg bounces impatiently.

"Goddess, you are so *loud* with your emotions," I say. I hand him a mug and settle myself down. "Now, what was so important that you had to meet me in person to tell me?"

Kane stares at me for a long time as though he's sizing me up.

"What?" I say, shifting in my seat a little.

"Did you know?" he says again.

"Know *what*?" I ask, taking a sip of coffee.

"About Luca Fortuna's estate?"

My throat tightens at the name of the sorcerer. "What are you talking about?" I say, searching his eyes. "Why would I care about that bastard's estate?"

Again, that long, assessing stare. His nostrils flare.

"Are you scenting me?" I ask, raising my eyebrows. "What's going on?"

"He named a business successor."

"Okay...?" I say uncertainly.

Kane leans forward. "Luca Fortuna was the sole owner of Ensanguine Enterprises, the multimillion-dollar conglomerate. Besides his three now deceased children, he had a wife and two mistresses. And that is not even taking into consideration his extended family or the half-dozen close confidantes he was grooming for future roles in the company."

Clearly Kane has done his homework on the family since we've been apart.

The shifter levels a look at me, one that desperately makes me want to look away. "Guess who Luca named to inherit his empire?"

Some sick emotion wells up in me. "You told me this was about Memnon."

"It is."

Kane reaches into the pocket of his running shorts and pulls out his phone. He taps on the screen, then slides the device over to me. I stare down at an image of a document titled "Ensanguine Enterprises Board of Directors Meeting Minutes."

"Look right there," Kane says, reaching across the table to point to a section of the page titled *Succession Plan*. "Read what it says."

My eyes scan the text.

*In the case of Luca Fortuna's death, the leadership of Ensanguine Enterprises passes to Leonard Fortuna, Sophia Fortuna, Juliana Fortuna, and Memnon Uvagukis.*

I can't breathe for a second.

"Luca Fortuna named your mate as the heir to his company," Kane says. "Along with, of course, his three legal children, who are all now conveniently dead."

Horror trickles down my spine.

Kane studies me, his nostrils flared. "You really didn't know," he finally says, like he only now believes it.

"Where did you get this?" I ask.

"Ensanguine Enterprises is a publicly traded company. The succession plan was made public a few hours ago, and one of my pack mates brought it to our alpha's attention."

I press a hand to the tightness in my chest and shake my head. "I don't...understand."

Only, I do. I understand the killing, the *claiming*. That was all a part of the Sarmatian ethos two thousand years ago. A king didn't just defeat an enemy; he moved in and acquired his land and wealth.

Kane sighs, his whole body relaxing. He runs his hands through his tousled hair.

"Memnon didn't destroy the Fortunas' empire last night. *He took it over.*"

The unbreakable oath's magic cinches tighter around my windpipe. It now feels uncomfortably like a noose.

Est amage, Memnon calls down our bond, breaking through my thoughts, *I hope you're ready. It's time to get married.*

# Acknowledgments

If I could describe my feelings about *Bespelled* in a single sound bite, I would say this book was pure indulgence. It is full of scenes that made me thrill and seethe and tense and swoon. While there was a satisfying flow to the book, it wasn't necessarily easy to write. I have a book's worth of removed lines and scenes, bits and pieces of *Bespelled* that weren't quite right so I had to cast them aside.

The one person who listened to me through the entire life of *Bespelled*—from its inception to its conclusion—is my husband, Daniel. It's strange to give thanks to what has become such a fundamental part of our relationship, like thanking a friend for having the same interests as you. But I want to thank you anyway, because I am eternally grateful for the weekly—if not daily—chats about stories and writing and all the beautiful places it takes us. I'm thankful to always, always have your support, for this book and all the others, and for the fact that you celebrate my wins as though they were your own. I love you—may it be forever.

To my agent Kimberly, I don't know what good deed I did to get to work with you, but I am beyond fortunate and so grateful for all the love and support you pour into my books. Thank you to Aimee, who lost sleep over this book so she could give me feedback.

Christa Désir, you are incredible at what you do, and you're an absolute delight to work with. Thank you for the wicked good feedback. Your excitement and belief in my stories is so, so humbling.

Sabrina Baskey, thank you for making this book sing! I appreciated each one of your comments and revisions. You truly added the polish to *Bespelled*.

A huge shout-out goes to my mom, who stayed with me during the end of my edits simply so that I could get them done in time. I'm going to try not to get weepy about this, but the truth is that it meant a lot to me. I love you, Mama. Thank you.

A big, heartfelt thank you goes to my dad, whose brain I picked about succession plans. And a secondary thank you goes once again to my husband, who reassured me a retrofitted skyscraper in San Francisco would remain standing even after a portal to hell ripped through part of its foundations. I'm sure your architecture professors back at Berkeley are super proud you could use your knowledge for such important and sobering matters.

I want to thank my family as a whole for supporting me in so many ways during this book's journey. There were so many shared posts and so much love showered on me, and I'm honestly still moved by it.

To my lovely kiddos, though you both in the most literal sense did not help with the book, you helped quiet the mess of my mind and gave me your laughter and your curiosity and sweet mischief.

To Naomi, Janett, Kel, Patricia, Lacey, and so many others—thank you for loving this series and believing in me and reaching out to me even though I'm a writing gremlin who is terrible at communication. I deeply appreciate all the love and excitement you've shown.

Lastly, thank you, dear reader, for taking a chance on my books and my characters. I will forever be grateful for the opportunity to share my stories with you.

# About the Author

Found in the forest when she was young, Laura Thalassa was raised by fairies, kidnapped by werewolves, and given over to vampires as repayment for a hundred year debt. She's been brought back to life twice, and, with a single kiss, she woke her true love from eternal sleep. She now lives happily ever after with her undead prince in a castle in the woods.

…or something like that anyway.

When not writing, Laura can be found scarfing down guacamole, hoarding chocolate for the apocalypse, or curled up on the couch with a good book.